'You'll find nothing worth stealing in this house. I suggest you leave. Immediately.'

Instead of reacting with the horrified dismay she sought, the man took his time straightening. Still with that leisurely air, he raised his candle to illuminate Genevieve where she stood. His face was covered with a black silk mask such as people wore to masquerade balls. Not that she had any experience of such events. 'You're dashed well protected if there truly is nothing worth stealing.'

Her hand steady, she raised the gun she'd taken from the drawer. 'We live on the edge of the village, as you no doubt noted when you chose this house as your target.' A horrible thought struck her and she waved the pistol at him. 'Are you armed?'

He stiffened with shock, as though the question offended. To demonstrate his non-violent intentions, he spread his hands wide. 'Of course not, dear lady.'

This rapscallion was a most bizarre burglar. Her knowledge of the criminal fraternity was limited, but this man's assurance struck her as remarkable. He spoke like a gentleman and didn't seem particularly concerned that she had a weapon. Her lips tightened and she firmed her grip on the pistol. 'There's no "of course" about it. In your line of work, you must expect opposition from your victims.'

'I make sure the house is unoccupied before I start work.'

'Like tonight,' she said coldly.

He shrugged. 'Even master criminals make the occasional mistake, Miss Barrett.'

THE SONS OF SIN
by Anna Campbell

Seven Nights in a Rogue's Bed
March 2014

A Rake's Midnight Kiss
July 2014

What a Duke Dares
November 2014

A RAKE'S MIDNIGHT KISS

ANNA CAMPBELL

Published in Great Britain 2014
by Mills & Boon, an imprint of Harlequin (UK) Limited,
Eton House, 18-24 Paradise Road, Richmond, Surrey, TW9 1SR

ISBN: 978-0-263-24653-7

009-0714

Harlequin (UK) Limited's policy is to use papers that are natural, renewable and recyclable products and made from wood grown in sustainable forests. The logging and manufacturing processes conform to the legal environmental regulations of the country of origin.

Printed and bound by
CPI Group (UK) Ltd, Croydon, CR0 4YY

Anna Campbell was the sort of kid who spent her childhood with her nose buried between the pages of a book. She decided when she was a child that she wanted to be a writer. When she's not writing passionate, intense stories featuring gorgeous Regency heroes and the women who are their destiny, Anna loves to travel, especially in the United Kingdom, and listen to all kinds of music. She has settled near the sea on the east coast of Australia, where she's losing her battle with an overgrown subtropical garden.

The first book in THE SONS OF SIN series, *Seven Nights in a Rogue's Bed,* has generated some wonderful reviews and a number of awards, including favourite historical romance from the Australian Romance Readers Association. Anna was also voted favourite Australian romance author at the ARRA Awards.

Anna loves to hear from her readers. You can contact her through her website at www.annacampbell.info.

PRAISE FOR ANNA CAMPBELL

'*Seven Nights in a Rogue's Bed* is a lush, sensuous treat. I was enthralled from the first page to the last and still wanted more.'
—Laura Lee Guhrke, *New York Times* bestselling author

'The fast pace and slightly gothic atmosphere make the pages fly. She keeps readers highly satisfied with the plot's tenderness and touching emotions that reach the heart.'
—Kathe Robin, *RT Book Reviews*

'Campbell matches up two proud, wary victims of abuse in this smart Regency romance...delightful insight and... luscious love scenes. Readers will cheer for these loveable and well-crafted characters.'
—*Publishers Weekly*

'Truly, deeply romantic'
—Eloisa James, *New York Times* bestselling author on *Captive of Sin*

'Regency noir—different and intriguing'
—Stephanie Laurens, *New York Times* bestselling author on *Claiming the Courtesan*

A RAKE'S
MIDNIGHT
KISS

Prologue

Packham House, London, March 1827

T he whole world knows you for a slut, madam."

The impassioned declaration dropped into one of those lulls that occasionally affected a crowded room. Like everyone else crammed into Lord Packham's ballroom this uncommonly warm spring night, Sir Richard Harmsworth craned his neck to see who had spoken. And, more interesting, to whom.

His height offered an advantage and he quickly identified the players in the conflict. Then wished to God he hadn't. Damn it to hell, the family dirty linen endured another public washing.

Near the main doors, a pale-haired stripling faced down a beautiful older woman with dark hair. A faintly pitying smile curled the woman's lips and she betrayed no trace of chagrin. While Richard couldn't place the furious boy, he had no difficulty identifying the lady labeled a trollop.

Augusta, Lady Harmsworth, was his mother. Much good it had ever done him.

From long habit, Richard plastered an affable expression on his face, as if none of this could possibly matter. Still, his gut clenched with old, futile anger as he started toward the brouhaha. What a dashed pity that he was thirty-two years too late to prevent scandal.

The extravagant crowd parted before him as if he was Moses contemplating a seaside stroll. He felt hundreds of eyes burning into his back. As an acknowledged arbiter of fashion, he was accustomed to attention. Tonight, that attention contained no admiration. Instead the avid interest indicated that society scented blood. Richard and his mother knew better than to give it to them. He wasn't so sure about the distraught young man.

Out of the corner of his eye, he saw his best friend Camden Rothermere, Duke of Sedgemoor, striding in the same direction. Then his gaze focused on his mother. It must be five years since he'd seen her and she'd hardly aged a day. Clearly sin was good for the complexion, he thought sourly.

"No need for that, Colby." Lord Benchley, one of his mother's regular escorts, raised his quizzing glass and subjected the trembling youth to a derisive inspection. "Take your dismissal in good part and don't make a fool of yourself."

Richard identified his mother's accuser. Lord Colby was just out of Cambridge and new in Town. Augusta always gathered a coterie of handsome young men although, to give her what little credit she deserved, she rarely accepted these greenlings into her bed. She saved that privilege for more experienced paramours like, reportedly, Benchley.

Richard might resent his mother, but some painful compulsion meant that he kept track of her admirers. To the world, he pretended not to care a fig for her or her behavior. Beneath his languid, fashionable shell, he reluctantly admitted that was far from the truth.

"And here comes her bastard," the boy said bitterly as Richard approached. "Or at least the one we know about."

Everyone in the glittering gathering seemed to release a combined gasp of horrified delight. The musicians scratched into silence. A lanky fellow behind Colby grabbed the youth's arm. "Shut up, Colby. Harmsworth's a crack shot. Do you want a bullet for your trouble?"

Colby shook him off. Now that Richard was near, he saw that the young lordling verged on tears. Blast her to Hades, yet again his mother wreaked havoc, as she'd wreaked havoc throughout her son's life.

"Good evening, Mother. I see you still know how to make an entrance," he said drily, pointedly ignoring the obstreperous cub. One would imagine that after being tarred a bastard so long, the word would lose its sting. Unfortunately the rancor knotting his stomach indicated that it hadn't.

Knowing how closely they were observed, Richard bent over her hand in a show of respect. Long experience had proven that the slightest betrayal of genuine emotion would have society tearing at him like wolves.

His mother was even better at hiding her reaction, if any, to insults. Or to meeting her estranged son after such a protracted interval. She stared back at Richard steadily and her lips curved in the smile that had caused untold trouble among the masculine half of the population. Going right back to Richard's father, whoever the hell he'd been.

Spiteful gossip had long speculated that a stablehand had tupped Lady Harmsworth while Sir Lester was away on a diplomatic mission to Russia. When Sir Lester returned to an heir after a sixteen-month absence, there was no hiding his wife's adultery. The scandal didn't upset the succession. Sir Lester had never openly questioned Augusta's faithfulness and Richard was duly accepted as the next baronet, however dubious his bloodlines.

"One would so hate to be dull," his mother said coolly.

Richard tilted an inquiring eyebrow at her as his rage coiled like a cobra. Since his schooldays, he'd suffered mockery, scorn, and violence because of his mother's wantonness. Pride might have taught him to hide resentment but had done nothing to soften it. "Indeed."

"Lady Harmsworth, a pleasure to see you." Cam finally made it through the crowd.

"Your Grace." Her exquisite curtsy conveyed a hint of defiance. Richard would dearly love to hate everything about his mother, but he couldn't quite make himself despise her courage. He knew what it cost to hold one's head up against the world's contempt. "Here to pour oil on troubled waters?"

Cam smiled at her. "Merely to offer myself as a partner for this dance."

Augusta turned to Richard. "And, my son, what are you doing here? Don't tell me you mean to fight a duel over my honor."

A faint titter from behind him greeted that outrageous statement. Richard read the devil in her eyes as she dared him to challenge her claim to honor. Part of the agony of all this was that he and his mother weren't so different, even down to the way they deployed imperturbable elegance to discourage insolence.

Usually it worked.

His neutral expression didn't falter. "I don't shoot inebriated children, however naughty they are."

Colby's friend latched more firmly onto his arm. "Come away, Colby. And be grateful that you escaped with your life."

"Yes, I'll go." Stubbornly Colby stood his ground and glowered at Richard. His voice was raw with emotion. "I'll forsake the lady's raddled charms and I'll overlook the presumption of a blackguard who can't name the man who sired him. Not even the Harmsworth Jewel could make either of you fit for decent society. Your names are filth."

This time the snickers were more pronounced and the crowd surged forward like a turbulent sea, threatening to suffocate Richard. God rot Colby; why must he parade his broken heart in the middle of this crush? The urge to flatten the unmannerly whelp with one blow jammed in Richard's throat, even as he forced out a light reply. "The Harmsworth Jewel? Good Lord, nobody's seen that bauble since the Wars of the Roses."

He was astonished that Colby knew of the jewel's existence or the legend that its possession confirmed the Harmsworth heir. Richard exaggerated to say that the artifact had been missing since the fifteenth century, but it had certainly been lost to the main branch of the family for more than fifty years.

"Raddled charms?" At his side, Augusta's silvery laugh rang out. "My dear Colby, you wound me."

"You're in remarkable looks, Lady Harmsworth. Ignore this puppy." Cam, no stranger to family scandal himself, stepped forward, his air of authority cowing even the fuming Colby. "Shall we dance?"

Cam signaled to the orchestra as if he were the host rather than Lord Packham. A waltz began as he and Augusta proceeded to the floor with a regal assurance that dared anyone to utter an impertinent word. Not for the first time, Richard was grateful for his friend's aplomb in a sticky situation.

With palpable disappointment, the eager audience began to disperse. Yet again, the Harmsworths had skirted outright disgrace, although Colby's tantrum would provide a deli-cious *on-dit* to spice reminiscences of the ball.

"Take his lordship home," Richard said to Colby's com-panion. For once he couldn't conceal his weariness. He was so bloody tired of all this. Tired of disdain. Tired of pretend-ing that every insult slid off his immaculately dressed hide without leaving a mark. Tired of his mother's sins crashing down upon his head. Tired above all of being the Harms-worth bastard.

The rage twisting in his belly cooled, set into a determi-nation as hard as an iron bar. He'd find the deuced Harms-worth Jewel and he'd turn the gewgaw into a pin for his neck cloth. He'd brandish it beneath the ton's noses like a banner of war until they admitted that while he mightn't be the right Harmsworth, he was the only Harmsworth they were going to get.

Then let any man call him bastard.

Chapter One

Little Derrick, Oxfordshire, September 1827

D amnation!"
A thud followed by a low masculine curse stirred Genevieve from sleep. Even then she needed a few seconds to realize that she was slumped over the desk in her study upstairs at the vicarage. Her candles had gone out and the room's only illumination was the dying fire. In that faint glow, she watched a dark shape below the windowsill lengthen upward until a man's form blocked faint starlight from outside.

Choking fear held her motionless. Fear and outrage. How dare anyone break into her home? It felt like a personal affront. Her father and aunt were out, dining with the Duke of Sedgemoor at his local estate. The duke never visited this isolated corner of his vast holdings, so everyone was agog to see him. Genevieve had been invited too, but she'd wanted to stay and work on some research. The servants were away for the evening.

The man at the window remained still, as if checking that the room was empty before launching his nefarious activities. The charged silence extended. Then the tension eased from his lean body and he stepped toward the fire. From her dark corner, Genevieve watched him set a candle to the coals.

Blast his impudence, he'd soon learn he wasn't alone.

Quickly her hand found the desk's second drawer and tugged it open, not bothering to conceal the noise as she grabbed what lay hidden inside. The candle flared into life, the intruder turned his head sharply in her direction, and Genevieve lurched to her feet.

As she stepped around the desk on shaky legs, she forced a confidence she didn't feel into her voice. "You'll find nothing worth stealing in this house. I suggest you leave. Immediately."

Instead of reacting with the horrified dismay she sought, the man took his time straightening. Still with that leisurely air, he raised his candle to illuminate Genevieve where she stood. His face was covered with a black silk mask such as people wore to masquerade balls. Not that she had any experience of such events. "You're dashed well protected if there truly is nothing worth stealing."

Her hand steady, she raised the gun she'd taken from the drawer. "We live on the edge of the village, as you no doubt noted when you chose this house as your target." A horrible thought struck her and she waved the pistol at him. "Are you armed?"

He stiffened with shock, as though the question offended. To demonstrate his nonviolent intentions, he spread his hands wide. "Of course not, dear lady."

This rapscallion was a most bizarre burglar. Her knowledge of the criminal fraternity was limited, but this man's assurance struck her as remarkable. He spoke like a gentleman and didn't seem particularly concerned that she had a weapon. Her lips tightened and she firmed her grip on the pistol. "There's no 'of course' about it. In your line of work, you must expect opposition from your victims."

"I make sure the house is unoccupied before I start work."

"Like tonight," she said coldly.

He shrugged. "Even master criminals make the occasional mistake, Miss Barrett."

Her belly knotted with dread. This time not even her strongest efforts steadied her voice. "How do you know my name?"

The lips below the mask twitched and he stepped closer.

"Stay back!" she snapped. Her heart banged so hard against her ribs, surely he must hear it.

Ignoring her pistol with insulting ease, he lifted the candle and subjected her to a lengthy and unnerving inspection. Genevieve's sense of unreality built. Everything around her was familiar. The shabby comfort of her favorite room. The jumbled items on the desk. The pile of pages covered in her writing. All was as it should be, except for the tall masked man with his indefinable air of elegance and his smile of indulgent amusement. She had an irritating intuition that the reprobate played with her.

Bracing under that assessing regard, she made herself study him like she'd study an artifact, although with his face covered she would never be able to describe him to the authorities. Candlelight glinted on rich gold hair and found fascinating shadows under the open neck of his white shirt. He wore breeches and boots. Despite this basic clothing, his manner screamed privilege. And while she couldn't see his face, something about the way he carried himself indicated he was a handsome man.

A most bizarre burglar indeed.

"A good thief does his research." He answered the

question that she'd forgotten she'd asked. "Although research occasionally lets one down. For example, village gossip indicated that you attended a soiree at Leighton Court tonight."

"I wanted to—" She realized she responded as if to any polite enquiry. The hand holding the gun showed a lamentable tendency to droop, pointing the barrel harmlessly at the floor. She bit her lip and hoisted the gun in what she prayed was a convincing gesture. "Get out of this house."

"But I haven't got what I came for."

He shifted closer, making her feel more at risk than at any time since he'd arrived. At risk as a woman was at risk from a man. Her skin tightened with awareness of their isolation. She hadn't missed how his gaze had lingered on her body. Before recalling that any show of vulnerability delivered him the advantage, she backed away. She pointed the gun at his chest. "Get out now or I'll shoot."

His frown indicated that her demand galled his sense of decorum. "Dear lady—"

She stiffened. Somewhere she'd lost control of this encounter. Which was absurd. She was the one with the gun. "I'm not your dear lady."

As if acknowledging that she'd scored a point, he bowed. "As you wish, Miss Barrett. I've done you no wrong. It seems excessive to menace me with murder."

Astonishment almost made her laugh. "You broke into my house. You threatened me with—"

He interrupted. "So far, any threats have emanated from your charming self."

"You mean to steal," she said in a low, vibrating voice.

"But I haven't. Yet." The expressive mouth above the intriguingly hard jawline curved into a charming smile. "Temper justice with mercy. Let me go free to seek redemption."

"Let you go free to find some other innocent to rob," she said sharply. "Better to lock you in the cellar and summon the local magistrate."

"That would be unkind. I don't like small, confined places."

"In that case, you've chosen the wrong profession. Somewhere someone will catch you."

Disregarding the gun, he took another step forward. "Surely your compassionate heart abhors the thought of my imprisonment."

She retreated and realized that he'd boxed her against the desk. She tightened her grip on the gun to counteract her slippery palms. "Move away or I swear I'll shoot."

He lit one of the candles on the desk and blew out his own smaller candle, dropping it smoking to the blotter. "Tsk, Miss Barrett. You'll get blood on the carpet."

"I'll—"

Words escaped on a gasp as with surprising speed he grabbed the hand holding the gun. A few nimble turns of that long body and he caught her against him, facing the open window. Pressed to him, she was overwhelmingly conscious of his power. His leanness was deceptive. There was no denying the muscles in the arms holding her or the breadth of the chest behind her. He embraced her firmly across her torso, trapping her arms. While she still held her weapon, she couldn't shift to aim it.

The barbed but oddly flirtatious conversation had calmed immediate dread. Now fear surged anew. What in heaven's name was she thinking, bandying words with this scoundrel? As if she enjoyed herself, when if she despised anything in this world, it was a thief.

She caught her breath on a frightened hiccup and struggled. "Let me go!"

His arms tightened like straps, controlling her with mortifying ease. Genevieve was a tall, strong girl, no frail lily, but the thief was taller and stronger. She'd never before measured her strength against a man's. It rankled how easily he restrained her. She'd never been so aware of another person's physical reality. The experience was disturbing beyond her natural terror of an intruder. "Hush, Miss Barrett. I give you my word I mean no harm."

"Then release me." She panted, her wriggles achieving nothing beyond the collapse of her never very secure coiffure.

"Not unless you put the gun down."

She maneuvered to elbow him in the belly, but his grip made it impossible. "Then I'll be at your mercy," she said breathlessly.

A grunt of laughter escaped him. "There's that to consider."

He was so close that his amusement vibrated through her. The sensation was uncomfortably intimate. A few more of those blasted deft movements and he snatched her weapon. He placed it beyond reach on the desk.

"I'll scream."

"There's nobody to hear," he said carelessly, and in that moment, she truly hated him.

"You're despicable," she hissed, trying and failing to free herself. Her heart galloped with fright and anger. With him, and with herself for being a stupid, weak female, prey to an overbearing male.

"Sticks and stones."

He drew her into his body and took a sliding step backward. She became conscious not just of his size and strength—those had been apparent from the moment he caught her up—but also of his enveloping heat and the way that he smelled pleasantly of something herbal. Fresh. Tangy.

This ruffian took the trouble to wash regularly.

He reversed another step and opened the door with a rattle, containing her struggles beneath one arm with humiliating ease. Fear spurred rage. She wrenched hard against him and tried without success to sink her fingernails into his forearm.

"No, you don't," he huffed, tugging her closer.

"I'll have your liver for this," she snarled, even as his scent continued to prick her senses. What was that smell?

"You'll have to catch me first."

She wished she didn't notice how laughter warmed that deep, musical voice. Any angry response died in furious shock as he brushed his cheek softly against the wing of hair covering her cheek.

"*Au revoir,* Miss Barrett," he whispered in her ear, his breath teasing nerves she didn't know she possessed. Then he shoved her away from him hard.

By the time she'd regained her footing, he'd slammed the door and locked it from outside with the key he must have palmed when he fiddled with the latch.

"Don't you dare ransack the house, you devil!" she shouted, rushing forward and pounding on the door. But the vicarage doors were of solid English oak and hardly shook under her determined assault. "Don't you dare!"

Gasping, she stopped and pressed her ear to the door, desperate to work out what he was up to. She heard a distant slam as though someone left by the front door. Could her presence have deterred him from his larcenous plans? She couldn't imagine why. From the first, he'd had the best of the conflict.

Her hands fisted against the wood as she recalled his barefaced cheek in holding her so . . . so *improperly*.

"Improper" seemed too weak a term to describe the

sensations he'd aroused when he'd captured her like a sheep ready for the shears. Like that sheep, she was about to be well and truly fleeced. She was in no position to stop the villain from taking what he wanted. Nobody would let her out until her father and aunt returned from the duke's, and heaven knew when that would be. The Reverend Ezekiel Barrett adored hobnobbing with the quality. He'd be there until breakfast if Sedgemoor didn't throw him out first. She'd have to go out the window the way the villain had come in.

Tears of frustration stung her eyes. However illogically, she felt the radiating heat of the burglar's body against hers. It was like he still touched her. She wasn't afraid anymore, at least not for her person. If the rascal had wanted to hurt her, he'd had plenty of opportunity. Her principal reaction, now that fear and unwilling fascination ebbed, was self-disgust. She'd acted a ninnyhammer, the sort of jittery female she despised. She'd had a gun. Why hadn't she forced him from the house?

The ominous silence extended. What was the black-guard doing? Would there be anything left by the time he finished? She glanced over to the desk and thanked the Lord that the only genuinely valuable item here had escaped his notice. For a sneak thief, he wasn't very observant, although he hadn't struck her as a man deficient in intelligence. Or, she added with renewed outrage, impertinence. Neverthe-less, any professional would immediately purloin the gold object on the blotter.

Something landed on the carpet near the open window. Curious, nervous, Genevieve grabbed the candle from the desk and lifted it high. On the floor lay the key.

Astonished and outraged, she rushed to the window, but darkness and the elm's thick foliage obstructed her view. In the distance someone started to whistle. A jaunty old tune.

"Over the Hills and Far Away." Apt for an absconding thief, she supposed. Not that he'd betrayed any panic. Again, his confidence struck her as puzzling. The music faded as the whistler wandered into the night.

With shaking hands, Genevieve scooped up the key and balanced it on her palm. One completely unimportant fact threw every other consideration to the wind. She'd finally identified the smell that had tantalized her when he'd held her.

Lemon verbena.

Chapter Two

Richard drained his brandy and rested his head against the back of the leather armchair in Leighton Court's library. Housebreaking left a man in dire need of a drink. The black mask draped disregarded from a bookshelf. He'd felt like a confounded mountebank wearing it, but as things turned out, it had been a wise decision. After six months of detective work, he'd found his treasure.

"She's got the jewel, all right, after playing coy with my agents about whether Great Aunt Amelia left it to her. When I climbed through the only open window I could find, it sat on the desk, plain as that big beak on your face."

"No need to get personal." Camden Rothermere, Duke of Sedgemoor, rose from the matching chair across the hearth to refill Richard's glass. The duke's green eyes below his ruler-straight black hair lightened with the humor that only his friends saw.

Right now, Richard knew he took advantage of that friendship. Only a good friend would rusticate on this obscure estate to support a pal when he could be enjoying the delights of his principal seat in Derbyshire. Cam's house in Little Derrick gave Richard a base in the neighborhood. Cam's name would provide an introduction to the locals.

Cam hissed with impatience. "Why the devil didn't you steal it then and there if the damned thing was ripe for the taking? Nice quick job. You can slink back to the fleshpots and I can go north to supervise the harvest at Fentonwyck."

"Bad form to steal it, old man, bad form." A faint smile tilted Richard's lips as his free hand dangled to toy with his dog's ears. Sirius, a hound of indeterminate breed, snoozed on the floor beside the chair, his long nose resting on his front paws. He hadn't appreciated missing out on tonight's excitement. "I'll give the chit a chance to sell it to me first. If I steal it, I can't brandish the bauble to demonstrate that I'm the title's incumbent and society had better bloody well respect that."

Richard spoke more casually than circumstances warranted. Until tonight, he'd only seen the jewel in watercolor sketches in the family papers. The urge to pocket the gold and enamel trinket had been deuced strong, but tonight's burglary had always only been a reconnaissance mission.

His agents had approached Miss Barrett several times to purchase the jewel and none of them could get the damned woman to admit that she had the troublesome artifact. She'd neither denied nor confirmed, although every trail ended at Little Derrick's vicarage. Tonight's burglary had been a last-ditch attempt to discover whether to proceed with the plan that even he admitted sounded outlandish.

The rage that had gripped him in Lord Packham's ballroom still soured his days. Laying his hands on the jewel had become a quest to assert his worthiness to a world too eager to discount him as a sham.

"I'm glad I don't have to add theft to your list of misdemeanors." Cam eyed Richard without favor.

"I'll try persuasion first." He sipped his friend's excellent brandy, his pleasure in recalling the vicar's fiery daughter vying with the anger that had simmered for six months. Longer. His whole life. "Anyway, Miss Barrett had a gun."

A surprised gust of laughter escaped Cam. "Did she, by Jove? Good for her. I wondered if you'd encounter the mysterious Miss Barrett when her father and aunt turned up to dinner without her, but it was too late to warn you that the vicarage wasn't empty. I swear the reverend gentleman could talk the leg off an iron pot. Even if you'd caught a bullet, I had the worst of the evening."

"I owe you." Richard stretched his long legs across the blue and red Turkey carpet. Pleasant weariness weighted his limbs.

"You do indeed. Although I have to say Leighton Court is dashed appealing. I should have been quicker to check out Uncle Henry's bequest after he turned up his toes last year." Cam subsided into his chair. "So was the scholarly spinster what you imagined? Bad skin? Round shoulders? No bosom? A squint from poring over all those dusty tomes?"

A surge of purely male appreciation warmed Richard's blood. The body he'd held had definitely sported a bosom. Quite an impressive one if he was any judge of women. Which of course he was.

"The lady is...interesting," he said musingly, fingers stilling on Sirius's shaggy head. The dog grumbled softly at the cessation of attention.

"If she countered your nonsense with a pistol, she certainly is. I take it you're proceeding with this ramshackle scheme."

Richard smiled, recalling the girl facing him down as cool as you please. Instead of a dried-up old maid, he'd encountered a glorious Amazon. Tall. Blond. Flashing silver eyes to make mincemeat of his unflattering expectations.

"Richard?" Cam prompted when the silence extended.

"Hmm?"

"Stop mooning over the damned filly. I gather she was something of a beauty. Answer me."

"Of course I'm going on." Richard rose and without invitation refilled his glass. He waved the decanter at Cam, but his famously abstemious friend shook his head. "I can't see I've got much choice. I could go through the courts and prove Aunt Amelia had no legal right to bequeath the jewel to Miss Barrett, but chancery cases take forever and you never know how those blasted judges will rule. Miss Barrett won't deal with my representatives, even after they said I'd give ten thousand guineas for the jewel."

"Money clearly doesn't move her."

"Something will, and I'll discover what that is. Luckily for me, her father takes in paying students. It's a matter of infiltrating the household and keeping an eye for the main chance. Everybody has a price—I'm sure I'll learn the female prodigy's."

Cam still looked unconvinced. "She'll know what you want the minute she hears your name."

Richard's lips curled in a sly smile as he lounged against the mantel. "Meet Christopher Evans, rich dilettante from Shropshire."

Cam's voice flattened. "You mean seduction."

For one blazing instant, the prospect of plundering Genevieve Barrett's Viking charms dazzled Richard, until reluctantly he shook his head. "No need to sound so disapproving, old chum. I'll soften her up with a bit of flirtation, but I won't ruin her. I don't mean the girl any harm, whatever dance she's led me over the jewel's whereabouts. I'll give her a few weeks of masculine attention and a nice fat purse, then leave her with a smile and the jewel in my pocket."

"A female who holds you off at gunpoint mightn't be an easy conquest."

Richard shrugged. "I know enough to get round an innocent country miss. She'll be eating out of my hand in no time."

"If tonight's any indication, she's more likely to bite your fingers off. You're sounding like such a coxcomb, I'd almost like to see that."

Richard's laugh held an acid note. "I can act the charmer when I have to. Good God, I learned that lesson long ago. My amiable ignorance in response to insult saved me a parcel of beatings from our dear schoolfellows."

He shuddered, recollecting the tortures their friend Jonas Merrick, also illegitimate, had undergone at Eton because he was too stiff-necked to play the game. Well, Jonas had had the last laugh last year when he'd been named Viscount Hillbrook. Richard intended to have the last laugh too, even if only to irritate the high sticklers by flashing the legendary Harmsworth jewel under their supercilious noses.

Cam looked unimpressed. "Nothing will change the circumstances of your birth."

"Perhaps not," he said with a bitterness that he'd reveal to nobody else. "But surely you of all men understand the need for defiance."

The murky details of Cam's conception had been subject to even more spiteful gossip than Richard's. Cam's mother, the duchess, had divided her favors between her husband and his younger brother. Nobody, including reportedly the duchess, knew which Rothermere had fathered her son. Scandal of that magnitude at the highest levels never lacked repeating.

All their lives, Richard and Cam had paid for their parents' sins. At Eton with Jonas, they'd forged a bond based in shared adversity. Until recently, Jonas had gone his own way, but Cam and Richard's friendship had never faltered, despite Cam being a pattern card of decorum and Richard's flair for outraging the prudish. In a rare contemplative moment, Richard had concluded that Cam strove to live down his notorious parentage by proving himself worthy of his title.

Still, through his harum-scarum existence, Richard had reason to be grateful for this steadfast friendship. Take the case in point. Loyalty brought Cam, even if vociferously objecting, to this small Oxfordshire estate.

"Any victory will be purely symbolic," Cam said.

"Symbols can be powerful." He summoned a smile as he returned to his chair. "Come, Cam. Let me have one last adventure before life becomes odiously flat. This next season, I intend to become a respectable married man. High time I set up my nursery with a virgin whose unimpeachable pedigree will restore some prestige to the sadly tainted Harmsworth name."

Cam didn't look any happier. "Marrying a woman you love can be an adventure."

"Love, my dear fellow?" Richard's laugh rang with cynicism. "I plan a fashionable marriage. No mawkish attachment. All I require of a wife is an unquestionably legitimate heir."

"You're selling yourself short. If any man deserves a happy family life, it's you."

Richard shifted uncomfortably. That was the confounded problem with old chums; they saw beyond civilized boundaries to places in a man's soul that he never wanted to visit. "Dash it, Cam, I never thought to hear you turning sentimental."

Cam's expression remained grave. "I can't help envying what Jonas and Sidonie have. He's a better man for knowing her. It makes me think love is worth seeking, whatever the risks."

Richard wasn't fool enough to dismiss the genuine love Jonas shared with his wife, nor the joy he'd found as father to his daughter. "Jonas is a lucky devil. But Sidonie's one in a million. I wouldn't wager sixpence on the chances of finding a woman to equal her."

But as Richard lounged in Cam's luxurious library, so different from the dilapidated room he'd invaded earlier, he couldn't help thinking of another woman. Prickly, clever, and surprisingly appealing Genevieve Barrett with her sharp tongue, snapping gray eyes, and voluptuous body. After tonight's escapade, he found himself anticipating the coming days with an eagerness that would have astounded him this afternoon. Luring the vicar's daughter into surrendering the Harmsworth Jewel promised entertainment beyond compare.

Chapter Three

First Genevieve noticed the dog.

She sat by the window staring vaguely outside, her embroidery ignored on her lap. The vicarage's parlor overlooked a back lane running off the Oxford road. Across the room, her widowed aunt strove to entertain Lord Neville Fairbrother, who had called to see her father. This afternoon the vicar was with a parishioner and Lord Neville, to Genevieve's regret, had decided to wait instead of returning to his nearby manor Youngton Hall. His lordship funded her papa's scholarly endeavors, but she couldn't like the man. Something about his deep-set eyes made her skin crawl and his oppressive presence sucked the air from a room.

When a large mongrel trotted along the lane, she straightened with surprise. In Little Derrick, stray dogs received scant welcome. The brindle hound sat on his haunches and checked back toward the corner. Within moments, a high-perch phaeton of an elegance rarely seen in these parts bowled into view.

Curiosity glued Genevieve to the window. The driver

wore a beautifully cut coat and a beaver hat tipped at what even she recognized as a rakish angle. With the merest touch of his fingers, he controlled the pair of showy chestnut horses drawing the yellow and black carriage.

What brought such a swell to deepest Oxfordshire? He must be lost. The narrow lane led only to the vicarage's stables. No man of style would find their humble abode of interest. Actually she couldn't imagine why a man of style associated with such a déclassé mutt. The gypsies camped by the river would disdain such a dog, yet it was clear from the animal's cheerful bark that he belonged to the driver.

The carriage and its spectacular horses, trailed by the less spectacular hound, disappeared around the wall surrounding the back garden. The man would discover his mistake soon enough and turn around, she supposed.

Genevieve waited for the man and his dog to reappear. A small drama to punctuate a dull afternoon. An afternoon that would have been considerably less dull if Lord Neville hadn't hindered her scholarly pursuits. She had plans in train to change her life and his lordship's presence interfered with their progress.

When the carriage didn't immediately return, she lifted her needle with a sigh. She had little talent for embroidery, but it gave her an excuse to avoid talking to their visitor.

Dorcas, their maid, opened the door, clutching a small cardboard rectangle in her hand. Aunt Lucy had struggled to inculcate the habit of placing calling cards on a salver, but Dorcas couldn't see the necessity. So far, Dorcas was winning that particular war. "Begging your pardon, missus, but the vicar has a visitor."

Aunt Lucy stood to take the creased card, then passed it to Genevieve. *Christopher Evans*. The name meant nothing to her. "Did you say my father isn't home?"

"Yes, miss. But he asks to wait." Dorcas's cheeks flushed a becoming shade of pink. "He's ever so handsome, miss. Pretty as a picture. And such a gentleman."

Despite herself, Genevieve glanced at Lord Neville. He didn't bother to hide his disapproval of Dorcas's flutterings. "Tell the fellow to make an appointment, girl."

How Genevieve would love to remind the arrogant oaf to mind his manners, but her father would never forgive her for alienating his patron. The vicar's living and scholarly work covered essentials, but luxuries came thanks to Lord Neville's support. "It could be something important."

"Indeed." Aunt Lucy ignored his lordship's interjection. "Please invite Mr. Evans to step into the parlor."

Genevieve laid aside her embroidery frame. Rising, she smoothed the skirts on her plain green muslin gown. The man who strolled into the room was the phaeton's driver, as she'd expected. Although for the life of her, she couldn't imagine what business such a tulip of fashion had with her father.

While Dorcas might lack refinement, there was nothing wrong with her eyes. Mr. Evans was, indeed, handsome. Remarkably so.

"Good afternoon, Mr. Evans. I'm Mrs. Warren, the vicar's sister-in-law."

"Your servant, Mrs. Warren." Mr. Evans bowed over Aunt Lucy's hand. Genevieve noted her aunt's dazed admiration. "Please forgive my intrusion. Last night at Sedgemoor's, the vicar was kind enough to ask me to call."

Last night, the vicar had attended another dinner at Leighton Court. He'd come home in an incoherent lather at the attentions he'd received from the duke and his guests.

The newcomer's voice was smooth, educated, and oddly familiar. Genevieve frowned as her mind winnowed where they'd met. Unlike her father, her life was not awash with new acquaintances. The only stranger she'd encountered recently was her mysterious burglar four days ago on the night of the vicar's first visit to the manor.

Half-formed thoughts hurtling through her mind, she studied the stranger. Mr. Evans shared the burglar's height but not his bright gold hair. This man's hair was dull brown. His hair was the only dull thing about him. His face was lean and distinguished. His jaw was firm and determined. His clothing was remarkably elegant, for all that he dressed for the country.

What a fool she was to imagine a fleeting similarity. The Duke of Sedgemoor would hardly play host to a sneak thief. Her nerves were still on edge after the break-in.

"He didn't mention your call," Genevieve said steadily.

Mr. Evans turned to Genevieve and dark blue eyes, guileless as the sky, surveyed her top to toe. Lord Neville inspected her in a similar manner at every meeting. This time instead of aversion, she felt a frisson of feminine awareness. Every nerve tightened with warning. This man had predator stamped all over him.

"Is this an inconvenient time? I can come another day." A quizzical expression lit Mr. Evans's face and Genevieve realized he'd misunderstood her scowl. Apparently awkward social behavior at the vicarage wasn't confined to the maid. Color pricked at her cheeks.

"Mr. Evans, I'm—"

A storm of screeching and hissing drowned her answer. Hecuba, her aged black cat, leaped onto Genevieve's shoulder, dug her claws in, then launched herself at the high shelf lined with china plates. The dog barked once, then settled at his master's heel.

"Good God!" Lord Neville jumped back. Aunt Lucy

shrieked and cowered against her chair. Mr. Evans, who had until now struck her as a rather languid gentleman, moved with impressive speed to save a blue and white Delft plate that Genevieve had always hated.

"I'll put Sirius outside," he said calmly, handing her the dish.

The dog regarded her with reproach. He was behaving perfectly, so she felt like a traitor when she agreed. "That might be wise."

"But first I'll rescue your cat."

"Hecuba doesn't like men," Genevieve said quickly, but Mr. Evans had already reached up. To her astonishment, Hecuba dived into his arms as fast as a gannet plunged into the sea after a herring.

"I see that," he said solemnly. Somehow she knew that beneath his grave demeanor, he laughed at her.

"How bizarre," she said, momentarily distracted from the chaos. Even from a few feet away, Genevieve heard purrs of delight as the big, lean man cradled Hecuba to his dark brown coat. She'd rescued Hecuba as a kitten from neighborhood lads attempting to set fire to her tail. Since then, the cat couldn't abide the touch of any human male.

With a gentleness that made Genevieve's foolish heart skip a beat, Mr. Evans passed Hecuba across. Hecuba's reluctance to forsake her new beau was audible. The man snapped his fingers at the dog. "Come, Sirius. Outside."

Genevieve still recovered from her odd reaction to the sight of those capable, deft hands handling her cat. She bent over Hecuba, hoping that nobody noticed that the usually unruffled Genevieve Barrett was indisputably ruffled.

Who was this fellow? Gentlemen of such address never came within her orbit. Or her father's. Well, apart from the Duke of Sedgemoor. But he was so far beyond her touch, he hardly counted as a mortal man. Lord Neville might be well-born, but he lacked the newcomer's polish.

"Let Sirius stay." She cursed her breathless tone. What on earth was wrong with her? At twenty-five, she was well past the giggly stage. Yet Mr. Evans had an extraordinary effect on her. He made her feel as though her world span out of control. And he'd done it with an ease that she couldn't help resenting.

The man glanced at her and the laughter in his eyes stirred another shiver of awareness. She straightened against unwelcome giddiness. Mr. Christopher Evans was far too charming for his own good.

Or for hers.

"Thank you. He really is well trained." As if to prove it, he clicked his fingers again and Sirius trotted to his side. Once more, Genevieve was struck by the contrast between the man's breeding and the dog's disreputable appearance.

"Allow me to make introductions." She hoped Mr. Evans wouldn't notice the catch in her voice, but she had a sinking feeling that he knew his power over susceptible women—among whom, apparently, she must count herself.

"This is my father's friend, Lord Neville Fairbrother." Genevieve couldn't help contrasting Lord Neville's blunt, swarthy features with Mr. Evans's spare elegance.

"I hope I'm your friend too, Genevieve," Lord Neville sniffed. He gave the stranger a distinctly condescending nod. "Evans."

"Lord Neville."

"And I'm Genevieve Barrett. Please sit down, Mr. Evans." Her aunt had abdicated her duties as hostess in exchange for the delights of ogling their visitor. "I'll ring for tea."

"Thank you." With a flourish, he settled on the spindly chair beside her aunt. The dog, as promised, behaved perfectly and lay at his side without glancing at Hecuba.

"My father is on parish duties." Genevieve retreated to the window seat, still cuddling Hecuba.

The man smiled and Genevieve's heart, which had almost settled into its usual rhythm, jumped again. Handsome? Mr. Christopher Evans, whoever he was, was downright beautiful.

"No matter. I hoped to extend my acquaintance in the neighborhood."

Her skin prickled with preternatural warning. This didn't sound good. This didn't sound good at all. This sounded like he wasn't just passing through. She wasn't usually at the mercy of animal instinct, but every atom insisted that Mr. Evans wasn't what he seemed. The moment he'd spoken, her heart had known him for a liar. And just what was he doing in Little Derrick?

"You'll find no entertainment in this backwater," Lord Neville said snidely as he resumed his chair.

"La, Lord Neville, you are unkind."

Genevieve cringed at her aunt's archness.

"Not at all." He barely disguised his derision. "Beyond our scholarly circle, there's precious little of interest."

"His Grace recommended the scenic beauties of this corner of Oxfordshire." Mr. Evans focused on Genevieve with intent that even a bluestocking couldn't misread. "He didn't exaggerate."

Stupid, stupid blushes. She tried to hold Mr. Evans's gaze, but her nerve failed and she stared out the window. She could already tell that he was an accomplished flirt. Even when the only female within reach was tall, awkward Genevieve Barrett with her ink-stained fingers.

Her hands tightened in Hecuba's silky coat. The cat complained and wriggled free. Ignoring the dog, she twined around the furniture to leap into Mr. Evans's lap.

Immediately those hard capable hands curled around the black cat. Genevieve suppressed another discomfiting reaction.

A rattle along the back lane diverted her troubled thoughts. "Papa is here."

"Excellent," Lord Neville said. "He promised to show me that illuminated manuscript Carruthers sent."

"I hear it's a peach." Mr. Evans's enthusiasm wouldn't shame the keenest medievalist.

Shocked, Genevieve met his brilliant eyes. "You're an antiquarian, Mr. Evans?"

The doubt in her question had her aunt frowning. Poor Aunt Lucy. She'd lived at the vicarage since her sister's death fifteen years ago, and she'd spent most of that time struggling to instill manners into her niece. With little success, Genevieve regretted to admit.

The mobile mouth quirked, although Mr. Evans answered politely enough. "In this company, I'd hesitate to describe myself as such."

Too smooth by half, my fine fellow.

Her father bustled into the room, saving her from responding to their guest's false modesty. "Lord Neville! An unexpected pleasure." Then he turned and spoke with an unalloyed joy that set Lord Neville wincing. "And Mr. Evans! If I'd known you visited, I'd have put off my business. I so enjoyed our discussion last night. Have they given you tea? No? Goodness, what will you think of us? A bunch of country mice, begad."

The vicar wasn't a quiet presence. His voice bounced off the walls and set the dog twitching. Genevieve's father strode across the room to wring Mr. Evans's hand with a zeal that made Genevieve, inclined to disapprove of the newcomer, bristle with resentment. Her father was a man of international reputation, however ill-deserved. He didn't need to toady to the quality.

She sighed, heartily wishing that Mr. Evans would slouch back to wherever he came from. Already she could foresee conflict between him and Lord Neville, and she didn't feel up to dealing with another of her father's crazes.

Fleetingly Genevieve observed her father as a stranger might. Tall, graying, distinguished, with a distracted air that indicated a mind fixed on higher things. Once she'd believed that. Now however much she loved him with a stubborn affection that never wavered, she couldn't contain the coldness that crept into their relations. Her father looked like an Old Testament prophet, but at heart he was a selfish, weak man.

Dorcas chose that moment to bring in the tea tray. The small parlor became uncomfortably crowded. Advancing toward the table, the maid danced around the vicar. Genevieve blushed to see milk splash from the jug. Mr. Evans really would think they were bumpkins. Then she reminded herself that she didn't give a groat what Mr. Evans thought.

Genevieve managed to serve tea without tripping over any of the room's occupants, animal or human. Lord Neville drew her father into a discussion of some scholarly point. Her aunt engaged Mr. Evans in conversation about local amenities. Genevieve retired to the window seat and retrieved her embroidery.

She inhaled and struggled for calm. Absurd to let a handsome face affect her so. She'd always accounted herself immune to masculine attractions. Certainly none of the men in her father's circle had set anything but intellect buzzing. Her reaction to Mr. Evans had nothing at all to do with intellect and it frightened her.

"How charming to see a lady at her sewing."

Skeptically Genevieve glanced up. Mr. Evans leaned against the window frame, watching her. In his arms, that hussy Hecuba looked utterly enraptured.

"I like to keep busy, Mr. Evans." She didn't soften the edge in her voice. He needed to know that not every denizen of Little Derrick's vicarage was ready to roll over and present a belly for scratching. However, the picture of lying before him begging for caresses was so vivid, her wayward color rose. She prayed he didn't notice.

When he placed Hecuba on the floor, the cat regarded both humans with sulky displeasure before stalking away. He plucked the embroidery frame from Genevieve's hold. She waited for some complimentary remark. For purposes that she hadn't yet fathomed, the man seemed determined to charm.

A silence fell. Genevieve dared a glance. He maintained a scrupulously straight face.

"It's a peony," she said helpfully.

His mouth lengthened but, to give him credit, he didn't laugh. "I ... see that."

"Really?" She retrieved her embroidery and inspected it closely. Even she, who knew what it was supposed to represent, had trouble discerning the subject.

Without invitation, Mr. Evans settled on the window seat. He crossed his arms over his chest and extended his long, booted legs across the faded rug. Surreptitiously she inched away.

"I believe you assist your father with his work."

Unfortunately, he couldn't have said anything more liable to annoy her. Her eyes narrowed and old grievances cramped her stomach. "I am most helpful, sir," she said flatly.

The evening light through the window lay across his hair but caught no shine in the brown. Hecuba rubbed against his ankles, purring fit to explode. Catching Lord Neville's glower from across the room, Genevieve bent over her sewing. Surely he didn't imagine she encouraged this decorative interloper. And even if he thought that, he had no right to censure her behavior.

"At Leighton Court last night, the vicar praised your abilities."

"Are you surprised to hear of a woman using her brains?" she asked with a sweetness that would warn anyone who knew her.

He sighed and leveled a surprisingly perceptive regard upon her. "I have a nasty feeling that somewhere I've taken a wrong step with you, Miss Barrett."

For a bristling moment, she stared into his face and wondered why she was so certain that he had ulterior motives.

"It hardly matters." She should turn his comment aside. After all, he wasn't likely to become a fixture in her life. Even if he lingered in the neighborhood, the vicarage's fusty medievalists would soon bore him.

"If I've inadvertently offended, please accept my apologies."

Curse him, he'd shifted closer and his arm draped along the windowsill behind her. She stiffened and, abandoning pride, slid toward the corner. "Mr. Evans, you are presumptuous."

His lips twitched. "Miss Barrett, you are correct."

"Pray be presumptuous at a greater distance."

His laugh was low and attractive. "How can I argue when you're armed?"

She realized that she brandished the needle like a miniature sword. Despite her annoyance, the scene's absurdity struck her and she choked back a laugh. She stabbed the needle into a full-blown peony that sadly resembled a sunburned chicken. "You waste your attentions, sir."

"I hate to think so," he said with a soft intensity that had her regarding him with little short of horror. Was that a challenge? And how on earth should she respond?

Luckily her father spoke. "Mr. Evans, Lord Neville wants to see that codex. Are you interested?"

The vicar's question shattered the taut silence. Mr. Evans blinked as if emerging from a trance. She realized she'd been searching his face with as much attention as she gave a historical document.

He turned toward her father. "Of course, sir. Lead on."

Without the gentlemen and Sirius, the parlor felt forlorn. As though Mr. Evans's departure leached the light away. Genevieve glanced across to where her aunt stared into space, hands loose in her lap.

"What a lovely man," she said dreamily.

Genevieve stifled a growl and stood to collect the teacups and place them onto the tray. "He thinks he is."

Aunt Lucy's stare was surprisingly acute. "Because he treated you like a woman and not some moldy book from your father's library, you've taken against him."

"Don't be a henwit, Aunt. That kind of man flirts with any female in reach. Today that's you, me, and Hecuba."

Hearing her name, Hecuba curled around Genevieve's ankles. "It's too late to make amends, you minx."

"I hope he'll be a regular visitor," her aunt said. "I worry that you'll never find a man to marry."

Shocked, Genevieve nearly dropped the tray. "Aunt! Don't be absurd. Even if I liked Mr. Evans—and I don't, he's too conceited—I don't want a husband. I've got my work."

It was a familiar argument. Her aunt was a conventional woman and couldn't bear for her niece to die a spinster. In Aunt Lucy's eyes, any halfway eligible man who wandered into Genevieve's vicinity was a likely match. She'd once even suggested Genevieve set her cap for Lord Neville. What a nauseating thought. The man was at least twenty years too old, he was bullying and dictatorial, and his touch made her skin itch with revulsion.

"Work won't keep you warm at night." Aunt Lucy paused. "I suspect Mr. Evans would be very . . . warm."

Chapter Four

To Genevieve's chagrin and Hecuba's delight, Mr. Evans stayed for dinner. Carefully Genevieve watched for any disdain for their humble fare or the country hour of the meal. Obscurely it griped her more than any sneer would when the fellow expressed his pleasure with arrangements and tucked in with hearty appetite.

As usual, discussion focused on the vicar's scholarly preoccupations. At present, he was obsessed with proving that the younger prince in the Tower had survived. While her father harangued an apparently fascinated Mr. Evans, Genevieve caught the disapproving arch of Lord Neville's eyebrows. He'd also joined them and now sat beside her. Thank heavens, they had leg of mutton and there was plenty, although plans for using the leftovers for cottage pies faded with every mouthful.

"Do you intend to stay long in the neighborhood, Mr. Evans?" she asked when her father finally lifted his wineglass, allowing someone else to squeeze in a word.

Mr. Evans, on her father's right beside her aunt, smiled

at Genevieve with practiced charm. She could imagine that smile had set countless female hearts fluttering. Unfortunately for Mr. Evans, Genevieve Barrett was made of sterner stuff. Or at least she wished she was.

"I hope so. I'm in the fortunate position of having leisure to follow my inclinations." A mocking light in his eyes hinted that he guessed how his efforts to please irked her.

"You're acquainted with Sedgemoor, I believe," Lord Neville growled, slicing at his mutton as if it were Mr. Evans's hide.

Genevieve could imagine how Mr. Evans's friendship with Camden Rothermere grated on Lord Neville. Lord Neville might dismiss what he termed the fribbles and flibbertigibbets infesting London society, but she'd long ago recognized the pique behind his derision. His lordship wasn't sparkling company and wouldn't shine outside antiquarian circles. Even in scholarly circles, he earned respect more for his family and fortune than for his intellect. While he was far from a stupid man and he had a magnificent collection that she'd been privileged to work on, Lord Neville remained a dilettante.

Mr. Evans sipped the fine claret that Lord Neville supplied to her father and answered with a coolness that only emphasized his lordship's churlishness. "We were at school together. I'm proud to call him my friend."

"Where are your people, Mr. Evans?" Until now, Aunt Lucy had sat quietly. The price of sharing her brother's roof was enduring arcane discussions that held no shred of interest for her. "Evans is a Welsh name, is it not?"

"My family is in Shropshire. Perhaps we were Welsh originally." His voice warmed as he addressed her aunt.

"Wouldn't an enthusiastic amateur historian investigate?" Genevieve had no idea what Mr. Evans hoped to gain from his association with her father, but she'd wager every penny she had that he harbored no genuine interest in the Middle Ages.

Her question didn't unsettle him. She reached the conclusion that Mr. Evans would retain his sangfroid standing naked between the French and English lines at Waterloo. While she'd never met a rake, something told her that Mr. Evans played the rake to perfection.

If he was a rake, perhaps he contemplated seduction. But surely she was beneath his touch and the only other female under thirty in the house was Dorcas. The idea of elegant Mr. Evans pursuing the scatterbrained maid tempted her to giggle into her gravy.

"I'm hoping your distinguished father will guide my research."

"Hunting a noble ancestor?" Lord Neville scoffed, earning a frown from Aunt Lucy. "Some Welsh princeling?"

Mr. Evans's affability didn't falter. "We're not a grand family."

But wealthy with old money, Genevieve could tell. It wasn't just that everything about him screamed expense. It was also his assurance, as though he found a welcome everywhere because of who he was. This man had never had cause to doubt himself.

"What about your wife, Mr. Evans?" Aunt Lucy asked with wide-eyed innocence.

Genevieve kicked her aunt under the table. Or at least that was the plan. Mr. Evans released a soft huff of surprise and shifted in his seat. Dear Lord. Now she'd demonstrated that she had the manners of a drunken cowherd. She must be as red as a tomato.

"Alas, I'm not married, Mrs. Warren. Perhaps I'll discover some lovely ladies in Oxfordshire." His lips curved in pure devilment. "Of course, no ladies could be lovelier than the two sharing this table."

"Sir, you flatter us," Aunt Lucy simpered.

She'd been a pretty girl, the toast of Taunton. Much as Genevieve discounted Mr. Evans's flummery, she couldn't begrudge her aunt the chance to relive her youthful triumphs. The soldier she'd married had died within a year on the Peninsular campaign. Aunt Lucy was born to mother a brood of children and cosset a doting husband. Instead she'd landed up as companion to an eccentric, self-centered brother and his gawky daughter.

"Not at all, Mrs. Warren." Mr. Evans raised his glass. "To my beautiful hostesses."

"Stuff and nonsense," her father interrupted with his usual insensitivity. "Lucinda's too old for such flannel. Fifty if she's a day."

Genevieve bit back a remonstrance.

"True beauty knows no age," Mr. Evans said firmly.

The flash of anger in his blue eyes mitigated Genevieve's hostility, although it didn't make her trust him any further. She still couldn't work out why a man who looked ready to grace a royal banquet sat at her lowly table.

Richard enjoyed his evening more than expected, although meeting the beauteous Genevieve four days ago should have prepared him. The prospect of a leisurely flirtation while he convinced her to sell the Harmsworth Jewel became more appealing with each moment.

He even found the scholarly discussion interesting. At Oxford, he'd been an erratic student. Life had offered too many other amusements for a presentable young man of immense fortune. But apparently he'd picked up more in his history tutorials than he'd thought.

Dr. Barrett's academic reputation was a puzzle. Before Richard embarked on this scheme, he'd read some of the vicar's articles. They were clever and incisive, revealing a mind of breathtaking subtlety and imagination. After several hours in his company, none of those adjectives matched Richard's impressions of Little Derrick's vicar. Richard also picked up a trace of discord between the vicar and his daughter. Now, what in Hades was that all about? And how would it affect his plans?

Under cover of listening, he observed his companions. For an obscure country village, they were an intriguing lot. The aunt was charming and patently interested in forwarding his acquaintance with Genevieve. Lord Neville didn't appreciate competition and bent more than one possessive glance at the oblivious girl. He wondered why Mrs. Warren didn't promote that union. All the Fairbrothers were disgustingly wealthy, including this man's nephew, the Marquess of Leath. Lord Neville was too old for the chit, but otherwise he'd make an enviable husband. Or so common sense insisted. Richard's gut revolted at the idea of Genevieve's beauty and spirit in thrall to the condescending rhinoceros.

They retired to the parlor for tea. Richard fell into conversation with Mrs. Warren. Aunt Lucy liked him. As did Hecuba, the man-hating cat, who purred on his lap. Sirius was tied up outside, sulking. What a pity the vicar's daughter was as far from purring as Richard was from Peking. He had no idea what he'd done to raise her hackles, but she watched him as if expecting him to purloin the silver. She couldn't recognize him as her burglar. He'd been masked that night, his hair was now a different color, and Sedgemoor had vouched for him.

In fact, it surprised Richard how easily everyone accepted him as rich Mr. Evans from Shropshire. He wasn't used to meeting people without the scandal surrounding his birth tainting introductions. It was both appealing and galling, reminding him yet again of the barriers his bastardy placed between him and the world.

"Genevieve, leave those dusty books and help me sort my wools," Mrs. Warren called.

"Papa wants to show me this document." Genevieve didn't shift from the table where she, Lord Neville, and the vicar pored over a manuscript.

"Tomorrow. You're neglecting our guest."

Richard caught the twinkle in Mrs. Warren's eyes. He knew what she was up to. And she knew that he knew. Genevieve was aware too, but without overt rudeness, couldn't ignore her aunt's request.

He watched Genevieve approach. Today before arriving, he'd wondered whether he'd idealized her attractions, but one glance at that beautiful face, severe in his presence, and he knew that this was a gem worth the mining. A treasure to rival the Harmsworth Jewel. This afternoon, she'd played the cold goddess. Now in candlelight, she was all gold and shadows.

The pity of it was that she was a respectable woman. Honor precluded seduction. Although with all the lies he told, his honor grew grubbier by the hour.

"More tea, Mr. Evans?" Genevieve's chilly question made him want to shiver theatrically.

"Please, Miss Barrett."

Mrs. Warren turned to him. "Were you in Little Derrick for last week's excitement, Mr. Evans?"

"Aunt, I'm sure Mr. Evans has no interest in local trivialities," Genevieve said repressively.

"On the contrary, I'm all ears." He hid a smile when she all but lashed her tail. Everything indicated her inexperience with men. A more worldly woman wouldn't fling challenges with every flash of those arctic-gray eyes. She hoped to freeze him into retreating, whereas with her, ice burned.

"Genevieve saw off a thief!" Mrs. Warren's breathless announcement earned a derisive glance from her niece. "Only shooting at the rascal saved her."

Richard regarded Genevieve with exaggerated admiration. "Good heavens, Miss Barrett, you're Boadicea reborn."

Her lips flattened as she refreshed his tea. Heat bubbled in his veins as he remembered holding her. She'd been soft and fragrant. Her hair had slid against his skin like warm silk. Hecuba complained as his lap firmed. He stroked the cat and strove for control.

"The man was a coward. When he discovered the house occupied, he scarpered with his tail between his legs."

For shame, Miss Barrett. It seems I'm not the only liar in the house.

"Isn't my girl brave?" The vicar left Lord Neville at the table.

"Hardly, Papa," Genevieve said uncomfortably. "I told the fellow to leave and he went. By then, he'd probably guessed that there was nothing worth stealing."

She deuced well should be uncomfortable, fibbing to her nearest and dearest. The encounter mightn't have gone completely Richard's way, but she hadn't scared him off like a panicked rabbit.

"You're quite the heroine," Mrs. Warren said. "I would have fainted into his arms with terror."

Richard was pleased to note the color lining the girl's slanted cheekbones. She hadn't fainted, but by Jove, she'd been in his arms. At the time, he'd considered kissing her. He'd certainly wanted to.

"I'm sure you wouldn't, Aunt. He was a most unimpressive

specimen. Skinny and half-starved. Why, Hecuba could have taken him." She glanced at Richard. "Are you all right, Mr. Evans?"

He realized he'd replaced his cup on its saucer with a loud clink. The urge to wring her neck—after kissing her within an inch of her life—rose. His voice remained even. "Perfectly, thank you, Miss Barrett. I've realized how late it is."

As if to confirm that it wasn't late at all, the hall clock struck nine.

"Must you go?" It was Mrs. Warren, not her niece, who asked. The niece's expression indicated that she was happy that he left the vicarage and she'd be even happier if he left the neighborhood for good.

We don't always get what we want, Richard thought as he rose. "Indeed I must. Thank you, Dr. Barrett and Mrs. Warren, for your kind hospitality. Lord Neville." He bowed to Genevieve. "Your servant, Miss Barrett."

"Are you sure you won't stay? Our groom has gone for the night. It's no trouble to make a bed." Mrs. Warren gazed at him as if he carried the map to the Promised Land. Poor Genevieve, if her aunt subjected every male visitor to such matchmaking. No wonder she was testy.

He needed to regroup, to shake off Genevieve's surprisingly powerful influence. And something told him his strategy was better served by leaving. "I can manage my carriage."

"If you insist." The vicar didn't hide his disappointment.

"Genevieve, show Mr. Evans out," Mrs. Warren said.

Flushing with chagrin, Genevieve put down her tea. "Very well. Mr. Evans?"

"Miss Barrett." He took her arm as she stood.

She stiffened beneath his touch and the instant they'd passed through the door, she jerked free. "It's only three steps."

*   *   *

Genevieve abhorred this fluster. She'd always considered herself above female foibles; the thrill at spying a handsome man, the primping and preening. Yet even now, she was painfully conscious that she'd spilled ink on her sleeve and her hair hadn't seen a comb since this morning. Next to Mr. Evans's perfect tailoring, she felt shabby and disheveled and inadequate.

She shut the door to keep Hecuba in the parlor. Mr. Evans stopped, blast him, in the flagstoned hall. The space had never felt so small. He turned to her, puzzlement darkening his features. "Why don't you like me, Miss Barrett?"

She couldn't help herself. She laughed. "Hasn't anyone ever disliked you?"

He had the grace to look slightly shamefaced. "If I say no, I'll sound like a complete ass."

"Although nobody ever has disliked you, have they?"

He shrugged. "Generally not young ladies."

Her lips quirked with wry agreement. "I can imagine."

He stepped closer. With difficulty she held her ground, although every feminine instinct screamed to run. "I'd like us to be friends."

Now it was her turn to be puzzled. "Why?"

"Your father hasn't told you?"

A chill presentiment of disaster oozed down her spine. "Told me what?"

"The vicar has invited me to study with him. I'm moving out of Leighton Court tomorrow and coming here."

"Oh, no." Genevieve only realized she'd spoken aloud when humor turned his face to brilliance.

"Tell me what you really think."

No other man made her blush like this or provoked her to say such idiotic things. And their acquaintance only started.

The idea of sharing the same roof made her stomach cramp with dismay. Still, she'd been appallingly rude and to give him credit, he'd taken it in good spirit. "I'm sorry."

Mr. Evans collected his hat from the stand. "Perhaps you'll like me once we're better acquainted."

And perhaps cows might sing Rossini. But she kept that thought to herself. Was she learning discretion? She'd need to if Mr. Evans became her houseguest. She consigned her father to perdition, not for the first time, for his impetuousness. But he was the master of the house and he expected his womenfolk to obey his whims. The task that currently engaged her became more urgent with every day.

"How long are you staying?" she asked stiffly.

Something about Mr. Evans's smile made her step back. She'd feel less foolish if she could identify one particular element in his manner that unnerved her. Well, until he smiled at her the way he smiled now. He looked like a hungry tiger contemplating a lamb chop. Trepidation shivered along her veins and her heart thumped chaotically against her ribs.

"As long as it takes," he said softly. His eyelids lowered, lending him a disconcertingly saturnine air. For most of the evening, he'd played the perfect guest. But in the space of a second, he transformed into a man who clearly intended seduction.

She told herself she let the fright she'd suffered from the burglary turn her into a nervous wreck. Surely she mistook him. A dull bluestocking past first youth couldn't attract this Adonis.

"Stop flirting," she said firmly. "You're only doing it because there isn't another woman here."

This time he laughed out loud. The sound was attractive. Open. Joyful. Genuine. "You defeat me, Miss Barrett. How am I to work my wiles when you undo me at every turn?"

She didn't smile back, although something in his unabashed

delight tugged at her heart. "I don't want you to work your wiles, Mr. Evans."

"Your aunt likes me."

Genevieve's huff approached a snort. "My aunt likes any man who's breathing and unmarried."

Curse him, he shouldn't laugh again. Her glare did nothing to quell his amusement. "The longer we're alone, the keener she'll be to see your ring on my finger."

He slouched against the newel post and regarded her as if she provided marvelous entertainment. She was sure she did. He probably hadn't toyed with such an awkward female since his first dance lessons. Among the reasons he set her bristling like an angry cat was that she felt irredeemably gauche in his presence.

"You mention marriage with disdain worthy of a rake," he said drily.

"You'd know."

He arched one eyebrow. "I'm merely a country gentleman pursuing intellectual interests."

"Not even I'm green enough to believe that."

"Ah," he said softly. "So it's not that you don't like me, it's that you don't trust me."

She retreated until she collided with the wall. For one frantic moment, she wished she'd spent fewer nights over her books and more at the local assemblies. She was completely out of her depth with this urbane man. "Can't it be both?"

He stepped closer. "Is it?"

She stared at him, her heart racing. She'd never been kissed. Until this moment, she hadn't marked the lack. Right now, she had a horrible feeling that her unkissed days were numbered. Might perhaps end this second. She wondered why the prospect left her excited rather than outraged. She should itch to slap this Lothario's face.

"Please go." She cursed her husky tone. "Aunt Lucy will post the banns if I'm not back in the library within the next five minutes."

"You're not really at your last prayers, are you?"

Color flooded her cheeks and she spoke sharply. "I'm not praying at all. I'm not interested in marriage."

"Miss Barrett, you shock me."

She frowned, then realized he'd misunderstood. Deliberately. "I'm a scholar, not a courtesan," she snapped.

Did he lean a fraction closer? Or did her imagination play tricks? Heaven help her. He was moving into the vicarage. Eons of this torment stretched ahead. How on earth would she survive?

"Pity." He straightened and set his hat at a jaunty angle. "Until tomorrow, Miss Barrett."

And the day after that, she thought despairingly. Her father welcomed a wolf into the sheepfold.

She drew herself up, reminding herself that she was clever and strong and had never fallen victim to a man's stratagems. Not that the distant adoration she'd incited in her father's previous students compared.

She spoke with commendable conviction. "I can't see what amusement you'll find with a country vicar and his ape-leader of a daughter."

Did she mistake the sudden fire in his eyes? "I'll let you know if I'm bored."

"What do you want, Mr. Evans?" she asked dazedly.

He stepped back and bowed with an aplomb she envied. She must have mistaken that brief, intense flash of sexual awareness. A deep breath loosened the invisible band around her chest.

"Miss Barrett, once I thought I knew. But now? Now, the game has changed." He touched his hat with a confidence that reminded her why he irked her. "Good evening."

He lifted a candle with a gesture that stirred memory. Somewhere, sometime recently she'd watched a man like this lighting a candle in a shadowy room. But in her agitation, she couldn't tease any sense from the scrap of recollection.

"Good evening, Mr. Evans."

She wished she didn't sound so breathless. Dear Lord, he hadn't touched her, hadn't come within a foot of her. Yet she dithered like a besotted milkmaid. She needed to rush upstairs and bury herself in something dry and dull like the local shire rolls. Something as dull as she'd promised Mr. Evans his stay at the vicarage would prove.

Instead she lingered in the hall after he left. She didn't shift until she heard his carriage rattle away over the cobblestones.

Chapter Five

Once Richard moved into the cramped back bedroom, his visions of lazy days flirting with Genevieve Barrett evaporated under the reality of vicarage life. Dr. Barrett was overjoyed to have an assistant who paid generously for the privilege, and even more welcome, an audience for his endless theorizing. Lucy Warren provided more agreeable company and was remarkably confiding about her niece. But Richard was staying ostensibly to widen his knowledge of all things Middle Ages, so he couldn't devote too much time to the aunt without rousing suspicions about his historical interests. Lord Neville visited every day and proved an inconvenient presence, dogging Richard's footsteps as if fearing for the church plate.

While his acquaintance, congenial or not, developed with the vicarage's other denizens, Miss Barrett proved elusive. As did any chance to worm the Harmsworth Jewel away from her. If Richard hadn't seen the jewel the night he'd broken in, he'd begin to doubt the artifact was in the house. Nobody, including Miss Barrett, mentioned it.

After three frustrating days meeting her only at meals, not to mention learning more than he'd ever wanted to know about the Princes in the Tower, Richard resorted to drastic measures.

Quietly he opened the door to the small upstairs room where he'd first encountered Genevieve. It was so early, the sky was dark. In Town, he often saw the dawn, but as the end of a night's entertainment, not the start of a day's scholarship. Across the faded carpet, candlelight formed a circle around the woman bent writing over the desk.

His breath caught as he stood transfixed, astonished anew at her beauty. She sat slightly turned away, revealing her profile. Straight, autocratic nose; determined chin; lashes lowered against high cheekbones as she concentrated too deeply to notice her observer. The sleeve of her faded dimity dress drooped from her shoulder, revealing the strap of her shift. A striped pinafore protected the front of her gown.

In Richard's glittering world, female beauty was no rarity. But this dauntingly clever vicar's daughter was the loveliest woman he'd ever seen.

He suffered a momentary pang that he didn't pursue her as his real self. But then, Genevieve would despise the shallow Sir Richard Harmsworth. Hell, she didn't much like Christopher Evans.

Without Sirius's interruption, he might have watched forever, but he must have left his bedroom door along the corridor ajar. Sirius squeezed past him now and trotted up to the desk.

"Hello. Where did you come from?" Genevieve spoke with a warmth she'd never directed at Richard, damn it. When she glanced up, she started. Then her closed expression felt like a winter wind. To his regret, she tugged her sleeve over her pale shoulder. "Mr. Evans."

"Miss Barrett." At this hour, he couldn't help thinking that they'd both be better off in bed. His bed. Not that wanting did much good. Lusting after a chaste woman promised only frustration.

"You surprised me."

"Are your nerves on edge?"

She shrugged. "I'm jumpy after the break-in."

Guilt stabbed him. She'd been so indomitable facing down his burglar self, it hadn't occurred to him that she'd been genuinely frightened.

Masking her vulnerability, she extended a hand to scratch Sirius behind the ears. Ridiculous to be jealous of a dog, but Richard was.

"What are you doing awake?" she asked.

To confirm the uncivilized hour, a lark burst into a torrent of silvery song outside. He decided to be honest. Well, as honest as a man sporting a false name could be. "You're avoiding me."

She didn't meet his eyes. "Nonsense."

"I moved in three days ago and we've hardly exchanged a word since."

"You're here to work with my father." Her dry tone indicated that she questioned his dedication to scholarship. Clever girl. With a doggy groan, Sirius stretched out beneath the windowsill.

"You're more decorative."

She pursed her lips. The expression didn't look forbidding. It looked like she meant to kiss him. The thought lit the cool dawn to flame.

Gently he closed the door and stepped into the bookcase-lined room. Books and papers littered every flat surface. The shambles was endearing. The rest of the house was dauntingly ordered. When he'd broken in, he hadn't noted his surroundings. The woman had occupied his attention. The woman and the Harmsworth Jewel.

She set down her pen. "I need to help Dorcas with breakfast."

He didn't shift. "Dorcas is still enjoying the sleep of the just."

"We'll wake everyone if we talk here."

"I'll keep my voice down." The vicarage was old. Seventeenth century, he guessed. The walls and doors were so thick, no sound penetrated. After he'd locked Genevieve in, he'd barely heard her protests.

"It's inappropriate for us to be alone." She jerked to her feet, upsetting the horn cup of water on the desk. "Bother!"

He surged forward to hold her wrist. Her skin was warm and he caught a drift of her morning scent. Flowers and woman. "Let me."

"No, I'll fix it." Ink-stained fingers fluttered in protest without making contact.

When he released her, he heard her relieved exhalation. Her eyes fixed upon a gold object on the crowded desk. It proved how distracting she was that he only now realized that, as on the first night, the Harmsworth Jewel sat for the plucking, if he was so bold.

He wasn't so bold.

"I hope the water hasn't damaged anything." Drawing his handkerchief from his coat, he mopped up the spillage. Thank goodness, the cup had been nearly empty.

"Only some notes I'm working on." With little ceremony, Genevieve pushed him out of the way and grabbed a crumpled cloth from the floor. Carefully she sponged the sheet she'd been writing on. The ink blotched and she tossed the cloth into a corner with a sigh.

With every moment, the day brightened. Soon he'd have

no excuse to detain her. Richard wondered, not for the first time, if he'd find her so fascinating if she didn't prickle with hostility. Then he remembered her serene beauty in the candlelight. She'd attract him whatever she did. Something about her made him feel alive. Was it just that she saw him as a man, not as the notorious Harmsworth bastard? Or was it something more?

He looked around with a deliberately casual air. "What do you do in here?"

She cast him a suspicious look as he lifted a pile of papers from the desk and perched his hip on the space. "What do you care?"

He cared more than she imagined. In his peripheral vision, the Harmsworth Jewel shone red, blue, and gold. Strategy suggested an oblique approach to his real interest. His real *interests*. Genevieve's lure became at least as powerful as the family relic's.

He met her challenge with a level stare. "Why so secretive?"

She slumped into her chair and regarded the soaked page with a disgruntled expression. "Do you like working with my father?"

"Yes," he said, not altogether truthfully. He enjoyed reviving his rusty Latin and Greek, but the vicar wasn't the intellectual powerhouse reputation indicated. Richard was yet to glimpse the brilliance that illuminated the articles. "I thought you acted as his assistant."

"I do." An unreadable expression crossed her lovely face.

He'd caught vague hints of an estrangement between the vicar and his daughter, but now he was sure of it. Genevieve was yet to join one of his sessions with Dr. Barrett. That suddenly struck him as more significant than her merely avoiding a guest's company.

Idly he lifted a page covered with writing. She had a strong, almost masculine hand.

"Put that down!" She rushed around the desk and snatched uselessly at the paper.

"Indulge me." He stepped sideways and started to read, then frowned. He put down that page and reached around her for the next. After a few minutes, he replaced the pages and lifted his head to stare at her in shock. "It's you."

She scowled, panting with annoyance at his high-handed behavior. He rather liked that she made no attempt to charm him. Women always strove to turn him up sweet, however disreputable his birth. "What on earth are you talking about?"

"Dr. Barrett isn't the brilliant mind here. His daughter is. You write the articles."

Genevieve paled and backed against the desk. Her hand clenched on her ruined manuscript, crushing the damp paper into a ball. "Don't be absurd. I'm a mere woman."

He laughed, genuinely delighted. "That's the first coy thing I've heard you say."

Her jaw set in a mutinous line. "Any article written in this house is published under my father's name."

"It's all your work." He watched her struggle to deny the truth. But the lightning intelligence and sharp perception demonstrated in the articles, and lacking in the vicar, were clear from the first line. "Come, there's no point nay-saying. I *know* you're the scholar here."

Briefly he wondered whether he could turn this knowledge against her, use it to obtain the jewel. Would she sell him the heirloom in return for his silence on her authorship? He tucked the thought away to consider later, even as he recognized his reluctance to resort to blackmail. Ridiculous when the whole purpose of this masquerade was to winkle out the chit's secrets.

"I have no qualifications."

"Apart from a brain the size of St. Paul's. And a lifetime in scholarly circles." Still, he was impressed at what she'd achieved without formal education. Ignoring her resistance, he lifted the hand curled around the soggy paper and placed a kiss across her knuckles. For once he wasn't being seductive. "Deny the fact until Christmas, but it won't do any good. I'm in awe, Miss Barrett."

She cast him an uncertain glance under her lashes. Another woman might mean flirtation, but he'd concluded that Genevieve Barrett had never learned the wiles of her worldly sisters.

When he let her go, she began to shred the paper, her hands working nervously in front of her extravagantly pocketed pinafore. "You can't share your suspicions. They could destroy my father's reputation."

After lifting some books off the seat, he moved a chair from the wall to the desk. Dust flew and he sneezed. Sirius started up in surprise from where he lay in sleepy contentment. Sitting, Richard surveyed her with unfettered admiration. "Your brilliance should receive acknowledgement."

Her voice expressionless, she retreated to sit behind the desk. "Papa offered to credit me as coauthor after I turned twenty-one, but that is yet to eventuate."

Genevieve's careful neutrality indicated that this was a sore point. No wonder she resented her father. As a man familiar with parental betrayal, Richard felt for her. "Surely people suspect."

"There's no reason they should." In her eyes, he read displeasure at how quickly he'd uncovered her secret.

"I knew the moment I read that first page."

"A lucky guess."

"Perhaps we're particularly attuned, Miss Barrett."

Her expression didn't lighten. "Stop flirting. This is serious."

He laughed softly and leaned back in his chair. "Believe me, flirting is a serious business." He sobered. "Fairbrother must have an inkling."

Lord Neville strove to make Richard feel like an interloper. Richard had immediately recognized that the man protected his territory. The question was—what was his territory? Scholarly pursuits? The vicar? The vicar's dangerously unsuspecting daughter? Or all three?

A cynical light entered Genevieve's eyes. "Lord Neville's interest is his collection, not scholarship for its own sake."

An interesting opinion. And one that wouldn't please his overbearing lordship, Richard thought with unworthy satisfaction. "You can't hide in your father's shadow forever."

The tension drained from her shoulders and she answered with unexpected readiness. Perhaps the relief of sharing the truth with someone, even his unworthy self, encouraged confidences. "I'm publishing an article about the Harmsworth Jewel under my own name."

Holy God above. No wonder she didn't want to sell the artifact. He barely stopped himself choking with appalled astonishment.

He struggled to act as if this revelation incited only mild curiosity. "What?"

"That's it." She pointed at the enamel and gold object, as if he needed help locating it. "My findings should set the scholarly world abuzz. Or at least that section of the scholarly world interested in the Anglo-Saxons." Her tone turned wry as she acknowledged that this esoteric field rarely impinged on the wider public.

She lifted the jewel, her hands sure, almost careless. His belly clenched with conflicting impulses. The urge to grab the girl. The urge to grab the jewel.

"A wonderful old lady bequeathed it to me. She was a disciple of Mary Wollstonecraft and until you, the only person to guess that I wrote most of Papa's published works. It's a family heirloom."

Damn it, it certainly was. And not one that Amelia, Viscountess Bellfield, had any business handing on. Richard gritted his teeth against informing Genevieve that the jewel belonged to him.

"She must have been fond of you." He hoped to hell his voice didn't sound as strangled to Genevieve as in his ears. Patience, he reminded himself, patience. He'd get the jewel off her in good time.

"I loved her dearly too." Genevieve's admiration for Lady Bellfield was audible. "She was a noted bluestocking and owned an impressive collection of books and antiquities."

"One would think she'd keep something so valuable in the family."

"She'd had a falling out with the Harmsworths. She particularly disliked the current baronet. Some family scandal made him unfit to hold the title."

Despite himself, Richard winced. The hell of it was that the disgrace never died. Call him a slow learner, but he now understood that it never would, whoever possessed the Harmsworth Jewel. Which made him no less determined to restore the trinket to Polliton Place, the family seat in Norfolk. It belonged to the head of the Harmsworth family. And, bastardy or no, that was him.

He'd always liked Great Aunt Amelia, for all her fearsome reputation. A shock to discover that because he was a bastard, she couldn't abide him. Old anger tightened his gut. Anger and shame.

Luckily Genevieve studied the jewel, not his reactions. "That was a condition of inheriting. Under no circumstances was Lady Bellfield's great-nephew Richard Harmsworth to obtain the jewel."

God rot Great Aunt Amelia for an interfering old witch.

"I doubt the executors would prosecute if you sold it." Richard tried to sound disingenuous. Genevieve cast him a questioning glance that indicated he'd failed. Hardly surprising. Genuine innocence had been a casualty of childhood bullying. "I imagine you'd get a good price."

"Strange that you say that. A few months ago, Sir Richard discovered I had the jewel. He's pestering me to sell."

"At a bargain price?" He'd offered her a fortune. He waited to hear if any amount might change her mind. At least he now understood why his agents had failed. Part of him admired Genevieve's loyalty to Aunt Amelia, while another part cursed this complication.

"Money seemed no object. Odd when Lady Bellfield indicated Sir Richard wasn't interested in family history."

Little do you know, sweetheart. "The jewel is very beautiful."

"And reputedly powerful. There's a myth that Alfred the Great presented it to a Harmsworth ancestor for foiling a Viking assassination. The jewel passed from Harmsworth father to son, confirming the heir's right to inherit. Such tales abound in old families. That's one fascinating element of my research."

"Perhaps you should sell." A critical light in his eyes, he surveyed the shabby room. "Think what you could do."

She shrugged. "I owe Lady Bellfield better return for her generosity."

Damn, why must Genevieve be such a stickler? "Did she forbid any sale?"

If there was a ban on disposing of the thing altogether, he'd have to steal it. Which meant he could never display it openly. With every moment, his quest became more tangled.

"It's mine unconditionally, as long as I never sell to Richard Harmsworth or his heirs." She paused. "I hope that my article creates opportunities for me. I'd only sell the jewel out of dire necessity."

Relief flooded him. There was still a chance he could buy it. "Once your article comes out, people will know you wrote your father's pieces."

Irritation lit her gaze. "My father's work has been devoted entirely to the high Middle Ages. He isn't renowned as a Dark Ages specialist. Any similarities in style will be credited to my father being my teacher."

Unable to resist any longer, he reached out, "May I see it?"

Her hand curled around the jewel as if she mistrusted his intentions. By heaven, nothing was wrong with the girl's instincts. "It's very fragile."

"I'll be careful." He had more reason to respect the jewel than any man in England.

She sighed and he thought she might refuse. But after a hesitation, she passed it across.

The breath jammed in his throat and he lowered his eyes to conceal his possessive excitement. The gold was warm from her hands. What an intimate sensation, like touching her skin instead of inanimate metal. The jewel was unexpectedly heavy, as though it carried the weight of the centuries. Holding this heirloom left him surprisingly moved. Finally he claimed his right to the Harmsworth name.

He rose and stepped toward the window on mortifyingly shaky legs to inspect the piece in the light. And also to escape Genevieve's all-encompassing stare. She mustn't guess this moment's significance.

The drawings he'd seen didn't do the object justice. The jewel was about five inches long. A chased gold handle shaped like a dragon supported a gold oval containing an enamel image of a saint with large dark eyes like a child's drawing. It was a thousand years old; beautiful, uncanny, unique. The blue and red enamels were as vivid, he was sure, as the day they were fired.

Here in Oxfordshire, he played at finding the past as fascinating as the present. But touching this tangible link to generations of Harmsworths, he sensed something of Genevieve's passion for history. The need to guard this talisman was the most powerful emotion he'd ever felt. His hand closed around the relic. Every atom in his body revolted at the idea of relinquishing it.

He forced himself to look toward the woman, the woman he came to want almost as much as he wanted the jewel. "Shouldn't you lock it away in a strongbox or a bank?"

Genevieve looked troubled. "I need it for my work."

"The article is important enough to risk this priceless artifact?"

"My whole future depends on it." For once he had no doubt that she revealed her soul. "If I establish an independent reputation, I can support myself as an antiquarian, doing everything that I currently do for my father. I've told you that I'll never marry—a husband would constrain my pursuits—so I need an income."

And, he guessed from what she didn't say, a life away from the vicar.

Inconvenient it might be, but he couldn't help admiring that she'd refused to sell the jewel to his agents. Ten thousand guineas would set her up in her own household for life. "Does Dr. Barrett know of your plans?"

Guilt shadowed her features. "I haven't told him yet."

"He won't like the competition."

She raised her head, a plea in her silvery eyes. "I want

to present everything as a fait accompli." She paused. "You must think me unnatural."

He smiled and moved closer. "It's time you claimed your due."

"Thank you." She flushed and glanced to where he clutched the jewel as though his life depended upon it. Right now, mad as it was, he thought his life did.

Genevieve continued. "I'm surprised the thief last week didn't take the jewel. Aside from the historical interest, it's solid gold. I've thought over and over about what he hoped to find. Anyone can tell there's no money in the house, so why break in? The jewel is the most valuable item we have. Yet outside the family and Lady Amelia's solicitors, the only person who suspects it's here is Sir Richard Harmsworth. If Sir Richard sent the thief for the jewel, the fellow must have seen it. It was sitting on the desk as clear as day."

"Perhaps he was blinded by your beauty." Richard wasn't entirely joking, even as he cursed her clever brain for narrowing blame for the burglary down to his real self.

She sent him a quelling glance. "He wasn't much of a thief. We haven't found anything missing."

Bloody hell. What a stupid mistake. He should have lifted something worthless from downstairs. A burglar fleeing empty-handed aroused unwelcome curiosity. Too late now. "Would you rather he'd stripped the vicarage?"

"Don't be absurd." She sounded uncomfortable. Did she recall that thrilling moment when he'd held her close? It haunted his dreams.

He braced his shoulders. "Will you sell it to me? I'll double Sir Richard's offer."

Silence crashed down. Even his heart seemed to stop beating. Shocked silvery gray eyes focused on him and the hands she laid on the desk closed into fists.

Her reply seemed to take forever. "It's not for sale."

His relief made no sense. He was here for the jewel. Buying the bauble after a few days counted as a major victory. Or at least it should.

He forced himself to continue negotiations. "You'd be welcome to keep it until you've finished your article."

She already shook her head. "Thank you, but no."

So the game played on. He tried to tell himself that he was disappointed. Even he didn't believe that was true. It was a long time since he'd found a woman as intriguing as he found Genevieve Barrett. He wasn't ready to abandon her.

Her eyes sharpened. "Can I have the jewel back, please?"

Surrendering the jewel felt like treason. In the transaction, his hand grazed hers. She jerked back as if his touch burned. Heat shuddered through him.

Her gaze leaped to meet his and he read renewed wariness in her eyes. "You offer more than the jewel is worth."

He shrugged and stared hard at her. "When I want something, I go to any length to get it."

She paled. "You . . . scare me when you say such things."

His eagerness threatened to send her fleeing in fright. If he wasn't careful he'd lose both jewel and woman—it became increasingly inconvenient to remember that only a cad played fast and loose with a lady's reputation.

He might be a bastard, but he wasn't quite a cad. Or not yet.

"You mistake me. I merely found myself with a fancy to own a pretty thing." Two pretty things, in fact. He adopted an innocent air as he stepped away from the desk to stretch ostentatiously. "I'm off for a ride before breakfast."

"I trust you not to share anything we've discussed." Unsurprisingly she regretted her confidences.

"You have my promise." His carefree smile didn't

extinguish the doubt in her expression. "I'll see you later, Miss Barrett."

Beneath his nonchalance, his thoughts were troubled. Nor had he conquered the turbulent emotions that had stirred when he'd touched the jewel. After this morning, he knew more about the jewel and he knew more about Genevieve, but everything he'd learned fouled his path.

Chapter Six

As everyone sat in the parlor before dinner, Genevieve watched Mr. Evans from her place on the window seat as unwaveringly as she'd watch a cobra. He played some silly card game with her aunt, who would be his willing slave even without her unconcealed ambitions for marrying him to her niece.

Within ten minutes of his departure from her study this morning, Genevieve had realized her terrible mistake. Why, oh, why had she been so forthcoming? She didn't trust Mr. Evans. She hadn't trusted him from the moment she'd seen his too-handsome face. Now he knew her authorship and her hopes for the future. Her recklessness placed her firmly within his power. Would he use his knowledge against her?

Years of thankless devotion to her father had taught her that the last thing she wanted was to subject herself to another man's will. That was why she'd never marry—she longed to use her talents for her own purposes. Any husband would expect her to accept the helpmeet role she'd adopted too long with her selfish parent. Mr. Evans guessing her authorship wasn't quite as onerous as submitting to a husband, but he still might try to influence her choices. Now that freedom beckoned, she could hardly bear that.

The vicar and Lord Neville swapped opinions over a table covered in folios. New acquisitions of his lordship's, Genevieve supposed. She should be grateful that he shared his collection with the Barretts. But her charity with her father's patron was in short supply. Since Mr. Evans's arrival, Lord Neville had become a ubiquitous presence, like a grumpy rhinoceros guarding his territory. If she wasn't tripping over one gentleman, she tripped over the other. She wished them both to perdition.

It had been a difficult week. She'd only just come to terms with facing down her charming but inexplicably inefficient burglar. She supposed she should be grateful that Mr. Evans's arrival at least provided distraction. No longer did she jump at shadows. Instead she jumped at the sound of one particular baritone voice.

Mr. Evans glanced across to where she caught the evening light for her needlework. Behind her, the window was open in hope of attracting a stray drift of air. September had turned abnormally sultry and the parlor was stuffy. Or perhaps the crowded room was at fault. Her aunt, her father, Lord Neville, Mr. Evans. Not to mention Sirius and Hecuba.

Irritated with the heat, Genevieve brushed back stray tendrils escaping her chignon. Mr. Evans continued to stare. Did his gaze hold a conspiratorial light? Or was that her guilty conscience speaking? The secret of her father's work wasn't hers alone. She'd had no right revealing it to a stranger.

When the vicar had invited fifteen-year-old Genevieve to collate some notes on local churches into an article, she'd leaped at the chance. Any adolescent girl with pretensions to intellectual achievement would find such a request flattering. Especially motherless Genevieve Barrett who craved her father's attention. Even more exciting when the piece she wrote appeared in a journal.

So the deception had continued and thickened until Genevieve's work shored up the vicar's fame and any suggestion that he share credit made him sulk like a child. Her resentment had curdled over the last year, as she realized that her father was content for this arrangement to last indefinitely.

Then Lady Bellfield had bequeathed her the Harmsworth Jewel and her research had uncovered interesting and potentially explosive facts about the object. The chance of independence from her father had finally become a reality and she meant to seize it with both hands. When she'd told the interfering Mr. Evans that her whole future depended on the Harmsworth Jewel, she hadn't exaggerated.

But ruthless as she strove to be, that lost young girl still lurked in her heart. Even now when she was so angry that she could strangle her father with his clergy stole, she still loved him. She didn't want to destroy his reputation, however unjustified it was. She just wanted to claim her work and use it as the basis for a life of her own.

How on earth had Mr. Evans recognized her authorship so quickly? A sharp brain lurked behind those languid manners, but nobody would call her father's latest pupil an academic specialist. A premonition of disaster shivered through her—and Mr. Evans already made her as wary as a fox in hunting season.

Again she uselessly berated herself for succumbing this morning to guileless blue eyes and a ready smile and a voice that made her blood flow like warm honey. Mr. Evans had everyone dancing to his tune. Why was she the only person in this house to see that?

She stabbed her needle into her embroidery with a savagery that threatened to burst her bloated peonies. Neither her aunt nor her father heeded her suggestions that Mr. Evans should move back into Leighton Court. When Genevieve had insisted that she didn't trust the way Mr. Evans infiltrated their life, both had said she was unreasonable. Her aunt had gone so far as to accuse her of jealousy now that Mr. Evans monopolized the vicar's attentions. How ironic to hear that when Genevieve worked so hard to break free of her father.

"Your elephant grows apace, Miss Barrett." Mr. Evans abandoned his card game and crossed the room to stand beside her, regarding her woeful embroidery with a quizzical expression. Sirius trotted after him to sit at his master's feet. She liked Sirius. Genevieve wished the dog's master was nearly as easy to stomach.

"You know very well it's a peony garden, Mr. Evans," she said frostily. After this morning, she'd prefer he kept a greater distance, physically and otherwise.

Her chill tone attracted her aunt's notice, but no rebuke. Perhaps Aunt Lucy finally saw that her matchmaking was futile.

Mr. Evans remained unabashed. Of course. "That explains the pink. I thought perhaps the elephant was embarrassed."

"You have no manners, sir," she bit out, and bent over her embroidery frame, but not before she caught the unholy amusement in his eyes. He was a strikingly good-looking man, but when laughter lit his face, he was irresistible. Even she, who mistrusted everything about him, felt her heart beat faster.

"Sincerest regrets, dear lady."

She knew he wasn't sorry, so she didn't grace his apology with acknowledgement. Furiously she stitched at the central flower which, now she checked, did rather resemble a pregnant elephant. A blushing pregnant elephant, curse Mr. Evans.

Despite lack of encouragement, Mr. Evans showed no signs of leaving. He sat without invitation—he was smart enough to know no invitation would be forthcoming. "Clearly my eyesight fails."

He was dressed plainly, but even a country mouse like her noted his superb tailoring. He always made Genevieve feel a frump. Last night, she'd caught herself gussying up her yellow muslin with her mother's silver brooch. She pinned it to her bosom before realizing what she did. With an unladylike imprecation, she'd flung the brooch onto her dressing table.

"Clearly." She refused to give him the satisfaction of shifting away. Unfortunately, that meant remaining too near his long, lean leg, encased in fawn breeches, extended inches from hers. His boots were so shiny, she could see her face in them. How on earth was he turned out so beautifully without a valet?

Absently, Mr. Evans fondled Sirius's head with one elegant hand. Yet again, she wondered at the contrast between the man's sartorial perfection and the scruffy dog. Before she reminded herself that curiosity only inflated Mr. Evans's pretensions, she spoke. "Your pet doesn't befit your dignity, Mr. Evans."

She caught his quick frown and for a moment, he wasn't the impossibly polished man she feared, but someone considerably more intriguing. Then the expression vanished and he was once again someone whose motives she suspected to her last atom. "On the contrary, Miss Barrett. He's far too good for a rapscallion like me."

That she could believe. "I picture you more with a greyhound or a pug."

His low laugh vibrated along her veins like a distant storm. She didn't want to be aware of him as a male, but it became increasingly difficult to pretend that some deeply feminine and hitherto unrecognized element in her liked Mr. Evans very much indeed.

"A...*pug*? A hit. A palpable hit, madam. You seek revenge for the elephant, I see."

"A dog with a pedigree, at least."

At the mention of pedigree, a haunted expression darkened his eyes. She couldn't imagine why. He reeked of good breeding. "Pedigrees are overrated."

She frowned. Something stirred below this prickly, half-flirtatious conversation. Why did he clam up at the mention of pedigree? "How did you become Sirius's master?"

He smiled more naturally, confirming her instincts that discussions of bloodlines discomfited him. "I'm not sure I'm his master. His colleague, perhaps. He's been with me for three years. He turned up not far from my estate and seemed of a mind to stay. I'm glad. He's deuced good company. And far too clever for the likes of me."

Against her better judgment, Genevieve's hostility ebbed. It was hard to maintain virulent dislike for a man so openly fond of his dog. She reminded herself that Mr. Evans's kindness to animals didn't make him one iota more trustworthy. For once, the warning didn't strike true.

He glanced up from patting Sirius to stare into her face, catching her brief softening. Without her usual defenses, her heart stuttered to a standstill. Her entire body vibrated to his presence. Speech deserted her. She could only look. And admire. Never before had she been so aware of a man's beauty. The perfect planes of his face, the glittering dark blue eyes, the long, powerful body—all melted resistance. Mr. Evans was a dangerously beguiling man. Particularly dangerous if he drew this response despite her inchoate suspicions.

His gaze sharpened. "What is it, Miss Barrett?"

"I—"

With a sharp crack, her embroidery frame snapped in two. He frowned and reached for her hand. "Genevieve—"

Dear Lord, she couldn't let him touch her. Not when she was so on edge. Even as she cursed her betraying reaction, she jerked away before he made contact.

Her aunt chose that moment to rise and lift Hecuba from her snooze near the empty hearth. The hallway clock struck six. "Perhaps we should move through to the dining room."

Only the greatest exercise of will stopped Genevieve from bolting for the door. Anything to escape Mr. Evans and that terrifying interval where attraction had turned her into a lunatic.

Pride straightened her spine and insisted that she had nothing to fear. Then she risked a backward glance. Mr. Evans lounged on the window seat and his expression as he watched her tied her stomach into sick knots. She'd expected her erratic behavior to bewilder him. But he didn't look surprised. He looked like a man who eyed a prize for the winning. He looked like a man who put some great purpose into effect. He looked invincible.

Another chill rippled down her spine and she tore her gaze away. She revolted at the possessiveness that she read in his face. Even as unforgivably, unacceptably, excitement coiled low in her belly, reminding her that she might be a scholar, but she was also a woman. And the woman responded to Christopher Evans in ways that had no truck with intellect.

Slowly, his heavy eyelids lowered, hiding triumph. Her lips tightened and she whirled away to find Lord Neville regarding her with unmistakable disapproval. Her color rose and shame gripped her throat. As though she'd been caught dancing naked in a tavern or kissing a married man in church. For the love of heaven, was her every move under observation?

On a spurt of temper, she marched through to the hallway. Lord Neville followed. When he took her arm, sensitive as she currently was to overbearing males, she resented his proprietorial air. She tried to withdraw, but his grip tightened. Shocked, she looked up. The parlor door had swung shut, closing Mr. Evans and Sirius inside. Ahead past the stairs, the light from the dining room hardly penetrated this dark corner. For a fleeting moment, Lord Neville's expression struck her as menacing.

What a fanciful idiot she was. Clearly she still wasn't as easy with last week's burglary as she'd hoped. Although perhaps she should blame Mr. Evans rather than the thief for her nerves. She'd known Lord Neville most of her life. He wasn't her favorite person, but he had never hurt her. Nonetheless, she dearly wished he'd unhand her. And stop looming. She forgot what a substantial figure he made until he stood close.

"I can't like that young fellow," he said in a low voice. "He has an insinuating way about him."

"Papa likes him." She wondered why she didn't join Lord Neville in deriding Mr. Evans.

His lordship's smile was sour. "Your father is one of nature's innocents. And Mr. Evans flatters him."

This was nothing she hadn't thought herself, but still she found herself reluctant to agree. "I doubt that Mr. Evans means any harm."

What a lie that was. With Mr. Evans, she wasn't sure of very much at all, apart from his ability to turn her into a nitwit.

"But we don't know, do we?" Lord Neville's fleshy lips turned down. "He has no right to use your Christian name."

Her color rose. Hopefully the shadows concealed her embarrassment. "It was only once—"

"He offers you insult. And he has the run of the house."

Annoyance made her draw herself up to her full height. This time when she tugged, he released her.

"Do you imply there's something between Mr. Evans and myself?" Her voice was so cold, icicles practically hung from every word.

Even in the gloom, she read Lord Neville's dismay at her reaction to his well-meant if inopportune advice. "Genevieve, you're a woman of unimpeachable virtue. I lay no blame at your door. Any wrongdoing is entirely the gentleman's fault."

The apology didn't mollify. "My lord, none of this is your business."

Now she'd offended him. "A man of principle must speak when he sees a woman he...respects at risk of making a fool of herself."

His concern struck her as overweening. After all, he was a colleague of her father's, not a member of the family. "Lord Neville—"

Luckily for her relationship with her father's patron, the door opened and Mr. Evans emerged with Sirius at his heels. The parlor faced west, so it was purely a matter of geography that the setting sun lit him like a saint in a painting.

She had no idea what Mr. Evans saw, but he went still and his tall body radiated danger. Sirius stood alert at his master's thigh.

"Miss Barrett, are you all right?" he asked softly. With his back to the light, she couldn't read his expression. His voice was steady and he sounded protective. Or he would if she trusted his sincerity. Even so, she battled a traitorous surge of warmth.

Lord Neville lurched around. "You interrupt a private conversation, sir."

Did she imagine it or did Mr. Evans deliberately relax back into his easygoing self? "I go through to dinner, my lord."

No love was lost between them. But tonight for the first time she wondered if mutual antipathy might verge on something stronger. Something approaching loathing. She'd always considered Lord Neville a dominating character. But it was the older man who shifted on his feet and turned to stump into the dining room.

"I take it he warned you against me." Mr. Evans stepped into the hallway, clever enough not to crowd her. Right now she thought she'd clout the next man who tried to intimidate her with his physical size.

Genevieve glared at her rescuer, fleeting gratitude evaporating. "Shouldn't he?"

She waited for Mr. Evans to claim ignorance of her meaning, but she misjudged him. He leaned close enough for her to see his half smile in the gloom. "Do I make you nervous, Miss Barrett?"

With a flick of her skirts, she turned and headed for the dining room. "Not at all, sir."

She waited for him to challenge an assertion that they both knew was untrue. He merely gestured her ahead with the smooth dispatch that both attracted and frightened her.

Chapter Seven

Richard woke with a start. Lying motionless in his monastic bed, he tried to work out what had disturbed him. Everything was silent. Moonlight flooded through his open window. The night was stifling and he slept naked, although his clothes were conveniently to hand across the Windsor chair. His door remained open a crack for air.

Sirius stretched out under the sill, his brindled coat lost in the shadows. His great dark eyes glinted. Something had alerted the dog too.

Richard heard a door squeak down the corridor, then a surreptitious rustle as someone tiptoed toward the stairs. The rumble of the vicar's snoring next door, audible even through the thick wall, indicated that the old man slumbered. Dorcas slept in the attics. Which meant the nocturnal wanderer was Mrs. Warren. Or most intriguing of all, Genevieve.

Carefully so the bed didn't creak, Richard sat and reached for breeches and shirt. In this heat, even such light clothing felt constricting. As he tugged his boots on, he heard the snick of the kitchen door. Whoever left was as light-footed as a sylph.

He stood at the window. Below, someone wrapped in a dark cloak slipped through the back garden, plotting a deft path between cabbages and lettuces. The figure was anonymous, but he knew that swift grace to his bones. It didn't belong to middle-aged Lucy Warren.

No, another quarry roamed the Oxfordshire countryside this quiet night.

He traced Genevieve's progress toward the stables. If she glanced up, she'd see him. But she remained intent upon her errand, whatever it was. The nearly full moon lit her way.

So where did the enchanting Miss Barrett go?

Did she meet a lover? The thought pierced his gut like a saber. He'd never encountered a female so unaware of herself as a *woman*. Her unworldliness compounded the challenge, along with her intelligence and determination to dislike him no matter how he tried to charm her. He respected Genevieve's resistance. Although tonight in the parlor, for one blazing instant, attraction had spiraled unchecked between them. Now he faced the unpleasant possibility that his charm failed because her interest was engaged elsewhere.

Devil take that.

Within moments, he'd followed her from the house. At his side, Sirius padded soundless as a ghost.

Gingerly Richard opened the back gate, then realized he wasted his care. She was no longer in sight. It should be cooler outside, but the air was as still and heavy as a damp blanket. With an impatient gesture, he brushed his hair back from his forehead and bent to whisper in Sirius's ear. "Find her. Find Genevieve."

Sirius trotted toward the high brick wall separating the stables from the adjoining Leighton Estate. Feathery tail idly waving, he slipped through the rusty gate that sagged from its hinges. Feeling like he trespassed upon a fairy-tale realm, Richard pushed past the wildflowers tangled around the gate's base.

Sirius waited on a path leading into the woods. Once his master followed, he loped ahead. Under the trees, progress was more difficult. Richard picked his way forward, keeping an eye on Sirius. Luckily the trail was well trodden, indicating someone—Genevieve?—used it regularly.

It was cooler too. Fresh scents surrounded him. Leaf litter. Green foliage. Sirius's confident progress indicated that Genevieve was still ahead.

Unless, damn it, Sirius chased a rabbit.

The path ended so abruptly that Richard nearly tumbled into the clearing. Cursing his conspicuous white shirt, he slipped under an oak's shadow. He sucked in a breath, heart racing. Then another deeper breath as stabbing relief weakened his knees.

She wasn't meeting a lover. She'd wanted a swim.

As she stroked across the water, each ripple caught the moonlight, turning the pool to silver. No man with an ounce of poetry in his soul could fail to relish this scene.

Richard didn't know how long he stood, astonished and entranced. Something about her ease indicated she'd done this frequently, probably since she was a girl. She didn't check nervously for intruders, although surely that was a risk. But who would be about at such an hour? No poacher with his head screwed on right chanced his luck on one of Sedgemoor's estates.

Without conscious thought, Richard circled the pond, keeping to the dark, seeking to see without being seen. When he stumbled over a bundle under a rowan bush, he smiled with wolfish anticipation.

Reluctantly Genevieve swam toward the bank. The secluded pool in Sedgemoor's woods had worked its magic once again. She felt better. More like the woman she'd been before the break-in and everything turning topsy-turvy.

Soon after she and her father had arrived in Little Derrick, she'd started coming here in secret. She'd been a bewildered ten-year-old, mourning her beloved mother, coping with unfamiliar surroundings and unfamiliar people, not least an aunt she barely knew. In the fifteen years since, she'd never met another soul during her midnight swims. Sometimes she thought she was the only person on earth to know of the pond's existence.

Tonight she'd desperately needed the pool's tranquility. The week's events had troubled her soul. And fear of encountering Mr. Evans, not to mention memories of the aborted robbery, had confined her to her room every night since he'd moved in. In this oppressive heat, she'd stretched out on her bed, chasing a thousand useless thoughts around her head. She could have worked, but what she'd longed for was freedom.

She'd stayed out longer than intended, but she couldn't bear to leave the silky water. She found her footing and waded to the bank where she'd left her clothes and towel.

Something rustled in the undergrowth and she stopped, alert. Suddenly her recklessness in coming here while a thief prowled the neighborhood made her stomach cramp with disquiet. Just because there had been no trouble for over a week didn't make it safe to roam the woods like a gypsy.

"Who's there?" She cursed the quaver in her voice.

She edged toward her clothes, wondering if fleeing into the trees would be a wiser move. But she couldn't stay outside naked until dawn. Another rustle set her heart banging like a trip-hammer. If only she'd brought her pistol, but it was safely locked in her desk along with the Harmsworth Jewel.

Frantically her eyes scoured the darkness, but shadows defeated her. Moonlit in the clearing, she was completely vulnerable.

An animal ventured out to stand a few feet away. She was in such a state that she needed a few seconds to recognize Sirius's shaggy outlines. Relief made her legs feel likely to collapse.

"You scared me, you silly hound." She stepped forward to collect her clothes with renewed confidence. "How did you escape your infernal master?"

She'd developed a healthy respect for Sirius's intelligence. If he'd answered, she wouldn't be altogether surprised. On such a night, animals could talk and frogs might turn into princes.

Fumbling after her towel, she found only her gown. Puzzled, she kneeled, patting around the area. She raised her head. "Have you eaten my towel, Sirius? If you have, I'll sic Hecuba onto you."

"Don't blame Sirius," a familiar voice murmured from behind.

As she stiffened into horrified stillness, her towel dropped around her naked shoulders.

"Dear God..." Genevieve breathed, frightened, humiliated, and furious. With herself and with the vile Mr. Evans. She stumbled upright on trembling legs and whipped the linen strip around her body. Too little, too late, she acknowledged with a sick twisting in her belly. She whirled around in outrage. "H...how long have you been there?"

From a few feet away, he stood watching. Tall. Lean. Outwardly relaxed. But that didn't fool her. He was on the hunt and they both knew it. "Long enough."

Mr. Evans's calm response didn't quiet her panic. "You had no right—"

"Of course I had no right. But I defy any man with blood in his veins to abandon you to the moonlight, Miss Barrett."

She was such a fool. The worst of it, even as shame strangled her, was that he'd destroyed her sanctuary. Whether she never saw another person here, she couldn't feel safe again. He'd stolen this source of happiness as blatantly as her father stole her work. At this moment, she loathed Mr. Evans.

She chanced a quick glance at his face, his smug expression clear in the bright moonlight. She bit her lip as fury overwhelmed embarrassment. No man had ever seen her naked. This felt like a violation. "You're no gentleman, sir!"

"Come, Miss Barrett, you can do better than that." His laugh played a chromatic scale up and down her spine. "A woman with your vocabulary can summon an archaic insult or two."

"Well, you're a filthy sneak. Is that better?"

"Much."

Genevieve's hands tightened on her inadequate covering as she backed toward her dress. Bored with the conversation, Sirius trotted into the shadows. "This is such a joke to you, isn't it?" she snarled, fighting tears. "I'll thank you to go now."

"Surely the damage is done."

Carefully she bent, then straightened, her gown dangling from her shaking hand. "Ha ha. So amusing."

Her temper slid off him like the water trickling down her bare back. She shivered. As she stood dripping with the pond behind her, a wicked little breeze flirted around her.

"This sneak's reward was a beautiful naked woman."

Her cheeks threatened to combust. Self-righteousness was difficult to maintain when one only wore a flimsy towel.

She struggled for control, even as the need surged to scratch and kick at him until he was bruised and bloody. "Please leave, Mr. Evans."

"Wild horses couldn't tear me away, Miss Barrett." He stepped closer. "Given how our acquaintance has advanced this evening, can't you bring yourself to call me Christopher?"

"I can bring myself to call you a self-serving rat," she said coldly. He remained a few feet away, but that seemed too close. She retreated another unsteady pace, the grass scratching her bare feet.

"Aren't you cold?"

"I can't dress with you here."

Moonlight silvered his features into beguiling black and white. "I could promise not to look."

"You could demonstrate some honor and go." She struggled to sound defiant. This was the most mortifying thing that had ever happened to her. And she had nobody to blame for this catastrophe but herself. How could she have been so foolhardy as to chance a swim when she knew Mr. Evans watched her like a buzzard watched a field mouse?

"Or I could just turn my back." He suited actions to words.

For a fraught moment, she stared at him. She couldn't trust him, but nor could she stand here covered in a strip of linen. She let the sodden towel drop and hurriedly tugged her old muslin dress over her head, fastening it with shaking hands.

"Can I turn around?"

"Yes," she said sullenly, although she was angrier at herself than him. He'd only followed the dictates of his rodent nature. She should have known better than to come here.

"Do you feel better?" he asked neutrally, although the way his gaze ran over her body made her feel naked again. She resisted the urge to shield herself with her hands.

"Why did you follow me?" Although the answer was no mystery. He'd flirted with her from the first. Even without her flaunting herself, he'd leap at any chance to get her alone.

"I thought you met a lover." The edge in his statement made her frown in consternation.

"I don't have a lover," she said quickly, before remembering that her swains weren't Mr. Evans's concern.

He arched one eyebrow in a fashion that made her shiver. Not with cold. "I could fill the position."

This time she didn't bother to conceal her retreat. "If my father knew you pestered me—"

"Do you intend to tell him?" he asked, as if her answer was of purely casual interest.

"Yes." Although how could she? Anyone would say she'd asked for trouble by being out here. Anyone would be right.

Something dangerous flashed in Mr. Evans's eyes. The breath caught in her throat and she chanced another step back, only to slosh into the pond. The shock of cool water around her ankles made her gasp. She stumbled as her bare toes sank into the mud. Mr. Evans moved swiftly to catch her arm and save her from a spill.

"Careful." He spoke softly. She realized that he always did. Uncanny how much power that quiet voice exerted.

"Let me go." She hated her breathlessness. She hated the easy confidence of his hold—and its radiating heat. She hated the way her nipples tightened painfully against her bodice. Fumbling, she raised her skirts above the water. She tried to wrench free, but his grip remained adamant.

"Seeing I'm to be hanged anyway, it may as well be for a sheep as a lamb," he said thoughtfully.

Her belly dipped with dread and her knees wobbled. "What...what do you mean?"

He always watched her, but this time his gaze felt

different. This felt like he placed his mark on her, claimed her in some atavistic way. "I want to kiss you."

"You can't." Although if it cost only a few kisses to escape this disaster, she should be grateful.

"Indeed I can," he said with one of those flashing smiles that always set her heart pounding. This time, her heart already pounded nineteen to the dozen. With fear, she told herself staunchly. Definitely not with anticipation.

"I . . . I won't let you."

Another laugh. Warm and lazily amused. He lifted his hand and stepped back. "Then by all means, return to the vicarage."

She frowned, not leaving the water. "Just like that?"

"Just like that."

"Then I wish you good night, Mr. Evans," she said crisply, still not trusting him but desperate to escape.

Ignoring his proffered hand, she splashed out of the pond. She'd emerge unscathed from this encounter. Which was more than she deserved. Keeping a careful eye on him, she edged toward the trees, her sopping hem slapping her ankles.

She'd almost reached the woods before he spoke. "Such a pity."

Trembling, she turned. Moonlight transformed him into a statue of silver and ebony. She'd survived twenty-five years happily oblivious to masculine splendor, but something about Mr. Evans made her heart skip a beat. Then another. He might be rotten to the core, but he was disgustingly picturesque.

A bristling silence built and her skin tightened with longing that she refused to examine. Safety beckoned. Still she poised in the shadows. Night scents filled her nostrils, strangely seductive.

Eventually curiosity won out. "What's a pity?"

He tilted his hip, standing with a loose-limbed elegance that made her pulses race. "That you're such a coward, my dear."

"I'm not your dear," she said automatically.

"I suggest a little harmless flirtation and you retreat to your books and dry old men. For shame, Miss Barrett. I thought better of you."

He's taunting you. He just wants you back within pouncing distance. Go while you can.

"I have no intention of being ruined," she said coldly, while a sensation as far removed from cold as possible rushed through her veins.

"You have my word that I'll stop at kisses." He considered her thoughtfully. "Have you been kissed?"

Dear Lord. She felt giddy as forbidden images flooded her traitorous mind. "Mr. Evans, I'm twenty-five years old. It would be very sad if I haven't."

She'd hesitated too long. His features sharpened and his stare burned. Heaven help her, he guessed her embarrassing lack of experience. Although the lack only seemed an embarrassment in his company. Her flimsy dress felt invisible. From now until the end of time, she could never forget that he'd seen her as no other man ever had.

She waited for some derisive comment. But he merely nodded once as though confirming a theory. "Ah."

God above, what did that mean?

Run. Run.

"Men have wanted to kiss me," she said defensively, moving from one foot to the other but unable to convince those feet to remove her from this discomfiting conversation.

"I'm sure," he said softly.

She expected mockery but detected none. "I haven't wanted to kiss them."

"That may change once you discover how good a kiss can be."

"With you?" She wanted to sound sarcastic, but the words emerged as barely contained curiosity.

He shrugged, looking irritatingly at ease with himself as he folded his arms across his powerful chest. "Why not? I profess some skill and you're quite safe."

"Said the spider to the fly."

She shifted restlessly, only stopping when she noticed his close attention. His expression indicated that he knew more than she did. Of course he knew more than she did. He was a rake and she was a scholarly spinster who had never been kissed.

Which suddenly seemed cause for regret.

His voice deepened to velvet enticement. "Doesn't some part of you long for a man to touch you in desire?"

His voice possessed magic. That soft drawl made her think of all the wonderful, unprecedented things he'd do to her if she let him. She might be inexperienced, but some instinct insisted that when he claimed to be a skillful kisser, he wasn't boasting.

Goodness, likely he could fling her to heaven and back without trying. It was both exciting and terrifying. She began to wish she'd encouraged those callow young men who had shown an interest in the vicar's intimidating daughter. Mr. Evans had never found her intimidating. She suspected that Mr. Evans found very little intimidating.

She prepared to tell this encroaching charmer to leave her alone. Instead different words emerged. "This is purely an intellectual exercise. I'm not attracted to you."

His lips quirked. "Understood."

She stepped into the moonlight. In her loose, light frock with nothing beneath it, she must look completely brazen. Part of her howled protest at her intentions. But fascination and, yes, unwilling attraction kept her here.

After a couple of attempts to clear her throat, her voice emerged with gratifying firmness. "Show me."

Chapter Eight

God forgive him, he was such a devil. Richard played
games with Genevieve, games he knew he'd win. An
appeal to her curiosity never failed.

A gentleman would let her go on her way unmolested. A
gentleman wouldn't spy on her in the first place.

As she'd pointed out, he was no gentleman.

Nor was he blind. He counted himself a jaded fellow,
accustomed to female beauty. But Genevieve rising from
rippling water clad only in moonlight set his heart leaping
like a landed trout. She was the most glorious thing he'd
ever seen. He couldn't relinquish this astonishing chance to
explore the awareness simmering between them.

Even more astonishing, nobody had ever kissed this
incomparable woman. In the name of all that was holy,
what ailed the men of Oxfordshire? Did none of them have
enough backbone to take her on and turn all that spirit to
their service?

Richard Harmsworth was up to the challenge.

He'd have found the double entendre more amusing if

he wasn't aching with need. The memory of her nakedness would haunt him forever. Closing his eyes, he saw every glistening curve, the full breasts, the graceful dip of waist. The long, long legs. Legs that would bend around his back when he plunged into her.

Except that she was a virgin. And a vicar's daughter. And after he left, she'd have to weather any talk in the village. She wasn't one of his London lightskirts. He needed to remember that. Difficult when desire thundered through him like a herd of runaway horses.

"Are you quite well, Mr. Evans?" she asked.

He struggled to banish the image of his body thrusting into hers. Intensity would frighten her. He needed to be charming, superficial. Why was it so difficult? He'd spent his life playing a lazy, even-tempered man who cared for little, least of all society's disdain of his bastardy.

He spoke with unconvincing lightness. "Of course. Why shouldn't I be?"

"You groaned." Her tone was dry. "I wondered if perhaps you'd eaten something that disagreed with you."

Celibacy disagreed with him. Especially when he pursued an alluring, sharp-tongued hussy. The night was so still that he heard the soft pad of her feet as she approached. He fought the urge to seize her. *Control, man. Control.*

"Genevieve, you are beyond lovely." Admiration roughened his voice.

The downward flicker of her lashes betrayed a bashfulness that touched him as much as her defiance. "It's a very old dress."

That doyen of fashion Sir Richard Harmsworth should scorn the drab garment, but Genevieve's beauty transformed the worn muslin. He held out a hand, unsurprised to note that it wasn't steady. A distant warning clanged in his brain that with this woman he risked the detachment that protected him from emotion. But how could he heed caution's call with her standing so close?

"Come here," he murmured, taking her hand. Her skin was cool from her swim. Slowly he drew her nearer.

Hesitantly she advanced. Her shyness quieted the rapacious beast inside him, so gentleness came naturally when he slid his hand around her waist. Her innocence seemed precious and fragile. As precious and fragile as the Harmsworth Jewel. His heavily armored heart cramped with poignant longing and his grip turned coaxing, soft. Touch confirmed what sight had hinted. She wore nothing beneath the flimsy muslin.

"I'm sure this is a mistake." Her body lost its stiffness and she curved into his hand.

"I'm sure it's not." Which wasn't completely true, damn it.

He was accounted a master of seduction. He couldn't recall his first kiss. His first fuck had followed too closely upon it. But this tremulous, delicate anticipation made him feel like a boy with his sweetheart. He lifted the hand he held and placed it over his heart. Through his thin cambric shirt, her touch melted all remnants of calculation.

Experimentally she flexed her hand, spurring his heart into a gallop. "You're so warm."

"Let me warm you," he whispered.

Her chin tilted until glittering eyes met his. What he read in her gaze was no surprise. Trepidation. Questions. Courage. And something else. Something he'd longed to see since he'd climbed through her window little more than a week ago.

Desire.

He'd imagined when he kissed Genevieve, he'd be eager to stake his claim. That wasn't how he felt, holding her tall, trembling body in the moonlight and staring into her beautiful face. Perhaps the night indeed possessed magic. Or, much easier to believe, the woman did.

Genevieve remained motionless as Mr. Evans's mouth skimmed hers. The brief contact set her lips tingling. In the second between that kiss and the next, her head swam with a multitude of impressions. His height, his heat, the constrained power in his arms. The satiny texture of his lips. His clean, masculine scent.

He kissed her with a purpose and fervor that curled her toes against the grass and turned her knees to water. Lost, dazed, she hooked one hand around Mr. Evans's shoulder to keep her balance. That first tentative kiss had provided little hint of what was to come. Her girlish imaginings even less. This was like a whirlwind.

Behind closed eyes, the darkness was blacker than a starless night. Hot darkness. Beckoning darkness. Her hand clenched in his shirt, over his frantic heartbeat. She whimpered with longing against his lips.

He gave another of those low growls that reverberated not just in her ears but in her bones and slid his tongue between her lips. She tensed with surprise and tried to withdraw.

"Open for me, Genevieve," he whispered, brushing kisses across her nose and cheeks and forehead. It was the way one kissed a child, except that his determination mocked innocence.

"We've kissed now," she stammered, hardly aware what she said. "You can let me go."

"Devil take that for an idea." He cradled her face between his strong palms. "That wasn't a kiss."

"It felt like a kiss." She struggled to sound resolute, but only managed breathless and bedazzled. She could hardly blame Mr. Evans for responding with wry amusement.

"How would you know, my sweet little lamb?"

He kissed her again. This time his tongue's invasion didn't seem so alien. A thrill coursed through her, tightening her breasts and settling heavily between her legs. She shifted to relieve the building pressure.

The sensation wasn't uncomfortable. It was just...odd.

A kiss was astonishingly intimate. Her mind might insist that Mr. Evans meant trouble, but close to his big, strong body, she felt safe. Safe, yet brave and verging on some marvelous discovery. It was like entering a hitherto forbidden section of the library.

She should be frightened, but she wasn't. His touch was inexplicably familiar, as though he'd touched her before. As though she belonged in his arms. As though she'd waited all her life for this man to set his lips to hers.

By offering her mouth, she surrendered something of her soul. The experience was overwhelming, too complex to analyze. Instead she drifted into velvety pleasure where his lips lured her with what even a novice recognized as breathtaking expertise.

Tentatively she moved her tongue, copying him. This time Mr. Evans's growl expressed satisfaction. What remarkable communication he achieved without words.

Encouraged, she slid her tongue over his, then more daringly, she slipped it between his lips, tasting him as he tasted her. At first the activity had seemed outlandish. No longer.

Mr. Evans plunged his hands into her hair and angled her upward, changing the pleasure. This time the moan was hers. After exploring every inch of her mouth, he lured her with delicious nips and nibbles. She loved his rich taste. She pursued him, seeking more soul-melting kisses.

She was vaguely aware of Mr. Evans stroking her hips. When his hands cupped her buttocks, she started.

An intimation of danger pricked.

As her skirt inched upward, the breeze brushed her bare legs. A warning strove for purchase in her foggy mind. Mr. Evans had promised a kiss to enlighten ignorance. Now this encounter escaped those boundaries.

As if to confirm that thought, he pressed the small of her back, bringing her nearer. Inexperienced she might be. Stupid she wasn't. And she'd lived in the country all her life. She couldn't mistake that throbbing hardness against her stomach.

Roughly she broke away. "No."

She wasn't sure he heard. Or if he heard, whether he'd take note. Fear, long overdue, crammed her throat. Then to her relief, he released her and her skirt flopped to her ankles with a damp slap. He breathed unsteadily, but otherwise seemed unaffected.

Genevieve, on the other hand, felt like she'd barely survived a tempest. For one traitorous moment, her heart leaped with hope that his kiss had required feelings as well as technique. Then she reminded herself that she was safer by far if it hadn't.

Unexpectedly his expression turned sheepish. "I apologize, Miss Barrett. You were right to stop me."

She panted, still quivering with reaction. How could she have been so stupid to let this go so far? How could she have started at all?

The ghosts of his kisses lingered on Genevieve's lips and in her mind. Grimly she suspected the ghosts of his kisses would haunt her for too long. Well after Mr. Evans forgot her.

For the first time, she comprehended the full extent of her rashness. She'd trusted his honor, and thank goodness, he hadn't disappointed her. But after this glimpse of pleasure, the door to desire didn't close as readily as she'd hoped.

"I must go." Just as before, she didn't move.

"Yes."

Blast him. That monosyllable shouldn't sound like an invitation to stay and explore new worlds. She leaned forward to claim another drugging kiss before lurching back to reality and stopping herself. Her yen for this man terrified her, as did the possibility that he might reveal her foolishness to the world. "You can't say anything about this."

His lips lengthened in an unamused smile. "I thought you intended to tell your father so he banished me from the vicarage."

Admit that Mr. Evans had caught her swimming naked on Sedgemoor's estate? Admit she'd kissed Mr. Evans? Lord above, it didn't bear considering. "No."

"Thank you," he said quietly.

The silence extended. She knew they both relived those heady moments. She must go. Before he reached for her. Or heaven forbid, before she sprang at him and begged him to kiss her again and never stop.

"Good night, Mr. Evans." The formality was ludicrous, but she desperately needed to establish some distance between them.

When he wasn't being superior, he had a nice smile. "Good night, Miss Barrett."

Dear God, what was wrong with her? She mooned after him like a twelve-year-old. She straightened and struggled to summon the scowl that usually greeted his attempts at charm. Except he wasn't attempting charm. He *was* charming. And she was in dire trouble.

"To Hades with it," he muttered. He seized her shoulders in an uncompromising grasp. Before she could protest or run—not that she tried to do either—he hauled her into his arms and kissed her hard.

That inexplicable feeling of familiarity returned. Before she could examine it, he released her and strode away under the trees, Sirius following.

Genevieve stood trembling where he'd left her. The moon slipped behind a cloud and the night turned dark and lonely. She drew a breath redolent of clean male scent. Clean. Tangy. Lemony.

Lemon verbena . . .

Chapter Nine

Mr. Evans was Genevieve's inept burglar.

The next morning as she struggled to work in her study, the revelation still appalled her. How she kicked herself for taking so long to realize. The clues had always been there. The height. The subtle elegance. The beautiful voice. Curse him, the confidence with women. Although he'd been masked then, and now he dyed his hair. That dull brown had always seemed incongruous on such a spectacular man.

Now she understood why every instinct had leaped to alert the first time he'd sauntered into the parlor. No wonder his touch had always felt familiar. It wasn't some mystical affinity. He'd held her close when he'd disarmed her.

Last night she'd stormed back through the dark woods, determined to denounce Mr. Evans. How she loathed a thief. Her father had spent the last ten years stealing her work without an ounce of compunction. Now the first man to kiss her turned out to be a thief too.

Yet however much the double-dealing devil's betrayal smarted, bewilderment outweighed anger. While she might call him a thief, so far he'd stolen nothing except her peace of mind and a few kisses. For the life of her, she couldn't discern his motives for leaving empty-handed and then infiltrating the vicarage.

What did he want? Would she be better to discover his purposes before she exposed him? Even if she accused him, what proof did she have? How could she confess that she'd been close enough to Mr. Evans to recognize his scent?

Did he want the Harmsworth Jewel? It was the only thing here worth stealing. But so few people knew she had the artifact. Dr. Partridge at the Ashmolean Museum, who considered her article for publication. Her father was so focused on his princes that she wasn't sure he remembered Lady Bellfield's bequest.

Sir Richard Harmsworth...

Was Mr. Evans's arrival part of a campaign to retrieve the jewel? With a nasty start, she remembered Mr. Evans offering to buy the jewel. Did he want it for himself or for Sir Richard?

If Mr. Evans worked for Sir Richard, why hadn't he pocketed the jewel when he broke in? He must have noticed it. After these last days, she was convinced that his deceptively lazy gaze missed little. Even if he'd overlooked it that night, she, gullible idiot she was, had placed it in his hand yesterday.

And how on earth did Sedgemoor fit into the puzzle? He'd introduced Mr. Evans to the district as an old friend. Was the duke part of the plot? If so, why?

She sighed with frustration and impatiently shoved aside the half-written page lying on the blotter. So many questions. And no answers that made a jot of sense.

From now on, she'd carry the jewel on her. And one thing above all—no more kisses. Ever.

However necessary that decision was, it made her want to howl. Because the secret she'd take to the grave was that she'd loved Mr. Evans's kisses. However much she might want to skin him with the butter knife now, she'd never felt so alive as she had in that sneaking liar's arms.

"Ah, here you are. Your father is asking for you."

She was so focused on the duplicitous Mr. Evans, she needed a moment to realize that the man in the doorway was Neville Fairbrother.

"My lord." She was surprised to see him. He'd never ventured upstairs before. "You didn't need to fetch me."

Despite the lukewarm welcome, he approached. "I've always wondered where you disappeared each day."

Genevieve couldn't help contrasting his graceless trudge to Mr. Evans's tigerish prowl. Mr. Evans's every move proclaimed him a rake. So what did Lord Neville's gait say? That he asserted rights over everything and everyone in the vicarage?

As if to confirm that unpleasant thought, Lord Neville lifted the Harmsworth Jewel from the desk. She stifled the urge to snatch it back. Lord Neville's acquisitive streak was well known to her. Her father, taking advantage of Genevieve's expertise, had sourced many *objets d'art* for his collection.

"Good God, what is this?" Lord Neville twirled the jewel, setting the dragon's ruby eyes sparkling in the light flooding through the windows. "Is it twelfth century?"

She had even less desire to confide in Lord Neville than in Mr. Evans. Odd, when Lord Neville was her family's benefactor, and Mr. Evans was here under false pretenses.

"It's the Harmsworth Jewel." To her educated eye, the relic's design belonged to an earlier period, but she'd long ago learned that Lord Neville pretended more expertise than he possessed. "The family legend is that Alfred the Great presented it to an ancestor."

Lord Neville's hand fisted. Genevieve bit back a demand to take care. "Ninth century, then. What on earth is it doing here? And why hasn't your father offered it to me?"

Because I knew you'd want it the moment you saw it.

"It's mine," she said stiffly. "I inherited it from a friend."

"The Harmsworths have become lamentably rackety. The current baronet is reputedly a stablehand's bastard."

"I didn't know you followed gossip, Lord Neville."

He shrugged, not shifting his attention from the jewel. Her fingers curled against the leather blotter. She burned to lunge across the desk and pry the artifact from his grip. "I don't, of course. I focus on higher things. But the scandal has been the talk of the town for years."

Lord Neville's sneering tone made her range herself on Sir Richard's side, whatever his schemes. How horrible to have everyone sniggering over something he couldn't help.

"Can I please have the jewel back?" She rose behind her desk. "I'm sketching it."

He rotated the artifact. "How much do you want for it?"

She stared into his square face. Greed lit his eyes. "It's not for sale."

"Come, dear lady, price is no object. Name a figure."

When Mr. Evans called her dear lady, she didn't like it. When Lord Neville called her dear lady, she wanted to thump him with the inkwell. "Lady Bellfield left me the jewel. I will always keep it in memory of her."

"I'll pay ten thousand guineas."

Dear Lord...

"That's a fortune," she said in amazement. It was the same sum Sir Richard's representative had offered. She'd refused double that from Mr. Evans. Perhaps she should hold an auction. She'd be set for life.

"For something so rare, who cavils at price?"

Her brief amusement died. The hard light in Lord Neville's eyes made her distinctly wary. Or perhaps her nerves were on edge after cavorting in a scoundrel's arms. She extended her hand. "Please give me the jewel. I'd hate you to damage it."

"I know how to handle precious objects," he said, offended. "I'm a famous collector."

A famous collector who'd set his sights on her treasure. She didn't mistake his covetousness.

With visible reluctance, he surrendered the jewel. Genevieve resisted the impulse to whip the relic into the drawer, away from those beady eyes.

"So you accept my offer?"

Ten thousand guineas could change her life forever. "I told you, it's not for sale."

"Fifteen thousand."

She shook her head. "It's not a matter of money."

"Everything's a matter of money." He leaned across the desk and grabbed her arm. He wasn't hurting her, but she'd have difficulty shaking free. His touch always chilled her. "I'll go to twenty, but that's my final figure."

"My lord—"

"Twenty thousand guineas and a promise to keep your secret."

Horror flooded Genevieve. Had Lord Neville seen her with Mr. Evans last night? The thought made her sick with humiliation.

"S-secret?" she stammered, cursing the betraying fear in her voice.

Lord Neville looked more self-satisfied than ever. Something she would have thought impossible. "Don't play coy, my dear Miss Barrett."

Oh, dear God, he must have seen her at the pond. Shame kept her silent as she stared at him.

"I know you write your father's articles."

Stupid relief made her dizzy and she was almost grateful that he held her upright. Then she realized this was a disaster. Heartbreak and mockery loomed for her father if the true authorship became public. If she'd sometimes wondered whether she still loved her father despite his selfishness, the twisting fear in her belly now told her.

"What... what nonsense."

Lord Neville's laugh made her cringe. "Don't bother denying it. I've known for years. If you want to convince the world that you're nothing but a humble assistant, you should restrain your opinions at the dinner table."

Two people now knew the secret of her father's work. How ironic that her father's benefactor threatened to expose the truth, not the man she suspected was an out-and-out scoundrel.

She mustered her courage and glared at him the way her aunt would glare at a cockroach in her spotless kitchen. "Even if it's true, you can't use that information to force me to part with the Harmsworth Jewel."

"Can't I?" His stare turned assessing.

"Do you stoop to blackmail, my lord?" she asked sharply.

"Not at all." His hold on her arm tightened to bruising. "I merely point out that it's in your best interests to sell me the jewel. The treasure belongs in a great collection, not hidden in a drawer in a shabby vicarage."

Think, Genevieve, think. "If... if you reveal my father isn't the author of the articles, as his patron you risk looking a fool, my lord."

She caught a flash of displeasure in his deep-set eyes. He never appreciated opposition. "Not so much of a fool as the vicar will, my dear. And after all, I have a great name to save me from becoming a laughingstock."

"Is there some trouble, Miss Barrett?"

Mr. Evans might be a rogue, but at his question, her heart leaped with relief. He looked wonderful standing in the doorway, tall and strong. He was dressed for riding. From one leather-gloved hand, a crop dangled in unspoken threat.

"What business is this of yours, Evans?" Lord Neville snarled.

"None whatsoever," Mr. Evans said mildly, sauntering into the study. He cast a pointed glance at Lord Neville's grip on Genevieve's arm. Under that calm blue gaze, Lord Neville retreated. Genevieve snatched a shaky breath and slumped into her chair.

Lord Neville cast Mr. Evans a disparaging glare before he turned to Genevieve. "I can't be easy with such a valuable artifact lying unprotected. If you trust the Harmsworth Jewel to my keeping, I'll hold it safe until you decide on its disposal."

Until she decided to sell it to him, he meant. Genevieve wasn't so green that she misunderstood. Was she wrong to deny him? Twenty thousand guineas was more money than she'd see in a lifetime. And her father's secret would remain safe if she agreed. But every atom revolted at the idea of giving the jewel to the acquisitive lord.

"It's been safe until now."

"Not so, dear lady. What about the blackguard who broke in?"

How she wished he'd stop calling her dear lady. Deliberately she didn't glance at Mr. Evans. "I chased him off."

"Next time, you mightn't be so lucky," Lord Neville said.

She stood. "I must tidy myself before I go downstairs."

It was a dismissal. He must know she rarely bothered with her appearance before attending her father. For a moment, she wasn't sure that his lordship would go. But a glance at Mr. Evans seemed to convince him that right now, his plans to obtain the jewel wouldn't thrive.

She experienced a reluctant flash of gratitude that she hadn't seen Mr. Evans banished as a thief. Right now, his presence provided the only barrier between her and his lordship. The ache in her arm indicated that when Lord Neville wanted something, he wasn't always careful about how he got it.

"We'll discuss this issue once you've had time to think," his lordship said.

She could have told Lord Neville that he didn't need to emphasize the threat. Grimly she was aware that the matter wouldn't rest there. He was dogged in acquiring whatever took his fancy. And he'd taken a powerful fancy to the jewel.

"Coming, Evans?" Lord Neville clomped toward the door.

"I need a wash. I stink of the stables," he said amiably, although his gaze remained watchful.

"Indeed." Lord Neville's eyebrows arched at Mr. Evans's bluntness. He cast one last glance at Genevieve. "You are in many ways naïve, Genevieve. You'd do well to heed more worldly heads."

Thanks to Mr. Evans and Lord Neville, she became less naïve by the moment. "I won't change my mind, my lord."

"We'll see." He gave Mr. Evans a frosty nod as he left. "Evans."

Ignoring Genevieve's forbidding manner, Mr. Evans strolled across to lean on the corner of her desk. "What did the old mackerel want?"

"The Harmsworth Jewel." She aimed a pointed glare at him. Men! She'd happily consign the whole sex to the Bristol Channel and dance a hornpipe as they sank beneath the waves.

She still hadn't absolved Mr. Evans of plotting to steal the jewel, although she couldn't imagine why, if he wanted it, he hadn't taken it. After all, the jewel had been in her desk drawer until this morning. A man of Mr. Evans's initiative would make short work of the lock.

"And you, of course."

She hissed with irritation and pushed her chair back against the wall. Impossible to forget that he'd seen her naked. Humiliation pricked her nerves. To think only moments ago, she'd welcomed his appearance. "Don't be absurd."

He shrugged. "I suffer the same malady. I recognize it in another."

"I'd rather not refer to last night."

A faint smile flirted with his lips. He glanced down to where his long fingers played with her silver letter opener. Sliding it left and right. Up and down. "So I imagine."

"Then it never happened," she said stiffly.

Still he smiled. Still he moved the shining knife in casual patterns across the blotter. "It's not that simple, Miss Barrett."

The formal address mocked. Her hands fisted at her sides. How she longed to hit him. "Of course it is. A gentleman would—"

"You say I'm no gentleman."

"Nor you are."

He surveyed her beneath heavy eyelids, dark blue eyes brilliant with humor. And desire. Her pulses had rushed when he'd saved her from Lord Neville. They hadn't settled since and that glittering gaze didn't help.

"Harsh." His voice deepened as he balanced the paper knife on its handle. The action was inexplicably suggestive. "You left me burning, Miss Barrett. I caught nary a wink of sleep."

Nervously she checked the door. If Lord Neville overheard, he'd have something else to blackmail her with. "I slept like a log."

His eyes narrowed with amusement. "Liar."

"My father wants to see me." She cursed the quiver in her voice.

"Still running away?"

She refused to admit it. "Good day, Mr. Evans."

He leaned forward and grabbed her hand in an uncompromising grip, letting the knife bounce on the blotter.

She squeaked with shock. "This isn't private."

"Does that mean we can arrange a private meeting?"

"No, it does not." Angrily she tugged on her hand. How she longed to denounce him as a liar and a thief, but some shred of prudence reminded her that just now, he formed her best defense against Lord Neville.

"Pity."

He didn't sound particularly cast down. Of course he didn't. This was a game to him. If she forgot that, she was in trouble.

Heat seeped up her arm from where he held her, reminding her that she was already in trouble. To think that not long ago she'd only worried about establishing an academic reputation separate from her father's. Since then she'd dealt with burglars, kisses, and blackmailing, covetous noblemen. Not to mention a reluctant but immovable attraction for the rapscallion studying her as if he read every thought.

He probably did. She had a fair idea that Mr. Christopher Evans was no novice with the ladies. "Please, let me go. If anyone sees us—"

"Will you meet me later?"

"No."

"Then I must kiss you now."

"No, you mustn't," she said crossly. Then, horror of horrors, she heard footsteps on the stairs. Terror set pulses jumping. "For pity's sake, let me go."

"As you wish." He raised her hand and kissed it. The contact was so fleeting, she should hardly remark it. Why, then, did her skin still sizzle after she snatched free?

"Are you there, Genevieve? Dr. Mitchell has written from Glasgow with a new lead on the princes." Her father bustled in, brandishing a letter covered in spidery writing. "Ah, there you are, Mr. Evans. I was hoping I'd find you. You'll be interested in this."

His genuine pleasure at seeing his student weighted Genevieve's heart with foreboding. He'd become fond of Mr. Evans. Hardly surprising. Mr. Evans set out to please. But what happened when their visitor's falsehoods became known, as surely they would? However angry she was with her father, she was still his daughter. She hated to think of anyone hurting him. And right now her father was at risk from both Mr. Evans and Lord Neville.

"Excellent, Dr. Barrett." Mr. Evans slouched with picturesque ease against the far wall. He'd shifted without haste before her father appeared.

Genevieve hid a sigh. The safest choice was to avoid Mr. Evans as she had during his first few days. But now she recognized him as her burglar, she needed to watch him. And while Mr. Evans was with her, Lord Neville couldn't pressure her.

Feeling that her life whirled into chaos, she surreptitiously slipped the Harmsworth Jewel into her pinafore pocket and stood. Tonight when she was alone—no midnight swim, Mr.

Evans had put paid to that pastime—she'd sew a pocket into her petticoat to hold the jewel.

She stepped around the desk. "Shall we go downstairs, Papa? Lord Neville will wonder where you've got to." Speaking Lord Neville's name made her want to gag.

"Of course, my dear, of course." Her father bustled toward the door. Behind his back, Mr. Evans's blue eyes met hers. He was remembering their kisses. Curse him, so was she.

Chapter Ten

Over the next two nights, the memory of Genevieve's innocent kisses tormented Richard into sleeplessness, but his quarry had learned to be careful. Although the weather continued unseasonably hot, she didn't sneak out again. Conscienceless—and optimistic—fellow he was, he kept his door ajar so he'd hear if she left.

As he joined the family after dinner, he was grimly aware that he was still far from dazzling her into surrendering the jewel. There she sat across the parlor on her window seat, stitching doggedly at her grotesquerie of an embroidery. Beside her, Hecuba occupied the space that Richard wanted to claim. At the table, the vicar and Fairbrother pored over a parchment. Sirius snoozed in the corner. Mrs. Warren knitted in her usual chair.

Fairbrother, more omnipresent than ever over the last days, noted Richard's maneuverings toward Genevieve and rose to intervene. Until Mrs. Warren detained his lordship with a question. With ill-concealed reluctance, Fairbrother paused to reply, leaving Richard free to corner Genevieve. Mrs. Warren could teach Napoleon strategy.

"Your peonies still bloom, Miss Barrett," he murmured, lounging against the window frame.

"Mr. Evans, for shame." Her head jerked up and her cheeks turned pink. "My peonies are my business."

He laughed softly. How delightful. She must stew on their kisses if his remark struck her as indecent. "I merely admired your needlework."

She cast him a skeptical look. He couldn't blame her. The elephant had whelped a litter of malformed puppies. Or perhaps jellyfish.

He scooped Hecuba into his arms as he sat. Predictably the cat's rapturous welcome contrasted with her mistress's wariness.

Genevieve stuck her needle into the linen with an emphasis that made him suppress an "ouch." As she started to rise, he touched her arm. Nothing so blatant as grabbing her, but she stilled, trembling.

Oh, yes, she definitely remembered their kisses.

He released her. "I know you don't want to talk to me—"

"Correct, Mr. Evans." Her tone was repressive and temper set her lovely eyes sparkling.

He continued as though she hadn't interrupted. "But if you don't stay, Lord Neville will monopolize you."

Although her manner didn't thaw, she subsided onto the seat. "You imagine I prefer your company to his?"

"Don't you?" To his chagrin, the only times she welcomed Richard's presence was when Fairbrother was around. Being treated as the lesser of two evils wasn't especially flattering.

She shot him a disgruntled look. "You're insufferable."

He smiled. An insult from her lush lips was more arousing than another woman's fawning. If he wasn't careful, he'd find himself besotted with Miss Genevieve Barrett.

Which wasn't his plan at all. This was meant to be a short adventure, followed by a serious hunt for a suitable wife. "Absolutely."

"And conceited."

He heard how hard she fought not to laugh. "Probably."

"And lacking in principle."

"Now that's going too far." His tone indicated that while he agreed, he'd never admit it.

"I don't know why I bother with you."

"I'm entertaining?" he said hopefully, stroking Hecuba. The other night, Genevieve had purred. Too fleetingly.

"No, that can't be it," she said flatly. She tugged the needle free and placed two more clumsy stitches into her sampler.

"You're making progress."

She didn't look up. "If my hands are occupied, it keeps me from wringing your neck."

He flung his head back and laughed. Damn, but she was wonderful. He enjoyed her conversation almost as much as he enjoyed kissing her.

Richard's unfettered hilarity attracted attention. Objecting to the noise, Hecuba sprang to the floor. The vicar jumped as if someone had poked him with a sharp stick. Mrs. Warren appeared delighted, while Fairbrother looked like he contemplated murder. Richard plastered on a cool smile and stared down the odious lordling.

"So glad that I amuse you, Mr. Evans." Miss Barrett placed another stitch into the elephant's rump. Try as he might, he still couldn't make out any deuced peonies.

"I am too, Miss Barrett." He meant it.

"People are listening," she muttered, head bent over the embroidery.

"Don't worry. I'm careful of your reputation." He paused.

"More than you are, given what I caught you doing three nights ago."

She frowned as she looked up. "You have no right to censure my behavior, Mr. Evans. You're neither my father, brother, nor husband. You're a chance-met stranger."

"Who would like to be more," he responded smoothly.

She arched her eyebrows and her tone turned scathing. "My clandestine lover? I swoon with excitement."

"Careful, Miss Barrett. As you pointed out, we're not alone."

Color surged into her cheeks and she glanced around the room. Mrs. Warren and Fairbrother still watched intently. The vicar returned to his reading. "You make me forget myself."

"I'd certainly like to," he murmured, then exhaled with audible irritation. "Hell, I can't talk to you here."

Her smile hinted at triumph. "That's the general idea."

"So where can I talk to you?"

"Nowhere," she snapped. "You don't seem to understand, which is odd because you're not completely stupid."

This time he didn't contain his response. "Ouch."

She plowed on as if he hadn't spoken. "I don't want to see you alone. Given a choice, I'd rather not see you at all. Despite the other night's unfortunate encounter, I don't like you, Mr. Evans. I'd prefer that you devoted your attentions to your studies. And if you take yourself off to wherever you originated, be assured that I'll experience no pang upon your departure." She paused for breath. "I hope I make myself clear."

"Bravo." Fairbrother planted himself at her other side. Good God, the cat would be among the pigeons if his lordship had heard the more revealing parts of Genevieve's set-down. Richard struggled to smile through the burning need to plant his fist in the man's face.

"My lord—" Clearly Genevieve too had missed Lord Neville's approach.

"Glad to hear you put this upstart in his place." He extended his arm. "I'd like a private word, if I may. Your father has said we may use the library."

"We're in the middle of a conversation," Richard said in a silky tone, noticing how Genevieve paled.

Fairbrother regarded him as he'd regard a slug that crawled out from the salad. "You outstay your welcome, Evans."

"That's hardly for you to say, is it?" he asked lazily.

"Stop it, both of you." Genevieve slapped her embroidery onto the seat. "My lord, I'm sure Mr. Evans will grant us privacy here."

Fairbrother smirked. "Your father was most insistent that we speak alone."

"Very well." Her visible reluctance as she rose heartened Richard.

She disregarded the older man's arm and strode toward the door with the free, hip-swaying walk that Richard so admired. With a smug glance at his rival, his lordship followed. Left behind on the window seat, Richard pondered the significance of Fairbrother's gloating.

Genevieve resented how Mr. Evans transformed her into a woman she didn't recognize and wasn't sure she liked. She resented how he made her blood fizz. She resented how he made her feel alive, as though she'd spent the last twenty-five years buried in her books like some sleeping princess from a fairy-tale. A princess waiting for the handsome prince to ride up on his white steed and kiss her awake.

Mr. Evans was handsome. He wasn't a prince. More an evil genie.

The snick of the closing library door disturbed her perturbing reflections. She glanced up sharply from where she stood in the middle of the room. "My lord, please open the door."

Lord Neville ignored her request and stumped toward her. "I spoke to your father this afternoon."

She frowned. "You threatened to expose him?"

Lord Neville's smile didn't calm her nervousness. "I wouldn't be so blatant."

Curse him, she heard the word "yet" at the end of that sentence. "My father doesn't own the jewel. I do."

"Your modesty is outshone only by your beauty, Genevieve."

Seriously worried now, she backed away. His tone made the hair stand up on her skin. "I won't sell the Harmsworth Jewel."

"My dear girl, right now I'm interested in another treasure altogether." To her consternation, he dropped to one knee and grabbed her hand. "You must know how eagerly I long to make you my wife."

"My lord—" Shock jammed all response in her throat. Her stomach knotted in horror. Frantically she prayed for Mr. Evans to wander in and make some irritating remark.

Lord Neville frowned. "Our understanding has been clear for years."

With a desperate tug, Genevieve broke away and retreated until she bumped into her father's book-covered desk. "I'm flattered by your offer—"

"Your consent will make me the happiest man in the world." He didn't wait for her to finish. He never did. A habit unacceptable in a husband.

What on earth had she done to make him think she expected marriage? With a sick feeling, she realized that this proposal's timing wasn't coincidental. Lord Neville was worried about Mr. Evans's interest and staked a claim that until now he'd assumed uncontested. And if she married him, he'd get the Harmsworth Jewel.

Still, he'd been good to her father. Despite the blackmail, he deserved politeness. "I'm truly sorry, my lord, if I've led you to believe that I considered you anything more than my father's associate."

He scowled and lumbered to his feet. His amorous manner degenerated into aggression. "What's that supposed to mean?"

Although several feet separated them, she squeezed against the desk. "It means that I thank you for your regard, but I cannot accept your proposal."

Lord Neville's outrage swelled. "Do you expect me to court you?"

Actually if a man wanted to marry her, she did expect more than an abrupt proposal that already assumed her agreement. A romantic must lurk inside her, however often she'd told herself she was at her last prayers.

"I'm not playing coy games. Surely you know me better than that."

He rose on the balls of his feet in a threatening manner that made her stomach lurch. The library suddenly seemed cramped, the closed door ominous. "I know that you'd be living in penury without me and that you're a damned ungrateful wench to expect me to dance attendance. And don't forget that I can destroy your father's reputation with a word."

Appalled, she stared at him. "You'd blackmail me into marriage?"

"'Blackmail' is an ugly word."

"And an uglier deed." She straightened, temper feeding

a recklessness that she already knew she might regret. "Tell the world."

He scowled at her, although she read surprise in his eyes. "I may very well do that. When your father's life is in ruins, remember how you brought it about, missy."

She straightened, indignation swamping any remnants of fear. "You've requested my hand. I've refused. This meeting is at an end."

With a swish of her meager skirts, she headed for the door. Despite her outrage at his proprietorial air, disbelief still gripped her. How long had he plotted this match? Her blood ran cold to think Lord Neville had spent years imagining her in his bed.

"Don't you walk out on me!" He snatched her arm and dragged her closer. This time he didn't care about bruises. Blood mottled his jowly cheeks and his hot male smell made her dizzy. "I haven't finished."

She stumbled to a stop and glared. "My lord, you're under my father's roof and obliged to act with discretion."

His mouth twisted with contempt. "You should go on your knees in gratitude that a man of my station glances in your direction. I'm a Fairbrother and you're a nobody."

Could this get any worse? "In that case, I'm amazed that you lowered yourself to consider me as your wife," she said with poisonous sweetness.

"I do lower myself, madam." He shoved his sweating face into hers. "I'll overlook your discourtesy and renew my suit in a few days. In the meantime, take time to consider consequences."

She wrenched free. Her arm ached from his grip. She backed toward the door and fumbled behind her for the handle. "I'm not teasing," she said unsteadily. "My answer is no."

"That ridiculous boy has turned your head." A sneer distorted his fleshy mouth. "If you imagine that fellow intends anything but your ruin, you're sillier than I credit."

"Mr. Evans has nothing to do with my refusal," she said stiffly, tightening her grip on the handle.

He laughed dismissively. "I won't take his leavings."

"You exceed the bounds of propriety," she choked.

"Just so you know that I won't wait forever."

"You will indeed wait forever," she retorted, repelled by his arrogance.

He'd never believe that she didn't toy with him before an inevitable yes. If only her father had given her some warning. Then the horrible thought struck that her father must think she was eager to become Lady Neville Fairbrother.

"Mark my words about that cur sniffing around you. My bride will be a virgin. That's not negotiable."

Nauseated, she turned away from him. She dearly wanted to cry. "Good evening, my lord."

She escaped even as he protested. Carefully she closed the door behind her, just because the temptation to slam it was nigh overwhelming. She collapsed against the door, promising herself that she could cry once she reached her room.

If Lord Neville revealed the truth about her authorship, her father would never forgive her. Nor was she blind to the fact that a man with her suitor's connections could put paid to her own nascent career.

What the devil was she going to do?

"Genevieve?"

"Dear God—" Mr. Evans with his ever-watchful eyes was the last person she wanted to meet right now.

"Are you all right?" He sounded concerned, not like the flirtatious scoundrel who destroyed her peace. She didn't trust that voice. After the last half hour, she didn't trust any man.

She whirled to face him. "For pity's sake, leave me alone!"

On a betraying sob, she dashed upstairs. Mr. Evans remained below, silently observing her ignominious flight.

Chapter Eleven

D amn it, man, what the hell is taking so long?"

At Cam's impatient question, Sirius looked up from his nap on the stillroom's stone floor. Richard straightened the towel around his shoulders and stared disconsolately out the window at the rain sheeting onto Leighton Court's palatial stables. His hair was wet, and stinking with the paste for turning blond to the brown that he grew to loathe. A freezing trickle dribbled down his neck. He hated this part of his ruse—dyeing his hair made him feel like a blasted cicisbeo.

Cam hadn't finished. "You're not setting yourself up for life as the vicar's clerk. When I helped you put this together, I didn't imagine I'd be providing a cover story longer than a week. Your absence has been noted in Town. I'm assuming you don't want to become such a mystery that people start asking about you all over the country. That might let the cat out of the bag."

Richard contemplated the miserable morning. He'd been in a grim humor since Genevieve had fled him in tears three nights ago. He'd burned to comfort her. Whatever propriety's dictates, it felt wrong to ignore her distress.

Cam growled. "Confound you, answer me. Have you lost your tongue as well as your wits in this godforsaken backwater?"

Richard laughed wryly and finally met his friend's concerned eyes. Cam stood ruler-straight before the marble counter. Not for him the slouch that Richard affected. "What was the question again?"

"Good God, you're bloody lovesick, aren't you?" Cam pounded his fist against the counter. "That woman has turned your brain. You've always been so cynical about love. How the mighty have fallen."

Richard's gut clenched in denial. "Utter rot, dear fellow."

Cam snorted disbelief. Richard cursed old friends who didn't fall for his pose of good-natured vacancy. "I must meet this Genevieve Barrett. To think a prim bluestocking has you on your knees. I never thought to see the day."

Richard shivered. It was deuced chilly weather to sit around in his shirt with sopping hair. "You and your wild imagination. I'm making sure I do this properly."

"Do what? Steal the jewel or the girl's virtue?"

His lips tightened with an impatience that would have astonished those who believed that Richard Harmsworth reserved his deepest reactions for his tailoring. "I can't bloody well steal it. How can I taunt the ton with the deuced bauble if I do? The situation is more complex than I thought."

He hoped Cam didn't notice that he failed to comment on any plans for Genevieve's virtue. Playing the gentleman became more onerous every day. Especially since he'd kissed her.

"So how much longer?" The duke frowned with the displeasure that invariably sent minions scurrying. "Surely you tire of rural amusements."

Richard merely arched his eyebrows. If Cam knew the

delights of Genevieve's kisses, he wouldn't mock the rustic life. "I'm making progress."

Cam threw his hands up in disgust. "Not from what I see."

The urge arose to confide in Cam about Genevieve's work for her father. But his friend would only nag him to use the information to obtain the jewel. Richard wasn't sure why he hadn't taken advantage of the only secret he'd uncovered—unless he counted her propensity for swimming naked. Perhaps the unspoken threat in Fairbrother's manner toward her stopped him. Galling at his age to discover that a knight in shining armor skulked under his nonchalant demeanor.

"I'm taking the subtle approach."

"Well, that's novel."

He might fend off Cam's jibes, but the time he devoted to brooding upon Genevieve was disturbing. Not to mention these unfamiliar protective instincts. Inconvenient protective instincts. After all, he meant to soften her up until she surrendered the jewel, not keep her from harm all her days.

He had a sinking premonition that those protective instincts might stymie his wicked schemes. Hell, they already had. After she'd run upstairs crying, his pursuit had relented.

The memory of that night reminded him that he wasn't merely here for a scolding and somewhere private to dye his hair. "What do you know about Neville Fairbrother?"

"Leath's uncle?" Cam's dark brows contracted. "He doesn't appear in society. He has a property a few miles away. Youngton Hall. By all reports it's stuffed to the gills with treasures. I went up against him for that Titian in Rothermere House's library. He didn't take losing in good spirit."

"That's in character."

"I imagine he's plump in the pocket. All the Fairbrothers are."

"Have you heard anything to the fellow's detriment?"

Cam shrugged. "Haven't heard much at all."

"Can you find out?"

Cam's mouth flattened with reluctant humor. "I have got a life separate from your madcap stratagems, my friend."

"A word here, a word there. Not asking you to lay down your life, old man."

"Why?"

"Why aren't I asking you to lay down your life?"

Cam's eyes narrowed. "No. Why this sudden interest in the middle-aged second son of a marquess?"

"The bugger is after Genevieve." Even more unforgivably, he'd made her cry. For that, he deserved to have his kidneys poached.

Cam laughed. "Priceless. Not only is the bluestocking holding out, she has another suitor. Dear God, man, you'll end this escapade with your tail between your legs."

Richard had a bleak feeling that Cam's raillery was justified. He swam in deep water and right now, he was drowning. "The vicar told me that Fairbrother proposed three nights ago and Genevieve refused him."

"Did she indeed?" Calculation replaced Cam's amusement. "A penniless vicar's daughter is a comedown for a Fairbrother, even a second son. They're notoriously high in the instep."

"She doesn't like him."

"Says you."

"She's got too much sense to fall for that walrus's blather."

Richard awaited further mockery, but Cam regarded him with a frown. "A sensible woman would say yes. It's a big step up in the world."

"No sensible woman would marry Neville Fairbrother. He's a boor."

"Compared to you."

"At least I'm not thirty years older than she is."

"So you're contemplating marriage?"

Shocked, Richard jerked upright, losing his towel. Marriage? To Genevieve? If he wasn't stuck here with noisome gunk adorning his head, he'd march out. "Good God, you're talking madness. You know I need to marry a woman who can restore the Harmsworth name. A chit with exceptional lineage and no questionable interests."

Cam looked intrigued. "Questionable interests?"

Richard's lips tightened. His friend's query should amuse him. Instead, he wanted to punch Cam's aristocratic nose. "Miss Barrett's a lady of unblemished chastity. But the Harmsworth scandal will never die if I marry a lowborn bluestocking with a tendency to speak her mind."

"You've thought this through."

Richard's laugh was dismissive. "Not at all. Matrimony's the last thing on my mind. I'll set my course to seeking a bride when I'm back in Town."

"When will that be? After Christmas? Can you tear yourself away from the luscious Genevieve before then? She's got you in a lather and you haven't even tumbled her yet."

"It's only a passing fancy. I'm here for the jewel."

Cam shrugged. "You don't talk about the jewel. You talk about Miss Barrett. And in terms I've never heard you use."

Richard sobered. Strangely now that shock subsided, the prospect of marrying Genevieve didn't stir quite the horror he'd expected. Which was the most frightening admission of all.

She never bored him. If anything, she was a little too exciting. He wasn't used to women staying two steps ahead. If he wasn't careful, her brilliant brain might outwit him yet.

He spoke from the depths of his heart. "She's too good for me, Cam."

"Rubbish."

"Even if she isn't, she's determined on spinsterhood and a life of scholarship. She says right out that she won't marry. Can't blame her. A husband would try to crush her spirit. She's not exactly docile and I can't imagine her taking a fellow's direction just because she'd vowed obedience before a parson."

"She sounds likc she's got your measure."

Even if that was true, he damned well wasn't admitting it. "She's certainly interesting."

She was way more than that, but he'd exposed enough of this unwelcome obsession. Wanting a woman was perfectly acccptable, but this desire threatened to dominate his life.

Cam's expression became austere. "Richard, if you've decided you're interested in this woman as more than a brief flirtation, tell her the truth. You've already lied to a point where she mightn't forgive you. The longer you stay, the greater the chance that she'll discover you're not what you seem."

Richard's skin felt too tight and heat crept into his cheeks. How utterly bloody that his friend made him falter like a schoolboy. And squirm with guilt. "Don't be an ass. You see significance where none exists."

Cam didn't appear convinced. "Of course I do."

"Really."

"My mistake."

Richard's eyes narrowed, but Cam had turned to stare out at the rain. Instead of another harangue, Cam changed the subject. Unfortunately he chose a topic even less congenial than the beauteous Genevieve.

"Did you hear your mother is back from Paris? My sister Lydia saw her at the opera last week. Dazzling in some gown that has the modistes scrambling to catch up. And trailing two French comtes at least twenty years her junior."

Oh, merciful God. He didn't want to think about his mother right now. He *never* wanted to think about his mother.

"No, I didn't hear," he said with hard-won carelessness. "I pay no heed to my mother's antics."

Both he and Cam knew he lied through his teeth. But the reminder of his mother's peccadillos and the misery they'd caused him placed his fascination with Miss Barrett into perspective. He probably should thank Cam, much as he felt like pounding the insolence out of him for broaching this perennially painful subject.

Thanks to his mother, Richard had spent his life shoring up defenses against a hostile world. A man asked for trouble if he made himself vulnerable. If he'd learned anything after years of fending off snide remarks, it was that he couldn't risk any emotion deeper than a puddle.

Miss Barrett would prove to be only another woman in a long line of meaningless intrigues. A more complex and interesting woman than his usual conquests. A woman who right now he couldn't imagine leaving after a few weeks. But that mutton-headedness would pass, he was sure. She'd never leave a scar on his well-guarded heart.

Damn it. Cam would accuse him of protesting too much.

Chapter Twelve

"His confounded Grace knows too much for his own good," Richard told Sirius as they wandered along the bridle path toward the vicarage. Since discovering this shortcut when tracking Genevieve through the night, he'd used it regularly.

Needing thinking time, he led Palamon instead of riding. He'd pretended that Cam's remarks slid off him like snow melting off a roof. But Cam knew him better than anyone, and clearly his friend feared the consequences of this masquerade.

Around Richard, the trees were a striking combination of red, yellow, and green as autumn took hold. The newly emerged sun sparkled weakly on wet grass. Above, stray clouds massing in the sky reminded him of Genevieve's embroidery. Devil take it, he must be smitten, much as he hated admitting it. He even found her malformed stitchery endearing.

The path veered toward Genevieve's pool. The memory of her rising—however clichéd, he couldn't help thinking of Venus—from the water still disturbed his sleep.

"Genevieve's outside the usual run of female. That doesn't mean this affair is important."

Sirius glanced back with an expression eerily reminiscent of Cam's skepticism.

"Admittedly she's smarter than most women I've had in my sights. I need to be at the top of my form to match her."

Although what did he mean by "match"? Obtaining the jewel, obviously. Or did he mean kisses? *More than kisses?* He swallowed to moisten a suddenly dry mouth at the thought of seducing Genevieve, virtuous woman or no.

The devil whispered in his ear and he struggled against listening. Genevieve didn't intend to marry. Would Richard do irreparable damage if he explored the attraction flaring between them?

His voice turned husky. "She's halfway there. More than halfway."

Sirius's steady gaze didn't waver.

"Shut up," Richard muttered. "What do you know?"

Sirius gave himself a good shake and trotted ahead.

"You're not much of a confidant," Richard called after him. "Unless you lift your game, it's hardly worthwhile keeping you in bones."

Sirius barked sharply and loped into the undergrowth. Richard frowned and stared after him. He led Palamon onward, wondering what had set Sirius off.

His thoughts elsewhere—predictably with Genevieve's kisses—he approached the last turn of the path before the stable yard. The sound of running feet made him stop.

A curved body, soft, fragrant and disheveled, crashed into him and sent him staggering. Automatically he released the reins and his arms closed hard on his assailant. Behind him, Palamon snorted and danced away.

"What are you—"

"Let me go!" Genevieve struggled, panting. Her scent, warm woman and crushed flowers, made his head swim. His hands tightened even as she wriggled.

"Miss Barrett, what's the matter?" Although he should release her, he couldn't convey the command from brain to hands. No wonder. All the blood in his body flowed to one organ alone.

"Let me go, you idiot! They're getting away!"

"Who's getting away?"

She growled and broke free, hurtling past. She clutched a broom. What in Hades was going on?

"Miss Barrett? Genevieve?" He watched her vanish into the trees in a flurry of skirts. He went to pursue her before remembering that he couldn't leave Palamon. He caught the trailing rein.

"I'll look after him, Mr. Evans." Williams, the elderly groom, appeared at his elbow.

"What the devil's got into everyone?"

"Great doings this afternoon. Miss Barrett came back from her parish visits and surprised robbers. Second time the vicarage's been burgled in a month. Don't know what they expect to find. Just a lot of dusty old books in there, from what I see."

What the hell? And Genevieve chasing the intruders armed only with a broom? Didn't the woman have a jot of sense? Panic gripped him.

Shoving the reins at the groom, he took off at a run. What a deuced mess. He wasn't armed. But then he'd blithely imagined he was the sole villain in the neighborhood. Clearly he was mistaken.

"Genevieve, wait!"

Damn it, where was she? He strained to hear her crashing ahead, but the woods remained silent. Then Sirius barked and he sprinted in that direction. He prayed Sirius had found Genevieve. The dog was almost as valiant as the girl.

Richard had spent the morning denying any conscience concerning this woman. The sour, sick feeling cramping his gut proved him a liar. The prospect of anyone hurting even one hair on her head made him want to commit bloody murder.

Gasping, Richard broke into a clearing. Genevieve still ran ahead, Sirius at her side.

He dashed forward to seize her waist and nearly caught the broom on his head for his trouble. "Genevieve... Miss Barrett, it's all right. It's me. Rich... Christopher Evans." Good God, he'd better keep his wits about him or he'd betray himself.

His voice didn't calm her at all. "Let me go, you devil!"

Sirius, picking up the excitement, jumped around them barking. Still Genevieve writhed like a trapped eel. If Richard had doubted her strength, he had his answer now. He needed all his concentration to hold her. "Genevieve, hush, you'll injure yourself."

Her laugh was wild and bitter. Seriously worried, he twined his arms around her, drawing her into his body. Her struggles intensified. "I'll scream."

"Down, Sirius!" he snapped at the dog.

"Leave me alone!" She tried to clout Richard with the broom and this time he didn't fool himself that it was accidental.

He heard her genuine fear. She'd never been frightened of him before, even when he'd caught her naked. The knowledge sliced through him like a razor. Bewildered, he raised his arms and retreated. "Are you all right?"

"Yes," she said in a clipped voice, standing there trembling with anger.

"Williams said the vicarage was burgled." He ventured a step closer.

She raised the broom. "Don't touch me."

Disbelief kept him still, even if within the broom's reach. "I'm no threat."

"What do you know about this?" Her voice was hard. Sirius whined and pressed into Richard's hip.

Bewilderment made Richard pause. Did she accuse him of the break-in? Was it possible she'd guessed that he was her burglar? Her first burglar, damn it. Now it seemed there were genuine criminals on this patch.

"Nothing. I've been with Sedgemoor all morning. He's back for a few days." If he wasn't confident that his disguise was foolproof, he'd think she'd rumbled his scheme. He chanced a smile, but it aroused no answering warmth. "Please put the broom down. You make me nervous."

For a bristling moment, wide gray eyes peered into his soul. "Whoever did this knew that Aunt Lucy and I were out and that it was the maids' half day."

"But the vicar was home."

Genevieve looked unimpressed. "He wouldn't stir from his library if the house fell down about his ears."

She sighed and planted the broom on the ground, leaning on it. At least she no longer looked ready to kill him. That felt like major progress. Richard had no idea why she was so furious with him. Perhaps because he'd stopped her charging willy-nilly after the robbers.

She continued more evenly. "Mrs. Meacham wasn't well enough for visitors so I dropped off her basket and left. I came in through the back and noticed the kitchen door open. That seemed odd with the servants away. I called out. Then I heard a crash upstairs in my study."

"Of course, you rushed inside to see."

She stiffened at his disapproving tone. "Is there anything wrong with that?"

His response wouldn't lift his shaky credit with her, but he needed to say it. "You're reckless to thrust yourself into danger. How many men were there?"

"Two."

Dread tasted pungent in his mouth as he pictured what could have happened. "Did you recognize them?"

"No." She paused. "I only caught a glimpse. They pushed past then ran away."

"So you decided to chase them armed only with a broom?"

She flushed. "I couldn't let them escape." She spoke with an edge. "Although of course I did. Did you see anyone in the woods?"

"No. But just before I met you, Sirius took off after something. These robbers want the jewel."

She frowned. "That's a rash assumption. I know you do, but that doesn't mean the whole world does."

"It's the most valuable item in the vicarage, unless there's some hoard I don't know about."

"The library is full of rare manuscripts."

"Which argues a specialist's knowledge." His eyes sharpened. "Who knows you've got the jewel?"

There was a bristling pause as though she meant to pursue the argument. Then she spoke in a flat voice. "My father. You. Dr. Partridge at the Ashmolean. Sir Richard Harmsworth. Lady Bellfield's solicitors. Lord Neville. Perhaps my father mentioned it to a colleague. He conducts extensive international correspondence."

"It's Fairbrother."

"Surely not." She frowned as she considered Richard's idea. "Lord Neville is a rich man with a family name to protect. Why risk ruin? If he steals the jewel, he could never display it."

"But he wants it." *And you.*

"He offered to buy it. I told him no."

"And then he proposes marriage, Genevieve?" Richard should call her Miss Barrett, but when she stood before him beautiful and ruffled and in need of protection, she was Genevieve. Lovely, warm, sensual Genevieve.

She scowled, folding her arms. "How do you know that?"

He couldn't help noticing how the stance pressed her full breasts against her blue dress. "The vicar told me."

"My father had no right to share that information with a stranger," she snapped.

He suffered a pang at hearing himself labeled a stranger. "How long ago did Lord Neville discover you had the jewel? Was it that morning I stopped him bullying you?"

"He wasn't bullying me," she said without conviction. "Or no more than you do. Are you suggesting he only wants to marry me to get the jewel?"

"No." Richard had seen how the older man looked at Genevieve. With lust and a disturbing air of ownership.

Genevieve regarded Richard doubtfully as though expecting him to say more. He realized that he should ask about the jewel. Bugger, Cam was right about his confused priorities. "Did the thieves find it?"

She shook her head. "No."

He told himself that he was more relieved about the jewel's safety than Genevieve's. Not even he believed that. "They searched your study. Doesn't that tell you they're targeting the jewel?"

"If you imagine I've discounted the coincidence of your arrival with the criminal classes invading our unexceptional vicarage, I'd advise you to think again, Mr. Evans."

"Are you accusing me of something, Miss Barrett?" he asked, suddenly tired of fencing. If she recognized him as her burglar, she'd have to say so.

Her eyes narrowed and he wondered if perhaps she meant

to denounce him. Then what would he do? If ruthless men plundered the vicarage, she was in danger. He couldn't forsake her, whatever lies he'd told Cam about his lack of emotional involvement.

"Not right now."

Which was no answer at all.

With a flounce of her skirts, she marched off, still carrying the broom. When she was annoyed, her walk developed a swinging stride that heated his blood. She was such a passionate creature. His hands curled at his sides as he resisted the urge to catch her and turn all that passion toward him.

Still she strutted away. Tall. Straight-shouldered. Ready to take on a world of men and win. She should look absurd. What she looked was strong and brave and beautiful beyond his wildest dreams. And after today's incident, terrifyingly vulnerable.

It seemed Richard Harmsworth wasn't alone in marking Genevieve's beauty and the treasure she guarded. After today, he had a more important task than wheedling the jewel away from her. That could wait till Doomsday if it must. Ensuring Genevieve's safety couldn't.

Chapter Thirteen

After hearing garbled tales about rampaging mobs, Lord Neville slammed into the vicarage and didn't notably calm even after Genevieve downplayed the drama. He insisted upon bearding the vicar in his library.

Genevieve followed, although as a mere woman, her opinion wasn't sought. Her aunt stayed outside, but Mr. Evans joined them. Genevieve waited for Lord Neville to object to his presence, but perhaps even his lordship quailed from such presumption in another man's abode.

Genevieve stood near the hearth. This chilly afternoon, she appreciated the fire. Or perhaps the cold stemmed from awareness that the criminal fraternity had invaded her home. For a second time.

Could Mr. Evans be right? Was today's outrage his lordship's doing? Or, as seemed more plausible, was it like the last break-in, all up to Mr. Evans?

While she accepted Mr. Evans's story about being with Sedgemoor, he could easily pay someone to rob the vicarage. The thieves had rifled her study, although yet again, nothing was missing. Luckily the jewel was safe in her petticoat.

When Mr. Evans had caught her in the woods, she'd come so close to revealing that she'd identified him as her burglar. The accusation had trembled on her lips. Until she'd remembered the buffer he created between her and her blackmailing suitor. Right now, she didn't know whom to trust. Her strongest instinct was to trust nobody, stay silent, and watch for some clue to the truth.

"I cannot be easy with the vicarage unprotected." Lord Neville held forth from the center of the library as if he owned the house. "You and Genevieve must move into Youngton Hall until these thugs are apprehended."

Mr. Evans remained a silent observer. Sirius sat at his side, seeming to follow each argument.

"What about my parishioners?" the vicar asked in a quavering voice from where he sat—crouched really, like an animal at bay—behind his untidy desk. After the first break-in, he'd been nervy, but today's broad-daylight opportunism left him befuddled and frightened.

His lordship dismissed the vicar's question with a swipe of one hand. "If you're needed, they can send a message. I'll bring you over for Sunday services."

"I'm not sure." Her father was hardly an active shepherd to his congregation and usually he'd leap to partake of aristocratic bounty. But after today's events, Genevieve knew that abandoning his home for a strange place, even so luxurious a strange place as Youngton Hall, would unsettle him. "It's my duty to stay if thieves infest the neighborhood."

Lord Neville sighed with ill-concealed impatience and his hand clenched on the silver gargoyle on top of his cane. Genevieve was familiar with the piece, an elaborate copy of a carving in Lincoln Cathedral. She'd never liked it. The grotesque seemed steeped in malevolence. "Then send Genevieve to me."

She drew breath to refuse. Since his proposal, Lord Neville had treated her with resentment, punctuated with smothering solicitude. At least he hadn't renewed his blackmail threat since she'd called his bluff—except she had a discomfiting presentiment that he merely bided his time. She preferred his pique over his care, especially as his care became most overt in Mr. Evans's vicinity.

"That's hardly proper, my lord," her father bleated. "Your visits to Little Derrick raise no questions because you're here for scholarly purposes. But for Genevieve to stay in your house? As a man of God, I can't condone it, however innocent your motives."

Genevieve wasn't so sure about the innocent motives. To her irritation, she couldn't disregard Mr. Evans's insinuations about his lordship.

Lord Neville's smile dripped superiority. "You mistake me, Dr. Barrett. Your daughter's reputation is precious to me too. I would of course offer Mrs. Warren hospitality."

"I'm not leaving you, Papa." Genevieve hated that Lord Neville discussed her as if she wasn't present. His bombastic manner only made her grateful that she'd never contemplated marrying him—or any man.

Lord Neville was adamant. "Genevieve, prudence insists—"

"Miss Barrett has a right to decide whether she stays or goes, my lord," Mr. Evans said in the light, pleasant voice that indicated he was determined on his opinion prevailing.

"This doesn't concern you, Evans," his lordship snarled. Since Genevieve had refused his proposal, he'd foregone even minimal politeness to Mr. Evans.

"On the contrary, I take this outrage very personally indeed." As always, Mr. Evans gave no indication by tone or expression that he resented the other man's rudeness. As always, his coolness made Lord Neville look like a hectoring bully.

"Perhaps I should stay until the danger passes." His lordship subjected Mr. Evans to a narrow-eyed glare.

Her bugbear reclined against the mantel with an exaggerated languor that would make Genevieve laugh if she wasn't so on edge. "Lud, the place will be more crowded than Tattersall's on auction day."

"My lord, we have no chamber befitting your dignity." Genevieve glowered at Mr. Evans. He overdid the useless flower of fashion act. Especially when she knew that his beautifully cut coat concealed muscles that wouldn't shame a stevedore. This morning, she'd fought like a demon when he'd caught her and he'd hardly broken a sweat. "We know to be on guard. Between Williams, my father, and Mr. Evans, we should be safe."

Except she had a nasty feeling that Mr. Evans was the fox in this particular henhouse.

Lord Neville's mouth turned down. "A geriatric retainer, an unworldly scholar, and a namby-pamby fop. Pardon me if I consider arrangements inadequate."

Genevieve saw the fop's barely contained smirk. Her father struggled to his feet with a sudden display of spirit. "I may be an unworldly scholar, my lord, but I protect my own."

Lord Neville must have realized that he'd overstepped the mark. He bowed to the vicar, so briefly it was almost insulting, and again to Genevieve. "My counsel falls upon deaf ears. All I can say is that my offer of sanctuary remains."

"Will you stay to dinner, your lordship?" the vicar asked.

Lord Neville still sulked over his failure to get her to Youngton Hall. "Not tonight."

"Capital, my lord," Mr. Evans said with purposely grating

cheerfulness. "A man your age should beware the evening chill."

Genevieve watched Lord Neville stifle a blistering response to this blatant piece of cheek. Only because she observed Mr. Evans so closely did she note the satisfied glint in his eyes. Of course he was satisfied—he'd managed to banish Lord Neville for the evening. Yet again she thought what a manipulative devil he was.

"I take my leave, then," Lord Neville said grudgingly.

"Good evening, my lord." The vicar remained unaware, Genevieve knew, of the dark currents swirling through the room. Currents of resentment and jealousy and mistrust. "Genevieve, perhaps you should see his lordship out?"

Protest would upset her father further. Since he'd learned that she'd refused Lord Neville's proposal, the rift between them had deepened, but still she flinched from adding to his distress.

Mr. Evans stepped forward. "Let me show his lordship out."

Ten minutes ago, she'd wanted to strangle him. How nonsensical now to want to hug him for saving her from a cozy chat with Lord Neville.

"I have something particular to say to Genevieve," Lord Neville said.

"What's all this fuss? I can't abide all this fuss," her father complained. "Genevieve, go with Lord Neville. I want Mr. Evans with me. He's such a comfort."

Reluctantly Genevieve nodded and moved toward the door. A glance back at Mr. Evans restored her failing courage. Something in his stance told her that he'd rush to her rescue if she stayed outside too long.

Since when had she started relying on Mr. Evans to save her?

As she'd expected, his lordship resumed the argument

once they were alone. "I insist you come to Youngton Hall for your own protection."

"The thieves haven't been violent." She stepped as far back as the narrow space allowed. Since his lordship's clumsy attempt at blackmail and his boorish proposal, she could hardly endure his company.

"Yet." He paused. "You're a stubborn chit."

She shrugged, unmoved by the criticism. "I'm a self-willed woman. I have no wish to submit to a man's guidance."

It was a pointed reminder of what an unsuitable wife she'd make for a man of his station, not just in birth but behavior. The mulish angle of his jaw indicated that he disregarded her statement. "You can be schooled, my dear."

"Like an unruly horse?"

Her mocking response raised no amusement. She'd long ago remarked that Lord Neville lacked a sense of humor. Mr. Evans possessed a highly developed sense of humor. A quality she dearly wished she didn't find so attractive.

Lord Neville frowned. "Send Evans away. He means no good."

That was, she suspected, the truth. "My father likes Mr. Evans."

Lord Neville shook his head in disgust. "Your father lives in his own world. If he didn't, he'd keep a better eye on you."

Indignation soured her stomach, but she struggled to retain at least a patina of politeness. However she disliked Lord Neville, he had a hold over this family. "My lord, you broach subjects that, for all your generosity and care, aren't your concern."

He didn't retreat. He never did. He was always convinced that he was right. Like most males, she thought acidly. She wondered whether Mr. Evans hid a bully beneath his eye-catching exterior.

"Given your father's gullibility, I consider myself in place of a parent. A young man unrelated to you under the same roof injures your reputation. To the pure all things are pure, so I'm sure you're unaware of the gossip."

Her cheeks heated with vexation. And a touch of shame. After all, if anyone had stumbled into the woods several nights ago, they would have found plenty to talk about. "If you consider yourself my father, my lord, I'm surprised that you offered marriage."

"You take me too literally."

"Do I?" She straightened. This promised to become a pointless quarrel. "The house is bursting at the seams with chaperones. My aunt, my father, the servants can all testify that Mr. Evans and I have shared nothing improper."

Lord Neville had the grace to look slightly abashed. "My uneasiness is over Evans's behavior. After all, what do you know of him?"

That at the very least he was a liar. "I know that he's the Duke of Sedgemoor's friend. I know that he's unfailingly kind to my father and aunt. I know that he rushed after the thieves without thought to his safety this morning."

Now that she defended Mr. Evans, she realized that the rogue possessed more admirable qualities than just his sense of humor. Qualities that appealed considerably more than Lord Neville's arrogance. Mr. Evans was intelligent and spoke to her as if she was too. He liked animals. He was surprisingly interesting. He kissed like a dream.

Oh, no, don't think about that.

Lord Neville exhaled through his teeth. "There's no point talking to you. You're blind to your interests. I fear that man has bewitched you."

"Don't be absurd." She forced herself to sound conciliatory, even as her heart rebelled. "You know that I'm a contrary creature and your opposition only makes me defend Mr. Evans."

It was a warning, should Lord Neville take it. But he remained deaf to the message. "You've run wild far too long." He paused, as if realizing that criticism was unlikely to curry favor. His voice softened. "At least give me the Harmsworth Jewel for safekeeping."

She frowned. "Nobody outside my closest associates knows I have it."

"The criminal classes have sources honest folk cannot imagine."

"They haven't found it yet. The jewel's safe." The only way anyone could steal it was to knock her over the head and toss her skirts into the air. Thieves could search the vicarage until they were blue in the face.

"Are you certain? Where is it?"

Curse Mr. Evans and his aspersions. Curse Lord Neville for acting the cad. A week ago, a couple of days ago, she'd have confided in him. Now she found herself lying. "There's a secret niche in my study. The only time the jewel leaves its hiding place is when I'm working on it."

"You can work at Youngton Hall."

Her voice hardened. "I'd rather stay with my father and aunt." And Mr. Evans, although she didn't say that.

She didn't need to. Lord Neville read her thought. His eyes flared with temper and his tone turned frigid. "As you wish. Until you consent to be my wife, I have no authority over you."

Only with difficulty did she stop herself from retorting that she'd never grant him that particular honor. "I must let the kitchen know you won't be at dinner."

She saw Lord Neville consider changing his mind, but she stepped back and offered her hand before he spoke. She

welcomed a night without Lord Neville's smothering presence. It was odd—she suspected Mr. Evans's motives, yet
if she had to be locked in a small room with either man, she
wouldn't choose Lord Neville. Which said little for the intellect upon which she prided herself.

"Good evening, my lord."

He took her hand in his fleshy palm. For one blind
moment, she became suffocatingly aware of his size and
power. For years, he'd been a distant figure, one of her
father's associates. Since his proposal, he'd developed an
unpleasant physical reality that set her nerves jangling.

"I can still assert my authority."

It was as close as he'd come to blackmail. She stiffened and tried unsuccessfully to pull free. "I won't bend to
threats," she said coldly.

"We'll see." He bowed and for the first time, kissed the
back of her hand. "Good evening, Genevieve."

He turned to go. The urge to wipe her hand against her
skirts was overwhelming. If ever she'd considered marrying
Lord Neville, her reaction to his touch promised a lifetime of
misery if she did.

Chapter Fourteen

Despite the robberies, the intrigue surrounding the Harmsworth Jewel, and the looming scandal over her authorship, Genevieve refused to alter her routine. That would assign the forces massing against her too much power. On the morning after the break-in, she set out on parish duties. The villagers were accustomed to the vicar's daughter catering to their daily needs while Dr. Barrett remained in scholarly isolation.

It took her nearly an hour to realize that she had a shadow. As usual, Sirius gave the game away. She emerged from discussing church flowers at Miss Brown's cottage to a greeting from the dog.

"Hello, Sirius." She stepped into the street and patted him. She wasn't sure what she thought about the nefarious Mr. Evans, but she couldn't argue that he had a very nice dog. She grabbed Sirius's collar. Taking him home wouldn't disrupt her morning. "You shouldn't be wandering the village."

Sirius focused upon her, as if questioning her decision to haul him away. The cause for his bewilderment was soon clear. Glancing over his head, she saw a tall, lean man sauntering toward her.

Dear Lord, could she never escape Mr. Evans? She knew how the local foxes felt in hunting season. Irritation pricked her skin as she unwillingly noted the swing in his stride and the glinting eyes below his stylish beaver hat. He was dressed for Mayfair, not Little Derrick.

Releasing Sirius, she straightened without smiling. "Aren't you engaged with my father? Something about Edward IV?"

His lips twitched. "There are so many blasted Edwards. Almost as bad as the Henrys. How is a fellow to keep track of these deuced dead chaps?"

His appearance of intellectual laziness didn't gull her. "What are you doing here?" she asked in an uncompromising tone.

She'd never encountered him in the village before. Usually she could count on some peace when he worked with her father each morning. Apparently not this particular morning, curse him. Her grip tightened on the basket of provisions for the parish poor.

He shrugged. "I wanted some fresh air."

"Of course you did," she responded sarcastically, marching toward the next parishioner on her list, Mrs. Meacham with her arthritis and poor eyesight.

He fell into step beside her. "Let me take that."

She considered objecting, then decided that if he wanted to lug the heavy basket, it was the least he could do in return for hounding her. "Here."

Another twitch of those lips. To think yesterday she'd extolled his sense of humor. He had no right to mock her. At least she wasn't a thief. "Shouldn't you be hobnobbing with the duke instead of slumming it in Little Derrick?"

He cast her a thoughtful glance. "You know, Miss Barrett,

this is a public road and I'm perfectly free to use it without your permission."

"Except you're following me."

He laughed softly. "A chance meeting."

"And I'm a Dutchman." Now she'd reached Mrs. Meacham's house, she extended her hand for the basket. "I'll see you at the vicarage."

He looked up at the half-timbered façade. "Ah, dear Mrs. Meacham. I believe she received a letter from her son in the navy yesterday. She'll need someone to read it for her."

Genevieve gaped in astonishment. She had no idea that he'd infiltrated the village. Just what was he up to now? "How do you know that?"

"My crystal ball?"

"Don't be absurd. And please go away."

He still looked cheerful. Of course he was cheerful. She'd long ago realized that needling her was his favorite pastime. When he wasn't climbing through ladies' windows. "I promised I'd visit this morning."

She glared at him, ignoring the way that Miss Smith simpered at handsome Mr. Evans from across the road. Charlotte Smith was welcome to him. Lying weasel he was. "When did you meet Mrs. Meacham? She never leaves her house."

He shrugged again. "The vicar and I called the other day." He paused. "She didn't seem to mind."

"I'm sure she didn't." Arthritis hadn't affected Mrs. Meacham's appreciation for a fine-looking man.

The affectionate understanding in Mr. Evans's smile was almost as irritating as his teasing. She had a horrible feeling that he saw beyond her frosty exterior to the confused girl within. The girl who had relished kissing him. The girl who wondered if she could lure him into kissing her again.

The girl she didn't want to acknowledge, even in the quiet

reaches of the night when she lay awake, restless and long-ing for sin.

She made a low sound of displeasure and just managed not to stamp her foot. Nobody but Mr. Evans set her temper flaring like this. "Oh, you might as well come in."

He swept his hat from his head and knocked. "Thank you."

She regarded him with irritation. "As if I could keep you out."

This time he gave her a full smile and she blinked at the brilliance. She was always conscious of his exceptional looks. His spectacular appearance somehow seemed part of his deceit. But now and again, his masculine beauty struck with the force of lightning through a stormy sky.

"Of course you can't keep me out," he said in a low voice. "Haven't you realized that yet, Genevieve?"

Before she could object to his use of her Christian name, before she could muster any response at all to his discom-fiting question, the door opened and Mrs. Meacham's maid ushered them inside the neat cottage. Sirius trotted after his master, at home here as he was in the vicarage.

"Ah, Miss Barrett, Mr. Evans, how kind of you both to call." Mrs. Meacham struggled to stand, but Richard moved quickly to take her hand. She settled back into her chair with a concealed wince. "And Sirius. We saved you a nice bone from last night's joint."

"No wonder he's your friend for life," Richard said with a smile. He liked this widowed lady. He liked her courage and her dignity and the warmth with which she'd received him. He didn't like the speculative glance she cast Genevieve, but he'd known that when he escorted the vicar's daughter, he would set the village agog.

Under Genevieve's wary gaze, Richard read the precious letter from Charles Meacham. "All is well on the high seas.

Would you like a quick game of piquet before I accompany Miss Barrett to her next appointment?"

"You gamble?" Genevieve asked with disapproval.

"Like fiends," Mrs. Meacham said.

"I'll soon have to pawn my shirt," Richard added.

Mrs. Meacham giggled. "After my last triumph, you owe me half an hour of reading."

"Indeed. Miss Barrett, can you wait?"

Genevieve wanted to say no, he saw, but reluctantly she nodded. Mrs. Meacham was a favorite with her too and she often stayed for a chat. An abrupt departure would only stir the widow's interest.

Richard moved toward a side table piled with books. "I believe we were up to chapter fifteen of *Ivanhoe*. Gad, that fellow's insipid."

"Too insipid after Charles's adventures in the West Indies," Mrs. Meacham said. "I've got something better. My niece sent the London papers."

Another quality he admired in Mrs. Meacham was that despite her arthritis, fading eyesight and genteel poverty, she maintained a lively interest in the wider world. "We'll both enjoy those."

Which turned out to be not quite the case, damn it. The papers were a couple of months old and focused on high society. At that time, Richard Harmsworth had been prowling the marriage market, assessing the current crop of debutantes for a potential wife. A wife of perfect pedigree to polish the tarnish off the Harmsworth name.

The Harmsworth name that frequently appeared in print, even if inadequately disguised as 'H__msw__th.' It seemed his doings were familiar enough to Mrs. Meacham that she discussed him as if he were a naughty nephew.

His fear that something in the papers might expose his

identity faded. Luckily, the publications' sketch artists weren't nearly as accurate as their reporters. Several pictures purported to be him. But not even his best friends would recognize him as the dandified pretty boy depicted. Although at least they'd got his clothing right. Bitterly he recognized that what he wore carried considerably more importance than the man he was. He'd carefully cultivated his image, but the realization was nonetheless discomfiting.

"Poor Sir Richard," Mrs. Meacham sighed after a particularly lengthy and annoyingly accurate list of the ladies he'd danced with at Cam's sister's ball. One of the servants that night must have taken bribes—and detailed notes. "Will he ever live down the scandal?"

"Lord Neville mentioned something about his birth," Genevieve said.

Bugger him dead. Despite Great Aunt Amelia's hints to her, Richard had hoped that Genevieve would remain unaware of his illegitimacy. But even in Little Derrick, his name was tarred.

Eagerly Mrs. Meacham leaned forward. "He's a bastard, dear. Nobody knows who his father is."

Richard's skin itched with the familiar mixture of humiliation and anger. Worse this time because Genevieve heard the grubby story and in a place where he'd been welcomed at face value.

Genevieve frowned as if she pieced together clues. "But it sounds as if he's accepted everywhere."

Mrs. Meacham's expression remained avid and he caught a hint of the pretty girl she'd once been. "He's rich and handsome, and the previous baronet acknowledged him as the heir, even if everyone knew he was a by-blow. The gossip is that he's seeking a wife to restore the family prestige." She looked across at Richard, who battled the desire to fling the bloody scandal sheets into the fire. "Mr. Evans, you've moved in society. Have you met Sir Richard? According to the papers, he's a great friend of Sedgemoor's."

Hell, what could he say? Genevieve's fixed attention as she awaited his answer hinted at hostility. Perhaps because Richard Harmsworth wanted her treasure. If she only knew that Richard Harmsworth wanted considerably more than that from her.

"No, we haven't encountered one another." That wasn't completely a lie, although it sounded like one. He tossed away the paper with unconcealed contempt. "From what I hear, he's a paltry fellow."

Still Genevieve stared at him. He hoped she couldn't see past his careless response to the roiling rage inside. She had no reason to think him anyone other than Christopher Evans, but still he squirmed under her searching regard.

"He always sounds so dashing to me," Mrs. Meacham said. "Such a model of fashion and manners."

Genevieve looked unimpressed. "He sounds like a frivolous wastrel."

Richard couldn't restrain a wince, true as her assessment was. She frowned at him in puzzlement, even as Mrs. Meacham launched into a highly colored description of his past escapades and flirtations. All of which only served to paint him as more profligate.

"A man needs to do more with his life than tie a neck cloth to perfection," Genevieve said repressively.

How Richard longed to defend his real self, but his gut clenched in shame. When he'd set out to become the perfect society gentleman, he'd risen above the foul mire of his parentage. But this particular Phoenix had abandoned his self-respect in the ashes.

Chapter Fifteen

Genevieve was astounded to see the welcome that Mr. Evans received from Mrs. Meacham replayed throughout Little Derrick. She'd always assumed he spent his days with her father or riding the flashy gray thoroughbred that, along with his chestnuts, looked so out of place in their humble stables.

She marched up the village's single street, past the few shops and the tavern. Behind her trailed Sirius and behind him, whistling and looking hideously pleased with himself, Mr. Evans strolled. He swung her now empty basket as though he hadn't a care in the world. Which wasn't quite true. Those reports of Richard Harmsworth's caperings had upset him. A tightening over his cheekbones. A hint of chill in the blue eyes. His reaction intrigued her, given her suspicions that he played the libertine baronet's cat's paw.

Which stirred other doubts. It worried her to see a man she mistrusted making friends in the village, although how could she blame the local ladies for succumbing to Mr. Evans's charm? Even Genevieve found him charming, when she forgot that he was a mendacious snake. She desperately wanted to maintain her anger, if only because it stopped her longing for his kisses. Or at least it should.

She paused at St. Catherine's. Miss Brown had given her some embroidered hassocks to replace the church's worn furnishings. "I'll only be a few minutes," she said to the man behind her. "Please go ahead."

She didn't linger for a reply, but went inside, inhaling the incense-laden coolness. She glanced up at the stained glass window depicting St. Catherine with her palm frond and wheel. From red and gold glory reminiscent of the Harmsworth Jewel, the saint regarded her with disapproval.

"I can't help it. He annoys me," Genevieve muttered. Even in the church, she felt hedged in, confined, unable to evade Mr. Evans. Worse, she couldn't stifle the constant awareness that prickled at her skin and made her blood rush. "Everybody will talk about us."

Until today, despite Lord Neville's insinuations, she doubted if even the most avid gossips had suspected Mr. Evans of designs on the vicar's bluestocking daughter. Now any matrons with matchmaking instincts would be alert for an announcement.

"Can you use your influence to send him away?"

Before I do something I regret. Before I forget that he's a liar. Before I let him steal my heart as well as whatever else he's set his sharp eyes on purloining. Before he marks my soul so deeply that I never forget him.

The saint's face remained cold, untouched by murky mortal concerns. That was once how Genevieve had felt. Before Mr. Evans had disrupted her world. She longed to return to the time when she'd known exactly who she was and what she wanted. Now she was torn between her old desire for independence and the yen to explore the sensual pleasure Mr. Evans offered, whatever disaster that promised.

Tugging her bonnet off, she slid into a back pew and surveyed the empty church. Loving the past as she did, this dim stone space always calmed her. Since the eleventh century, the people of Little Derrick had come here for comfort and counsel and to mark important occasions. Yet today she found neither comfort nor counsel, and Mr. Evans's larcenous arrival was an occasion she could never mark publicly.

Finding no route through confusion, she sighed and stood. In a matter of minutes, she replaced the old hassocks with the beautiful new ones. Miss Brown was an artist with a needle and her work put Genevieve's sorry efforts to shame. She wondered if she had the hubris to present the bilious peony cushion to the church. Ostensibly that was her intention, but surely she'd gain more points in heaven if she burned it and scattered the ashes on the vegetable garden.

She took far too long tugging a few wilting flowers from last Sunday's arrangement. She knew she was hiding. But since Mr. Evans's arrival, she'd lost so many of her sanctuaries. Her study. The pond. Whenever she set foot in Little Derrick after today, she'd see the humor in his eyes and hear his warm baritone.

It wasn't fair. Before he'd appeared, she'd been content. She already knew that when he went—as he inevitably would; men of fashion didn't linger in rural backwaters—he'd leave her fatally unsettled. He made her wish for things she'd never had. He made her resent her narrow life in this isolated village. He made her aware of her body in an extremely improper manner for a woman standing in a church.

Blindly she stared at the carved stone altar, telling herself she could resist him. After she published her article and, if all went to plan, the world lost interest in owning the Harmsworth Jewel, everything would return to normal. She just needed to keep her head and outlast Mr. Evans. He was a patient man—and a kind one, she'd reluctantly noted when he visited her lonely old ladies—but surely he'd tire of this dull village before too long.

She shivered. It was cold in the church, and much as she might like to, she couldn't skulk in here all day. She wanted to work for a couple of hours. She'd almost finished the article. One last visit to Dr. Partridge at the Ashmolean Museum tomorrow and she was ready to draw the threads together.

The prospect of escaping the vicarage and the village and, above all, the back bedroom's troublesome tenant, beckoned like a green shore to a drifting ship. Perhaps from a distance, she'd view things differently.

A day away from Mr. Evans. She could hardly wait.

Smiling at St. Catherine, she tied on her shabby straw bonnet. The saint had been generous after all. With a lighter step than she'd managed since the night Mr. Evans had surprised her at the pond, she walked from the church and through the churchyard. To bolster optimism, the clouds broke up and sun lit the grassy area.

She approached the lych-gate with a swing of her skirts, assuring herself that her torments wouldn't last forever. Life would return to its gentle, even pace and she'd forget whatever madness had possessed her when she'd kissed a rake in the moonlight.

After the brightness outside, the gloom under the lych-gate left her momentarily blind. But sadly not deaf.

"I wondered if you'd sneaked out the back, you took so long."

Happiness instantly dissolved and the hunted feeling returned. She blinked to accustom her eyes to the dimness and saw Mr. Evans lounging full-length on the wooden bench that ran along the wall of the small stone building. Sirius sat in the corner near his master, still as a statue on a medieval tomb. Mr. Evans cradled her empty basket on his lap.

"You waited," she said flatly, stepping back although she knew she couldn't avoid him. Thank goodness, the church was at the village's quieter end and the only people likely to pass sought either the vicarage or private worship.

He'd tipped his hat forward as if napping. "Of course."

"I wish you hadn't."

Slowly he raised one hand and brushed his hat back. His eyes were steady and his voice was serious. "I see I must express my purpose blatantly, Miss Barrett. I'd assumed a smart woman like you could guess my intentions."

Humiliatingly, her heart accelerated like a bolting horse. All at the mention of 'intentions,' when she knew any intentions he harbored were of the worst.

"You're out to nettle me. Any fool can see that." She hoped he didn't hear the quiver in her voice.

That familiar half smile appeared. "Well, of course." He paused. "And I'm keeping you safe."

Shock turned her motionless as a pillar of salt. Briefly he didn't appear the louche, decorative creature she fought so hard to resist. Instead he looked like a man she could rely on, more fool her. "What?"

He sat up and placed his feet flat upon the ground, bending forward to dangle linked hands between his powerful thighs. "You've had two break-ins at the vicarage. Each time, they targeted your study, nowhere else. Someone's after the jewel. Someone ruthless and determined."

Yes, you are.

She fought the urge to challenge him with her knowledge

that at least one of those break-ins was his. But she was still curious about his purpose. Once she accused him, he'd be on guard. He might even scarper, leaving her at Lord Neville's mercy.

"Will you let me keep it for you?"

She retreated toward the far wall. Was his protection just another ruse to get the jewel? "No."

"Then will you tell me where it is?"

"No."

He looked regretful, as well he might. "I'm sorry you mistrust me."

This cut too close to the bone. She released an unladylike snort. "I can imagine."

Mr. Evans looked as grave as she'd ever seen him. "Please heed my warnings. For men like Fairbrother, possession is everything. The jewel would be his dirty little secret and he'd derive as much—no, more—pleasure from his illicit treasure than from announcing it to the world."

She desperately wanted to argue. Unfortunately over the last days, her longstanding wariness of Lord Neville had cemented into fear and dislike.

"He's not getting it." Her voice hardened. "The jewel is mine. You know why it's important to me."

Mr. Evans straightened against the wall, staring at her. "I'm still happy to buy it. Or if you sold it to Sir Richard, I'm sure he'd let you keep it until you finished your research. Given the family connection, he'd appreciate having the jewel's history confirmed."

She almost laughed. Mr. Evans was so clever and cunning and underhanded. And so utterly wrong about the jewel. She almost told him the truth about the artifact, just to put him in his place. Then she recalled what a coup her article promised, the kind of coup that launched a brilliant career, and she stifled the impulse. "I'm sure."

He frowned at her ironic tone, but couldn't, for once, read her thoughts. "Despite that balderdash you heard this morning, he can be a reasonable man. Sedgemoor knows him."

"The jewel isn't for sale." She couldn't, in conscience, take money for it.

"Then my company is yours until the threat passes."

"You tempt me to sell the jewel," she said drily.

He didn't smile. "Genevieve, I think the danger is genuine."

If he was behind the second break-in—and surely that was the most logical assumption—she didn't. Her suspicion that Mr. Evans worked for Sir Richard solidified with every day. But for all his plotting to frighten her into relinquishing the jewel to his employer, she knew Mr. Evans wouldn't hurt her.

She swallowed to moisten a dry throat. "Nobody is likely to leap on me in the middle of the village."

"Perhaps not. But you're not always in the middle of the village, are you?"

Her cheeks turned so hot, she thought they'd burst into flame. The reference to her midnight revels spiked her voice with resentment. "I haven't been back to the pond."

The smile that lit his face set her heart skipping, however much of a rogue he was. "I wish you would."

"I thought you feared for my safety when I'm alone."

Eyelids lowered over brilliant eyes. His smile developed a wicked edge. An edge that shifted her pulses from headlong charge to wayward tarantella. "Who says you'd be alone?"

His silky tone seeped through her skin. It was as if he put his arms around her the way he had beside the pond. Inconvenient heat swirled in her belly. "Stop flirting," she said in a hard voice, while her innards melted to warm syrup.

His smile deepened and with it, her liquid response. "I

can't help it. I tell myself I'll be strong, then you frown at me as if unsure whether to kick me or kiss me, and I'm snared again. You should take pity."

Her lips firmed against the impulse to smile. "I pity any woman who listens to your nonsense."

He collapsed against the stone wall behind him and closed his eyes with theatrical agony. "You never think I'm sincere."

She edged toward the street, partly because the impulse to jump on him and beg him to kiss her was so overwhelming. "You never are."

"Sometimes I am." He rose, sending the basket tumbling to the ground. In the enclosed space, she was unbearably aware of his height. His voice lowered and despite her accusation of insincerity, something in her opened to that persuasive baritone. "Genevieve, I mean it—take care. I'd hate anything to happen to you."

She told herself that his seduction was a means to an end. Obtaining the jewel. And if he got to tumble her too, well, that was a bonus. Her mind recognized the truth. Her body wanted to press against his tall frame like a hot iron flattened linen to the kitchen table.

She turned to go, but faster than a striking adder, he caught her hand.

Struggling to bolster fading resistance, she tried to escape. "Don't call me Genevieve."

"I can't address a woman I've kissed as Miss Barrett. It's against the laws of nature."

She summoned a scowl. "I prefer the laws of society, sir."

He laughed softly. "No, you don't, you little hypocrite. You're perfectly happy to bend the rules when it suits you."

She glanced around frantically, hardly listening. "Please. If anyone sees us, my reputation will be in shreds. I know you think I'm past the age of scandal, but this is a small village and people will say that something's going on between us."

"Something *is* going on between us, or do you intend to deny that too?"

"Blast you, Mr. Evans, let me go."

"Christopher."

She ceased wriggling and stared at him aghast. "I can't call you Christopher."

He still smiled. "Of course you can. Three syllables. Nice English name. 'Chris-to-pher.' Say it after me."

Her brief charity with the bumptious Mr. Evans evaporated. How she wished she'd shot him when she had the chance. "I don't want to call you Christopher. I don't want to call you anything but someone who has left the neighborhood."

He winced dramatically. "Cruel."

She lowered her voice and injected all her outrage into her tone. "If you don't let me go, I'll sneak into your room when you're asleep and smother you with a pillow."

Sensuality weighted his expression. He looked like he wanted to kiss her. What on earth would she do if he did? "If you come into my room, we'll do something much jollier than murder."

"Right now, murdering you offers enjoyment beyond my wildest dreams."

His laugh held a hint of admiration. "Ghoulish wench."

It was all too much. "Stop it," she said in a shaking voice. "For pity's sake, just stop."

To her astonishment, he released her. "I'm not acting the gentleman."

"You don't say." She rubbed her wrist. He hadn't hurt her, but the delicate skin tingled with his touch. She was getting heartily tired of arrogant males manhandling her.

Mr. Evans tilted his hat, becoming the man of the world instead of the impetuous suitor. "I'll escort you to the vicarage."

"You really mean to dog my footsteps?" she asked sourly. "You'll drive us both mad."

He extended his arm and his smile held secrets she resisted exploring. "I'm a big boy. I can bear it."

"I'm not sure I can." Reluctantly she accepted his arm. Surely it was her imagination that with the contact, warmth radiated through her.

"Soon you won't even notice I'm around."

How she wished that was true. But while she scorned his lack of principle, she remained aware of his every breath. It was like some horrible fairy-tale curse. And the only person likely to kiss her awake was this flirtatious rapscallion with questionable motives.

Heaven help her.

Chapter Sixteen

Early the next morning, Richard waited in his carriage. The sunlight lent scant warmth and he appreciated his greatcoat. Although the coat provided merciful little protection from Genevieve's icy stare when she stepped into the stable yard.

"Mr. Evans—"

"Good morning, Miss Barrett. We'll have a fine trip to Oxford."

In salute, he touched the handle of his whip to his hat. Truly, she was a sight to behold. She'd made an effort with her appearance and the dark green velvet pelisse and bonnet with its green ribbons were fiendishly becoming. Her ensemble might be a few seasons out of date, but he couldn't imagine anyone criticizing the way it clung to her impressive curves, nor how the rich color turned her creamy skin to living satin. Especially with annoyance tingeing her cheeks with pink.

"*I'll* have a fine trip to Oxford," she said sharply. "I asked Williams to have the gig ready."

"Williams and I had a word last night."

Her lips tightened. Richard found her temper arousing. Although, he had to admit, he couldn't think of much about Genevieve that didn't make him as hot as a geyser. Even when she and her father pursued some hopelessly abstruse argument about medieval history, Richard couldn't help imagining how she'd feel under him.

"You had no right to countermand my orders."

Richard set the brake, although his horses were too well trained to bolt. He leaped down and extended his gloved hand. "I'll take you to Oxford."

As expected, that raised her hackles. She turned toward the barn. "Williams will harness the gig."

"Then I'll follow. Won't that feel rather silly?"

"In that case, I won't go."

"Suits me," he told her retreating back, trim in its green velvet. "I can guard you more easily here."

She stopped without turning. Her voice vibrated resentment. "You are the most irritating man, Mr. Evans."

"I am indeed, Miss Barrett." He was a lost case. Even calling her Miss Barrett put him in the mood for bed sport. Perhaps because it sounded so prim and decorous, when he'd seen her naked. Still, he didn't want to bicker for the next ten miles. "Are you so set on winning the point that you'd delay your appointment?"

Slowly she turned and her lips curved in a triumphant smile. "It's inappropriate for us to spend the day alone together."

He smiled back. Rare enough that she smiled at him. He wouldn't carp at the reasons behind it. "I've had a care for your reputation."

As though he'd been listening—he probably had, if Richard knew anything about eleven-year-old boys—young George Garson rushed from the stables. He bowed breathlessly to

Genevieve. "Good morning, Miss Barrett." He jumped into the phaeton's fold-down rear compartment. "I'm ready, Mr. Evans."

"Where's Sirius?" Surprise and exasperation warred in her face.

"Tied in the stables and not best pleased. But he can't run all the way to Oxford and George has his seat."

"Will the boy be safe?"

"Of course. I designed it myself, even sat in it once or twice before I risked Sirius."

A tiny line appeared between Genevieve's brows as she surveyed Richard, the natty carriage and George. "Does your mother know you're away all day, George?"

The boy responded with a carefree grin. "Yes, miss. Mr. Evans promised her a crown, and a shilling for me besides."

"Aren't you lucky?"

"Will your pique deprive George of his shilling?" Richard adopted a deliberately pathetic expression.

Her scowl indicated that it failed to convince. "Pique is such a petty description for what I'm feeling," she said sweetly, but she firmed her grip on her satchel and approached the carriage.

"If only you had a gun handy," he murmured, taking her arm to steady her as she climbed into the vehicle.

He was a cad to notice how the movement ruffled her skirts to reveal a nicely turned ankle.

"How do you know I haven't?" She sat and stroked the scuffed leather satchel with menacing intent.

"What about the Harmsworth Jewel?"

Genevieve cast him one of those glances under her lashes that hinted at secrets. "It's safe."

"And so shall you be, my lady." He smiled at her and crossed to his side of the carriage. He settled beside her.

Surely it was fancy that her hip felt warm against his through several layers of clothing.

"Walk on," he said to the horses. He directed the vehicle toward the village.

Genevieve turned in surprise. "This isn't the way to Oxford. We should have gone left after the lane."

The carriage rolled past the grim ruins of Derrick Abbey. The Cistercian foundation had been destroyed during the Reformation and while Genevieve had spent hours exploring the site, she'd never liked it.

"I'm taking the long way," he said calmly.

"Hurrah!" George shouted over and over, waving madly to everyone.

Mr. Evans slowed the carriage and set the horses stepping high. Blast him. It became more and more difficult to dislike him.

On market day, the village was bustling and Genevieve caught smiles from the people who stopped to watch. Perhaps George wouldn't meet the strictest standards as a chaperone, but she caught no hint of censure in the faces they bowled past.

George saved his loudest cheers for his widowed mother and three older sisters, gathered outside their cottage to see the man of the house in his glory. Mr. Evans raised his whip in greeting to the family, who could definitely use the money he paid for George's company today. Genevieve noticed that all three girls blushed at the attention. Of course they did. Mr. Evans was a man who set women's hearts aflutter. Even sensible women like Genevieve Barrett.

Except sitting beside a breathtakingly handsome man as he tooled a stylish vehicle past people she'd known most of her life, she didn't feel like a sensible woman. She felt like a princess. And she realized just how dangerous Mr. Evans could be when he set his mind to something.

The parade lasted mere minutes, even at the leisurely pace Mr. Evans set. Little Derrick was designated 'little' for good reason. Once they reached the outskirts, he turned the carriage toward Oxford and set out at a cracking rate.

Genevieve had never ridden in a high-perch phaeton. She thought she'd be terrified, but Mr. Evans was such a fine whip, the carriage proceeded with impressive smoothness. For the first few minutes, she clutched her seat for fear of overturning. He didn't comment on her nervousness, but he cast her a sardonic glance when she finally ceased gasping at every bump.

"Go on, say it," he said drily without shifting his attention from the road.

"Say what?" Her grip tightened on her satchel.

"That it was nonsensical to give George his moment in the sun."

She lifted her chin and regarded him directly. "What makes you think I disapprove?"

"Your frown." He paused. "And let's face it, you rarely approve of what I do."

"I thought it was rather wonderful and very kind." She risked honesty. "You're an odd man, Mr. Evans. Every time I think I understand you, you confound me."

"There's not much to understand," he muttered.

She'd never seen him blush before. She studied him much as she'd study a historic document. Except Old English or Latin held no mysteries. And this man with his erratic generosity and concealed motives left her flummoxed. "You do yourself an injustice."

Smiling secretly she turned to watch the scenery. She'd resented the way he'd commandeered her expedition. But the moment she'd realized how he'd taken the trouble to please a small boy and his family, her heart had melted. He might be a liar and a flirt, but there was good in him somewhere. She'd wager the Harmsworth Jewel on it.

Genevieve concluded her meeting with Dr. Partridge more quickly than expected and on an encouraging note. After months of negotiations, he agreed to publish her paper under her name, despite her lack of formal qualifications. She had dates to send material for checking and printing. The whole project became concrete in a way that it hadn't when she'd worked in her study.

She swung under the museum's impressive portico with a jaunty step and excitement bubbling in her veins. Life offered possibilities. And justice after years of her father claiming her work. Not even the threats posed by Lord Neville and whoever targeted the vicarage spoiled her mood.

"You're looking remarkably pleased with yourself."

Slowly she turned to see Mr. Evans slouching against one of the Ionian columns. For a few marvelous moments, she'd forgotten Mr. Evans. His comment reminded her that just now, her life wasn't an uncomplicated march to success, but a navigation through dark and complicated influences.

She struggled to cling to the happiness she'd felt when Dr. Partridge had extolled her painstaking scholarship. Soon, Mr. Evans would be gone. Her work was with her always. "Yes. It went well."

He smiled and straightened to wander closer. His clothes were plain, but cut and worn with a dash that stood out, even here in cosmopolitan Oxford. "I'm glad."

She sought but found no hidden meaning in his response. "Thank you."

"Here, let me take that."

"N—"

Too late. He slid her satchel from her arms with a smooth competence that reminded her how he'd disarmed her in her study. Right now, with the sun shining and Mr. Evans regarding her as if she was the prettiest girl in Oxford, she was surprisingly grateful that she hadn't shot him.

He cast her a wry glance. "Relax. I promise I won't run away with the jewel."

The jewel was safe in her petticoat. She contented herself with a request to be careful with the bag.

He gestured with his gold-topped ebony cane. "It's a fine day. Shall we walk?"

She frowned. "We should go home. I've finished my business."

He was still smiling. She wished he wouldn't. That smile played havoc with her common sense. He tucked his stick under his arm and extended an elbow. "Then it's time for pleasure."

She regarded him warily. The word "pleasure" summoned heated memories of kissing him. "I don't trust pleasure."

His smile intensified. "You mean you don't trust me."

"That too." She glanced around. "Where's George?"

"At the stable I use for my carriage. They'll keep an eye on him."

"He loves horses."

Mr. Evans shrugged. "He's a good lad. I'd give him a job on my estate, but if he left Little Derrick, he'd break his mother's heart."

Startled, she stared at him, so astonished she didn't notice when he took her arm and escorted her down the steps to busy Broad Street.

"I'd give him a place with Williams, but we can't take on further staff right now."

"Given Williams has extra duties with my horses, perhaps George could come outside school hours." He paused. "I should have thought of it before."

She appreciated that he didn't point out that if she sold the Harmsworth Jewel, she could cram the vicarage with staff. "You're being kind."

Genevieve had a horrible suspicion that Mr. Evans *was* kind. In a self-effacing, untheatrical way that contrasted with his amiable languor and urbane charm.

After Magdalen College, the crowds thinned. She kept hold of his arm, although it was no longer strictly necessary. She even found, wicked girl she was, stolen excitement when his body brushed hers.

"Genevieve?"

Her name from his lips set up an enjoyable inner ripple. She'd given up insisting that he call her Miss Barrett. She was starting to feel silly addressing him as Mr. Evans.

"Shall we do that?"

From his tone, she guessed that it wasn't the first time he'd asked the question. Curse her blushing. "Do what?"

She sought the familiar mockery, but his expression conveyed fondness. While a somnolent heaviness in his blue eyes acknowledged the anticipation simmering between them.

"If his mother agrees, I'll pay George for a few hours each week under Williams's supervision."

Mrs. Garson would welcome the money and the chance of advancement for George. Genevieve couldn't imagine her saying no. Even if she was inclined to refuse, when Mr. Evans stared at Mrs. Garson the way he currently stared at Genevieve, she'd happily sell her son to the Grand Turk. Yet again Genevieve warned herself to beware this man's wiles. But here on this sunny street with his long stride matched to hers and his deep voice shooting secret thrills through her, her barriers crumbled.

"That's a good idea."

"Capital." He smiled. "That's settled."

It struck her that today produced yet another miracle. She'd managed a perfectly civil discussion with Mr. Evans about a matter of common concern without one whisper of hostility or innuendo.

Ahead the river sparkled. The velvet pelisse, suitable for an early departure, made her skin prickle with heat. She'd kill for a cup of tea. She supposed Mr. Evans meant to walk for miles. He'd packed a breakfast of rolls and cheese which they'd shared on the way—another sign of thoughtfulness; today abounded with them. That makeshift meal seemed a long time ago.

He drew her to a stop beneath a willow. She appreciated the shade and glanced around with interest. She loved Little Derrick, but it was exhilarating to visit this bustling town, packed with tradesmen and shoppers and students.

A man approached, carrying a large closed basket. "Here you are, Mr. Evans. Everything as ordered."

"Thank you, Tait. I'll have the punt back before sunset."

The man stowed the weighty basket in the bow of a long wooden boat that Genevieve only now noticed moored nearby. "You've paid for the whole day. And a mighty fine day it is. I can't think of a better way to pass it than on the river with a pretty lady."

"My thoughts exactly," Mr. Evans said.

"Miss." The man touched his hat and turned to leave, whistling.

"Mr. Evans?" she said faintly. "What are you doing?"

He smiled as he placed her satchel and his cane near the basket. "We're never alone in Little Derrick."

"Which is a good thing." She folded her arms across her bosom and regarded him with disfavor that felt, more than usual, manufactured.

"Do you think so?"

She studied him under the brim of her bonnet. She told herself he manipulated her again, but nothing stifled her quivering awareness. Much as she hated to acknowledge it, the need to be alone with him had tormented her too. Here in Oxford, nobody was likely to report them back to Little Derrick.

"You won't take liberties?"

His lips curved into that cursed appealing smile. "If I get too energetic, the punt will capsize. You're safe."

Excitement and uncertainty warred inside her. If she went with him, would he kiss her? She had a horrible inkling that she'd feel disappointed if he didn't. "On your honor?"

He crossed his heart. "On my honor."

She stared at him, wondering why fate dictated that she, plainspoken, difficult Genevieve Barrett, got to spend an enchanted afternoon with this gorgeous specimen of masculinity. He met her gaze as if guessing her decision.

Of course he guessed. He saw her trepidation, but he also saw her sensual curiosity. Sensual curiosity won.

"Very well, Mr. Evans. You have a passenger."

Chapter Seventeen

Richard refused to acknowledge quite how high his heart leaped when Genevieve agreed. He'd devised this scheme last night while he lay awake struggling against his yen to invade her virginal bed. Sleep had been a stranger since he'd kissed her and the added need for vigilance against intruders didn't help.

He knew Oxford well. He and Cam had been students here. It was simple enough to arrange the boat and picnic basket. Tait had been a well-paid accomplice in Richard's youthful adventures.

"You'll be too warm in your coat."

She unbuttoned the snug green velvet. "It was a gift from Lady Bellfield. I told her it was too extravagant for a mere vicar's daughter, but I love it."

Her uncertainty away from her books aroused a tenderness more unsettling than lust. "You're more than a mere vicar's daughter." He damned the betraying huskiness in his voice. "You're a beautiful, alluring woman."

He waited for some spiky response, but to his surprise, she smiled with shy pleasure. "Thank you."

He slid the coat from her shoulders. Beneath the spectacular pelisse, her dress was a becoming pale gold. She usually wore high necklines, suitable for a clergyman's daughter, but this dress scooped across her lush breasts. It was obviously her best, a fact that touched him too—most women in his circle had so many clothes, they never singled out a "best" dress.

In a London ballroom, her modest décolletage would incite scarcely a murmur. Here alone with her, his reaction to that slope of white skin thundered through him like a thousand cannons firing together.

She watched as he placed the folded coat in the boat. Shrugging out of his own coat, Richard bent to lift the long wooden pole at his feet. He stepped onto the punt's raised stern, automatically finding his balance.

When he helped Genevieve on board, her hand clung to his, the sun gleamed down, and the rest of the world receded. A warning clanged in his mind. His defenses, fortified through years of countering derision with a careless smile and an elegant shrug, fell dangerously low. Stifling his disquiet, he settled her in the prow against the satin cushions he'd had Tait buy new for today. The rich blues and reds reminded him of the Harmsworth Jewel.

His expertise with the punt swiftly returned. Genevieve removed her bonnet, one hand trailed in the water and a faint smile lifted the corners of her lips. Her legs stretched along the boat's narrow base, permitting a glimpse of her fine ankles. Her blissful expression as she closed her eyes and raised her face toward the sun made him yearn as he'd never yearned before, even kissing her.

Perhaps he burned so hot because he'd tasted her passion. The need to kiss her again built like lava inside a volcano. He stared at the river, his gaze focused over her head. If he kept watching her, God help him, he'd jump on her. And devil take the risk of the boat overturning.

"I've never been in a punt before." She broke the increasingly taut silence. She studied the way her fingers made lines in the water. "It's very pleasant."

Despite his overheated state, he smiled. "You're welcome."

She glanced at him from the corner of her eyes. It was astonishingly seductive. He stifled a groan. "I wasn't thanking you."

"A pretty girl like you should have been on the river hundreds of times."

She wiped her hand on her skirt. Briefly the material clung to the subtle curve of her belly and arousal stabbed him anew. Astonishing how even the most innocent movement fired him up. "I'm my father's assistant. I have no time for dalliance, Mr. Evans."

Hearing himself addressed as "Mr. Evans" rapidly palled. She'd call him Christopher before the day ended if it killed him. He crushed a longing to hear her call him Richard. Christopher Evans might wangle a chance at Miss Barrett's charms. The hellish reality was that all of Richard Harmsworth's lies exiled his true self from her favor forever.

"Your father mentioned young men who stayed as I have, to study. Surely one or two of those invited you on the river." He ached to banish the wistful note in her smile.

Her voice was low, as if she confessed something shameful. "I rather terrified those young men."

He only just stopped himself from commending that as a good thing. She needed a lover to match her, not some pimply stripling. "If they weren't at least half in love with you, they weren't fit to be called men."

Her lips pursed to dismiss a compliment that she clearly considered extravagant. "Papa didn't encourage his students to flirt."

Hmm. More likely the old fox wanted his daughter concentrating on the scholarship that ensured his fame.

Richard easily located the loop in the Cherwell where as an undergraduate he'd brought many an eager girl. In the dozen or so years since, the willows over the water had thickened, lending the secluded nook greater privacy.

Which suited him perfectly.

He dug the pole into the riverbed and angled the boat through the graceful fronds. Sun penetrated in long golden beams and lit Genevieve as if she were onstage. He was always aware of her beauty—good God, he was in such a lather of desire, he was aware of everything about her—but in the soft light, she was breathtaking.

She sat up and glanced around with the wariness he'd hoped to extinguish with the leisurely boat ride. "Mr. Evans, this place reeks of rakish intentions."

He didn't blunt the wicked edge to his smile. "You're such a clever girl. It's dashed refreshing."

She flattened her lips. "You said you wouldn't take liberties."

He shrugged. "I meant I wouldn't ask for more than a kiss or two."

"Christopher's Dictionary?"

"Precisely."

Instead of putting him in his place, she lounged against the cushions and regarded him with an unreadable expression. "I hope you'll feed me first. I'd hate to swoon at a critical moment."

A vibrating silence crashed down.

Her lips curved in a smug smile that he'd never seen before. "Cat got your tongue, Mr. Evans?"

He cleared his throat and struggled to speak. Where on earth was smooth-talking Richard Harmsworth? This

Christopher Evans was a deuced clumsy fellow. "If you swoon, it won't be from lack of sustenance."

A teasing light lit her silvery eyes. "I hope you live up to your promises."

Heaven help him, he hoped he did too. Right now, kissing Genevieve seemed the most important task he'd ever undertake.

"Lunch?" she asked hopefully when it became clear that he was out of witty responses.

He straightened and laughed, feeling like the world's luckiest man.

Mr. Evans's confusion was delicious. With a heady mixture of excitement and nerves, Genevieve waited for him to take up her invitation. All day awareness had vibrated between them. Since she'd ceased open hostilities, she'd danced to a symphony of unspoken need.

But true to his word, he kneeled to open the basket, revealing a feast. Chicken and salad and crusty bread and creamy cheese and shiny red apples. Even a bottle of champagne. Nobody had ever taken this trouble for her sake.

The basket contained gilded plates and crystal glasses. Mr. Evans picnicked in style. He filled her plate and passed it across with a damask napkin before serving himself. She waited for him to settle beside her in the prow, but he was more subtle than that.

Once he'd poured the champagne, he reclined against the stern. "Your health, Miss Barrett."

"And yours, Mr. Evans." She wrinkled her nose as bubbles burst against her palate. "Oh!"

He smiled. "A day of new experiences."

She glowered. "I've had wine before."

"Not champagne." He tilted her glass. "You'll like it once you get used to it."

Her stomach lurched on a shocked thrill. He wasn't only talking about champagne.

She rather liked the wine. It was dry and cool and left a lovely apple taste on her tongue. She took another sip then set her glass down. Only when she'd cleared her plate did she realize that Mr. Evans stared at her much as she puzzled over some difficult translation.

He sat back, one hand cradling his glass in his lap. In his shirtsleeves and with his hair ruffled by activity, he looked delightfully disheveled. "You aren't shocked."

Oh, heavens. She couldn't pretend to misunderstand. Well, she could, but it would make her seem nauseatingly coy. "That you harbored wicked plans? No."

His lips twitched and familiar desire tugged at her belly. She should be careful with the champagne. It had a deleterious effect on willpower.

Of course it was only the champagne.

She scowled into the glass she held, unaccountably half full. Surely she needed more alcohol than that to feel quite so…heated. She raised her eyes, feeling more daring than ever before in her quiet life. "I liked kissing you."

While his expression remained grave, amusement lurked in his dark blue eyes. "I liked kissing you."

"This seemed like a…safe place to do it again." She paused. "If you want to." She put down the champagne and smoothed her skirts with an uncertain gesture. "Don't misunderstand. I want you to kiss me. I don't want you to—"

One eyebrow arched. "Ruin you?"

Her cheeks were on fire. "I'm not in the habit of negotiating—"

"Pleasure?"

"I can finish my sentences, thank you," she snapped. "Over our acquaintance, I've come to realize that I've missed…experiences. Experiences that you're uniquely placed to provide."

This time she couldn't mistake the unholy laughter in his eyes. "I feel like I'm applying for employment. Should I supply references?"

She didn't smile. "I'll never marry so no husband will begrudge me a few kisses from a handsome scoundrel. And I trust your discretion."

For one aching moment, she wished she could trust more than his ability to keep his mouth shut. He kept his mouth shut now, just when she wanted the devil to speak. She'd blithely imagined she'd agree to kiss him and he'd leap like a frog to a mayfly.

"Mr. Evans, this is how a conversation works. I speak and you respond," she said crossly.

That disconcertingly perceptive gaze focused on her. "I'm thinking."

He refilled both glasses and started on his meal. Genevieve drank a little more champagne, hoping it might stop her stomach twisting into knots. It didn't.

Eventually the suspense became too much. "God forbid I force you into anything distasteful," she sniped.

He smiled faintly. "I can't enter into a carnal arrangement with a woman who calls me Mr. Evans."

"It's not a carnal arrangement. It's a few kisses."

The smile intensified several degrees, as if he contemplated deeds beyond an innocent's imagining. "Kisses can be carnal."

Oh, dear Lord. A thrill shivered through her as she recalled his mouth ravaging hers. "Will you kiss me?"

"Will you call me Christopher?"

"Must I?" A sly smile lifted her lips. "It's such fun watching you steam when I call you Mr. Evans."

She'd been teasing him? Richard slammed down his glass, sloshing wine over the rim. "You little witch!"

Panic flared in Genevieve's wide eyes as he surged forward, caging her between his arms and legs. "Be careful!" she cried as the boat rocked.

"What's my name?" He snatched her champagne, spilling it over her bosom as he shoved the glass carelessly behind him.

"Mr. Evans," she said defiantly, sliding up to sprawl against the cushions like some Oriental fantasy.

"Indeed?" He did what he'd wanted to do since she'd removed her deuced becoming coat. He kissed the slope of her breast. Champagne added exquisite piquancy.

"Mr. Evans!" She flattened one trembling hand on his chest. Through his shirt, her touch seared like a brand.

"For shame, Miss Barrett." He resisted the thundering urge to rip away her bodice. Instead he ran his lips up her neck to the nerve that set her quaking with response. "Permitting such liberties to a man with whom you're not on first-name terms."

"Mr. Evans, you're too demanding," she gasped, arching into him.

He studied her from beneath lowered lids. "Shall I stop?"

"Stop?" She spoke the word as if it made no sense. Her eyes were hazy with sensual confusion.

He bared his teeth. He was too edgy to manage a smile. Which for the unflappable Richard Harmsworth said a great deal. "What's my name?"

He wondered why the hell he was so set on this point. After all, Christopher wasn't his real name. But in the war they waged, his Christian name signaled her surrender.

"You're so stubborn." Need darkened her eyes.

"That's the pot calling the kettle black." He surveyed her impatiently. "You'll let me kiss you, but you address me as if we've just been introduced at bloody Almack's?"

"Don't tell me you mean to take me back to the Magdalene Bridge." She sounded disgusted, as well she might. "What kind of blasted rake are you, Mr. Evans?"

Mr. Evans? Still? "You know my requirements."

She made a low sound like a cat denied a treat and rose on her elbows. "Proceed, Christopher."

Chapter Eighteen

Christopher's expression transformed to wolfish anticipation. Thrilling trepidation quivered through Genevieve as he dragged her into his arms. Then coherent thought fled as his mouth crashed down.

There was none of the seeking gentleness she remembered. This was headlong demand. Shock held her motionless, then a dark wave of arousal overwhelmed her. On a broken moan, she raised her hands and buried them in his thick, soft hair.

The first time they'd kissed, she'd been untouched. Now she parted her lips for his invasion. His tongue stroked hers, stirring restless heat in her belly. She'd never wanted a man before Christopher. She'd had no idea the experience could be so delicious, yet so frustrating. A sensation of falling, then the cushions were slippery behind her back. His long body came down over hers, cloaking her with passion.

His passion... Hard fullness jutted into her stomach. She arched to test that intriguing weight and felt as much as heard him groan against her lips.

Tentatively, then with growing confidence, she ran her hand across his chest while her mouth danced with his, advancing, retreating, teasing, surrendering. It was a rhythm as complex as any music. Sweeter than the sweetest music. Lingeringly she ran her hands down the powerful column of his neck to his broad shoulders. She loved his shoulders. Their power. Their grace. The way they created their own horizon.

Encouraging his intoxicating rapacity, she turned her face up. She curled her fingers around his biceps then slid her hands across his back, feeling the subtle shift of muscle and bone under the thin shirt. Lower she ventured, tracing the line of his spine. Some distant warning made her pause before she reached firm masculine buttocks, however much she ached to discover all of him. He touched her too, no longer lashing her close as if expecting her to run. They both knew she had no intention of going anywhere, except too far along the primrose path.

Her whole body sang. She whimpered as she tore her lips from his and buried her face in his shoulder. He barely exceeded the bounds of propriety and already she felt overcome. His scent dizzied her. That cursed lemon verbena that should smell like betrayal, and instead promised joy. Beneath it the musky scent of a man's hunger, astonishingly familiar after those moments by the pond.

His hands cupped her hips, stroking her through her skirts. Heat welled between her legs. She opened her eyes to dazzling shafts of light piercing the graceful willow fronds. This bend of the river was a private, shining world where concepts like sin and virtue held no sway. There was just pleasure, endless pleasure.

Christopher raised his head and his flaring nostrils drew in her scent. His ferocious expression should terrify her but it only fed her excitement. As his mouth possessed hers, she dreamily imagined she could stay here forever. Nothing in scholarship matched this exhilaration. To think she'd wasted all that time learning Latin and Greek when a doctorate in kissing could increase her happiness so immeasurably.

He balanced over her, eyes vivid against the green, shoulders hedging out the world. "There's more."

Her hands slipped around his neck. Now that she wasn't fighting him, she could admit he had a wonderful face. "Show me."

He kissed her breast, making her tremble. Her nipples were tight and throbbing. She didn't know what she wanted, until he slid her bodice lower and nipped at the beaded tips. She gasped as the feeling, halfway between pain and pleasure, jolted to her belly. "Christopher!"

When he drew one peak between his lips, need spiraled. Distantly she knew that she should stop him. A few kisses fell into a gray area between flirtation and ruin. Brandishing her bare breasts crossed a line.

He kissed her until she writhed, muscles tightening toward an end she couldn't imagine. Still kissing her, he rolled her other nipple in long, sensitive fingers. She'd never felt like this. When he raised his head, she shook as if a strong wind buffeted her. Whereas the only storm assailing her was desire. Her hands fumbled to cover her chest.

Panting, he stared down at her, his arms supporting his weight. "You're so beautiful."

For the first time in her life, she believed it. Nervously she licked her lips and his heavy gaze focused on the movement. He shuddered and pressed forward, making her inescapably aware that he wanted her with a man's hunger.

"Kiss me again," she murmured, wondering who this demanding wench was. It certainly wasn't scholarly Genevieve

Barrett who only got excited about obscure facts in obscure volumes.

He smiled and slid along her body to rest on the cushions beside her. "With pleasure."

She wriggled in the confined space. "It's a tight fit."

Her comment amused him. His dipped eyelids indicated that he contemplated lechery. "It is indeed."

He leaned against the prow and arranged her pliant body across his lap. One powerful arm encircled her back as he lifted her hand from her bosom and kissed it. "Let me see you."

She struggled with her free hand to cover as much skin as she could. Sadly she was so ridiculously over-endowed, a mere palm and five fingers weren't up to the task. She blushed. She hoped by the time she'd finished with this reprobate that he'd cure her of that lamentable habit. "You've seen me."

"Can one get too much of a good thing?"

She sighed with impatience and fumbled her bodice over her breasts. "You can't mean to debate philosophy."

His lips quirked and his fingers moved upon hers in a caress that tingled to her toes. "It might distract me from what I really want to do."

He was hard against her hip. She'd ventured so close to yielding that while his desire daunted, it thrilled too. "We can't."

She prayed he didn't hear her piercing regret. How had he lured her so quickly to the brink? She'd thought to enjoy a few kisses, then take her merry way. Instead longing entangled her, made her want more. Knowing that more was a mistake.

"I know." Tucking her head under his chin, he cupped a possessive hand under one breast. He pressed his lips to her temple with a tenderness that stifled doubt. Almost.

Gradually passion subsided to a gentle flow, in tune with the river and the soft breeze shifting the willow. The erratic dance of the sunlight mirrored the erratic dance of her heart until even that slowed.

She'd never imagined lying quietly with him, breathing as if they shared one life. Always he'd picked and pried at her, making her as jumpy as a flea on a cat. While the warm afternoon drifted, Genevieve forgot time, although she never forgot whose arms encircled her in perfect peace.

Genevieve awoke to lazy pleasure. Behind closed eyes, she was aware of golden light. The day wasn't over. Slowly, not sure that she wanted to return to the real world of responsibility and consequences, she lifted her eyelids. Christopher studied her with heavy-eyed delight as he dipped his hand under her bodice to stroke her breasts. She shifted and realized that his other hand slid beneath her skirt.

Voluptuous enjoyment kept fear just far enough away to ignore. "What do you think you're doing?" she asked drowsily.

He kissed her briefly, then returned to kiss her more thoroughly. "Taking advantage, Miss Barrett."

His hand traced elaborate patterns under her drawers. With each pass, he ventured higher. Her sex ached for a touch where no man had touched her before. The distant alarm became a blaring shriek. Still she had to force herself to stiffen in his arms.

"I'm not Hecuba."

"You purr like she does," he whispered into her ear, his breath disturbing soft tendrils of hair.

"You promised."

He stared at her, his gaze steady. Almost trustworthy. "I give you my word you'll be as pure when I've finished as you are now."

"Take me back to Little Derrick."

Desperation lit his eyes. "Not yet. Please, not yet."

His need sliced at her heart. She felt as though she poised on a cliff. One reckless step and she tumbled down to the rocks below.

She took the step.

"Kiss me before I change my mind," she said, her throat tight with nerves.

His mouth took hers and the world faded to hot darkness. When his hand rose higher, she clung to his shoulders. Then his hand slipped between her thighs. The seeking touch so close to her center made her close her legs.

"You'll like this," he whispered.

"I'm sure I will," she said unsteadily. "But that doesn't make it right."

"I'll stop if you ask."

Despite apprehension and gnawing frustration, she gave a choked laugh. "Once you start, I won't want you to stop."

She sighed and loosened her thighs. Scattering thought, he kissed her again. Then he stroked her through the slit in her drawers.

She tensed with surprise. "Oh."

His thumb brushed a spot that set her trembling. She moaned against his lips as clever fingers circled and caressed. Her skin felt too tight. She shifted against his hand and the change in pressure throbbed through her. Hot moisture welled against his palm and she hid her face in his shirt, his musky, lemony scent intoxicating her.

Dear Lord, what magic his fingers contained. His body curled over her and still those deft fingers teased. She went rigid when he slid one long finger inside her.

She grabbed his wrist. "That feels strange."

Strange. Terrifying. Wonderful.

"Don't fight it, Genevieve," he whispered, curling his finger to coax another shudder of response. "Don't fight *me*."

Saying yes seemed too brazen. Saying no meant he'd curtail this astonishing journey.

She'd never imagined a man would touch her like this. Especially a man who made no promises beyond not hurting her. Beneath her cheek, his heart raced. If he'd remained unaffected, it would be so much easier to remember that she'd always been chaste.

When she didn't speak—coherent words were beyond her—he stroked his finger in and out, setting up a driving rhythm in her blood. His arm tightened around her back, bringing her closer. She lay across his lap, as open as a door flung wide in welcome.

The pressure deepened. Exquisite sparks lit her blood. He invaded her with two fingers. Gently, inexorably, he pressed inside. She trembled at the glorious fullness and tightened her grip on his shirt.

This time when he withdrew, she instinctively lifted her hips to follow. He buried his head in her hair, muttering encouragement. His jagged breathing filled her ears as he fueled her response. He stoked a fire inside her, a fire that flared higher and higher until it raged out of control. She gasped her frustration against his chest.

Suddenly, torment dissolved into brilliant light and her body flowered into pleasure. She cried out in surprise and delight and rose toward that adept, tormenting hand.

Chapter Nineteen

As they drove home, Christopher remained quiet. At first, Genevieve was grateful. His silence gave her a chance to come to terms with what they'd done. But as they wound along the country roads, she began to wonder if her wantonness disgusted him. The pelisse covered her rumpled dress and he'd helped to fix her hair, but she had a painful suspicion that what had happened on the river was written across her in letters a foot high.

Long after she'd succumbed to those unearthly sensations, he'd held her tight against him. He'd kissed her when she'd floated back to earth, but not since, and his smile when at last he'd released her had been strained. With hardly a word, he'd packed up the remains of their meal, then while she settled onto cushions that carried the scent of their bodies, he steered them back to Oxford.

Conflicting emotions had gripped her as she'd watched the willow grove recede. Surprise. Shame, although not as sharp as it should be. Satisfaction.

Her response to his touch had been a revelation. So much

for clever, self-contained Genevieve Barrett. She'd all but fainted in his arms. Even now, as she sat beside him in the elegant carriage, the glow lingered. The frightening truth was that she loved his touch. She wanted him to touch her again. And if he did, she had a horrible inkling that the encounter wouldn't stop at kisses.

They'd collected an exhausted and overexcited George from the stables. The boy now slept behind them, wrapped in a rug that Christopher had produced from beneath the dog seat. Another rug covered her legs. The evening wasn't cold, but it had cooled since the day. Or perhaps she'd been too occupied this afternoon to notice any temperature other than her own. She bent her head under its bonnet and contemplated the rug's plaid pattern.

What was in Christopher's mind? His demeanor offered no clue. He used that inscrutable expression to distance people. Now he turned it on her and she hated the experience. With George so close, she couldn't ask. Instead she stewed over her rashness.

Christopher took a corner at what felt like dangerous speed and she reached under her rug to curl her fingers around the edge of the seat. Ahead lay a straight stretch, empty of traffic. Christopher spoke a word to the horses who settled to a trot. He caught the reins in one hand and tore the leather glove off his other hand with his teeth. Genevieve watched from the corner of her eye and wondered what he intended.

He lowered his bare hand and slid it beneath her rug. She tensed with appalled denial. Surely he couldn't plan more seduction. George might wake any second.

Then she felt the glance of Christopher's little finger against hers. A brush, almost accidental. He touched her again.

Such insignificant contact. Yet she felt it. In a strange way, as strongly as she'd felt those brazen caresses on the river.

Her turmoil eased. She chanced another peek at his face. He concentrated on the road ahead, but a softness about his mouth indicated that he too felt the bond. She stared unseeingly over the horses' pricked ears as warmth seeped up from that chaste, sweet communication.

Everything would be all right. Everything would be all right.

Richard drew up outside Mrs. Garson's cottage as evening edged toward twilight. He leaped to the ground and strode around to lift George into his arms. The boy was sound asleep. He hadn't been much of a chaperone, praise heaven.

Keeping George wrapped against the nip in the air, he carried the boy up the path. Before he reached the door, it banged open and Mrs. Garson rushed out. "Thank heavens you're back, Mr. Evans. And Miss Barrett too. Such goings-on."

"What's happened, Mrs. Garson?" Gently, he handed a stirring George to his mother, even as foreboding settled in his gut. The day had been perfect. Its very perfection tempted fate.

Mrs. Garson broke into a confused tale about strangers breaking into the vicarage. Genevieve climbed down. "Is my father unharmed?"

Mrs. Garson hardly paused. "Tied Vicar up, they did, and locked him in his library. Goodness knows what else."

"Dear Lord..." In a whirl of green skirts, Genevieve hurtled toward the vicarage.

Richard scrambled into the driving seat and whipped the horses to a speed risky in the high street. He clattered around the back of the vicarage and drew the vehicle to a juddering stop. Williams emerged, almost hopping in his urgency.

"Mr. Evans, Mr. Evans, you've heard then."

Richard flung the reins to the groom and jumped down. "What happened?"

"I'd taken Vicar's cob to the blacksmith and Dorcas was doing the marketing. The buggers must have been waiting. Locked the vicar and Mrs. Warren up right and tight and ransacked the house."

Hell. Richard should have made sure the vicarage was safe before he went to Oxford. He'd been too busy worrying about Genevieve to pay proper attention to her family. "Is Dr. Barrett hurt?"

"He's pretty bad shaken up."

Whatever the hell that meant. "Did you see the intruders?"

"No. They were gone before I got home. I headed out to see my sister after dropping the cob. Only got back half an hour ago. Vicar was nigh gaga with fear when I let him out."

Poor Dr. Barrett. Poor Mrs. Warren. They'd been through the mill, by the sound of it. Richard clapped Williams on the shoulder and told him he was a good fellow, then strode through the kitchen.

Each room he passed was in chaos. Pictures. Crockery. Furniture. Hundreds of books. All lay scattered. From the front of the house, he heard raised voices.

As he neared the parlor, the voices sorted themselves into the vicar's whine in response to Genevieve's urgent questions. And Fairbrother's unctuous tones. Richard should have guessed that Fairbrother would hover like a vulture at a massacre.

"So that's agreed?" Fairbrother said from the center of the room as Richard appeared in the doorway. "I'll make arrangements for my man to move in tomorrow."

Richard hardly heeded Fairbrother's blatherings. Instead, he sought Genevieve. Today in the willows, she'd claimed at least part of his soul. Probably all of it.

She kneeled beside her father, her attention on the old man. The vicar hunched in a low chair near the fire, a knitted shawl around his shoulders. He looked small and frail, his shaking hand curled around a posset cup. For the first time, Richard saw him as something other than an absurd creature with a nasty habit of claiming undeserved credit.

Pity jammed Richard's throat. Pity and envy. Despite her father's sins against her, Genevieve loved the old man, just as she loved her aunt. Genevieve belonged to a family, something he'd never had.

"Let me help, Papa." Genevieve steadied the cup. Her sweet concern made Richard's belly cramp with futile remorse. Damn it, he should have prevented this.

"Was anyone hurt?" Richard entered the room.

Mrs. Warren summoned a smile from her usual chair, although she looked haggard and not her rosy-cheeked self. He hated to imagine her terror while ruffians vandalized her home. "Mr. Evans, we've . . . we've had quite the excitement."

He admired her spirit in making light of what must have been a hideous experience. "I heard. Are you unharmed?"

"I've got a few bruises. Ezekiel was in his library so all they needed to do was bundle me in with him and barricade the door. We shouted and shouted, but nobody heard until Williams came back."

Every ounce of chivalry revolted at her maltreatment. "How many were there?"

Genevieve still hadn't looked at him. He hoped she didn't feel guilty because of what they'd been doing while this outrage occurred.

"I saw three. There could have been more."

"Did you recognize them?"

"No, they were masked." Again, Mrs. Warren answered. Genevieve continued to murmur softly to her father.

"What about their voices? Were they local?"

"Apparently they sounded like Londoners," Fairbrother said.

Richard didn't even resent the arrogant lordling answering. To prevent a recurrence, he needed to know everything.

Was the jewel safe? He hardly cared. At that moment, he admitted that he stayed for Genevieve Barrett. The Harmsworth Jewel became almost irrelevant.

His gut knotted. Hell, if Genevieve had been here, she'd have fought back. She could have been seriously hurt.

Except Genevieve hadn't been here.

That struck him as significant. Whoever had planned this knew about comings and goings at the vicarage. Inevitably Richard's suspicions focused once again on Fairbrother. "Did they take anything?"

"With the house in this state, who can tell?" Mrs. Warren said.

"But they didn't touch the library?"

"They did. Oh, they did. My poor books," the vicar quavered. "They tied me to a chair, the savages, and went through everything. Word of my discoveries must have spread. Once I make my findings about the princes public, the cat will be among the pigeons, never you doubt it."

Richard did doubt it. These thieves searched for something of more tangible value than academic glory. Had they found it? Genevieve still hadn't addressed him and something in her tense, pale features stopped him asking.

Mrs. Warren stood, her hands fluttering at her waist as if she was unsure what to do with them. "We can't leave the house like this." She glanced out the window. "Goodness me, what do they want?"

Richard stepped to her side, taking her arm. A crowd of villagers marched up the back lane. He leaned out the window. "Mrs. Garson, the vicar's in no condition for visitors."

"We're not visiting, Mr. Evans," the widow called up. "We hear everything's a right old mess. And that silly girl Dorcas isn't up to much beyond pushing a duster. We'll have the house shipshape and Bristol fashion before you can say boo to a goose."

By God, Richard liked these people. With a few exceptions like Cam or Jonas, he couldn't imagine any of his so-called friends rallying to his assistance if he was in trouble.

"Mr. Evans, you should go home," Fairbrother said coldly behind him. "With the vicarage in disarray and violence brewing, the Barretts need some peace."

"No, no, not Mr. Evans," the vicar wavered, clutching the shawl to his throat despite the fire burning in the grate. "Thieves wouldn't dare threaten me with a strong young man in the house."

Richard waited for a sign of approval from Genevieve, but she turned to stoke the fire. He frowned. What was wrong?

"They attacked today." Impatiently Fairbrother slapped his gloves against his beefy thigh. "Evans wasn't much use."

"He wasn't here," the vicar retorted with unexpected energy. He looked past Genevieve to where Richard leaned against the window. "Please say you'll stay. Surely it's not presumptuous to call upon our friendship."

For one burning moment, Genevieve's glance fell on him. But when he tried to catch her eye, she fussed with refilling the posset cup.

"Of course I'll stay," he said, disregarding Fairbrother's huff of disgust.

Curse his preternatural awareness of Genevieve. Her back was turned, but he saw her shoulders stiffen. Why wouldn't she look at him? It seemed deuced queer when not long ago she'd begged him to touch her. Was it shame? Or had something else upset her?

What a fool he was. Of course she was distraught. Her home had been pillaged. Her quietness wasn't aimed at him.

"Capital," the vicar said, and Richard's conscience twinged at the relief flooding the old man's face. After all, while he'd never intended injury, his purposes were murky.

"I'll let the ladies in." Mrs. Warren looked less bereft now that she had a task.

"No, I will," Richard said. When he reached the door, he turned briefly to find Genevieve at last watching him. Her face was stark with hatred.

Chapter Twenty

"Lord Neville is right. We need to send Mr. Evans away." Genevieve linked her hands at her waist to hide their shaking.

It was the afternoon following the burglary and she stood in the center of the parlor, at last mercifully free of predatory males. Lord Neville pursued his own investigations. Christopher, aftcr shadowing her without encouragement since yesterday, had taken Palamon for a gallop. With just her father and aunt present, Genevieve snatched the opportunity to denounce the man she blamed for their trouble.

"Why on earth should we do that, dear?" Her aunt laid her knitting on her lap. She was still edgy, but calmer since restoring the house to order. "I feel safer with him here."

"No, no, Mr. Evans must stay," her father said urgently. "What flummery is this, Genevieve?"

Her father still started at the slightest sound and he'd taken to locking his library door. Right now he huddled near the blazing hearth, wrapped in the ubiquitous shawl.

Genevieve forced out the accusation she should have

made after Christopher kissed her in the moonlight. Identifying him as a villain shouldn't be so difficult. She knew his every word was a lie, but still her recalcitrant heart grieved at his duplicity.

Self-hatred rose like bile. How could she have kissed the swine without tasting his corruption?

Until now she'd been willing to consider Christopher's suspicions of Lord Neville, but she now recognized the allegations as a clever way to distract her from his vile intentions. The evidence against the man who made her stupid with kisses was overwhelming. He'd broken in once already. And yesterday he'd delayed her in Oxford while his henchmen brutalized a helpless old man and a defenseless woman.

Most mortifying of all, Christopher's hands had touched her body while the burglary took place. Her cheeks stung with shame. She was so gullible. Any fool could see that a sophisticated man like Christopher Evans would never desire an awkward bluestocking like her. There had to be an ulterior motive for his seduction.

"Mr. Evans is behind the break-ins." Her voice was scratchy after too many tears. The deceitful cad wasn't worth one sleepless minute, which hadn't stopped her tormenting herself through the night.

She'd never expected her family to believe her immediately, but it was an unpleasant shock when her aunt laughed. "Don't be silly. He's a gentleman to his bootstraps."

Genevieve stoutly refused to recall moments when he'd been less than gentlemanly. And she'd been less than a lady. He'd betrayed her; he'd flown her to heaven. She still couldn't reconcile those two facts. Her stomach heaved with humiliation and outrage. Outrage above all. How could he touch her like that and all the while plot this cowardly crime?

"He broke in that night you went to Sedgemoor's." Curse her distress. It made her sound like a weepy female when she had to appear strong and sure.

"Nonsense," the vicar said sharply. "That man was masked, wasn't he? And you described a horrible ruffian when Mr. Evans has the prettiest manners. I despair of you, Genevieve, slandering a good man."

"Papa," she said helplessly, even as her heart sank at his stubborn expression. When he looked like that, nothing would shake him. "Trust me about this."

"You took against Mr. Evans from the first. Heaven knows why." His jaw jutted at an ominous angle. "Now, when you know the comfort I derive from his presence, you seek to deprive me of my one security. It's too bad of you, Genevieve. Too bad."

"Mr. Evans was in Oxford with you when it happened," her aunt said. Genevieve found the sweet reason in her tone harder to counter than her father's querulousness.

"Doesn't that strike you as suspicious?" Genevieve couldn't, she just couldn't, confess that she'd recognized Christopher as the intruder after he'd kissed her.

After he'd gone riding, she'd searched his bedroom for incriminating evidence. But the scoundrel kept few possessions with him and she found nothing to prove him a villain. Instead, she'd spent far too long breathing lemon verbena, an inevitable reminder of what he'd done to her. Should she need such a reminder, curse her.

Her aunt looked unconvinced. "If he was with you, how could he rob the vicarage?"

"He hired thugs. Whoever arranged this knew that the household lay unprotected."

Her aunt resumed knitting, clearly dismissing Genevieve's suspicions. "That could be anyone passing through

Little Derrick. Why would you think Mr. Evans has wicked intentions?"

His intentions were wicked in all sorts of ways Genevieve didn't want to recall. She flushed. "I remember his voice from that night."

Her aunt regarded her as if she was mad. "After all this time?"

"Our troubles started when he arrived," Genevieve said, even as she recognized that nothing would persuade either Aunt Lucy or her father that Christopher Evans meant them harm. She'd reviled his fatal charm before, but never with such virulence.

"Coincidence." In other circumstances, she'd welcome the vicar's spark of authority. Since yesterday, he'd been so cowed, it had wrung her heart, no matter his sins against her. "I won't hear a word against him."

"Papa—"

"I agree with your father, Genevieve." Aunt Lucy's voice softened. "We're all upset and jumping at shadows. But that doesn't mean you should leap to conclusions about innocent bystanders."

Christopher was an innocent bystander the way she was a society belle. "You're wrong," she said flatly.

The disapproval in her father's expression could still make her squirm. "I'd appreciate it if you kept these wild surmises to yourself, girl. If you bother Mr. Evans with this twaddle, he may take offense and leave."

Which would be a fine thing in Genevieve's opinion. She choked back a bitter sigh. It hurt that her family refused to listen to her. It hurt almost as much as discovering that Christopher had connived to keep her away from the vicarage yesterday.

"Genevieve?" her father said sternly when she didn't

reply. "I want your word that you'll never mention this silliness again."

Frustration welled, prompting her to tell them exactly why she knew Christopher Evans was false. But her courage failed. Even after she exposed her shame, they'd probably still take his side.

She straightened and stared back at her father, wishing she felt angry rather than devastated. "I promise not to accuse Mr. Evans."

Her father nodded, his brief vigor fading. "Very well. We'll speak no more of this."

No, they wouldn't. From now on, she'd watch for incontrovertible evidence of Christopher's crimes and pray that nobody got hurt in the meantime. The vicarage's defense fell to her.

God help her.

"So she hates my guts." Arms braced against the marble mantel, Richard stared into the roaring library fire.

It was almost a relief to be at Leighton Court, away from the vicarage's simmering tensions. At least tonight he was sure that Genevieve and her family were safe. Thanks to Cam, half a dozen armed footmen watched the place.

He was worried sick about Genevieve. Lord Neville wasn't finished, he just knew it. After orchestrating two unsuccessful burglaries to find the jewel, threatening her would be the logical next step. The problem was convincing her that she was in danger. The second problem. The first was getting her to listen to him instead of treating him like Satan incarnate.

"Does it matter that much?" Jonas Merrick, Viscount Hillbrook, slouched in his chair, contemplating his brandy.

Jonas had reluctantly abandoned his beloved wife Sidonie and baby daughter to dine with Cam and Richard.

"Damn it, yes, it does," Richard snapped, irritated at his friend's bored tone.

He wondered if he could explain how he felt without revealing how he felt *really*. All his life, he'd struggled to hide his vulnerabilities beneath a careless façade. Although he had a grim perception that his friends knew him well enough to guess that more occurred here than a flirtation gone to the dogs.

As if to protest that description, Sirius opened one eye from where he snoozed on the hearth rug. Richard bent to fondle the dog's ears. "I know I've made a deuced mess of it, old fellow. No need to scowl at me as though I'm a bottle short of a dozen."

"I've never known you unable to charm your way into a woman's good graces—and more." Cam, ever the perfect host, rose to refill his friends' glasses.

Three armchairs ranged before the flames. Jonas sat on the left, his scarred face masklike. Cam subsided into the center chair, watching Richard with an annoyingly knowing expression.

Enduring friendship and the loosening effects of liquor meant that Richard could no longer pretend an impersonal interest in Genevieve's safety. Especially as he'd dearly love to enlist Jonas's help.

"For you, one woman is much the same as the next," Jonas said easily. "If this one resists, however lowering to your vanity, you'll find another quickly enough."

Cam understood him better than anyone, even Jonas. "I believe in this case, Richard has discovered that no other woman will do."

Good God, he was blushing. What the hell was wrong with him? "Putting it too strongly, chum."

Cam's eyebrows rose eloquently although he merely said, "No doubt."

Richard's fist clenched against the marble. "I'm sure she blames me for this last break-in." Either that or she felt devilish guilty about what they'd done at Oxford. "When she must know that I'd never place her family at risk."

Cam's brows remained elevated. "Must she?"

"Hell, yes." Richard prowled across to stare out the window. The night was stormy, the wind rattling the sash windows, not at all like the idyll when he'd kissed Genevieve by the pond.

Jonas, who had heard a condensed version of Richard's adventures in Little Derrick, spoke. "Perhaps she's guessed that you're an imposter."

Richard shook his head. "If she had, she'd have me tossed out on my arse."

"Maybe she merely discourages your interest," Cam said from his chair. "She was a virtuous woman."

"She *is* a virtuous woman," Richard said shortly, wheeling restlessly to survey his friends.

"Good. I never approved of you ruining a girl who has to hold her head high in a small village."

Richard felt his cheeks heat, like a naughty schoolboy brought before the headmaster. Cam always did the right thing. The fellow was no monk, but he confined himself to women who suffered no harm from his attentions, and like everything the duke did, he pursued his sexual interests in moderation.

Richard would lay money Cam had never been as hungry for a woman as he was for Genevieve. Lucky sod.

"So where is the jewel?" Jonas asked. Until his legitimacy had been confirmed, he'd lived outside high society, amassing a fortune that wouldn't disgrace an emperor.

He still thought like a man of business instead of a louche aristocrat.

Richard shrugged. "She wouldn't tell me. Damn it, she won't give me the time of day. I'm guessing from the lack of panic that it's still stashed somewhere. If I were wagering on Genevieve outwitting a band of sneak thieves, Genevieve would win hands down. Her brainbox puts even yours to shame, Jonas."

His childhood friend laughed softly. "I never thought the day would come when I'd hear you praising a female's intelligence."

Richard sighed. His friends' mockery grew tiresome. They acted as if he'd bedded anything in skirts, whereas he'd always had high standards of beauty if not wits in his amours.

Cam stood and strolled forward. "Don't you think it's time you gave this up?"

"Gave what up?" His friends should know to take that dangerous tone seriously.

Of course Cam didn't quail. "This whole misbegotten scheme. You set your heart on the jewel in a fit of temper. What difference will possessing it make? It can't undo your bastardy."

Richard's hands curled at his sides. From any other man, that remark would invite a punch in the nose. "It confirms the succession."

Cam's expression conveyed his scorn. "Nothing can change Sir Lester Harmsworth's sixteen months in St. Petersburg before your arrival."

"Take care," Richard murmured.

Cam sighed. "You're wasting your time here. And getting in much deeper than you should, both to your detriment and to the detriment of Little Derrick's residents."

Richard flung away, knowing he behaved like a boor but unable to stop himself. Where, oh where was the sophisticate who had adorned a thousand London ballrooms? He'd felt likely to split into pieces ever since Genevieve had turned her back on him.

How right he'd been to fear her power. Although his wariness had done bugger all to stop him tumbling head over heels in love. What would his friends say if he declared that mawkish sentiment? They'd laugh themselves into next Sunday.

"Do forgive me," he said with heavy sarcasm. "I'd so hate my racketing to smear your sterling reputation, Your Grace."

Cam didn't fly into a rage. He never did. Devil take him, Richard occasionally wished that something would ruffle that perfect façade, unearth some passion beneath the decorum. Instead Cam's face tightened with sympathy. Hell, he didn't want his friends feeling sorry for him.

"You know that's not my primary concern." Cam paused. "Although, yes, the longer this continues, the more likelihood of disaster and scandal. For you. For Dr. Barrett. For Miss Barrett. For me. After all, I introduced you to the neighborhood."

"I want the jewel," Richard said through tight lips.

From under lowered lids, Jonas observed his friends. "You're doing precious little to get it."

"I'd say he's doing nothing at all," Cam affirmed.

Richard shifted uncomfortably. He'd never taken advantage of the secrets he'd unearthed at the vicarage. Cam had a point, to Hades with him.

"I'm waiting for the optimum moment." He paused. "Right now, I can't do a blasted thing because bloody Fairbrother has posted a watchdog."

His festering resentment since that perfect day in Oxford

had only been exacerbated by the arrival of the bruiser Hector Greengrass. Fairbrother had infiltrated Greengrass into the vicarage ostensibly to protect the inmates. More likely to spy on Genevieve and Christopher Evans. But the decision had been made before Richard could lodge an objection. Greengrass slept above the stables and devoted his days to dogging Richard's footsteps.

Aside from the man's presence stymieing all attempts to get Genevieve alone, Greengrass struck Richard as a criminal type. It was like setting the cat to defend the mouse hole.

"Keep an eye on Fairbrother, Richard." Jonas's expression was serious. "Cam asked me to make inquiries. I hear disturbing rumors about sharp practices and stolen goods."

Now, that was interesting. "Enough to set the law on him?"

Jonas shrugged. "Nothing substantiated, but my sources indicate that he's a man with expensive tastes and an eye to acquisitions fit to empty a maharajah's treasury."

Richard frowned. "There. I can't leave Miss Barrett at the swine's mercy."

"You've got a barrel of excuses for staying, old chum," Cam said.

"If you wanted the jewel, you'd have it by now," Jonas said ruthlessly.

"I want it."

"Not enough," Jonas retorted.

Cam sighed. "Stop glaring at me like an angry bear and come back to the fire. You need another drink."

Richard didn't comply with his friend's half-humorous invitation. The reference to his bastardy had cut. It underlined how much he liked being legitimately born Christopher Evans.

"What can you achieve?" Jonas's unreadable black eyes

sent a cold chill through people who didn't know him or who had reason to fear him. Even Richard, who considered him a man of unshakable honor, suppressed a shiver as that obsidian regard settled upon him. "Surely you don't plan to devote your life to playing a rustic Romeo?"

Richard stiffened and stared down his friend. He spoke the thought that had crept into his mind so many nights when he'd lain awake longing for Genevieve down the hall, impossibly far away. "I could stay here. Why not?"

Cam groaned with disbelief. "Why not? A million reasons why not. You've taken leave of your sanity."

Stubbornly Richard turned to the duke. "What million reasons? Name them. Name one."

Again Cam sighed. "Let's start with the fact that you're not Christopher Evans, landowner from Shropshire. You're Sir Richard Harmsworth and sure to be exposed as such. Sooner rather than later. You've been lucky so far that nobody has recognized you." He made another irritated sound. "You have a real life outside this backwater. You have friends and family and responsibilities to your estates. What is your mother to think if you disappear off the face of the earth?"

The mention of his mother conjured a black mist behind Richard's eyes. Cam, it seemed, liked living dangerously. He might yet get that fist in the mouth. "My mother has her own life."

Cam didn't back down. "Which doesn't mean she'll accept you vanishing like the morning dew. You could end up the subject of a criminal inquiry."

"Tosh. Nobody—especially Augusta Harmsworth—cares if I leave London."

"When I was at White's last week, your absence was a hot topic. You surely can't expect to disappear from the civilized world without people wondering where the hell you've gone—and why. There are even bets in the book about your whereabouts."

"Anything I can make money on?" Jonas asked with a flash of the dark amusement so essential to his nature. "After all, I've got inside information on the elusive baronet."

Irritated, Cam turned to him. "Dear God, I don't know. There are a hundred theories as to where this dunderhead is skulking. He's joined the army. He's run off with an opera dancer. He's decamped for the Continent because he murdered his tailor."

"Sykes died?" Richard asked in shock. He was genuinely fond of his tailor, which was more than he could say for the frivolous clodpolls wagering on his location.

"Not as far as I know. But the general consensus is that only a sartorial mishap is likely to rouse Richard Harmsworth to murder."

"Ha ha," Richard said flatly. "And to think I looked forward to a pleasant evening with my oldest friends."

Cam's voice lowered to urgency. "Richard, this masquerade can't continue forever."

Defiance surged. "I like Little Derrick. They're good people, better people than I've met hanging around society, pretending that nobody sneered at me. No one here gives a rat's arse about the fall of my cravat or the cut of my coat. Damn it, they like Christopher Evans. *I like Christopher Evans.* I never had much truck with Richard Harmsworth. He was a dashed scurvy fellow."

Cam's expression softened, but his tone remained uncompromising. "That's as may be. But you can't spend your life hiding under an alias in deepest Oxfordshire. You know you can't."

"No, I don't know," Richard said stubbornly. "Does this mean you intend to expose me as an imposter?"

"Of course I won't." Cam sighed again and turned to Jonas. "Can you talk some sense into him?"

Jonas shrugged, then surprisingly smiled with a spark of devilry. "You know, I'd pay good money to set eyes on Genevieve Barrett. She must be one exceptional woman."

Chapter Twenty-One

From the chaise longue, Genevieve surveyed her glittering surroundings. The Duke of Sedgemoor had invited his neighbors to dine and the guests gathered to begin the evening. So far, all she'd had to do was smile, but still she felt out of her depth.

His Grace's drawing room at Leighton Court probably couldn't compare to the accommodations in his larger houses. But to a girl from a humble vicarage, the gilt and white room with its ormolu mirrors was breathtaking. No wonder her father had returned from his first visit babbling with excitement.

She sipped her champagne, wryly amused that the expensive wine almost seemed part of everyday life. Whatever else she thought of Christopher, he'd broadened her horizons. Recalling the afternoon when he'd ignited those horizons into a thousand blazing suns, she shifted on her chair.

She hated him. Or at least she tried very hard to hate him. But nothing banished her heated recollections of that day on the river. She loathed the way that, despite knowing he was a liar and a thief, her body didn't despise him at all. Her body wanted him to do it all again.

Do more.

She sought distraction by contemplating Sedgemoor's guests. From her place before the open French doors—summer made one last, brief return—she could see everyone.

They were a disparate bunch. Sedgemoor was immaculately dressed in black and white and she required no special intuition to recognize a man of uncommon power. She'd expected that. What she hadn't expected was how handsome he was, in a chilly, too immaculate way. Which was probably unfair. He'd greeted her with apparent pleasure,

He spoke with polite interest to Lord Neville and her father. More accurately, the duke listened to the vicar's views upon the princes. If Sedgemoor was lucky, he might escape the intricacies of York and Lancaster before pudding.

Her gaze settled next upon Christopher. He lounged against the wall opposite, a sulky expression on his handsome face. Since returning from Oxford, she'd rebuffed his every approach. She couldn't bear more deceit. Worse, she couldn't trust herself to resist him.

Earlier he'd walked over to see the duke and Lord and Lady Hillbrook, who she gathered were old friends. He too was in black, stark tailoring only emphasizing his manifold attractions. He wore his fine clothing with an elegance that put even Sedgemoor in the shade.

Apart from the duke, the only people she didn't know were the Hillbrooks. Even in Little Derrick, she'd heard about Jonas Merrick. The papers had covered his arrest for murdering his cousin, then the miraculous change in his fortunes when he'd been declared both legitimate and a viscount. Appalling scars marked his saturnine features. Just looking at them made Genevieve wince with compassion.

The bond of affection he shared with his wife Sidonie was palpable, even to a stranger.

The Hadley-Childe sisters, two spinsters from a manor in the next village, completed the party. Both looked overawed in such grand company.

"Everyone tells me how clever you are." Lady Hillbrook sat beside Genevieve. "I was rather daunted to meet you."

Genevieve smiled at the lovely dark-haired woman. "That can't be true."

"Believe me, it is." Compared to Lady Hillbrook's stylishness, Genevieve felt a dowd in her cream satin at least four seasons old. Even fresh from the village seamstress, it hadn't been the first stare. "When Jonas returned to Barstowe Hall yesterday and told me about Little Derrick's female prodigy, I was intrigued. Intimidated but intrigued."

"I'm not that frightening," Genevieve responded with a laugh.

The viscountess tipped her chin toward where Christopher chatted with Genevieve's aunt. "That gentleman appears ill at ease in your company."

Genevieve made herself look at Christopher again, although it hurt less to pretend he wasn't there. As if sensing her attention, he turned his head until his dark blue eyes stared into hers. Ridiculous, but she felt as though he crossed the room and hauled her into his arms and kissed her. Heat flooded her.

She scowled at him and he glanced away, but not before she caught a flash of what looked like pain. As if she could make that false wretch experience any real compunction.

"Mr. Evans?" She prayed that her airy tone sounded more convincing to Lady Hillbrook than to her.

The woman's gaze was unaccountably intent. "Is that his name? I missed it in the introductions."

Genevieve frowned. "I thought you knew him."

The viscountess appeared discomfited, before she lifted her glass to hide her expression. "Why would you think that?"

"He mentioned that old friends were staying at Leighton Court. I must be mistaken." Although Christopher's familiarity with Lord Hillbrook indicated long acquaintance.

"My husband has many business contacts."

That must be the explanation. If Christopher and his lordship were friends at all. Bother the man. He made her suspicious of everyone. "For some inexplicable reason, he's boarding with my father to brush up on medieval history."

The lady looked startled. "I thought you were an enthusiast."

Genevieve smiled wryly. "I am. But I've never fathomed why such a man should eschew the social whirl for scholarship."

It was perfectly clear, seeing Christopher in this aristocratic setting, that he was at home in the highest echelons. Genevieve struggled not to remember how at ease he'd been with Mrs. Garson and George and everyone in the village. She'd always known that he and Sedgemoor were friends. Which still struck her as odd. If Christopher was a sneak thief, how had he inveigled his way into the circle surrounding England's most powerful nobleman? If he pursued some scheme against Sedgemoor, he took massive risks. Sedgemoor would make a dangerous enemy.

"Perhaps there's more to him than you credit."

"I doubt it." She flushed, realizing she betrayed herself to a stranger. "Have you been to this part of the country before?"

Lady Hillbrook shook her head, gracefully accepting the abrupt change of subject. "No. But Jonas and His Grace are such friends, we simply had to call when we were nearby in

Wiltshire. I hope my daughter Consuela settles and we can see something of the area."

Thank goodness, the mention of Consuela saved Genevieve from further discussion of Christopher. But as she listened to a devoted mother's anecdotes, the back of her neck prickled. Sharply she turned to catch Christopher out. And found Lord Neville glowering at her.

Despite the warm night and the fact that she was as safe in the duke's drawing room as in the Tower of London, she shivered. She turned back to Lady Hillbrook, while unease soured the champagne on her lips.

To Genevieve's disgust, Christopher was placed beside her at dinner, with Lord Hillbrook on her right. At the foot of the gleaming mahogany table, Lady Hillbrook played hostess.

Genevieve awaited some expression of triumph at his successful maneuvering, but Christopher's expression was truculent as he slid into his chair. She didn't trust it. She didn't trust *him*.

"Now you'll have to talk to me," he murmured, swirling the hock in his glass.

"I could concentrate on my food," she hissed back. "It can't be nearly as tasteless as you are."

Christopher's lips compressed. His voice reverted to the lazy drawl that she hated. "Rest easy, dear lady. Sedgemoor supplies an excellent table. Why, even the humble pie is delicious."

"Very funny," she said flatly.

"I'm accounted a deuced witty fellow. You'll be in stitches before the night's out."

"I'm sure."

"Or you could stop treating me like I carry some contagious disease and tell me what bee's got into your bonnet."

His tone lowered. She cursed the way the soft baritone brushed like velvet over her skin. "What is it, Genevieve? What made you go from purring to snarling within an instant?"

She was a coward to avoid challenging him with her suspicions, but she couldn't trust her unruly emotions. The prospect of screaming like a fishwife, or, even worse, bawling like a motherless calf because he'd let her down twisted her stomach with nausea.

Furious at how susceptible she still was, she didn't have to manufacture a chilly response. "Don't pretend ignorance."

He sighed and it was a sign of his disturbance that he made no attempt to mask his irritation with charm. "Isn't that like a woman? You expect a man to be a mind reader, then condemn the fellow to perpetual exile when his simple masculine brain can't track his way through the labyrinth of your thinking."

She stared at him balefully. "Try very hard, Mr. Evans."

He winced at the way she bit out the formal address.

Lord Hillbrook turned to her. Humiliation burned her cheeks. Christopher seemed to have forgotten that they weren't alone.

"I've looked forward to meeting you, Miss Barrett."

"Thank you," she responded to the social nicety, then realized that his black eyes studied her with a concentration belying his bland comment. Now she was more accustomed to his scars, she saw past them to features vivid with intelligence and sensuality.

"I'd heard you were remarkable."

Surprise made her speak more frankly than she should. "That's very flattering, but I can't imagine how. His Grace only met me tonight."

A smile tugged at Lord Hillbrook's mouth. Did she

imagine his gaze flickered past her to Christopher? From the corner of her eye, she saw her Nemesis staring into his wine as if it contained hemlock. And as if he had a mind to drink it.

She bit her lip and told herself she didn't care. She turned back to Lord Hillbrook, although she was so upset, she could barely focus.

"General report. We were all agog to see you. Now that we have, can I say we're not disappointed?"

This was an exceedingly odd conversation with a stranger. Before she could answer, Christopher spoke from behind her left shoulder. "Stow it, Jonas. Miss Barrett won't play your damned games."

Lord Hillbrook's heavy black eyebrows arched at the rudeness. "Are you in a position to speak for the lady?"

Genevieve shot Christopher a fulminating glance. "No, he's not." She muffled her voice to a whisper, although Lord Hillbrook was too close to miss what she said. "What on earth is wrong with you? You're behaving like a lunatic."

"Driven mad by a pair of silver eyes," Christopher muttered, taking a reckless gulp of wine before signaling to a footman for a refill. Genevieve frowned, wondering how much he'd had to drink.

"Then go mad quietly," she snapped and deliberately turned her back. She began what became an absorbing discussion about Lord Hillbrook's extensive collection of antiquities.

The dinner party was conducted upon informal lines, with conversation passing up and down the table and across it. The Hadley-Childe ladies remained on best behavior, but it soon became clear that Sedgemoor, Hillbrook, and Christopher knew each other too well to stand on ceremony, and that Lady Hillbrook was perfectly capable of holding her own.

Genevieve had dreaded the evening. She'd worried about dealing with Christopher, and that the duke would be insufferably patronizing. But while Sedgemoor's remarks were more circumspect than those of his friends, his dry wit supplied a fascinating counterpoint. To her surprise when Lady Hillbrook rose, signaling for the ladies to withdraw, Genevieve was sorry to leave the men to their port. And thanks largely to Lord Hillbrook, she hadn't boxed Christopher's ears.

She'd always imagined people of fashion would be shallow and self-centered, but brilliance spiced the wit. There was nothing contemptible in the Hillbrooks or the Duke of Sedgemoor. In this company, even her father appeared to advantage. Only Lord Neville remained outside the charmed circle, his swarthy features set in disdain. The thought might be ungenerous, but Genevieve interpreted his displeasure as pique. Here he wasn't everyone's social superior as he was at the vicarage.

Even Christopher had abandoned his megrims and played an essential role in the lightning interactions. His ease in this great company didn't mollify her anger. Instead, it spurred curiosity. Why did a man who bandied quips with dukes lurk in her shabby back bedroom?

Worse, he made her feel like a country mouse. At the vicarage, surrounded by books, she could pretend that they were equals. Here, she couldn't help thinking that his pursuit conveyed a hint of King Cophetua and the beggar maid. That wasn't a pleasant sensation. Christopher had been right about the excellent dinner, but the idea of playing peasant to his prince curdled the *poulet à la perse* in her stomach.

Who was Christopher Evans? There was more to the relationship between these three men than she gleaned from observation. Once the duke had vouched for Christopher, nobody but Genevieve had questioned his background. Did

Sedgemoor covet the Harmsworth Jewel too? It began to seem like the whole world schemed to steal it. She wondered if she should reveal the shocking truth about the heirloom, whether it preempted her academic coup or not.

"I must speak to you," Christopher said urgently as she stood.

"No, you mustn't," she said, back where she'd been when the meal started, quarreling with Christopher Evans.

"Please, Genevieve." He reached for her hand, then curtailed the movement.

"I have nothing to say, Mr. Evans," she said icily. "In fact, the most agreeable thing you could do is to leave in the morning."

He went white and for one reverberant moment, he didn't look like the careless, handsome man she knew, but like someone capable of genuine feeling. "You don't mean that."

She glared. "I do."

If he left, she'd no longer feel confused and restless and unhappy. She'd return to the woman she'd been, busy, productive, purposeful. Not this desperate, yearning creature he'd created. Since that day in Oxford crammed with joy and betrayal, she could hardly bear to live with herself.

She watched him struggle to form some argument before a surreptitious glance around the table confirmed that their fraught discussion attracted general interest. She made a fool of herself. It was the last straw. She stalked from the room, back straight, head high and heart aching with misery.

After lingering behind the departing guests to finish a brandy he didn't want, Richard trudged toward the entrance hall. It was well past midnight. The evening had been such a success that it ended considerably later than the usual country entertainment. Everyone except Genevieve, Fairbrother, and Lucy Warren congregated near the door.

"Rich...Christopher, we wondered where you'd got to." Thank goodness Cam had caught himself before he let the cat out of the bag.

Before he could answer, Mrs. Warren emerged from the dining room. "My fan wasn't there. I hope Lord Neville won't mind waiting while I check the drawing room again."

"You can come in the gig," the vicar said. "Genevieve and Lord Neville have gone."

His words struck Richard like a blow from a shovel. Cold talons of dread scored his gut. From the first, he'd mistrusted Fairbrother. He'd seen how the toad looked at Genevieve. Now her bloody father delivered her into the devil's clutches.

"Ezekiel, that's hardly proper," Mrs. Warren protested.

"It's only down the driveway and his lordship's an old family friend. You'd just be in the way, Lucy." Clearly the vicar hadn't yet relinquished hope of a match between his daughter and his patron.

Damn, damn, damn. This sounded worse each minute. "How long ago?"

"What's the matter, Richard?" Sidonie forgot to call him Christopher.

He hardly noticed. He already strode toward the open doors past the wide-eyed Hadley-Childe sisters. "I've got to stop them."

The vicar frowned. "Young fellow, his lordship has known Genevieve since childhood. There's no impropriety in sending her home in his company."

"How long since they left?" Richard asked again.

Jonas answered. "Only a few minutes."

Richard clapped him briefly on the shoulder as he rushed

past. "Thanks. If I cross the park, I'll catch them before they reach the road."

The footman with custody of his pistols advanced to present the weapons. Since the last break-in, Richard had taken to traveling armed. Although God forgive him, he'd never imagined an evening at Sedgemoor's promised danger.

"Why on earth do you want to catch them, Mr. Evans?" the vicar asked. "And what are those guns? I cannot like all this fuss. I cannot like it at all."

Mrs. Warren's gaze focused on Richard with dawning concern. "Do you have reason to worry?"

Given that escalating violence had marked each attempt to get the jewel, of course he had reason to worry. He lied to placate her. "I hope not."

But as he dashed across the drive, heels clipping sharply on the gravel, he couldn't forget the fear in Genevieve's eyes after the proposal. Nor could Richard ignore the fact that as he wasn't behind the recent break-ins, that left Fairbrother as the most likely culprit. The man who had expressed an interest in not only the Harmsworth Jewel but the vicar's virginal, beautiful, and perilously unworldly daughter.

Chapter Twenty-Two

Without Aunt Lucy's company, Genevieve would never have agreed to travel home with Lord Neville, however short the journey. Even with Aunt Lucy, she was reluctant, but her father had fretted so volubly when she demurred that eventually she'd conceded to save embarrassment.

Stifling misgivings, she settled opposite his lordship inside the carriage. The footman shut the door and Lord Neville knocked the ceiling with his cane, signaling to Greengrass, who played coachman, to drive on.

Startled Genevieve turned from staring out the window. "What about my aunt?"

"She'll come with your father."

Misgivings transformed into raw fear. "She's just gone inside for her fan."

He raised one hand to display what he held. "This one?"

In the lamps, Lord Neville's smile was smug. Black terror jammed Genevieve's throat. It didn't matter that she'd known Lord Neville all her life. It didn't matter that he had never hurt her. She needed to get out of this carriage. Now.

"Stop," she said breathlessly, snatching for the door handle. "I'd like to return to the vicarage with my father and aunt."

"Too late." He snapped the fragile fan in two and tossed it to the floor.

She started at the sharp crack. "We've hardly gone ten feet."

Not even the most optimistic listener could dismiss the menace in his soft chuckle. The carriage swayed as it gained speed. "Ten feet too far, my love."

"I'm not your love." Her heart beat so fast, she felt dizzy.

Hand trembling, she shoved the door and felt it give. She lurched to her feet, fighting for balance against the rocking vehicle. Jumping was risky, but right now she'd rather take her chances with Sedgemoor's immaculate drive than his lordship.

The door opened a few inches before Lord Neville grabbed the edge and slammed it shut. "No, no, no, Genevieve." He caught her wrist in a brutal grip. "I have plans for tonight, and you breaking your neck in some melodramatic fit isn't on the agenda."

Gasping, she struggled to pull free. "My lord, you're scaring me."

He laughed again. She wished he wouldn't. "You've led me a pretty dance, but you must have known you'd end up marrying me."

Ignoring her resistance, he bundled her back into her seat, then squeezed beside her. His bulk crushed her, bruising her.

"I don't want to marry anyone."

He captured her other hand. "Of course you do."

She strove to sound calm, reasonable. To appeal to whatever goodness lurked in his heart. Although right now, she had a sick feeling that Christopher had been right all along about Lord Neville.

"Stop this nonsense." Injecting iron into her demand was difficult when her heart fluttered against her ribs like a frantic bird. "You've had your little joke."

"There's no joke, my dear. Tonight I'll have your maidenhead. Tomorrow we'll post the banns."

Choking horror made speaking painful. "Do what you like, I won't marry you."

"A ruined vicar's daughter in a small village faces a bleak future. Especially when the man in question is eager to redeem her sin with marriage."

"Marriage to you means a bleak future."

Of course he didn't listen. He never listened. "You were born for me."

Her false composure crumbled under an avalanche of terror. She tried to kick him, but her legs twisted to the side and she couldn't gain any purchase. "No, I wasn't."

She lunged for the door, but he caught her and hauled her across his knees. When she tried to strike him, he wrapped his arms around her, trapping her against his barrel-like chest. She'd never felt so physically overwhelmed. His musky odor suffocated her. She opened her mouth and screamed.

"None of that," Lord Neville said negligently and slapped her face.

Agony exploded through her head. "How dare you?"

"And how dare you?" Past the ringing in her ears, she heard him inhale. "How dare you cavort with that bastard Evans? How dare you flutter your eyelashes and push up your bosom and whisper with him in corners?"

His seething anger made her belly cramp with dread. "I didn't."

He grabbed her shoulders and shook her so hard that her head whacked the wall. "Has he had you?"

"Let me go." Her fists battered his chest, but it was like trying to dislodge a mountain. She raked her nails down his cheek.

"Bloody hell! You cat!" He seized her flailing hands and used his weight to force her into the corner, driving the air from her lungs. Fighting blackness, she screamed until he crashed his mouth into hers.

He was hot and immovable as a stone wall. His mouth was wet and he tasted unpleasantly of stale food. His tongue felt like a slug. Wanting to vomit, she struggled, but the sloppy lips kept sucking.

Through fury and revulsion, she felt the wheels' rhythm change. The carriage left the driveway and bumped over grass. Grim despair clawed at her. At least on the drive, there was hope of rescue.

Panting with lust and excitement, he raised his head. "If you're no virgin, the marriage is off. Damaged goods have no place in my collection."

"I'm devastated to hear that," she snarled.

His hold on her wrists tightened, twisting the fragile bones together. He hauled her forward until she lay across the seat. His body squashed her legs and pelvis into immobility.

"You know," he said almost idly. "I'll enjoy teaching you obedience."

When his swollen rod prodded her stomach, she yowled with disgust and jerked helplessly. Her fear attained such a pitch that she abandoned all pride. "Please don't do this. For the love of God, have pity."

His silent laugh vibrated against her. "Capital. Already you're learning."

Inexorably he flattened her onto the seat and kneeled over her, a figure from a nightmare. She kicked uselessly and screamed again, although nobody would hear except this spawn of Satan.

"I hate you," she spat, wrenching her head aside when Lord Neville slobbered over her neck.

As the carriage juddered to a stop, he pawed at her skirts. Loathing Lord Neville as she'd never loathed anyone, she bit her lip and prayed. Although surely even God couldn't save her now.

Breathless, Richard broke from the trees and dashed across the driveway to pound on the gatehouse door. "Open up, for God's sake! It's an emergency!"

The gatekeeper's grizzled head appeared from an upstairs window. "Has there been an accident?"

"Did Lord Neville Fairbrother's carriage pass?"

The man, thank heaven, didn't waste time asking questions. "Nobody's gone yet."

"Thank you!" Richard shouted as he sprinted back up the drive.

He almost missed the break in the shrubbery where the carriage had turned off. And that distant, muffled sound could be a bird's cry. Except that he was so attuned to Genevieve that he immediately recognized the scream as hers.

That fucking, sodding, hell-ridden mongrel Fairbrother. Richard crashed through the rhododendrons.

"Get down or I'll blow your skull to dust," Richard snarled to Greengrass. When the thug didn't immediately abandon the driver's box, Richard raised his pistols until the metal barrels glinted in the carriage lamps. "If you imagine I'll show the slightest hesitation, you underestimate quite how much your spying has irritated me."

"Hold your fire, damn you." Greengrass scrambled to the ground.

"Stand over there and don't move."

Richard waited until the man lumbered clear of the coach. The silence was ominous. Why the hell wasn't Genevieve shrieking her head off? Keeping an eye on Greengrass, Richard stepped up to the vehicle and flung open the door.

It banged against the carriage's body like a cannon shot. Inside, lamps illuminated a scene that Richard would never forget, no matter how long he lived. His blood froze to icy sludge and his belly lurched in sick rage.

Fairbrother's massive form forced Genevieve into the bench. All Richard could see of her was the pale tumble of skirts to the floor and the cascade of golden hair against dark leather.

Fairbrother jerked sideways. "What the fuck are you doing, Greengrass?"

Unbelievably, the cur had been too busy subduing his victim to notice Richard's arrival. Richard's anger flared to white heat when he saw one beefy hand plastered across Genevieve's mouth. Above Fairbrother's paw, her eyes were wide and shining with tears.

"Get off her." He didn't recognize the voice as his.

"Evans?" Fairbrother sounded shocked rather than afraid.

"Move before I put a bullet in your stinking hide." Richard bit off each word.

"This is unconscionable!" Fairbrother staggered upright to block the doorway. The fact that his trousers were still fastened did nothing to calm Richard's rage.

Fairbrother's bulk prevented Richard getting a good look at Genevieve. Why hadn't she spoken? What had this pig done to her?

"Genevieve, are you all right?"

Fairbrother puffed up. "Refrain from addressing my intended bride."

"That's a damned lie." Richard gestured with one gun. "Step down or take the consequences."

Fairbrother's lips curled in a gloating smile. "I'm unarmed."

"I don't give a rat's arse."

Richard was almost sorry when Fairbrother descended to shuffle toward Greengrass.

He heard a rustle from inside the carriage. Then Genevieve stood swaying on the step. Anguish speared Richard's gut. She looked as though every hope had been stripped away. Her glorious hair flowed about her shoulders. Shaking hands clutched her torn bodice. Abrasions marked her shoulders and neck. When her stricken gaze sought Richard, he almost forgot the danger and swept her into his arms. She hunched against his stare. He was appalled to read shame in her beautiful face.

Richard made himself smile, although his soul bayed for Fairbrother's liver. It took every ounce of will to sound reassuring. "Let me take you home, Miss Barrett."

Slowly she straightened and raised her chin. Richard's heart swelled with love as he watched her gather tattered courage. Staggering slightly and catching at the doorframe, she stepped from the carriage.

Richard wound his arm around her waist. She trembled as reaction set in. Much as Richard burned to make Fairbrother suffer, he needed to get her away. In this light, he couldn't see how badly she was hurt. Any injury at all made him feel like he'd swallowed a volcano.

He turned to Fairbrother. "If you touch her again, I'll kill you. Nothing, not pity, not the law of the land, will save you. And if you or your henchman utters one word about what happened tonight, I'll hunt you down and end your miserable lives. Do you understand?"

Fairbrother regarded Richard with virulent hatred. "Roast in hell, you bastard. Nobody makes a fool of Neville Fairbrother, let alone some trumped-up cit who thinks the gold in his pocket compensates for breeding."

All his life, people had called Richard bastard and mongrel. He waited for the familiar anger. Instead he found he couldn't care what this evil, selfish old man thought of him. All that mattered was to get Genevieve to safety and place himself at her service.

"Can you walk?" he asked softly, backing her into the shadows and keeping his guns trained on Greengrass and Fairbrother.

"Yes," she whispered, although he felt her unsteadiness as she moved.

His hold firmed. "Let's get out of here."

Chapter Twenty-Three

O nce they were well clear of the carriage and Gene-vieve had stopped mistaking every noise for pursuit, she wriggled free. She dearly needed to bolster her pride, although Christopher's embrace offered the only sanity in a world gone mad. "Where are we going?"

He stepped back, granting her distance as he pocketed his pistol. "To Leighton Court. Your father and aunt are there."

Terror had lodged behind her tonsils. "I want to go home."

She waited for an argument, but didn't get one. "Very well. But you can't be alone."

Still that annoying lump wouldn't vacate her throat. "Dorcas is there."

"Dorcas can't look after you."

"I don't need looking after." Even as her soul cried out for him to wrap his arms around her forever.

The compassion in Christopher's face brought her closer to crying than Lord Neville's assault had. He touched the hands she twined together at her waist. Her belly, only just settling, lurched in reaction. His hand, there against her solar plexus, felt breathtakingly intimate.

"Just tell me if you're hurt," he said quietly. "You don't have to say anything else."

She closed her eyes, reliving those hideous moments before the door opened and the man she believed was a scoundrel transformed into a hero. "You don't want to know what happened?"

His fingers curled around hers. He'd touched her so often, but this was different. Calm. Reassuring. Comforting. No trace of seduction. "I want what you want."

That wasn't true. That wasn't true about any man. When one came down to it, they were all selfish monsters. They hid their agenda under ineffectuality like her father or, like Lord Neville, they blatantly expected the world to bow down in worship. She opened her eyes and tried to summon a defiant answer, but the words wouldn't come.

"You're cold." He released her to shrug off his coat and drape it around her shoulders. His tenderness made her eyes prickle with tears. Strange that she'd stayed strong resisting violence, but gentleness split her in two.

"You've made a powerful enemy," she said hoarsely, huddling into the coat. His scent enveloped her. Clean male. Lemon verbena.

Christopher shrugged. "I can live with that."

She loved his careless courage. "He was jealous that my father favored you."

"Don't be a goose, Genevieve. He was jealous because you liked me."

"You risk making a fool of yourself, saying such things." She tried to dampen his presumption, but for once, her heart wasn't in it.

His brilliant smile always made her witless with longing,

even when she'd believed him an unrepentant miscreant. "I made a fool of myself over you long ago. But of course you know that, don't you?"

Did she? She knew he wanted her. She had no idea what else he felt. Except that tonight he acted like he cared. She was too tired and heartsick to talk herself out of the idea that perhaps he did. In his fashion.

"You were clever to scream," he said.

"I wasn't clever. I was terrified." She pressed an unsteady hand to her aching throat. "He...he choked me to keep me quiet."

"Hell, I should have shot the bugger."

Once more he took her hand. She returned his clasp, preternaturally conscious of the strong bones and long, sensitive fingers. His warmth made those horrid moments with Lord Neville seem distant and unimportant. "Shooting's too good for him."

"I could lock him in a room with your father and an alternative theory for the demise of the princes."

Surprisingly she laughed. It was strained and short-lived, but nonetheless it was a laugh. Tonight she'd thought laughter lost to her.

Something rustled behind them and her amusement evaporated. Panicked, she cringed closer to Christopher, who raised his pistol.

"Surely they wouldn't—"

"Shh," he said gently, pressing her to his side.

She hid her face in his shoulder, his silk waistcoat slippery beneath her cheek. She couldn't bear to see Lord Neville or to remember his hands on her. Although the grim reality was that she'd relive those suffocating moments in the coach for a long time to come. Beneath her ear, Christopher's heart pounded and his body vibrated with wariness.

He relaxed when Sedgemoor and Hillbrook emerged from the trees carrying lanterns.

"About time you turned up." Christopher sounded relieved as he lowered his pistol. She gathered her torn bodice although the coat preserved most of her modesty.

"We let you play Sir Galahad," Hillbrook drawled. "You've had so few opportunities."

"Very droll, old man." Christopher kept his arm around Genevieve. She should object, but fear had cut too deep tonight for her to stray from his side. "Better aim your barbs at Fairbrother."

"You needed to step in?" Hillbrook sounded like he already knew the answer.

"He tried to force Miss Barrett's consent to marriage."

"The sodding scum."

"Good evening, Miss Barrett," Sedgemoor said calmly from beside Hillbrook. "I hope you're unharmed."

"Yes, thank you, Your Grace." Shame burned her cheeks. At being found with Christopher. At her fatal naïveté in going with Lord Neville. At the way that both these men would surely speculate on what had occurred in that carriage.

"I'm appalled that this happened." The duke struck her as a man who concealed his emotions, but now she couldn't doubt his outrage. "Where's Fairbrother?"

Christopher pointed back through the bushes. "He and his bully boy are armed. Be careful."

"Miss Barrett, your father and aunt remain at Leighton Court while we await news. It's so late they're probably better staying in the rooms I arranged." The duke spoke as if finding his friend clutching a lady was nothing out of the ordinary. Perhaps it wasn't. Even that thought didn't scare her enough to disentangle herself. "Would you like to join them?"

"Thank you. But my maid is at the vicarage."

"Your men are still on watch, aren't they?" Christopher asked.

"What men?" Genevieve asked sharply. Tonight had produced too many revelations, turning her perceptions topsy-turvy.

As usual when he'd done something commendable, Christopher looked sheepish. "After the last break-in, I asked Cam to set a guard on the vicarage."

An hour ago, she'd been convinced that Christopher was responsible for terrorizing her aunt and father. She should be surprised to discover that he'd been guardian, not enemy. But since he'd saved her, she'd admitted that out of every man in the world, she trusted this one. "Thank you."

"Confounded little good it did." Christopher said wearily, then turned to his friends as Lord Hillbrook passed him a lantern. "Please remember that a lady's name is at stake."

The duke sighed. "Good God, man, we're not complete dullards. I can handle Fairbrother without damaging Miss Barrett's reputation."

Once Hillbrook and Sedgemoor left, Christopher extended his hand. The lantern created a golden circle of intimacy around them. "Let's go."

Without hesitation, she took his hand. Odd that earlier tonight she'd wanted to brain him with the soup tureen.

He stepped ahead, white shirt glowing like a beacon. She followed, sinking into a daze where all she knew was his touch and the vivid reality of his nearness. Every moment in this dark forest, the bond between them strengthened without a word spoken. It was like that day on the river, but deeper.

They reached a familiar part of the woods. "Stop," she said breathlessly, feeling like she emerged from a trance.

He raised the lantern to see her. "Do you need to rest?"

"No." Although the hike in evening slippers hadn't been easy. The wet grass was slippery, and damp soaked through her soles, chilling her feet. Her body ached, every step a reminder of Lord Neville's violence. "Can we go to the pond?"

Her request, seemingly out of the blue, made him frown. "The pond?"

"It's through those trees." Once they left this forest, she'd lose her nerve. Or weigh consequences.

Right now, she didn't want to consider consequences.

She waited for some remark about their meeting there. But he merely shrugged and turned down the overgrown path. When they reached the water, the lantern light spilled across the still, dark surface. Painful yearning rose in her like a spring tide. Yearning to wipe away tonight's cruel events. Yearning to replace ugly memories with something beautiful.

His coat slid to the cool grass. She straightened her spine and took one uncertain step forward. "Kiss me, Christopher."

Kiss me, Christopher.

Genevieve's words hung in the air as if etched in letters of fire. Slowly he turned toward her, the lantern dangling forgotten from his hand.

She faced him, shoulders straight and luxuriant hair drifting around her. She looked so beautiful, she made him want to weep. And of course he couldn't touch her. Hell, he still didn't know what Fairbrother had done. At the very least, the swine had frightened and brutalized her. The last thing she needed was another rapacious male mauling her.

Standing before Richard in her torn dress, she was breathtaking. Irresistible. Still, he had to resist. He ground his teeth on a silent prayer for control to a God who by all rights should ignore such a miserable sinner. Frustration roughened his voice. "Let's make for the vicarage. It's cold out here."

She flinched as if he'd struck her, but didn't budge. "No, it's not."

"I'm cold."

Her lips curled into a seductive smile that set his heart capering. "I doubt that."

Good Lord, what was she doing? Desperation frayed his question. "How can you want a man near you? After—"

"He didn't rape me."

Richard dragged in his first full breath since she'd left Leighton Court. "Thank God. I thought... When I found you... He was..."

He stopped. No woman except Genevieve reduced him to incoherence.

Her gentle expression pierced his heart. "So will you kiss me?"

He faltered back. "After tonight, you should hate every man alive."

"What happened tonight made me feel... sullied." Her voice emerged low and fervent. "When you touch me, I never feel like that. When you touch me, I feel... beautiful."

Astonishment and guilt struck him speechless. After all his deceit, he didn't deserve her longing. Or her agonized honesty. He fought against taking her into his arms. So difficult to do what was right when she offered everything he wanted.

He couldn't give in to her. Once she returned to her senses, she'd hate him forever. Hell, he'd hate himself. "Genevieve, let me take you home."

Her jaw set in a stubborn line. "Kiss me first."

His fist clenched so hard over the lantern handle that metal bit painfully into his palm. "You can't want this."

Her eyes settled on him with an unreadable expression. "You have no idea what I want."

Well, that was true enough. He'd imagined that she'd jump a hundred feet if he approached within a whisper. After what she'd been through, she deserved his indulgence. The problem was that he wasn't sure he could stop at kissing. Even now.

Wanting Genevieve was selfish and destructive, unworthy of her and increasingly unworthy of him. This whole bloody scheme to retrieve the jewel had been ill-conceived from the first.

Cam was right. Cam, blast him, was always right.

The abduction had jolted Richard into admitting that he wasn't much better than Fairbrother. He too sought to bend Genevieve to his purposes without care for end results.

"We have to go." Feeling like he scraped out his kidneys with a spoon, he turned away from the pond and its passionate memories.

"I'm not going until you kiss me."

"I could carry you home." Against his better judgment, he chanced a glance back.

A faint smile hovered around her lips. "You could, but you won't."

Hell, no, she was right. He couldn't play the barbarian after what she'd undergone tonight.

He bit back a groan. To think he'd once wanted her to beg for his kisses. This was torment worthy of the Spanish Inquisition. One thing he did know—if he didn't kiss her, she'd stand there studying him with that assessing expression until Kingdom Come.

Gathering every ounce of will, Richard placed the lantern

on the ground. The forest was silent as it had been silent when he'd first kissed her. Again there was that curious tension, as though the world held its breath to see what happened next.

Well, much as he hated to disappoint the dryads and demigods inhabiting these woodlands, what happened next was that he and Genevieve would share a quick kiss then he'd consign her to Dorcas's care. He'd then leave the vicarage so nobody said he and the vicar's daughter had slept unchaperoned under the same roof. Somewhere a demigod with an ironic sense of humor snickered at Richard Harmsworth's sudden concern for proprieties.

Still, it was only with the utmost reluctance that Richard stepped toward Genevieve. He scooped his coat from the ground and draped it across her shoulders in a futile attempt to create another barrier between them.

She linked her hands at her waist and studied him with a trace of uncertainty invisible from farther away. The vulnerability disarmed him as he tilted her face until starlight illuminated her loveliness. Need darkened her eyes before her lashes fluttered down.

He pressed his lips between arched brows. He tasted her skin, cool, satiny, sweet. The need to linger was sharper than a sword to his guts, but he stepped away, releasing her.

Her inhalation swelled her bosom against the tattered bodice. He tried not to notice. He really tried. This close, her shaky breathing was audible.

She opened eyes flashing with indignation. "What was that?"

"Good God, I must be losing my touch," he said huskily. The need to grab her and kiss her properly beat in his blood like thunder. "I'd call that a kiss."

She made a moue of disgust. "I wouldn't."

"Genevieve—"

"You won't hurt me."

"I'm trying like hell not to."

"I won't break."

After seeing her with Fairbrother, he wasn't so certain. Sighing, he caught her by the shoulders. She quivered under his hands and his touch became a caress.

He read no fear in her face, only yearning. Heroically he struggled not to glance at the sagging cream bodice. She didn't make it easy for him to become a better man.

His lips brushed across hers. He heard her tiny intake of breath, a soft gasp of excitement. Her lips parted as he withdrew. Her taste filled his head like wine. He itched to slake his thirst, but couldn't grant himself the freedom.

"I kissed you." His voice was choked. "Let's go."

Her hands curled in his shirt. "Please make me forget what happened tonight."

Oh, God, God, God. She sounded so hurt, so wretched. So bereft.

He stared blindly above her and hoped darkness hid the bulge in his trousers. "No."

"Oh."

He struggled to ignore the sad little syllable. He released her and waited for her to unhook her grip on his shirt. But she didn't. Instead she searched his features as if seeking proof that he was a liar.

The problem was that he was a liar. A liar had no right to lay his filthy liar's hands on Genevieve Barrett's pure body. Which didn't mean he wasn't frantic to touch her. He wanted her so much, he was likely to explode into a million pieces.

He strove to sound like the man he'd pretended to be, the careless rake Sir Richard Harmsworth, who never lacked an appropriate response. He'd always been so easy with his amours because he'd never cared. Not caring made his non-chalant manner a doddle. With Genevieve he cared to his bones, and he had no idea how to make this right.

Still, he must try. "A man needs his rest after he's battled villains like Fairbrother."

She flinched at his tone as much as at what he said, he knew. Still she didn't unhand him. She swallowed as if speaking proved difficult. He wished to hell she wouldn't speak. He wished to hell he was in Cathay. Or the East Indies. Anywhere but here with paradise inches away, yet completely beyond reach.

"Then sleep with me."

What the hell? His heart slammed to a stop. He caught her hands and managed to liberate his shirt. He should release her, but some things exceeded his powers. "Genevieve, this is wrong."

"You didn't think it was wrong in Oxford."

When she raised eyes glittering with tears, he felt like she punched him in the gut. Much as he loathed acknowledging it, he recognized how his rebuff had wounded her. He wasn't a fool. He knew what that offer had cost her. And she'd sought neither assurances for the future nor promises of love.

The irony was that for the first time, he could honestly tell a woman he loved her. Yet the vow stuck in his throat. Not just because he quailed from saying it, but because he couldn't declare his affections after so many lies.

"I've seen the light since Oxford," he said wryly. If he could, he'd laugh at himself. Sending Genevieve home as innocent as the day she was born was more excruciating than having a tooth drawn. She should be grateful. Hell, she should be lauding his chivalry to the skies.

Contrary like a woman, she lost her temper.

"I can't believe you're saying no. You've spent days trying to seduce me. Here I am, ready and willing." Her voice cracked into silence. Revealing a luscious expanse of bosom, she spread her arms.

His cock, already hard and aching, swelled against his trousers. By all that was holy, at this rate he'd lose himself like an impulsive boy. Then what would she make of his denials? Luckily she was too furious to note his physical discomfort.

"Time to go, Genevieve," he said gently, burning to gather her into his arms and comfort her. But too afraid of the devil inside to chance even that much contact. Those two chaste kisses had whittled his control to a sliver.

Abruptly she turned away and he felt another phantom blow to the belly when he realized that she wept. What an excruciating night she'd had. Fairbrother's assault. Now this rejection.

How he wished he could explain. But his lies divided them like a dank, foul canal. Too deep and wide to cross. He stood on one bank; she stood on the other. He could never cross the stinking mire to tell her how much he loved her.

Without looking, she extended a shaking hand toward him.

Damn it, he couldn't touch her. It was too risky.

But no man with a heart could ignore the plea in that trembling hand.

Knowing that he tested his principles but unable to do otherwise, he seized her hand. Her fingers clenched hard around his.

"I can't resist you," he muttered, hoping she wouldn't hear.

She straightened and faced him, bewilderment clear in the flickering light. "I don't understand."

For one moment more, he held back. If he'd marched her to the vicarage when she first offered, he'd have kept his hands to himself. But what could a man do when he wanted a woman as badly as he wanted this one and she promised to make all his dreams come true?

"Hell, Genevieve," he groaned in defeat and swept her into his arms.

Chapter Twenty-Four

Lightning blasted in Christopher's eyes as his barriers against her finally tumbled. Genevieve braced for ravishment.

Instead of flinging her into a world of unfettered hunger, his touch remained gentle. Delicious warmth surrounded her as he drew her into his body. Warmth that dissipated the chill lingering since Lord Neville's assault. His mouth touched hers. With a wordless protest, she moved closer. Still he teased. Soft kisses. Quick kisses. She wanted him to remake her with his passion, yet he seemed determined to tantalize her to death.

"Christopher!" she muttered in the space between one glancing kiss and the next.

"Yes?" What a hopeless case she was. The mere sound of his voice turned her into a molten puddle of longing.

"Kiss me properly."

"I don't intend to be proper at all, my love."

"So you say." She struggled to ignore the endearment as her hands tangled in his shirt. "Stop tormenting me."

Kisses on nose, forehead, jaw. He kissed her neck, setting a thousand nerves jangling. Her toes curled in her damp slippers and she pressed against him, silently begging him to stop treating her as if she was likely to break. Still he held her as delicately as he'd cradle a baby bird in his palm. His lips returned to hers and his tongue dipped between her lips for a fleeting taste.

This hint of controlled power crashed through her like cymbals. On a sigh, she sank into him. His teasing had brought her to a pitch of surrender that left her blind to everything but him.

When Lord Neville had touched her, she'd felt revulsion and fear. When Christopher touched her, she just wanted more. The hot weight settling in her belly was familiar now, yet new. She felt disconnected from the everyday world. Lost in Christopher's arms.

Her body couldn't contain these responses. She must shatter into a million stars. On an incoherent plea, she rose against his hips, pushing into his hardness. She built the pressure in a vain attempt to relieve the ache between her legs, but every slide of her body only increased her need.

Somewhere she must have pulled away his neck cloth. Or he had. Her lips traced smooth skin, redolent of male, lemon verbena and Christopher, the scent that she'd recognize from all the scents in the world.

He nibbled his way up her neck. His unrelenting, intense gentleness left her quaking, dizzy, overcome. His mouth traced the side of her face. The touch was soft as the brush of a feather, but pain splintered delight. She whimpered and jerked away.

"Darling . . ." He withdrew and stared at her.

Guilt darkened his expression. The hands gripping her arms—dear Lord, he hadn't touched her body at all and already she quaked—eased so that it felt as if his hold was as delicate as a single thread of silk.

Oh, no. No, no, no. He wasn't stopping now. Not when finally his kisses promised oblivion. Frantically she buried her hands in his hair, pulling its soft thickness. "Keep going."

"You're hurt."

"He hit me." Curse Christopher, he must know she didn't want to talk. She, a woman who spent all day juggling words, wanted only to feel. "It will hurt me more if you stop."

He kissed her tenderly, sending her heart swooping. "I won't stop."

She stretched up to kiss him, using her tongue in silent demand. When he hesitated, she tugged his hair until he kissed her back.

At last, at last, he cupped her breast. In aching welcome, the nipple pearled against his palm. She shivered as he bared her to sweet exploration. Moisture welled between her thighs and she shifted restlessly.

He kissed her neck again, stirring more shivery reaction, but for all her eagerness, she wasn't ready to lie down on the bank. "Come with me," she forced out, as his teeth scraped a sensitive spot on her neck.

Through the steamy haze in her mind, she realized he was caught in this whirl of pleasure and hadn't heard. She cleared her throat and spoke more loudly, "Not here."

He growled with frustration and lifted his head. "Where?"

With every second in his arms, the horror of Lord Neville's assault receded, submerged in a wild, reckless elation that turned the night brighter than the Harmsworth Jewel. She fumbled for his hand. "Follow me."

With her other hand, she tugged her bodice across her breasts and wrapped his coat around herself. Modesty was absurd after he'd touched her so carnally. But she was reluctant to wander the woods half-naked like a nymph.

He groaned. "This is revenge, isn't it? For the times I teased you about your embroidery or interrupted your work."

Laughing softly, she squeezed his hand. Sweetness leavened desire until her heart brimmed so full, it must surely burst from her chest. She hardly noticed Christopher collecting the lantern. She turned toward the end of the pond, shrouded in thick trees and bushes.

Richard struggled to leash his urge to tumble her where they stood. She seemed so eager, but he couldn't forget how she'd looked crushed beneath Fairbrother. She needed a perfect lover now, a man to worship her, treat her the way he'd treat antique lace or Venetian glass. Richard wanted her so much, more than he'd wanted any other woman, but tonight of all nights, he couldn't let his selfishness rule him. This was about restoring Genevieve's bruised spirit.

In a daze of anticipation, he followed her through the dark woods. She pushed through low branches. Richard was so focused on Genevieve, he needed a moment to identify the structure rising from the undergrowth as if planted there. But it was manmade. And completely hidden from anyone passing a few feet away.

"I had no idea." In amazement, he stared at the tiny white temple shrouded in greenery.

Genevieve led him up cracked marble stairs, littered with dead leaves. "I found it not long after we came to Little Derrick." She paused. "My mother died just before that. This provided the perfect place to hide and grieve."

"Darling—" Fierce compassion pierced him. Tenderly he raised her hand and kissed the knuckles.

She turned in the doorway, shaking her glorious hair back from her face. "Welcome."

His breath caught at the sight of her. She gleamed gold in the lantern light and her face was as pure as an angel carved on a cathedral front.

With a cursory glance at his surroundings, he stepped through the columned entry. The space was astonishing enough to occupy his attention, if the woman he loved hadn't stared at him as though he brought the stars down from the sky to set at her feet.

"Good God." With a shaking hand, he set the lantern on the marble floor with its geometric patterns. She'd furnished the summerhouse with candles and a table. And, praise the Lord, pillows. Pillows and cushions stacked against columns. Pillows and cushions piled to form a bed worthy of a harem.

She smiled. "Do you like it?"

He smiled back and gently drew her down to the bed until they kneeled facing one another. "Yes. You must tell me about it." He caught her thick fall of hair in his fist, revealing the graceful curve of shoulder and neck. She was so delicious, he could eat her up. "Much later."

He swung her close for a drugging kiss. She responded without hesitation, her mouth open and ravenous. Her hands curled around his arms.

Giddy with love, he kissed her throat. Her scent invaded his head. Warm flowers. Female musk. Genevieve. Above all, Genevieve.

He nipped her earlobe. Her breath escaped in humid little gasps and she arched, the peaks of her breasts grazing his chest through his shirt. She was no passive lover. Her capable hands grabbed his open collar. He waited for her to push his shirt aside, but her impatience exceeded his. With a grunt, she tore his shirt in two, then rose on her knees to skim her mouth across his pectorals.

Her desire fed his. Made him ready to take on the world and win. How had he lived without her? Still he couldn't forget her ordeal with Fairbrother. The memory tempered passion, made him careful, as he couldn't remember being careful with a lover.

He caught her face in his hands, chary of her bruised cheek. "I want to see you naked."

Her eyes were dark and mysterious. "I want to see you naked too."

For all her boldness, her hands trembled as she brushed his ruined shirt from his shoulders. Then slowly, so slowly that it was excruciating torture, she touched him, learning him with her fingertips. His heart threatened to burst under the powerful sensations.

Her fingers glanced across one nipple and he jerked with shock. She stopped and regarded him uncertainly. "Should I stop?"

"Hell, no." He loved the drift of her hands. Even more than her touch, he loved her wondering expression. As though his body was the gateway to a magnificent kingdom that she'd never dreamed existed.

With a few deft movements, he rid her of coat, dress, and corset, then pulled her torn shift over her head. Her torso rose from the froth of white petticoats like a perfect flower. When he took her beaded nipple into his mouth, her taste made his head swim.

His fumbling fingers—no woman in years had made him fumble, but Genevieve demolished practiced technique—released the tapes fastening her petticoats. The need to see her pounded like an army of drummers. He edged her back into the cushions. He drew away petticoats, then slippers, scuffed and dirty after tramping through the woods. Then stockings. With unsteady hands, he tugged her drawers down her long legs.

Dear God in heaven. He'd caught a hint of how exquisite she was when he'd surprised her at the pond. But nothing compared to this moment when she lay bare before him, flushed with desire.

Genevieve's hands coiled nervously at her sides. He knew she desperately wanted to cover herself.

"You're lovely," he said in a choked voice.

Vulnerability shadowed her eyes as she bit her lip. "When you look at me like that, I feel lovely."

In the light, she was a creature of gilt and shadow. Nothing could match her. He prayed for the skill to do this superb woman justice.

He kneeled between her legs, sinking into the cushions. Her hot scent made him crazy. She stroked his shoulders and chest until his muscles twitched with longing. Then she lowered her hands to his trousers, brushing his cock.

"Hell—" He grabbed her hand and stared at her in desperation.

"Can't I touch you?"

He hissed through his teeth and battled for control. "I want you so much."

"I want you too," she said softly.

She pressed her lips to his in a kiss that his former supercilious self might have considered clumsy. For the man who had discovered his heart, the kiss was as destabilizing as an earthquake. He kissed her back, tasting need and innocence.

Awkwardly, hurriedly, he ripped open his trousers. His cock sprang free, hungry and throbbing. She sighed, eyes fluttering shut, and lifted her hips.

Tenderly he cupped her mound, feathery hair beneath his

palm. In Oxford he'd had to coax her into accepting such familiarity. Tonight, praise the Lord, her legs swiftly fell open. She was wet, gloriously, lusciously, sumptuously wet.

He pressed his forehead into her satiny shoulder and tested her with one finger, then two. *Yes*...

Chapter Twenty-Five

Genevieve felt a seeking pressure between her legs, where she was aching and empty. She yearned for Christopher's possession with a hunger she'd never known, even when he'd touched her on the river.

Breathing raggedly, Christopher braced his weight upon his arms. "I'll hurt you."

She hooked her hands around his back. "Don't stop."

"I don't think I can." The raw voice didn't sound like the familiar self-possessed man.

He shifted his hips and pressed deeper. Her damp heat eased his passage; still he stretched her. She bit back a whimper and he paused.

Beneath her hands, his back was slippery with sweat and she felt his trembling tension. New sensations overwhelmed her. Sensations that left her shaking. Her body tightened to expel the invader.

He bit down on the nerve in her neck that turned her boneless with pleasure. A jolt of response shot to where their bodies joined. On a shocked inhalation, her muscles loosened a fraction.

He growled with satisfaction. Raising his head, he stared at her as if she was his most precious treasure. The fear lurking below her determination blossomed into warmth. As he kissed her, she shifted to take him deeper. She strained up to prolong the kiss and in that moment, he thrust. Stiffening, she cried out against his mouth.

"Don't cry, please, darling, don't cry." He placed urgent kisses over her face and neck.

He looked tortured to the edge of endurance. He looked like his suffering far exceeded hers. Especially now that the pain ebbed and her body subtly adjusted. Her lips caught his with a fierceness that made her blood rush.

He groaned and shifted. The new angle sparked a cannonade of sensations. Astonishing, almost pleasurable sensations. She moved, rubbing her breasts against his chest.

Supporting himself on one hand, he stroked her. She moaned and closed hard around him. This time tightness delivered pleasure not discomfort.

As he slowly withdrew, Genevieve felt every inch. "Don't go," she begged brokenly, tugging the damp hair clinging to his nape.

"I'm not going anywhere," he responded softly. With smooth power, he pushed inside again.

Her shocked gaze met his. "Oh."

He smiled with the brilliance she'd come to believe was only for her. "Oh, indeed."

He retreated, setting every nerve to shouting hallelujahs. Again he joined her, deeper than before. Dear Lord above, this was wonderful, unlike anything experienced or imagined. She felt restless and yearning, cherished yet frustrated. The next time he thrust, she instinctively raised her hips. Liking what happened, she repeated the action. She watched savage enjoyment flare in his face before she closed her eyes and surrendered to a blazing new universe.

Higher and higher she flew. She was an invincible, immortal eagle soaring into the incandescent sun. Her hands dug into his shoulders, her only anchor in a whirling world. Behind her eyes, the light was blinding.

Up and up she climbed. She shook and moaned with the fever. Her fever was desire. Desire twisting so tight that surely she must disintegrate.

Finally, at the point where she could no longer bear the twisting ascent, longing ignited into fire. She clenched to keep him. He groaned, the sound guttural. He tautened and jerked once, twice, three times. Liquid heat flooded her womb, augmented the overwhelming sensations.

When he collapsed gasping upon her, wonder held her still. His essence cloaked her. Lemon verbena and satisfied man. She couldn't doubt his satisfaction. His back loosened under her stroking hands as if he'd exhausted all strength. Against her cheek, his hair slid damp and cool.

Her body felt stretched and used. Her face ached where Lord Neville had slapped her. Christopher was heavy, cramming her into the pillows. His weight reminded her that this bed wasn't designed for love, but as a place to read a book on a quiet afternoon.

Now she'd found a new way to pass her idle hours. The wry thought added an edge of amusement to glowing pleasure.

Richard clung to the dark oblivion of sexual repletion as long as possible. How to measure the time he took to return from the stars? Genevieve's musky, female scent filled his nostrils, the sweetest perfume he knew. That shattering climax still rumbled through him like a distant storm. He'd never found such pleasure with a woman.

Genevieve remained quiet, arms draped around his waist. He wondered if she slept. He must be crushing her, but he couldn't bear to move. If he moved, his conscience might decide that he was willing to listen. And he damn well wasn't.

But his conscience caterwauled until he could block it no longer. Making love to Genevieve had been the transcendent experience of his life. And unquestionably it had been wrong.

Groaning, he rolled away and sat up on the rumpled cushions, raising his knees and burying his head in his hands. From bliss to wretchedness in a heartbeat. This felt like the most God awful hangover. A spiritual hangover. Much nastier than the effects of too much brandy.

"I've made such a bloody mull of this," he muttered, wrenching at his hair as if the small pain could compensate for the evil he'd done this woman.

"Well, that's what a girl wants to hear after she's taken a lover," Genevieve said sourly.

He didn't look at her as she scrambled away. He missed her proximity. Almost as much as he missed those luminous but unforgivable moments when he'd been inside her and she'd clasped him tight as if she'd never let him go.

"This is no joking matter." He pressed the heels of his hands into his eyes until he saw colored lights. When what he should see was the engulfing flames of hell.

He heard her moving about. "I'm sorry I didn't meet expectations."

Horrified, he raised his head to watch her marching around the temple lighting candles. She'd tugged her dress on, although without petticoats, her gown was nearly transparent.

"Don't be silly, Genevieve," he said grimly. The light blooming around him didn't brighten his inner darkness.

She halted before him, glowering. She was so beautiful. A louse like him didn't deserve to touch the hem of her skirt.

With a furious huff, she blew out the taper. "You certainly know how to make a girl feel like a princess."

He didn't smile. He felt lower than a snake's belly, too low to summon his usual tricks to keep a lady happy once he'd tumbled her. With Genevieve, his tired old lines seemed cheap and shabby. *He* was cheap and shabby. And a damnable liar.

The lies were the problem. Lies as black as pitch and stinking like a fart from Satan's arse.

Unsteadily he rose to tug on his trousers, then he slumped onto the makeshift couch to stare at her in despair. "Sit down, Genevieve."

She folded her arms, pushing her lush bosom up. He was definitely a louse. Even now, his cock twitched with interest. His cock didn't care that he was rotten to the core. His cock wanted to plant itself between Genevieve's creamy thighs.

Stifling his baser impulses, he extended his hand toward her. "Please."

Without touching him, she dropped onto the cushions. Her body was so tense he thought she might crack if he touched her. "Are you married?"

"Good God, no."

On a shuddering breath, her shoulders relaxed. Guiltily he realized how his behavior must unnerve her. "Well, that's something."

He stared blindly at the candles on the rickety table across the room. His belly cramped like he'd eaten bad fish. Life had been considerably easier before he'd given a damn.

Dear Lord, what if he'd got her pregnant? She'd curse the day he was born.

"There's something I need to tell you," he said bleakly, knowing that he should have told her before he took her virginity. That he should never have lied at all.

Too late. Too late.

He braced as if expecting a blow. But he owed her the foul, damaging truth. His voice emerged as flat as Lincolnshire. "I'm not who you think I am."

"I know you're not," she said equally expressionlessly. "You're the thief who broke into the vicarage and locked me in."

Bloody hell. *She knew?* Astonished, he turned. She studied him with severe, focused attention. Against expectations, she didn't appear to hate him. Yet. "What did you say?"

"You broke into the vicarage."

"The first time. Never after that," he said quickly, before reminding himself that he could only seek absolution after a full confession.

He didn't deserve absolution. How he wished he could take back the last hour. Or more accurately he wished that he wished he could take it back. His unparalleled satisfaction didn't outweigh his long overdue scruples.

Then the significance of what she'd said struck like a hammer on brass. "How the hell do you know?"

Her lips curved in an unamused smile, although her gaze remained watchful. "You're not as clever as you think you are."

That was something she didn't need to tell him. "Apparently." He struggled to order reeling thoughts. "How long have you known? Not from the first, surely? You wouldn't have let me move in."

He saw her consider making such a claim, but she was much more honest than he. "The first time we kissed."

Another shock shuddered through him. "What did I do?"

"It wasn't what you did. It was how you smelled." Despite the fraught moment, a reminiscent light entered her lovely eyes. "Lemon verbena."

"Blast. I was so careful."

"The dyed hair fooled me for a while."

He wasn't made for subterfuge. He should have realized that a woman as sharp as Genevieve would quickly penetrate his disguise. Still he had more questions than answers. "Why in heaven's name didn't you say something? Especially after the other break-ins."

"I waited to see what you were up to."

Unable to resist touching her, he lunged for her hand. There was a distinct possibility after he told her everything that she'd never let him touch her again. "I could be a villain of the worst sort."

"I'm not sure that you aren't." She tried to break free, but he, being the villain he claimed, wouldn't let her go. "The best explanation I can come up with is that you're working for Sir Richard Harmsworth to get me to sell the jewel. Although your efforts have been fairly half-hearted. You could have blackmailed me about my father's work. Lord Neville tried to."

Fleeting disgust distracted him. "The devil he did."

She nodded. "But you didn't. Are you working for Sir Richard?"

His stomach felt like it was made of lead. In his mouth, self-hatred tasted like rusty nails. He groaned again and buried his head in his knees, resting his brow on their clasped hands. He'd never loved her so desperately as now when he faced eternal banishment. Once she found out who he was, she'd never forgive him. "It's worse than that, my darling."

Her voice shook with trepidation. "Tell me."

He braced as though expecting the roof of the charming summerhouse to collapse. Of course the temple wouldn't collapse. What collapsed was his life and hopes.

He raised his head and spoke quickly to lessen the pain. "I *am* Richard Harmsworth."

Chapter Twenty-Six

I'm so stupid," Genevieve whispered.

Of course he was Richard Harmsworth. It was both the most obvious and simplest solution to the mystery of his interest in the Harmsworth Jewel. She snatched her hand free and rose on shaky legs.

"I'm sorry," he said in such a low voice, she strained to hear. He stared at the hands linked around his knees. Even now, even after this revelation of his identity and how he'd misled her, she couldn't stop her heart turning over at how beautiful he was.

"Is that enough?" Because the temptation to touch him remained so strong, she stepped away. She knew how his skin felt beneath her hand, smooth and warm and alive. She knew how his long muscles tightened and released when he moved. She couldn't erase the experience of pleasure.

"No," he said dully.

Candlelight lit him like an actor on a stage. Of course an actor was what he was. Nothing was real. An hour ago, she'd gloried in her recklessness. Right now, she felt sick to the stomach with remorse.

The weight of hurt and betrayal left her crushed. "Why didn't you steal the jewel that first night?"

When he glanced up, despair shadowed his blue eyes. She almost believed that he suffered, until she remembered how convincingly he lied. "I never planned to steal the jewel."

"Then why are you here?"

He shrugged faintly, an unhappy version of his usual nonchalance. "You'll hate me."

Her lips tightened. Lord Neville's attack and what Christopher—no, *Richard*—had done had left her sticky and sore. She desperately wanted a bath. She desperately wanted to return to the woman she'd been before she met this deceitful Adonis. "Who says I don't hate you now?"

He flinched. Although the truth was that she was unsure what she felt. For days, she'd known he had an agenda. Yet she'd brought him here and let him have his way with her. Such a banal description for that unforgettable journey to the stars. Worse, she had a horrible suspicion that if he touched her with intent to seduce, she'd fall as readily as before.

Mind and body had always been at war over handsome Mr. Evans. Who wasn't Mr. Evans at all, but a rich and rakish baronet. The stories in Mrs. Meacham's London papers taunted her with the knowledge that this man moved in a world far beyond her humble circle.

He straightened upon the cushions, sitting there pale and serious as she'd rarely seen him. "When you told my representatives that even if you had the jewel, you'd never sell it to me, I decided to inveigle it away from you."

It was her turn to flinch. "Seduce me, you mean?"

He flushed with shame. "I never intended to ruin you, but the moment I saw you I wanted you."

Her tone descended to sarcasm. "Wonderful. At least you didn't need to pretend enthusiasm."

"Genevieve, I realize how bad this looks." He stood and reached for her. His tone deepened into sincerity, but she'd learned to mistrust him. "You must know there's more between us than my half-baked quest for the jewel."

She backed away, staring at his hand as if it sported long jagged teeth. "I don't know anything. Until a few minutes ago, I didn't even know your name."

"You can't despise me more than I despise myself." He drew himself to his full height. He'd never looked more magnificent, candlelight flickering across his lean, muscled torso and his shoulders straight and proud. The light gleamed on his hair and she realized that the dye faded to reveal shining gold.

It broke her heart to look at him, although she knew she'd invited this pain. She turned away and bent to scrabble through her petticoats. She flushed with humiliation to see their discarded clothing.

She faced him, hand tightly closed. "Neither of us deserves accolades."

Swallowing hard, she struggled to forget those miraculous minutes when their bodies joined, how she'd felt beautiful and wanted and free. How she'd felt loved. If she thought about lying in his arms, she'd start to cry. Now she needed to be disdainful and strong.

Slowly she extended her hand and unfurled fingers stiff with the pressure of her grip. He'd ripped her heart out. Nothing mattered anymore. "Seduction worked."

His eyes darkened at her bitter statement and a muscle flickered in his cheek. Then his gaze dropped to what she held. The object glittered as though it was alive. "It's the jewel."

"Of course it's the jewel," Genevieve snapped, then stopped. Screaming like a banshee wouldn't convey the impression that she required. She intended Sir Richard to remember her as proud and queenly, not as a hysterical termagant. She wanted him to walk away with some corner of his heart regretting what he'd tossed away.

A likely outcome.

"You carried it with you." His eyes glinted with admiration. "That's why nobody found it."

"At least your henchmen didn't."

His lips turned down with displeasure. "Genevieve, you have no reason to believe me—"

"That's the first honest thing you've said to me."

He ignored her jibe, although his fists clenched at his sides. She was savagely glad to needle him, to repay some of the pain ripping her to shreds. "I'll never lie to you again. I told you I was only responsible for the first break-in, and that's the truth."

"You wouldn't know the truth if it kicked you in the teeth." As she longed to do. She braced against swelling anger. Inside her there stirred a beast that burned to claw that sad, concerned expression from his face. Until his skin lay in tattered strips and she exposed the reality under the gorgeous mask.

Proud and queenly, Genevieve.

"I know you hate me—"

"More frankness. Good heavens, Sir Richard, in no time at all you'll pass as an honest man."

His lips compressed, but he continued in the same reasonable tone. "But I never intended you harm."

That was so patently untrue that she had to blink away hot, furious tears. She wouldn't cry. Not now. Not ever. He wasn't worth one tear. He wasn't worth the dirt under her feet. "Take it."

He frowned as if she spoke a foreign language. She shoved

her hand at him like a punch. Her best efforts couldn't control her trembling. Given a choice, she'd pitch the jewel at him, but it was delicate and valuable and deserved better use than as a missile against a faithless lover. "Take it, and may you be damned."

No wonder he'd been so interested in her research into the family legend. No wonder he'd contrived to make her his creature. But there were things he didn't know about the jewel, things that would give her the last laugh. When her article appeared, she'd have her revenge.

If only the prospect was more satisfying. Right now, all she wanted to do was crawl into a dark corner and cry her eyes out, whether he was worth her tears or not. If the chance to huddle forever in that dark corner arose, she'd snatch it as fast as she expected Sir Richard to snatch the Harmsworth Jewel.

Although to be fair, he wasn't acting like a heartless Machiavellian blackguard. Which did nothing to mollify her anger.

Very gently he cupped his hand under hers. Someone this cold-hearted should be clammy like a frog, but he was warm. Memories of those hands on her skin pricked at her determination to loathe him. She beat the weakness back, but with more difficulty than she liked.

"I don't want it, Genevieve."

She stiffened with horror. Did he guess the secret, the discovery that would make her article the talk of the academic world? Surely not. That was impossible, even for the great Sir Richard Harmsworth. "Of course you do."

He shook his head and with more of that searing gentleness, he closed his hand, curling her fingers around the jewel. "Keep it."

"Do you want me to beg you to take it? You overestimate your charm."

He sighed. "Right now, I don't feel very charming."

Raising her hand, he kissed her knuckles. For one lost moment, yearning surged. Then she remembered his deceit and wrenched her hand away.

"You'll regret this sacrifice after you've gone."

He frowned. "Gone?"

"I want you out of my life."

Stubbornly he shook his head. "No."

She forced herself to confront her brazen behavior. "You'll never touch me again. You've got everything that you'll ever get."

Unhappiness shadowed his face. "Genevieve, don't torture yourself like this."

Torture herself? How wrong could he be? She was a queen punishing an unruly subject. "Tonight was a mistake."

He smiled slightly. It was the first hint of humor since he'd confessed his identity. "A magnificent mistake."

She flushed. The horrid thought struck that tonight might result in repercussions. She'd known from the start that she played with fire, but it had seemed more important for Richard's caresses to erase all traces of Lord Neville from her skin. Now she wondered at her idiocy. "I never want to see you again."

His faint smile remained. "I'm sure that's true, but you're in danger. I won't abandon you."

She laughed harshly. "Who protects me from you?"

He didn't react, although that muscle in his cheek continued its dance. "You have nothing to fear from me."

"I'll never offer you the jewel again."

"You're the only jewel I'm interested in."

He was such a liar. Anger that felt more like desolation made her stagger back a step. "Pretty words, Sir Richard."

He remained inhumanly calm. Probably he didn't care

enough to be angry. "Fairbrother must realize now that the jewel's not in the vicarage. He'll come after you."

"So you're offering to keep it for me?" Sarcasm weighted the question.

He shook his head. "I told you, I don't want it. But you can trust Cam."

Her temper flared again, although it had hardly subsided since he'd admitted his name. "The duke's a liar too."

He winced, but his voice emerged as measured as ever. "He hated being party to this deception. Cam's as fine a man as you could meet."

His defense of his friend rankled. A snake like Sir Richard shouldn't demonstrate qualities like loyalty. "I'm beginning to think there's no such thing as a man worth the air he breathes."

Sir Richard made a convulsive move as if to take her into his arms. His voice vibrated with urgency that she couldn't let herself credit. "I'm sorry, Genevieve. I'm sorry I hurt you this way. I know I was wrong. I'd do it all so differently if I could. But I didn't count on you. I didn't count on how you'd change me. I didn't count on what all this would mean."

She stepped back before her needy heart lured her closer. He was right. She was hurt and angry. But she wasn't fool enough to throw herself into the furnace where she'd been burned once already. "And what does it mean, Sir Richard?"

Unwaveringly he stared at her. For a moment, she wondered if she might get an answer. Not that she'd believe him.

He straightened, dark blue eyes somber as she'd never seen them. "One day I'll tell you. When you're ready to listen."

She tightened her hand around the jewel until the metal bruised her. "I'll never be ready."

Unable to withstand the steady gaze that seemed to

demand something of her, something she didn't understand, she moved around the temple collecting her clothing. Carefully she wrapped her torn shift around the jewel. She avoided glancing at the jumbled pillows in the center of the floor.

Genevieve feared that in taking her body, Richard had marked her forever. That unwelcome perception fortified outward hostility, while inside she quivered like one of Dorcas's jellies.

"Go back to London, Sir Richard. I'm sure the fine ladies there appreciate your cruel games."

Arms overflowing with undergarments, she headed doggedly for the entrance. This man, Christopher, Richard, whoever in blazes he was, had wrecked another of her sanctuaries. He left her nowhere to hide. And she'd never needed a haven more.

He stepped in front of her. His eyes glittered with a wild light as his hands hooked around her forearms. Fear shivered through her. Fear and reluctant excitement. His touch sparked sensations she'd battled to deny since learning that he wasn't a dream lover but a lying reptile.

"Let me go."

He ignored her. She couldn't blame him. She wasn't exactly struggling. "This isn't over, Genevieve."

"Yes, it is." She stared at him, striving to detest him.

"I'll prove that I'm worthy of the privilege you granted me tonight. I'll prove that you've turned a shallow fribble into a man of honor."

She blushed hot as fire. "Prove it by leaving."

His jaw hardened into an obstinate line. "Not while you're at risk."

"You're the risk."

"In that case, you're safe. Your safety is all I want."

Her eyes narrowed. "But that's not all you want, is it?"

She meant the jewel. But as his eyes sparked and his grip firmed, she realized that her phrasing had been fatally imprecise. Academic suicide. Unwise too, when dealing with half-naked men.

"Right now, I want you to remember this." His hands cradled her head with a ruthless tenderness that set her heart cartwheeling.

Run, Genevieve, run.

But her feet remained pinned to the floor. Idiot, idiot girl she was, even now, she wanted one last kiss. One last kiss before she forever banished this dangerous magic he conjured between them.

This close, it was impossible not to recall his body sliding into hers. His masculine scent teased, made her dizzy with desire she didn't want to feel. Her hands clenched in her petticoats as she struggled against touching him.

She prepared for aggression. But he was too subtle for that. A man lacking subtlety couldn't have seduced her. A man lacking subtlety would have stolen the jewel that first night and saved her a mountain of heartache.

Oh, how she abhorred a subtle man.

His lips were soft, reminding her how careful he'd been when he'd taken her. His gentleness brought tears closer than they'd hovered since his confession. Impossible to cling to anger when he kissed her.

She told herself to break away. He wasn't holding her tightly. If she fled, he wouldn't pursue.

At least not tonight.

She closed her eyes and familiar dark delight flowed through her veins, drowning outrage in desire. She fought to stay rigid and unresponsive. But as he sipped from her lips with endless patience, her iron backbone bent, melted, turned to honey. She struggled to recall his deceit, but pleasure flooded her mind, turning her blind to all other considerations.

His tongue traced the seam of her lips, tasted the corners, flicked against the sensitive philtrum. She trembled and a moan crammed against her closed lips. But he heard. She knew he did. His hands moved in her hair, stroking away tension, hatred, resentment, and luring her toward surrender.

Inevitably, her lips parted and her body curved toward his, crushing her underclothing between them. His hands slid around her back, bringing her closer, but not close enough. Lost to everything but physical need, she made a muffled protest.

The contact stayed light, teasing. She'd sensed temper when he'd seized her, but this was all persuasion and sweetness. His hands played up and down her spine in a beguiling rhythm that set her heart racing like a greyhound. She made another wordless complaint, desperate for those provoking lips to settle, plunder, ravish.

He taunted her until she was near mad with need. Then at last his kiss turned to fire. Arousal streaked through her like flame in a dry hay field. Heat flooded her body. She was at the point of flinging her arms about him, insisting that he take her.

When he wrenched free, she'd forgotten everything except hunger. He was panting and pale, apart from a flush along his high, slanted cheekbones.

Acrid shame flooded her, made her belly heave. How could she have done that? She forced herself to meet his eyes. They were dark and intent and alight with knowledge of her weakness. For one trembling moment, she stared at him, hating him more than she'd ever hated anyone. Even Lord Neville.

"And that was the cruelest game of all," she said through lips that felt made of glass.

Genevieve saw him whiten as she firmed her grip on her petticoats. She bent to collect the lantern before she shoved past him toward the door. All the time, she raged at herself and the scheming Sir Richard Harmsworth, curse his black soul to hell.

Chapter Twenty-Seven

"Papa, Lord Neville assaulted me last night." Genevieve placed her hands flat on her father's desk and leaned forward to capture his attention.

She'd only had a couple of hours' fitful sleep, pistol under her pillow in case Lord Neville returned. Or that wretch Richard Harmsworth tried his luck. But nobody had appeared until Dorcas arrived with tea.

Some foolishly optimistic corner of her heart had imagined that her father might check that she was unharmed. Instead, after returning from Leighton Court he'd retreated to his library. By now, she should be inured to her father's disregard, but every time he proved how little he cared, it cut anew. Her aunt had fussed about her all morning, horrified at the abduction and cursing Lord Neville for a villain.

"What nonsense." Her father looked annoyed as he glanced up from his book. "You caused a deal of trouble last night, Genevieve. I can't be pleased with you. It quite spoiled the evening."

"Lord Neville pressed his attentions." This morning she

felt completely battered. Her body sported bruises, and more insidiously, the untried muscles between her legs ached. "You must forbid him the house. And Greengrass too."

Her father looked troubled. "His Grace made this ridiculous claim last night. I don't know what you all hope to achieve with this slander. I told him then that Lord Neville is a gentleman."

"What about this?" She straightened and touched the mottled bruise on her cheek with a trembling hand. A fichu hid the bruises on her neck. "I'm not in the habit of imagining men attacking me."

"Genevieve, his lordship wants to marry you." Her father's hands twisted in his lap.

"Haven't you heard a word I've said?" Outrage choked her. Surely her father couldn't think that after last night she'd want to be in the same room as Lord Neville, let alone marry the swine. "He tried to force me."

Her father shook his head in disbelief. "It's a good match, Genny. If you marry him, you'll be settled, secure. What will become of you when I'm gone? There's no money."

Her father hadn't called her Genny in years. The nickname only pressed the knife deeper into her heart. She considered telling him of the offers for the Harmsworth Jewel, then realized that he'd still choose toadying to his patron over protecting his daughter. Anyway, she couldn't sell the artifact. Not knowing what she did.

"Even before last night's events, I couldn't marry him," she said dully. "He's too old for me."

Her father's anger flared. Not, she noted with chagrin, on her behalf. "He's been generous."

She regarded him with horror. "So I should sell myself to him?"

A hiatus in his hand wringing. "You'd be a lady in a great house and close enough to continue working with me."

Of course his convenience was paramount. If she married Lord Neville, her father retained patron and assistant in a neat package. An ocean of disappointment drowned her rage. She should have guessed that her father wouldn't take her side. That liar Richard Harmsworth was the only person prepared to stand up to Lord Neville for her. What an appalling revelation.

"Don't you care that he hit me?" she asked in a small voice.

Her father looked hunted. "You mustn't dismiss his many kindnesses because of a childish spat." He adopted the pious expression reserved for his sermons. "We can't be unchristian."

"No, let's not be unchristian," she said bitterly, turning away to hide her distress.

He stood and touched her arm. "Genny, I know that something's frightened you. But for your own sake, consider Lord Neville's proposal. I'm sure today he's repentant. Your innocence makes you blind to a man's passions."

Shamed color flooded her cheeks. After last night, she was innocent no more. But her voice remained steady, even as wretchedness weighted her belly. "Lord Neville attacked me. I won't overlook that for the sake of your comfort." She steeled herself to say what she should have said long ago. "And I'll no longer let you claim credit for my work."

Her father snatched his hand away and retreated. "What is this? You're getting above yourself, my girl. You've been an able assistant, but purely an assistant."

She jerked her head up and stared at him. The morning light through the window lay plain on his face. He looked tired, petulant, and completely sure of himself. She'd long ago accepted that fundamentally he was weak and self-centered. But this denial tested the boundaries of credulity. In the last five years, the vicar hadn't written one published word. Even commissions to authenticate some item or confirm an obscure piece of family history had been her work.

The tantamount importance of her article about the Harmsworth Jewel had never been so clear. How glad she was that she'd kept the truth about the artifact to herself. She needed to establish her academic reputation. And she needed to do it soon.

"I've been more than an assistant," she said shakily.

Her father's jaw set in an obstinate line. "Years ago Lord Neville approached me about making you his wife. I should have arranged the wedding before pride gained this hold over you. You've become arrogant, Genevieve, and rebellious. Remember what we both owe Neville Fairbrother."

Bile rose in her throat. Her father resented her upsetting his cozy world. He'd forgive her if she allowed everything to continue as before. No, even worse, he'd forgive her if she bolstered the lies about his work and married Lord Neville.

She'd rather die.

Richard awoke to shadows and the unmistakable aroma of horses. The bed beneath him was unaccountably hard and rough beams supported the ceiling above his head. He blinked, sneezed and wondered where the hell he was.

Immediately he remembered. Bundling his coat into a makeshift pillow, he'd slept in the vicarage stables. Even with Cam's footmen on watch, he couldn't leave Genevieve unguarded. Then the night's exertions had taken their toll and he'd nodded off, bugger it.

"Who's there?" a husky voice asked.

He recalled now what had disturbed him. A woman's

crying. Fierce concern banished all drowsiness. He rolled onto his side in his dark corner of the loft and discovered Genevieve huddled against the far wall.

"Genevieve? What's the matter?" He rose into a crouch, struggling to see her. Sun forced its way through the cracks in the boards, but he discerned little beyond her outline. She curled into the wall with her knees raised and her shoulders slumped forward.

She stiffened and hunched away. "What are you doing here?" she asked, the snap failing to mask her voice's rawness.

His lovely girl was crying as if her heart broke. Over what he'd done last night? The thought winded him.

"I slept here last night." He stood and stretched tight muscles. "I meant to stay awake to make sure you were safe."

"But you didn't." She sounded bitter and unhappy.

"I'd have heard if there was trouble." As he brushed away the straw clinging to him, he hoped to God that was true. Desperate not to scare her into scarpering, he strolled across to the narrow window and pushed the shutters open. The sun was high in the sky. Sweet air flooded the loft, dissipating the equine tang.

He turned back to Genevieve. Even with the window open, it was difficult to see. He could just make out the discoloration on her cheek where Fairbrother had hit her. Richard tamped down his fury at the sight.

He shrugged with assumed carelessness. "If you and I were alone in the house with only Dorcas as chaperone, it would look bad."

Her wariness was so powerful, it felt like a physical presence. "As if you care."

He frowned. "Of course I care." More than she knew, although after their quarrel, now wasn't the time to declare his feelings. He sucked in a breath redolent of hay dust and warm air and sneezed again. "That covers why I'm in this deuced inconvenient rat hole. What's your excuse?"

"I don't want to talk to you," she said sullenly, raising one unsteady hand to brush away her tears.

"Too bad," he said easily, dropping to sit beside her. The urge to take her into his arms gnawed, but after last night, he was uncertain about touching her. It was patently obvious that she was still furious. Rightly so, he reluctantly admitted.

"Leave me alone," she muttered, burying her head in the arms she propped on her knees.

"No," he said in the same pleasant tone. He rubbed his hand over his bristly jaw. He needed a wash and a shave. He needed a clear conscience. None were likely to come his way in the next little while. "Tell me why you're crying."

"I don't have to tell a liar and a fraud anything. If you had the sensitivity of a...a brick, you'd go away. Far, far away."

He winced at her description. But how could he leave her when she was unhappy? Her tears made him feel like she peeled his skin away an inch at a time.

Still pretending serenity, he stretched his legs out and propped his bare shoulders against the roof sloping behind them. Light was dim in this corner. Which was undoubtedly why she'd chosen it. He sneezed again. All this movement kicked up a devil of a dust storm. "I'm a blockhead of a man, my darling. No sensitivity at all."

She glared at him out of eyes swimming with tears. "I hate you."

His heart clenched into an excruciating fist, but he made himself sound calm, uninvolved. "I'm sure I deserve it. Did I make you cry?"

"As if you could."

The temper narrowing her eyes was an improvement. His

lips stretched in a wry smile. "That's a relief." He paused. "If not me, who?"

With her hair covered in dust and cobwebs and her face stained with tears, she seemed heartbreakingly young. He had a glimpse of the child Genevieve, mourning her mother in the hidden temple. She'd have been a difficult girl, curious, intelligent, prickly. Adorable.

She scowled. "Why don't you mind your own business?"

"Where's the fun in that?" He dared to tug a wisp of hay from her untidy hair. He was a scoundrel to find encouragement when she accepted the intimacy. "You may as well tell me. I'm not going anywhere until you do."

Briefly he thought she might resist. After all, they were both aware that he had no real claim on her. Resentment firmed her jaw, offset by her mouth's vulnerable softness. "My father wants me to marry Lord Neville."

"Like hell he does!" Richard stared at her, too disgusted to be angry, although anger lurked close.

"I told him to ban Fairbrother from the house." Hopelessness glazed her eyes.

She looked so alone. Genevieve against the world. Richard longed to stand as her champion. But to his regret, his lies made the offer unconscionable. She wouldn't believe him anyway.

"So he should. What about the abduction?"

Her delicate throat moved as she swallowed. "Apparently I exaggerate."

Richard began to stand. "I'll tell him exactly what happened. He can't keep living in Cloud Cuckoo Land. You're not safe as long as Fairbrother's got the run of the house."

She grabbed his arm, dragging him down again. "No."

Despite his wish to play the gallant protector, he was only human. Her touch shuddered through him like lightning.

"He won't listen to me because he knows I'm not Christopher Evans?"

She shook her head and her hand tightened around his bare bicep. Dear God, how he wished he'd rescued his shirt last night. Sitting here half-naked gave him too many ideas. "I didn't tell him who you are. He's had so many shocks lately."

Just like Genevieve to consider the old man's feelings, no matter how badly he'd treated her. Richard's shoulders relaxed with ill-deserved relief. He'd assumed that today the vicar would show him the door and he'd have to scuttle back to Leighton Court.

"Then why can't I add my account?" How it must chafe that her father wouldn't accept her word. Or perhaps the old reprobate did, but refused to jeopardize his comfort.

She blushed and looked away, releasing him, although the imprint of her fingers lingered like a brand. His gut knotted when he realized that she was deathly ashamed. "He might wonder what we got up to last night."

Privately Richard thought the selfish old haddock wouldn't care what his daughter did as long as it didn't affect his convenience. "I gave one of Cam's footmen a note for the duke, saying that if the vicar asked, I returned to Leighton Court and you slept at the vicarage. It was the best I could do to save your reputation."

She didn't look particularly reassured as she faced him directly. "I wish you'd go. I'll never sell you the jewel. You destroyed any chance of charming it away from me last night."

He gave a huff of hollow laughter. God help him, he'd moved way beyond conniving to obtain the jewel. Right now, he'd happily fling the blasted gewgaw into Sedgemoor's pond and applaud as it disappeared into the mud. It had caused nothing but trouble.

"I won't leave you unprotected," he said flatly.

"I've got my gun."

"With you now?"

"No."

"I've got mine. Fairbrother won't catch me napping."

"I did."

"I know," he said glumly, folding his arms over his upraised knees.

To his dismay, tears welled in her eyes once more. She leaned away to hide her loss of control, but not quickly enough.

"Darling, I hate to see you cry," he said helplessly. He reached for her, then pulled back. He'd scuppered all chance of mercy the moment he'd admitted his identity.

"Leave me alone." The hands over her face muffled her voice.

"Genevieve, I'll fix everything." He hoped like hell he wasn't lying again.

Her shoulders heaved and a strangled sob escaped. She wriggled away, but he had her boxed against the angled roof. He stared at her in despair. London lauded his social adroitness, yet he blundered around Genevieve like an elephant in a peony garden. No wonder she couldn't stand a bar of him.

Another sob. Her head bent and her nape under the untidy chignon seemed heartbreakingly vulnerable. She was a strong, determined woman, but right now she looked as fragile as glass.

Hesitantly, knowing she despised everything about him, he cupped that warm, smooth skin under the line of hair. Automatically, he stroked her, soothing her much as he'd soothe Hecuba.

Her breath hitched. He waited for her to wrench away.

She stiffened. Preparing to reject him, he guessed.

Oh, well, he'd asked for it. He couldn't accuse her of leading him on. She'd made it perfectly clear that she wanted him to leave the barn. Then preferably leave her life altogether.

Her muscles bunched under his hand. Would this be the last time he touched her? The prospect shriveled his heart like a grape in the desert sun. Touching her was life to him. The greatest punishment she could inflict was to send him away.

He struggled to imprint this moment on his memory. The warm autumn sunlight limning her with gold. The flaxen tumble of hair. The soft skin under his palm. The faint scent of flowers and Genevieve.

He'd never forget her. He'd love her till he died.

She made a strangled sound, then shifted. Not away but forward. A drift of hay, a scrabble of limbs, a twist of her body and two arms lashed around him as if expecting protest.

Protest? Not in this life. He was in heaven.

"My darling…" he choked out and caught her against him.

Chapter Twenty-Eight

G enevieve was in trouble. Worse trouble than the madness of again surrendering to this man. Even when she'd been so angry with him that she'd wanted to shoot him where he stood, leaving Richard last night had been like hacking off a limb. Now that he held her, she felt whole again. It didn't matter that he'd lied. It didn't matter that he stayed for his own purposes and his purposes promised grief for Genevieve Barrett.

Those things should matter, but when he wrapped his arms around her as if he'd readily defy the world for her sake, she couldn't make them matter. She was a lost cause.

She was about to become more lost.

Frantically she stretched up, rising awkwardly on her knees. She mashed her mouth against his. Last night when she'd marched away, she'd told herself she never wanted to kiss him again. That proud resolution crumbled to dust mere hours later. He tried to jerk free, but she grabbed his shoulders to keep him near.

"Genevieve, you don't want this. You hate me, remember?"

"I hate you," she growled, straining against the hands holding her away.

This close, his features were out of focus, making it impossible to read his expression. But she could smell his arousal. Before last night, she couldn't have identified that hot scent, but now, she recognized that his hunger matched hers.

His voice was hoarse. "I'm that odious rascal Richard Harmsworth. I'm the man you wished to Hades last night."

"I still wish you to Hades." She did, as long as he took her with him.

"Then why are you touching me?" His voice vibrated with wild despair as his hands kneaded her arms.

"Don't you want me to touch you?"

"I don't want you to hate me more than you do."

He'd resisted last night—at least at first. Then, as now, he'd struggled to act with honor. The thought shuddered through her, made her realize that he wasn't a complete swine. Of course he wasn't. He'd saved her from Lord Neville, and she was almost sure he'd done it with no ulterior motive. Then he'd tried to return her safely to the vicarage.

The chink of light in his dark, dark soul made her more determined than ever. "You talk too much."

Triumph surged as his resistance faltered. Not that he'd pushed back very hard. He groaned, then kissed her as if he'd die if he stopped. His mouth was searing, heavy, ruthless. None of last night's control. He seized her in his arms and rolled her over into the soft hay. Dust flew around them, catching shafts of sunlight until it was like being trapped inside the Harmsworth Jewel.

She closed her eyes in elation. How heady to have this powerful, sophisticated man mad for her. His weight anchored her, placed her in the world as nothing else did. Her misery receded. Her anger too. With Richard, with Lord Neville, with her father.

His shaking hands brushed aside her bodice. He plucked at her nipples, shooting hot arousal to her belly, making her moan. He rose above her, shoving her skirts up and stroking her thighs.

Her hands were busy too. Rediscovering the hard pads of muscle on his back, the ladder of his spine, the sinewy shoulders. Thank heaven he wasn't wearing a shirt. She thought she'd etched every detail into her mind, but each touch felt like exploring a new country. She bowed toward him, kissing his chest, tasting him, lingering over his nipples when he hissed in pleasure.

Daringly she ran her hand across the hard plain of his stomach to where he swelled against his trousers. Automatically her hand cupped his thickness. His response was a shuddering groan.

She opened her eyes. He angled above her, leaning to one side to keep his weight off her. His face was stark with desire. His jaw clenched hard and his eyes were black with need. Without conscious decision, she rubbed him, marveling at his heat.

He felt so large. How on earth had he fit inside her?

The memory of him pressing into her built anticipation. Clumsily she tugged at his trousers. A button ripped and rolled into the hay. Finally she found his pulsing rod. He groaned again and jerked his hips forward.

"Show me what to do," she said in a strained voice.

His hand covered hers to demonstrate the action. He felt marvelous. Satiny skin over iron. Hot. Vital. He caught her hand and brought it to his lips. With breathtaking deftness, he untied her drawers. She wriggled to help him. What point coyness? She wanted him more than she had last night.

Finally, finally, he touched her sex. She gasped at the liquid surge of need. The wild ride began. As she tilted her hips toward his hand, he withdrew.

"Richard?" she asked uncertainly.

The skin stretched tight over his face. His hair flopped across his forehead, lending him an uncharacteristically vulnerable air. "I can't wait," he gritted out.

"I don't want you to." Right now, she felt like his equal, not his dupe.

"You deserve better." Beneath desire, she heard anguish. As though he hated himself for what he did.

"Probably." Despite her urgency, a tremulous smile curved her lips. He was a better man than she gave him credit for. Better than he gave himself credit for, she came to understand. She ran one hand down his face, his beard bristling beneath her palm. She hoped he wouldn't recognize the gesture's poignant tenderness. His eyes changed, focused, lost their blind black sheen. She suspected something in him responded to her yearning.

She opened to him. "But the unfortunate truth is that you're the one I want."

"I won't let you down," he groaned, moving over her.

"Don't make promises you can't keep," she taunted, trailing her hands down his bare back. She dug her fingers hard into his firm buttocks, coaxing him to initiate that dazzling dialogue of pressure and power.

Genevieve was wet and hot. Richard glided into her with delicious ease. Last night, he'd feared hurting her. Now they moved together as if created for this dance. Her muscles tightened and she arched up with a sigh that sounded like perfect happiness. That soft huff of surrender wrote itself on his heart like an inscription in stone. Last night, she'd been miraculous. Right now, as he plunged deep, love transformed him. He'd never be the same again.

He retreated, relishing how she clung. He thrust again. Her gasps of pleasure set his blood swirling. A wave of need overwhelmed what shreds of control he retained. He closed his eyes, rose on his hands, and drove her hard. He knew he was a barbarian. But the compulsion to claim this woman in the most primitive way soared beyond kindness or consideration.

He wouldn't last. He knew he wouldn't. The threat of leaving her unsatisfied beat like a curse. But he couldn't stop. Then as blackness smashed against the back of his eyes, she gave a sharp cry and convulsed.

He braced every muscle against his deepest instincts and prepared to pull out. Through the thunder in his head and the agony in his balls, he knew that he couldn't risk a child as he had so recklessly last night. He straightened his arms to rigidity and inhaled roughly, swearing he wouldn't lose himself, he wouldn't lose himself.

She tilted her head back and opened her eyes, staring at him with such joy that his heart cramped. She clenched around him in a burst of heat, fingers clawing at his shoulders, bare breasts straining above her bodice. Her lips parted, revealing small white teeth and the mysterious interior of her mouth.

Her generosity sliced through his scruples like a knife through butter. He groaned in self-loathing, then again in endless satisfaction as he ceded the battle and flooded her with his essence.

He rolled onto his back, still inside her. With a sigh of repletion, he encircled her with his arms. Briefly he basked in the illusion that nothing could part them. Her breasts flattened into his chest and her hair flowed around him like tangled silk. Sunbeams through the rafters highlighted the rich color. She was a golden girl, gold to the bone. More precious than the tawdry jewel that had lured him here. She felt as fragile and graceful as a reed, as strong and brave as a lioness.

He closed his eyes and waited for his heart's headlong gallop to slow. Making love to Genevieve was an all-encompassing experience. She left no atom of body or soul untouched.

She stirred, disturbing his blissful doze. He firmed his grip. He didn't want her to move. He didn't want her to talk. Not when she was sure to remind him of the barriers separating them, rather than how sweet it was to lie together. He held the woman he loved while the unknowing world went on its way, unaware that this loft encompassed paradise.

The unknowing world…

What was he doing? He ought to be bloody horsewhipped.

"Sweetheart, wake up," he hissed, shifting to his side. He missed the connection the instant it was broken.

"What?" she asked huskily, brushing her hair away from her face with a sensual gesture that made the rake inside him want to tumble her back into the hay. "What is it?"

"We're in your father's barn," he whispered urgently.

"I know we are." She frowned as though questioning his sanity.

"What if someone comes in? Or heard us?" A horrible presentiment struck him. "Where the hell is Williams?"

She rose on one elbow to study him. Her faint smile hinted that she discovered more of his secrets than he wanted her to. He'd also rather she pulled her bodice into place. Otherwise she risked another swiving, Williams or no Williams.

"He's teaching George to ride," she said calmly. "They'll be outside at least until noon."

That meant nothing to Richard. He'd woken, he'd seen Genevieve, and he'd lunged. He had no idea what time it was. Struggling to his feet, he closed his trousers with all the aplomb of a schoolboy.

Genevieve, what a wreck you make of this particular rake. And you don't even know the power you wield.

Although another glance at her expression indicated that if she didn't know yet, she would soon. The glint in her eyes looked discomfitingly like mockery. As if she found his flutterings and fussings deeply amusing. "Worried about your reputation, Sir Richard?"

"I'm worried about yours, my girl," he snapped. He prowled across to the crumpled black rag that had once been his coat. His valet would have a fit if he saw what became of the exquisite tailoring.

Richard picked up the coat and shrugged it across his shoulders, knowing he must look like a beggar. He tugged his watch from his pocket. Relief weakened his knees. It was only half past ten.

"How sweet," she said softly.

"Sweet?" Growling, he swung toward her.

She sat up and, luckily for his self-control, restored her bodice. He told his stirring cock that under no circumstances would he tumble her again. Not when he risked an almighty scandal.

She still watched him with that quizzical expression that made him want to smash something. "Yes, sweet."

He stalked across to her, hands opening and closing at his sides. "I'm many things, madam. Never sweet."

"Stop scowling and kiss me." She caught one painfully tight fist.

Bewildered he stared down, even as his tension ebbed. He didn't understand what was happening, but one thing was clear—she didn't hate him anymore. "You're not angry."

Her lips twisted. "I'm not sure I'd go that far."

He sighed and let her draw him down beside her. "Why the hell do you want to kiss a man who's lied to you?"

"I'm insane." She leaned forward in encouragement.

He caught her chin and held her still. She closed her eyes, looking like a little girl awaiting a treat. His heart filled with tenderness so profound, it hurt. Gently he explored her mouth and received in reward a drift of honey through his soul. When he raised his head, the world seemed a glorious place.

Slowly she opened her eyes. "See? Sweet."

He growled again, but his heart really wasn't in proving himself king of the beasts. "You know nothing about men, Miss Barrett."

"I think—" Her shyness contrasted beautifully with burgeoning assurance. "I think that while I mightn't know anything about men, I'm coming to know something about you."

"I thought I was a villain and you never wished to see me again."

He should hustle her from the stables, but curiosity delayed him. His hand traced the shoulder under her sagging bodice, down her arm to her hand. He had a horrible inkling that anyone who saw him holding hands with Genevieve would concur with her assessment. Right now, he *was* sweet, confound it. If she wanted to punish him, this vulnerability was the punishment of the damned.

His voice lowered into seriousness. "I deserve your anger."

"You do." She responded with characteristic candor. "But you're not utterly irredeemable. And you kiss like an angel."

Like an angel? He barely resisted the impulse to preen like a blasted peacock. He arched his brows. "Just kiss?"

She blushed. What an intriguing mixture of inexperience and sensuality she was. "And other things. Stop cadging compliments."

He shrugged, then voiced the nagging question. "Why did you just give yourself to me, Genevieve?"

Chapter Twenty-Nine

As the silence extended, Richard's expression resumed the affability that he raised against the world. Genevieve was shocked to realize that somewhere in their tumultuous interactions, she'd peered beneath the mask. The perception was reassuring, fortifying her instinct that despite his lies, she'd glimpsed the true Richard Harmsworth.

"Forgive me. I have no right to ask." His grip on her hand loosened.

Curse him, she didn't want him to release her. She wanted him to hold her close forever. It terrified her to the bone quite how much she wanted him to stay.

"You push and push," she said resentfully. "Then when I cooperate, you question me."

She could hardly accept that she'd become a fallen woman, let alone put it into words. Last night, she could blame her recklessness on heightened emotions after the abduction. This morning, she'd had no excuse but lust.

"Because you push back. You were livid last night."

"I was." In the last hour, she'd accepted that while he'd

undoubtedly deceived her, he'd intended her no harm. If he had, she couldn't have thrown herself at him as she had.

Lowering her head, she studied her fingers curled around his, paler, smoother than his tanned skin. Something about the capable elegance of Sir Richard's hand made her feel safe and...loved.

Dear God, she really was in trouble.

He cupped her jaw, tilting her face until she met his eyes. His dark blue gaze was steady and concerned and made her feel like the only woman in the world. Stupid, stupid, stupid. But still she couldn't shake the impression. He looked like someone she could trust.

Could she?

"You no longer believe I pursue you for the jewel?" he asked softly.

She was now convinced that his desire at least had always been honest. "Perhaps at first."

He still looked troubled. "No, you were always the prize. Now I've ruined you." To her regret, he slid away, disturbing a cloud of dust.

She felt on stronger ground here. It saved her from admitting how she yearned for him. "You tried to do the right thing."

His laugh was bitter. "Much good that did me. I can't resist you."

She looked away. "As I can't resist you," she confessed.

When he didn't jump on her, she was almost disappointed. Heavens, she really took to vice with gusto.

After a taut silence, he sighed. "Aren't we a pair?"

If only they were.

Surely he wouldn't stay in Little Derrick. He must have duties and obligations, not to mention the fashionable world clamoring for his return. A fashionable world closed to a bluestocking with no connections, no fortune, and no polish. A fashionable world adorned with women who had shared his bed and women who would share his bed. The idea of those trollops touching Richard made her itch to scratch their eyes out. And there was that wife of perfect pedigree that he sought, according to the papers.

Her fingers formed talons in her crumpled skirt. She had no rights over Richard. But that didn't stop her heart screaming "He's mine" when she contemplated anyone else sharing those breathtaking intimacies.

And not just physical intimacies. She didn't want him sharing private jokes. She didn't want him studying another woman with that sweet, intense concentration. The same sweet, intense concentration he devoted to her now.

She was a jealous, possessive shrew. So much for proud independence. He'd forsake her for his real life. And she'd miss him forever, curse him.

"I could have made you pregnant," he said grimly.

A baby would cause such problems, she couldn't bear the thought. Which made her recent activities rash to the point of lunacy. But regret and fear seemed so distant when her body still quaked from his possession. "Can we cross that bridge when we come to it?"

Surprisingly he laughed. "What a pragmatic creature you are."

The comment sounded like a compliment rather than criticism. Still, thinking of blue-blooded brides, she prickled. "You must be used to more sophisticated company."

He caught each hand and kissed her knuckles with a tenderness that eased the ache in her heart, without banishing it. "You're more fun."

"Fun?" Her mouth dropped open with astonishment.

"You're the most interesting girl I've ever met."

"You can't—"

Below, the door squeaked. There was a sharp bark. Sirius.

Before she could react, Richard launched himself over her, rolling her into the hay. He pressed into her back, his heart banging against her. His breath moved the loose hair at her temple. Dread tightened every muscle to the point of pain. Her nose smashed against the dusty floor. She closed her eyes and prayed she wouldn't sneeze.

Lemon verbena flooded her senses, headier than wine. Especially mixed with the salty musk of sexual satisfaction. She shifted surreptitiously, bumping her hips against Richard, and he groaned in her ear.

"Behave yourself," he hissed. "If they find us, there's the devil to pay."

"You did well, lad," Williams said. The groom stood directly below. All urge to tease disintegrated.

With the soft clop of hooves, George led her old pony inside. These days Lightning didn't justify the name. "Thank you, Mr. Williams. When can we go again?"

Bubbling happiness rang in the boy's voice. She felt Richard smile against her cheek. In that moment, she gave up pretending to possess a scrap of sense where he was concerned. She'd fallen utterly in love with him. The emotion had been present so long that she didn't know where it started. Perhaps right back when he'd locked her up, then wandered off whistling.

She was hopelessly in love with Christopher Evans. She was hopelessly in love with Richard Harmsworth. She was hopelessly in love, and she had no idea what to do about it.

Luckily Williams chose to escort his pupil home, leaving the stables to Sirius, the horses and two miscreants in the loft.

When Richard was sure the barn was empty and likely to

stay that way, he rolled off Genevieve with a muffled groan. All that proximity had tested his control and he was as hard as an oak staff. The last few moments confirmed, as if he hadn't always known, what risks he took tumbling Genevieve. Risks he couldn't countenance if he made the smallest claim to honor.

Slowly she sat up and a pang of concern penetrated his sexual frustration. He stared up at her. "I'm sorry. I squashed you."

Her lush mouth curved into a smile that sent another jolt of hunger through him. "Actually it was rather . . . enjoyable."

"You're a tease, Miss Barrett." He stood and extended his hand.

"You're leading me astray." Once upright, she patted and straightened her skirts. She wasted her time. With her loose hair, creased clothing, and indefinable air of fulfillment, she looked thoroughly tupped.

Dear God, what he'd give to have her again. Lying over her, he hadn't been able to think beyond her accessibility. The merest hitch of her skirts and he'd take her from behind. She'd squirm deliciously and make those luscious sounds that became more addictive than brandy to a drunkard.

He stifled the urge to keep her here. They'd already had one close call. He couldn't chance another. He led her toward the edge. "I'll go first and make sure it's safe."

When Richard set foot on the ladder, Sirius barked and trotted forward. "Quiet, you blockhead."

As if the dog understood—Richard wasn't entirely convinced that he didn't—he sat on his haunches as his master descended.

"Stay there. I'll check outside," he called to Genevieve, who peeped down, thick golden hair framing her face.

His heart turned over. If he'd been close enough to haul

her into his arms, she wouldn't be going anywhere until tomorrow morning. If then. Prudence be damned.

Sirius watched with cool consideration. He shot the hound a quelling glare. "Mind your manners."

"What did you say?" Genevieve asked from above.

"Nothing," he muttered.

After checking the stable yard, he returned to the ladder. "Nobody's around. Can we get back into the house without being seen?"

"I hope so. I can't stay up here forever."

How he wished she could. How he wished he could stay with her. She descended as he held the ladder steady. He couldn't help regretting that she'd put her drawers on.

She glanced down with laughing disapproval. "Stop looking up my skirt."

"You have the most magnificent legs. It's a crime not to admire them."

She blushed. "Arrant nonsense."

He caught her round the waist and swung her to the floor. Then inevitably he kissed her. If she protested, he'd stop. Well, he'd consider it. But Genevieve, foolish woman she was, responded with a passion that set his blood rushing.

Eventually he raised his head. "We can't."

She was rosy and heavy-eyed, resting against him as if she had no thought of being anywhere else. "Will you come to the summerhouse tonight?"

He tightened his embrace, basking in her lithe warmth. With her, the anger that had smoldered most of his life faded. Even vanished. With her, he was free as never before. "We're being reckless, my darling."

She tilted her head. "I've never been reckless before. I'm beginning to enjoy it."

"Only beginning?"

She laughed softly. "You're so conceited."

"With you in my arms, I feel like a god." He pretended to tease. Whereas the woeful truth was that she made him feel immortal. By Jove, if a dragon poked his scaly head through the barn door, Richard would repel the beast with his bare hands.

"Will you meet me?" Her smile faded, revealing a need that stoked his own.

His heart crashed hard against his ribs. He bent and kissed her quickly. Anything more and he'd let the world hang itself from the nearest tree while he bundled her up the ladder into the fragrant hay. "I can't stay away."

She stroked his beard-roughened cheek. "Good."

He smiled, loving her frank desire. Still he couldn't let her go. "First we must decide what to do about Fairbrother."

He loathed the way the swine's name stole the joy from her eyes. He took her hand and drew her toward the door, Sirius trotting behind. After the barn's dimness, the light outside was blinding. Richard squinted as he stepped into the yard. Sirius growled, low and menacing.

Genevieve released a horrified gasp. Richard's vision cleared. Hector Greengrass sauntered through the gate, beefy arms crossed over his barrel chest and a sneer on his thick lips.

Chapter Thirty

Mortification paralyzed Genevieve. She cursed herself for lingering in the loft.

"What the hell are you doing here?" Richard snarled. His grip on her hand tightened, as if to stop her running.

Greengrass's sneer deepened. "I work here."

"No, you don't," Genevieve snapped. "Neither you nor your vile master is welcome."

With a knowing leer, the thug cocked his hip in a relaxed pose. "I figure only Vicar can give me the sack." He sniggered. "Wonder how happy he'd be to know you two are so cozy. My, my, who'd think Dr. Barrett's stuck-up daughter was such a goer? You might want to get the straw out of your hair before the village ladies come to tea, Miss Barrett."

With an inarticulate exclamation, Richard released Genevieve and surged forward to plow his fist into Greengrass's self-satisfied face. The man gasped and staggered back.

"Fucking hell!" With impressive speed, Greengrass regained his balance and aimed one meaty fist at Richard's head.

"Richard, look out!" she screamed, lunging toward the two men.

Then she stopped, shocked and trembling, as she watched the man she'd once dismissed as a lightweight—intellectually, emotionally, and physically—dodge with a grace that lifted her heart. Greengrass's blow connected with air, sending him stumbling within Richard's reach.

Richard landed another punch, then another. Still Greengrass didn't fall, but his movements became sluggish as he lurched vainly after Richard.

"Stop your bloody dancing, you bastard," Greengrass demanded.

Blood trickled from his nose while Richard hardly broke a sweat. Despite his commanding manner with Lord Neville last night, Genevieve had never considered Richard a man of action. How wrong she'd been. She forgot her humiliation. She forgot her fear of scandal. She even forgot that if Greengrass gained the upper hand, unlikely as it seemed, he'd turn on her.

Instead she clung to the barn's doorframe and watched in speechless admiration as Richard Harmsworth, the famous dandy, demolished a man twice his weight. Richard's fighting technique was like ballet. Light. Sure. Devastating. In no time, Greengrass gasped like a landed mackerel, every strike swinging wild.

The fight didn't last long. A clean clip to the jaw finished Greengrass. The big man wavered, almost recovered. Then his eyes flickered shut and he slammed onto the cobblestones in an ignominious heap.

With one foot, Richard nudged Greengrass. When there was no reaction, he glanced at Genevieve. He shook his right hand, then lifted it to blow upon the knuckles. With his unshaven face and wearing only coat and trousers, he looked like a gorgeous ruffian. A golden gypsy prince. "The bugger has a jaw like iron."

Genevieve stepped forward. As she caught his scent, clean sweat and Richard, need tightened her belly. Watching the man she loved defending her honor stirred primal emotions. "You're magnificent."

To her surprise, he blushed. "Doing it too brown, darling."

She shook her head and cradled his poor bruised hand, wincing at the grazes across his knuckles. They must hurt, although nothing to compare to Greengrass's headache when he awoke. "How on earth did you do that? He never laid a finger on you."

Richard still looked uncomfortable. She cringed to realize that despite all her needling, he wasn't a vain man. He used his diamantine façade to keep the world at bay, but he had no personal conceit. It appalled her how much she, the supposedly clever Genevieve Barrett, had got wrong because she'd accepted appearances instead of probing deeper. She'd misjudged this complex, wonderful man so badly.

His lips took on a wry twist. "Good to think I didn't waste my time with Gentleman Jackson."

"You must be his star pupil." She kissed the torn skin.

"Careful, Genevieve," he said quickly. "Someone could see."

She made no attempt to conceal her craving. "I don't care."

His laugh held a hint of self-derision. "Good God, if only I'd known you'd look at me like that after I floored some unsuspecting chap. I'd have done it weeks ago."

"Don't joke. He could have killed you."

Richard cast an assessing glance at his fallen foe. "He's mostly fat once you get over his size. If he sat on me, he'd do serious damage. Otherwise I was pretty safe."

She didn't believe him for a moment. "You're too modest. I felt like a damsel in a legend."

"Casting me as St. George, Genevieve?"

She shrugged and released his hand. However much luring him back into the loft appealed, she reluctantly recognized that they'd taken too many chances. It was surprising that nobody had seen the fight. "If the armor fits."

He scooped a bucket of water from the horse trough and flung it over Greengrass. "Get up, you scum."

The man jerked upright, spluttering and shaking his head. "Fuck me dead!"

The curse emerged thickly through his torn mouth. With his good eye, he scowled at Richard with malevolent intensity. The other eye was swollen shut and turning purple.

Richard tossed the bucket to the cobblestones. "Get off this property. If I catch you here again, you'll suffer more than a good thrashing."

"You and whose army?" From his dirty puddle, Greengrass's bombast struck a false note.

"Get out. And tell your swine of a master that he's not welcome either."

Greengrass stumbled to unsteady feet. "His lordship won't take this lying down."

Richard's voice hardened. "Too bad."

Greengrass cast a salacious glance at Genevieve. "Aye, I'll go. But wait till his lordship hears how Miss High-and-Mighty Barrett is spreading her legs."

She flushed but refused to cower. Richard took a threatening step toward Greengrass. "Unless you're gone in the next thirty seconds, I'll horsewhip you back to your master."

Sirius growled.

"Call off your mongrel," Greengrass snapped.

A daredevil smile curved Richard's mouth. Genevieve's

yen for him, barely restrained since the fight, surged anew and made her ache to take him into her body. Right now, she wanted to claim him as hers and to the devil with the world's disapproval.

"Sirius, chase," he said softly.

The dog bounded forward with a happy yip. Sirius was so well trained, he hadn't moved a muscle during the struggle.

"Bugger me!" Greengrass limped at a clumsy run toward the gate, Sirius worrying at his heels.

Richard bent over the trough and splashed his head and shoulders. When he looked up, dripping hair clung to his face. He smiled at Genevieve with that glowing fondness that always made her belly cramp with longing. "I doubt we'd pass muster at Almack's."

"I never aspired to elegance." She made herself smile back, but the reminder of his real life punctured her foolish hopes that he'd stay.

"I certainly did. I'd be tossed out of my clubs if they saw me now."

Richard's breathtaking display of skilled violence had fended off immediate danger, but other, long-term threats remained. Greengrass wouldn't hesitate to attack her reputation. She'd face scandal alone while Richard was far away in London. Choosing a diamond of the first water to marry, if Mrs. Meacham's magazines had it right.

Richard's lips quirked as he strolled forward, drops of water sparkling on his coat in the bright sunlight. Under the coat, ridges of muscle banded his bare torso. She should have realized long ago that his lean strength was handy for more than turning a lady's knees to custard.

"I think you look very nice," she whispered. As he approached, shyness gripped her. Which was insane, given what they'd done.

"Passion has turned your mind." He spoke lightly, but the hand that curled around the back of her head was hard and his kiss sizzled with a fierce possessiveness that made her shake. She'd loved his gentleness last night, but his ardor today thrilled her beyond imagining.

Far too soon, he raised his head. His tender smile threatened to make her even more besotted, curse the reprobate. "We're asking to become the talk of the town, standing here."

She curled her hands around his biceps, this time recognizing the power beneath the grubby superfine coat. She forced a practical tone. "We can use the elm to climb into my study. I hear that it's an effective way to break in."

His face lit with laughing admiration. "Only the best people arrive via the window," he said solemnly and extended his hand. "Come, Juliet. Let's get you onto your balcony."

While Genevieve slept upstairs, Richard commandeered the parlor to write to Cam, suggesting a meeting to plot Fairbrother's comeuppance. Apart from Dorcas, Richard and Genevieve were alone in the house. Daylight added a respectability that darkness lacked. The vicar called on a parishioner—and dodged his daughter—while Mrs. Warren visited Mrs. Garson. She hadn't wanted to leave her niece, until Richard had alerted her to the watching footmen.

Fairbrother should hang for attempted rape and kidnapping, but involving the law meant unavoidable scandal. Scandal already loomed too close. Greengrass wasn't well liked in the village, but his tales of Genevieve's fall from grace would find an avid audience.

The quiet afternoon shattered. Upstairs, glass smashed. Richard leaped to his feet and sprinted toward the noise before conscious thought kicked in. On the landing, his beloved hovered in front of her study.

"Are you all right?" He strode toward her.

"I was in my room." She turned to him, pale with fright. She wore her scholarly outfit, a pale blue muslin dress under a dauntingly efficient pinafore sewn with multiple pockets. "Someone's thrown a rock through the window."

"Come here." He opened his arms and as naturally as a snowdrop grew upward in spring, she flung herself at him, pressing her cheek to his heart. His poor, reckless, longing heart.

Too soon she withdrew and stared up at him. To his astonishment, he read trust in her eyes. He'd never imagined she'd look at him like this. Damn it, now that she did, he never wanted that radiance to fade. "I hate being on edge all the time. I hate being at the mercy of these thugs."

"We'll come through this." He glanced past her to the study. Shards of glass littered the threadbare carpet. His eyes sharpened. Perhaps this wasn't merely an act of wanton vandalism. There was a sheet of paper tied around the stone that had caused the damage. He moved past Genevieve and crunched across the glass to pick up the rock.

"What is it?" she asked, just behind him.

"Be careful. The glass could cut through your slippers," he said, even as he untied the string holding the note.

"What is it?" she repeated more urgently as he unfolded the crumpled sheet of paper.

Disbelieving fury set the words dancing before his eyes. "Fairbrother has Sirius. He'll shoot him unless you deliver the Harmsworth Jewel within the next half hour."

Chapter Thirty-One

Pulse skittering with nerves, Genevieve crept through the trees toward the ruined Cistercian Abbey that had once dominated Little Derrick. Her sweaty palm tightened around her pistol.

She'd expected shouting, but she only heard murmuring. Strangely that scared her more than raw aggression. Her belly clenched with trepidation. Not only because of Lord Neville's proximity, but because Richard wouldn't appreciate her going against his instructions.

He'd been adamant that he'd rescue Sirius alone. He'd refused to take the Harmsworth Jewel, although she'd begged him to carry it in case he needed to exchange it. Which if nothing else convinced her that somewhere during the last day she'd learned to trust him.

He seemed sure that a brace of pistols and self-assurance could vanquish Lord Neville. Genevieve wasn't so sure. Lord Neville now knew that Richard was handy in a fight, and despite his lordship's stipulations that Genevieve come alone, he must assume that she'd turn to last night's rescuer.

But with time so short, she couldn't persuade Richard to take her. Instead he'd sent her to alert the duke and Hillbrook. She'd found George and given him a note for Sedgemoor, then she'd rushed to this isolated spot.

She was terrified for Richard. Lord Neville had every advantage in this meeting. Well, every advantage save what she knew about the Harmsworth Jewel.

"...no jewel, no dog, I'm afraid."

Lord Neville's oily tones made her skin itch with loathing. Just seeing him took her back to those suffocating moments when he'd crushed her beneath him. She sneaked nearer, crouching behind a pile of stones.

"I haven't got the jewel." Richard sounded careless and confident. "It belongs to Miss Barrett."

She chanced a peek. Richard stood with his back to her while Lord Neville lounged against a lichened tomb, gun in hand. The scratches on his face stood out vividly, she noted with bloodthirsty satisfaction.

"Not for much longer." Lord Neville's other hand held Sirius on a short rope leash. Coarse twine bound the dog's muzzle shut. Even from yards away, Genevieve saw dried blood marking his hide. Pity welled in her throat.

"Just what have we here?"

Rough hands seized her from behind and hauled her to her feet. Greengrass shook her like Sirius would shake a rabbit. She struggled to aim her pistol, but he plucked it from her with a painful wrench to her wrist.

Self-disgust held her mute. She was so cursed stupid. She should have guessed Lord Neville's henchman would be on guard.

"Genevieve!" Through her horror, she heard the despairing anger in Richard's voice. Why, oh, why had she come? He'd warned her to stay away.

Lord Neville regarded her with a complete lack of surprise as Greengrass dragged her kicking and fighting into the clearing.

"Ah, I thought you might join us," Lord Neville said archly.

"Be still, you little bitch." Greengrass flung her down. She cried out as she crashed into the grass. Just beyond reach, she saw Richard's guns on the ground.

Richard helped her up. "Are you all right?"

"Careful," Greengrass grunted, his face a rainbow of bruises.

"Don't touch your weapons, Evans," Lord Neville said behind her. "That would be very unwise. Especially now that I have two hostages."

Genevieve stared at Richard, despising her impulsiveness. "I'm so sorry."

"We'll be fine," he said softly, his grip on her hand firming.

Genevieve found her balance and turned to Lord Neville. Sirius strained choking at the rope. "I'll give you the jewel. Let Sirius go."

"Here, hold the mongrel." Lord Neville thrust the leash at Greengrass.

"Genevieve, don't do this." Richard shifted to stop her approaching Lord Neville.

Evading him, she fumbled in her pocket. When all was said and done, the jewel was only metal and glass. It wasn't worth blood. "I have to."

"I knew you were a sensible woman." With sickening greed, Lord Neville's eyes fastened on the object in her palm.

"You won't have it for long," she retorted. "I'll report the theft."

He sniffed contemptuously. "I'm a Fairbrother. Nobody will believe I stole it."

"They will when you display your ill-gotten gains."

"You mistake the collector's passion. The joy is in ownership." He grabbed the jewel as if afraid she still meant to keep it. "This perfect object belongs with me. Unlike its slut of a custodian."

"Mind your tongue, sir," Richard said sharply, shifting toward Genevieve. His protection sparked a tiny ember of warmth, even in this fraught moment. "Last night you wanted to marry the lady."

"Marry that round-heeled trull?" Lord Neville's eyes glittered with malice, while Greengrass's snicker made her gorge rise. "The trollop fucked a scoundrel instead of accepting my honorable offer."

"Abduction and assault don't count as an honorable offer," she snapped, even as shame speared her.

Lord Neville's expression settled into a smugness that made her wish she'd clawed his eyes out, not merely bloodied his cheek. "It's more of a proposal than you've received from this knave, I'll warrant."

Her heart leaped to think that Richard might claim her. Although surely the magnificent Sir Richard Harmsworth would never stoop to wed a dowdy vicar's daughter with an unfeminine interest in people dead before 1600.

"Enough." Richard's voice was a whiplash. "You've got the jewel. I want my dog and I want you away from Little Derrick."

Genevieve's surge of illogical, irresistible hope shriveled. How stupid to expect a declaration. Especially at such a time.

Mesmerized, Lord Neville studied the jewel. "It's exquisite."

"A fine example," she said coldly.

He looked up, eyes gleaming with triumph. "Better you'd taken the money."

She ignored his jeering. "Untie Sirius and let us go."

Lord Neville's hand closed around the jewel. "That's not convenient."

"Not convenient?" A quick glance at Richard revealed no shock on his face. He'd expected double dealing. She was a fool that she hadn't.

Suddenly Lord Neville's cool response to her threats of exposure struck her as ominous. Fairbrother or not, if she alerted the law, he couldn't be sure of emerging with reputation intact. A premonition of disaster pressed down and she edged closer to Richard.

"As you pointed out, you and your lover can cause me a deal of trouble. Easier by far to dispose of you."

"What...what do you mean?" she asked shakily. Richard's hand gripped hers. While she knew he couldn't save them, the contact was welcome.

"Genevieve, Genevieve, I really will consider your cleverness overrated if you can't work out that it's better for me if you two are dead."

"You mean to kill us?"

Disbelief overwhelmed her. She realized that Lord Neville was base. Good heavens, hadn't he attacked her last night? But staring into his self-satisfied face, she couldn't help remembering how he'd been a guest in her house, eaten at her table, praised her work. The idea that someone she knew planned to shoot her left her staggering.

"Not in so many words." He waved the gun at them. "If you please?"

Richard's hold firmed in silent reassurance. Because she couldn't think how to defy the fate bearing down upon them, she walked with him toward the chapel's east end. Ahead rose empty stone tracery that had once contained glorious stained glass.

Genevieve stopped, astonished. The stone altar, worn and covered in lichen, had shifted to reveal a gaping hole beneath.

"Move." Lord Neville's gun poked her in the kidneys.

"How—"

"You never guessed that the altar covered the crypt's entrance, did you?" he scoffed. "I found the abbey papers in my nephew's library."

"You're not going to shoot us?" Richard asked steadily.

Lord Neville shook his head. "Too quick and easy. The altar can only be moved from above. Once down there, you're caged like rats until you starve or suffocate."

"People will look for us." Blind terror overcame Genevieve at the prospect of being buried alive.

Lord Neville smiled. "No, they won't. You two are the talk of the village. When I announce that I saw you eloping on the north road, nobody will doubt my story."

"Aye." Greengrass dragged a stiff-legged Sirius toward the crypt. "Every bugger knows you're gagging for it."

Genevieve muffled a sound of distress. Lying in Richard's arms, she'd felt brave and strong. Listening to Lord Neville and Greengrass, she felt dirty.

"You have no need to be ashamed, Genevieve," Richard said softly.

But the truth was that she did. She'd given herself to a man outside wedlock. She'd die at Lord Neville's hands with that stain on her name.

Pride bolstered failing defiance. "I regret nothing."

Lord Neville laughed. "You will before you're done."

"What about Sirius?" Richard asked.

Lord Neville shrugged. "I could shoot him here. Seems kinder."

"Don't," Richard snapped.

"For you, dear sir, I make the concession." He pointed the gun toward the descending staircase. "Pray take your places."

As if his thoughts were written on a parchment, she watched Richard consider throwing himself at Lord Neville. But with him unarmed, Genevieve's presence made heroics too risky. Again she berated herself for following him.

With a grace that made her heart dip in admiration, he stepped over the stone rim and onto the descending staircase. As calmly as if he asked her to dance, he extended his hand. "Come, Genevieve."

"With pleasure," she responded steadily.

Surprisingly she meant it. While her response to Lord Neville had been pure bravado, she realized that at this moment, she didn't regret a second of what she'd done with Richard. She'd acted out of love.

There were worse epitaphs.

Perhaps they'd win through. It was impossible to see Richard standing tall and steadfast, staring at her as if she carried the moon in her hands, and accept that Lord Neville had prevailed.

No, they weren't beaten yet. And something in Richard's eyes told her that right now, he considered her the best companion a man could have in adversity. His unconditional belief made her straighten and step forward. She couldn't disappoint him by playing the coward.

His hand closed around hers and he helped her onto the worn stone steps, letting her enter the crypt first. She had a second to take in a cavernous space lined with stone tombs. Then with a scrabble of paws, Sirius tumbled after her.

"I wish you peaceful rest," Lord Neville taunted from above.

The sharp report of a pistol made her jump. Greengrass marking his triumph, she guessed. With a loud scrape, the stone shifted, narrowing the light to nothing. Thick darkness slammed down, heavy with the stink of dust and ancient misery.

Chapter Thirty-Two

A bove them, warm autumn lingered. Down here in the dark, it was permanent winter. From the base of the stairs, Genevieve heard Richard murmuring reassurance to a whimpering Sirius. The mere sound of his voice rescued her plummeting spirits. Her crippling horror of suffocation receded. Panic constricted her lungs, not lack of air.

She fumbled toward the nearest tomb. The stone she sat on was cold and she shifted, seeking a more forgiving position. There wasn't one. The blackness seemed infinite, beyond possibility of light, like a living, malevolent entity. Something brushed her nape and she shivered. It was probably only a stray drift of air, but she felt as jumpy as a cat in a thunderstorm. She was a scholar and a skeptic, yet in this charnel house, malicious ghosts seemed to ogle her.

She shuddered. She didn't want to die in the cold and dark.

"I sent George to the duke with a note." Guilt stabbed her anew. She shouldn't have come. Alone, Richard might have escaped.

"Cam will look for us, then." His voice sounded odd. Thin. A trick of acoustics, she supposed.

But the duke didn't know about the crypt beneath the altar. Nobody did. Fear wedged in her belly, along with bleak awareness that this underground chamber would likely become their grave. Air seemed short again.

She shook her head to banish discomfiting thoughts and fiddled in her pocket. Within moments, frail light bloomed. Choking dread receded into the endless emptiness surrounding them.

"Good God, Genevieve. You're an enchantress indeed."

She smiled at Richard where he kneeled on the stairs. "I always carry candles and a tinderbox in my pinafore."

"For exploring underground passages?"

She struggled to pretend that this was a normal conversation in normal circumstances. "You'd be astonished how often I need light. I do practical research as well as read musty documents, you know."

"I beg your pardon, Madam Adventurer."

She rose and approached Richard, who struggled to remove Sirius's bonds. One of Richard's elegant hands smoothed the tangled fur, calming the shivering dog. He'd succeed, she knew. Richard Harmsworth's touch held magic.

"Madam Adventurer has a knife. Would you like it?"

His gallant smile set her heart thumping with love and crazy hope that they'd survive. "If you've got a knife, I'll ask you to marry me."

She ignored his teasing. Odd to recall that mere minutes ago, she'd regretted the lack of a proposal. Right now, all that mattered was that they were alive. And together. She dug into a pocket. "Here."

As he reached out, she caught his swiftly concealed wince. "Richard, what is it?"

Fear banished fragile optimism. Her gorge rose as she recalled the gunshot. Trembling, she lifted the candle. In the uncertain light, a patch shimmered wet on his black sleeve.

Nausea tightened her throat. When her lungs began to ache, she realized she'd drawn a breath and never released it. It hurt to exhale. "Dear God, you're bleeding."

"Greengrass holds a grudge." His drawn face contradicted his casual tone.

"For heaven's sake, why didn't you say something?" Anguished concern sharpened her question. Her hand shook so violently that the candle flared wildly, sending shadows hopping over the walls.

"I was being heroic."

His humor fell flat. "Idiotic, more like." On legs that threatened to collapse, she stepped closer. She reined in her futile need to rage at him. "Take your coat off."

He sawed at the rope muzzle. "Let me see to Sirius first."

"Men!" she snarled, snatching the knife and kneeling on the steps. The twine was thick, but eventually Sirius was free. He whined again and huddled into his master. Candlelight revealed blood caked around his mouth.

"Poor boy," she murmured, stroking his brindle back. He butted her with his head. "Poor old fellow."

Fortifying courage with anger, she turned to Richard. "I'd like to slap you," she said conversationally, placing the candle on a higher step to illuminate his wound.

"You can't hit an injured man."

"Which doesn't stop me wanting to." Still, her hands shook and sweaty palms threatened her grip on the knife. She firmed her hold and stretched his coat sleeve tight. She stuck the knife into the sodden material. "Don't move."

"What in Hades are you doing?" He jerked away, then hissed as the movement jarred his wound.

"I need to see how badly you're injured."

"I could take it off."

"Won't that hurt?"

"I can bear it."

"I'm not sure I can." She gritted her teeth. The wool parted under the blade. Sirius, bored with the lack of attention, wandered into the darkness.

"You must meet my tailor." Richard's sangfroid was unconvincing.

She hardly listened. Her jaw ached with clenching and the rusty stench of blood made her feel sick. "Why?"

"By the time you're finished, I won't have a decent coat left. He'll be in work for decades."

She didn't bother pointing out the odds against Richard escaping to need new clothes. "You were always overdressed for the country."

"By Gad, I wasn't!" He sounded mortally offended. "I always look *comme il faut.*"

"In Belgravia, maybe." A hard tug ripped the sleeve away. His stifled groan resounded in her bones.

"Genevieve?" he asked with no hint of teasing. "Genevieve, speak to me."

She made herself glance up from the saturated mess of his shirtsleeve. While all she saw was blood, blood everywhere.

"Take a deep breath and listen. It's only a nick."

Vaguely she was aware that she should reassure him, not the other way around. "How can you tell?" she asked thickly, her vision flooded with red. She struggled to focus on his face.

"It's not as bad as it looks. The bullet didn't stay in the wound."

She wouldn't cry. She wouldn't cry.

She cried.

"Darling—" He stretched out his good arm and curled her against his chest. For one weak moment, she rested there. Beneath her cheek, his heart beat with ineffable life, welcome proof that he wasn't at death's door.

She sniffed and without success, tried to sit up. "I have to clean your wound. Stitch it."

"To Hades with that idea. My social credit would never survive a pregnant elephant etched into my hide."

Laughter bubbled up, uncertain, unsteady, but restoring as a day at the seaside. His embrace was strong and sure. When he held her, she couldn't believe that they'd die without seeing the sun again.

She hid her face against him and struggled for composure. There was a miraculous hollow between his chin and shoulder perfectly shaped for her. "I've told you a thousand times, it's a peony."

Steeling herself, she straightened and shifted to his wounded side. This time, she handled his arm without swooning. Ruthlessly she tore his shirtsleeve off.

"Oh." She swallowed the bile stinging her throat.

"Is it that bad?" He watched her with an unquestioning trust that she didn't deserve.

"Doesn't it hurt?"

"Like the devil." Her jostling, necessary as it was, left him ashen.

"If you faint, I'll kill you," she said grimly. She eased away the tattered remnants of coat and shirt.

His lips, white with pain, stretched in a travesty of his usual grin. "Warning noted."

Using his shirt, she cleaned the wound. What she'd give for a bowl of warm water and some soap. What she'd give to be back in her parlor, battling to keep Richard Harmsworth from guessing that he attracted her like a magnet attracted iron filings.

"Will I live?" he asked after a long silence.

Would either of them live? Right now it seemed unlikely. But she took a lesson from him and answered with fabricated confidence. Not about his wound—he was right, and lucky; the bullet had merely grazed him. Despite the copious blood loss, she found no major damage. "You'll be dazzling the debutantes in no time."

This time his smile was a little more convincing, although she couldn't deceive herself about his discomfort. "My days of dazzling debutantes are over."

Ignoring his banter, she bent to inspect the wound. Now she'd cleaned the injury, she saw a long gash along the outside of his upper arm. At least it had stopped bleeding. She cast away the filthy shirt. "A new coat or two and you'll be your irritating self again."

She ripped the dirty hem from her petticoat and discarded it. She tore off a cleaner strip and wrapped it securely around Richard's arm.

"I'll owe you some new undergarments," he mumbled. He'd been stoic through the agonizing process, but the thready note in his voice indicated that his endurance faded.

She made herself smile. "More than one set."

"Brazen wench."

"That's me," she said lightly, even as apprehension gripped her. Given the blood he'd lost, she was surprised he'd stayed so chipper for so long. Now exhaustion shadowed his features. Suffering pared him down, made him much more like a regular mortal.

She tied the bandage as firmly as she could. "There's a comfortable tomb waiting. If you promise not to snore, I'm prepared to offer my shoulder as a pillow."

"I'd be honored." For once, he didn't sound like he joked. Another sign of failing stamina.

She rose and gently helped him up. For one frightening moment, he staggered. Then he found his feet and covered the short distance. He couldn't hide his weariness when he slumped to the ground, leaning heavily against the carved tomb.

Oh, Richard. Compassion squeezed her heart as she slid down beside him. She'd give anything to relieve his pain. But there was nothing she could do.

Except perhaps one thing.

Carefully she drew his ruffled head to her breast. Tearful gratitude thickened her throat when within minutes he sank into sleep.

"What the devil—"

Richard stirred in thick darkness. He was cold and sore and his arm throbbed like a drum. Yet well-being outweighed every other sensation.

"It's all right," a beloved voice murmured and he remembered. The clash with Fairbrother. The gunshot. Being trapped in this pit with Genevieve.

Genevieve who embraced him with a tenderness that banished the chill.

"Did the candle burn out?" He wasn't a fanciful man, but the air in this crypt oozed wretchedness. The prospect of perishing here with no glimmer of light was grim.

"No. But I only have two. Better to save them." She shifted. Even that slight movement jogged his wound. He bit back a groan. Nonetheless she must have heard because she stilled. "How are you feeling?"

Reluctantly he straightened away from her and rested against the stone behind him. "Not as bad as I thought I would." It was true. His arm was bearable and sleep restored his wits. "Your touch has healing powers."

"If only my touch had altar-shifting powers," she said bleakly.

"Where's Sirius?"

"He left about twenty minutes ago, I suppose. Should we look for him?"

"He's too smart to get lost."

Candlelight flared. "I should check the stone."

"It can wait. Cam will find us." Richard didn't say what they both understood—that she was unlikely to locate a convenient lever or button. Lord Neville might be a knave, but he was a deuced clever knave. He'd ensure that their prison was secure.

Richard grabbed her trembling hand. "I need to touch you."

Her frown melted into the smile he adored. "Yes, so romantic here among the decaying monks. Is that sound the rattling of bones or my beating heart?"

He laughed softly. Oh, she was brave. She was brave and beautiful and far too good for him, which didn't mean he wouldn't fight to keep her.

"Anywhere with you is romantic, darling." He raised her grimy hand and kissed her knuckles.

She shot him a skeptical glance. "I'm sure."

His courage failed at confessing that he meant it. "It sticks in my craw that Fairbrother got the jewel."

"Yes." One word, yet her detached tone pricked his instincts.

"You're taking the loss very calmly. It's incredibly valuable."

She shrugged. "What use is gold here?"

His gaze sharpened. He didn't trust her neutral expression. "What's going on, Genevieve?"

"Nothing." The corners of her lips deepened, bolstering his suspicion.

"Tell me."

She pulled free. "Lord Neville didn't get what he bargained for."

Richard frowned. "You gave him the jewel."

Amusement warmed her voice. "Do you remember I said that my article would establish my academic reputation?"

It seemed a non sequitur. "Of course." He remembered every word she'd said.

"My discovery was quite a coup. The Harmsworth Jewel is so famous. Not to mention very beautiful."

"And precious."

"And precious." Her smile intensified. "And a forgery."

He stared at her in shocked silence. Then he started to laugh.

Genevieve hadn't been sure how he'd respond to learning that he'd been mistaken about his heirloom. A lesser man—someone like Lord Neville—would be livid. Disappointment or dismay would be perfectly understandable. But when Richard Harmsworth discovered that he'd pursued a chimera, he reacted with an unfettered enjoyment that set her heart singing.

He laughed so hard that he bent over his raised knees. He ran out of breath and still whooped. She should make him stop. Surely this explosive mirth must damage his arm. But she couldn't bear to.

From the bottom of her soul, words she'd sworn never to say bubbled up, unstoppable as a flood. "Oh, Richard, how I do love you."

The moment the declaration left her lips, she was frantic to snatch it back. Humiliation closed her throat. Women from Land's End to John O'Groats must declare their devotion to Richard Harmsworth. She hated that she was just one more silly female head over heels with him.

Abruptly his laughter stopped and he stared at her with an expression she couldn't interpret. After his hilarity, the echoing silence seemed bottomless.

Furious with herself, she rose on shaky legs and stepped out of the light. Her fists clenched so hard at her sides that the nails scored her palms.

"You love me."

She'd never heard that tone before. Perhaps he offered her a chance to save her dignity. But having made the admission, she balked at denial. "Yes."

She stifled the urge to excuse or qualify. Rigid with humiliation, she braced for his response. If he was kind out of pity, she'd vomit.

A slow smile curled his lips. He looked happy. In fact, he looked completely elated. The silence extended until she wanted to scream. Still he smiled as though she was a magical treasure created solely for his delight.

"You love me."

For heaven's sake, hadn't they been through this? "Yes," she snapped.

He wasn't usually slow of understanding. Unless he was being deliberately cruel, she couldn't see why he belabored the point. He relaxed back and stretched his long legs toward her, every line of his body expressing satisfaction. "Well, I think that's altogether a fine thing."

"Do you now?" she asked on a dangerous note. She'd imagined nothing could be worse than pity. This strange, sardonic pleasure made her seethe.

He bent his good arm behind his head and regarded her with a lazy amusement that she couldn't like. How could she possibly love this ruffian? He should be hanged at the cross-roads. "By Jove, I do."

"Well, good for you," she said bitterly.

His smile became, if anything, more beatific. "Don't you want to know why it's a fine thing?"

"Not particularly," she said sourly.

"It's quite simple."

"Like you," she sniped, clutching unsteady hands in her skirts and telling herself she really, *really* couldn't thump him.

"Harsh." He leaned farther back, as comfortable as if he lolled on one of Sedgemoor's elegant chaises. "I'll tell you anyway."

"I'm all ears," she said sarcastically.

"I love you too."

"Charming."

Then she realized what he'd said. She stared at the beautiful, bedraggled man lounging against the tomb.

His smile developed a wicked edge. "Don't tell me you're lost for words. I never thought I'd see the day."

"What did you say?" she choked out, faltering toward him on legs that felt made of string.

"You heard."

"I'd like to hear it again."

His smile faded and she saw that under the teasing, he was as serious as she'd ever seen him. "I love you, Genevieve."

Radiant serenity slowly replaced turmoil. She'd never imagined him saying those words; now they struck her with the pure truth she found when she completed a perfect translation or comprehended the symbols on a carved ivory.

His face darkened with desperation. "If you don't kiss me in the next ten seconds, I swear I'll combust."

She didn't move. She wasn't sure her legs would support her. "That might be interesting."

"Genevieve," he groaned, rising to his knees and extending his good hand toward her. "Stop torturing me. I know I deserve it. I know I've been a bad, bad man. But have mercy."

"Oh, Richard," she sighed. Her feet hardly touching the ground, she flew across the distance between them.

Chapter Thirty-Three

Genevieve loved him. *She loved him.*

Richard kissed her, glorying in her untrammeled response. She was magnificent. From the first, she'd sent his soul soaring. She was the only one for him. He ached to become worthy of this gift. He had so bloody much to make up for.

"Take care with your arm," she said breathlessly. She sprawled across his lap. With tenderness that tore his heart, she rubbed her cheek against his bare chest.

"You're delicious." He kissed the curve of her shoulder. "And you're wearing too many clothes."

A gasp of shocked laughter escaped her. "We can't!"

"Of course we can. The monks are past minding." He pressed his nose to the satiny skin behind her ear. "I love your smell."

Another of those tremulous gulps of laughter, half-horrified, half-enchanted. "Thank you. I think."

His teeth scraped down her neck, making her tremble. "Your scent haunts me."

"Richard, we're stuck in a crypt. How can you possibly think about...that?"

He lifted his hands to unhook her dress then winced. He'd forgotten his wound. Love was a powerful drug indeed. "For the first time in my life, I've told a woman I love her. Against all odds, she says she loves me too. How can I possibly think of anything else?"

She stiffened in his arms, then pushed back to study his face. "The first time?"

The wonder in her eyes made his gut lurch with poignant joy. "The very first time."

Her throat moved as she swallowed. "I'm glad."

She linked her hands behind his neck and her kiss carved a rift in his soul. A Genevieve-sized rift. His hold tightened as he kissed her back.

"Let me show you how much I love you," he whispered, brushing his cheek along hers. He lifted his hips to demonstrate his readiness.

"You make me a wanton," she said huskily. "What about your arm? This is unwise."

"I'm a man in love. I don't need to be wise."

She cast him a quelling glance. "At least let me undress myself."

"Just what a fellow likes to hear."

"Stop flirting," she said repressively, but her lips curved.

His pulse kicked when she shifted away to shuck off the pinafore. "How can I help it? Ever since I first saw you, so serious and beautiful, poring over your ancient tomes, I've wanted to tease you."

"That's obvious," she said drily.

"I couldn't imagine such a smart girl giving me a second glance."

Beneath her lashes, she cast him a disbelieving look as

she rose on her knees. Reaching behind her, she tugged until her bodice sagged. His mouth went dry and his heart slammed against his ribs. "You're worth the occasional glance. You're quite decorative, you know."

Ridiculously his cheeks heated. "Flattery will get you everywhere."

"On my back at least." She didn't sound like she minded. The bodice drooped, revealing plain shift and corset. Pearled nipples pressed against the sheer white material. "Don't tell me you're blushing."

"Devil take you, Genevieve."

This time he couldn't mistake her amusement. "I begin to think you might love me, if I can make the rakish Sir Richard Harmsworth blush like a schoolboy."

He grabbed her hand. "Come to me."

"If I must." Her ennui was unconvincing.

"Surely you can't tire of the activity already." He tugged until she tumbled forward, warm and fragrant.

Laughing, she curved around him, lithe as a cat. But when she met his gaze, worry shadowed her features. "Richard, I don't want to hurt you."

"Trust me. We'll manage." Good God, right now, the pain in his balls outweighed the paltry wound Greengrass had inflicted.

Richard kissed her while his good hand lowered the precarious bodice. They both sighed with pleasure when he palmed one round breast. He smiled against her lips, tasting her gasp as his thumb tested the peak. "I love how you respond."

"I can't help myself," she admitted on another sigh. She rubbed her face across his chest, and the damp heat of her breath added another rich chord to the symphony of arousal.

When she stroked his cock, his hands fisted in the gaping back of her dress. "Damn it, Genevieve—"

Her laugh was husky. "Let me touch you. Let me find out what makes you desperate."

"You make me desperate." He leaned against the stone, surrendering his body. The thought of those clever hands discovering his secrets made him giddy.

She slipped off his lap to kneel so close that he barely needed to move to seize her. Clearly she liked playing with fire. She started innocuously, except that her merest touch made him quake. She ran her hand down his neck and along his shoulder.

"Does this hurt?" she whispered.

"Only with wanting you."

"Good." A faint smile teased her lips. The urge to kiss her built, but he resisted. He'd promised to show her how much he loved her. If it meant death by pleasure, so be it.

She stroked his clenched fists, learning each bone and sinew. He bit back the demand to hurry.

Flattening her palms across his pectorals, she buried her nose between them. She rubbed her face against the light covering of hair, then opened her lips on his skin, tasting him with a voluptuous enjoyment that made his teeth grind. His heart beat so hard, surely she must feel it.

Lower and lower she ventured. Hands and lips driving him insane. By the time she fumbled at his breeches, his breath emerged in great noisy gusts. Every sense concentrated on his cock. He wanted her to touch him more than he wanted air.

With agonizing slowness, she opened his breeches.

He loved the way she discovered her sensual power. He even loved the way she took her time, excruciating as it was. Then he realized that the torture only started. Tentatively she stroked him. He bit back a groan and she whipped her hand away.

"I'm sorry."

His smile must be a rictus grin. "Don't stop."

There was a pause. Then the soft slide of her fingers, from tip to base and back again. He couldn't shift his gaze from what she did.

She soon got the idea, thank God. Her depredations became more confident. She lingered at the tip, testing the betraying dampness. If he begged her to kiss him there, she'd be revolted. Probably just as well. Her clumsy yet hellishly arousing fingers made him see stars. If she put her mouth on him, he'd explode.

After an eon of provocation, her fingers curled around him. A shuddering sigh escaped him as she ran her fist up and down his length, before she intensified the agony by relaxing and tightening her hold. He groaned and tilted his head back against the stone. Fire burned behind his eyes. He hardly knew where he was.

He caught her hand. "Take off your drawers."

To his surprise, she complied immediately. Then he looked into her face and understood that touching him had inflamed her too. She tugged her dress over her head, revealing shift and stays. She removed her hairpins, letting her hair flow around her shoulders.

He wanted her to take off everything. He hadn't had nearly enough time to explore her body. Eternity wasn't enough time. But he was so eager, he stretched out his hand. "Come to me, my love. I hunger for you."

Her expression softened. A sliding movement, a graceful dip and she straddled his lap. His cock rose eagerly between her thighs. Her hands settled on his shoulders as she regarded him with a troubled frown. "This feels bizarre."

His good hand caught her supple waist. "You'll like it. You get to be in charge."

Her lips curved, although the way her skin tightened over her features indicated that she too tested the edges of control. "In that case, I probably will like it."

"Bring yourself down on me."

"Like riding?"

Despite his impatience, he laughed softly. "Exactly like riding." He paused. "No, more fun than riding."

"That's a big claim. I like riding."

"So do I." He leaned in to ravish her mouth. "I'm all yours."

She looked dazzled. He loved the way she flung herself headlong into passion. Her thighs gripped him as she rose. Her torn petticoat hid their joining, but he felt every move. Dear God, how he felt her.

When her humid heat grazed his cock's sensitive tip, he groaned and bit her shoulder. Her skin was dewy and she gasped in ragged little spurts.

"Take me, Genevieve," he grated, and he wasn't sure whether he meant answer this desire or take him forever.

Both.

"I take you." It sounded like a vow.

The moment dissolved into bliss as finally she descended. She was wet and ready, although he'd done little to prepare her. Her body offered exquisite resistance. Her muscles clung and released. She paused, breathing in whimpers.

"Are you all right?" he asked roughly, seizing her hips in shaking hands. His injured arm objected, but he was past heeding anything but Genevieve.

"Yes." She didn't sound certain.

He felt her tension. She clutched his bare shoulders. The scent of arousal mingled with the dust of ages. He closed his eyes against the darkness, diving into deeper darkness inside his head. The need to thrust was a pounding demand. But he wanted to show her that in loving him, she lost nothing of herself.

"Do it, my darling," he pleaded. She quivered on an instant of hesitation then sank fully over him, taking him deep.

Genevieve released her breath in a sob of satisfaction. The solid power of Richard's body inside hers answered heart and soul as much as physical need. Her hands tightened on his shoulders, his skin sleek beneath her palms. He pulsed inside her, breathtakingly virile.

"I love you, Richard," she said softly.

His expression was unguarded as it rarely was. She read wonder and joy in his eyes. "And I love you, Genevieve."

With a naturalness she'd never have imagined moments ago, she rose, relishing the thick, silky slide of his body. Teasing, she lingered at the peak before slowly descending. Again that completion. She leaned forward and kissed him hard, a fierce battle of tongues, lips and teeth.

She became a creature of instinct, rising and falling like the tide, the rhythm pulsing through her blood. Her ears filled with the sounds of lovemaking. The succulent meeting of bodies. Hoarse breathing. Her thundering heartbeat. These tumbling, tormenting sensations still astounded her. Her body tensed, seeking its incendiary goal. Tighter and tighter. Higher and higher.

Richard sank his teeth into her shoulder again and she shivered, but still relief hovered beyond her grasp. She bent her face into his damp, tangled hair, inhaling male musk and lemon verbena. Her movements turned clumsy, frenzied. Then he lifted hard as she lowered, and blackness exploded into a million stars.

She cried out at the shining waves rippling through her. Her muscles clamped around him and he groaned against her neck as he juddered into her.

The sky rained fire. For an eternity, they joined inside the inferno. Then, shaking, she fell against him, his arms surrounding her with love.

Genevieve stirred without opening her eyes, not wanting to shatter this moment. She draped across Richard. His scent filled the air the way his love filled her heart. She kissed the hard slope of his chest.

All her life, she'd feared love as a trap. She loved her father and had paid with years of thankless service to his causes. However much she'd resisted the prospect of marriage, she'd occasionally imagined falling in love with someone ordinary and malleable who shared her intellectual interests. "Ordinary" and "malleable" didn't describe Richard at all. So why, despite physical captivity, did she feel so free now? As though the world opened up before her like a book and she could turn to any page she wanted.

"Why are you smiling?" Gently he brushed aside the untidy mass of hair concealing her face.

"I never imagined it was possible to feel the way I feel right now."

"Me either," he responded softly. "You're my whole world."

Very slowly she raised her head. "I should be terrified, stuck here in the darkness." She met his unwavering gaze. "I'm not frightened because we're together."

His embrace firmed and he kissed her thoroughly. "We'll get out of this."

Sighing, she stood to retrieve dress and pinafore. "We're wasting time. We should check the altar stone."

His smile sent her heart on another of those disconcerting swoops. "I don't regret a moment. I can't get enough of you."

She blushed. Although what right a girl had to blush given what she'd just done, Genevieve couldn't think. "We might find the abbey treasury. It's rumored that the last abbot hid it from Henry VIII's men."

Richard rose, wincing when he bumped his arm against the tomb. "I've had my fill of ancient mysteries."

She watched him fasten his breeches. Observing the intimate action thrilled her, besotted creature she was. "This treasure would be genuine."

"Are you sure the jewel's a copy?"

"I'm surprised nobody else noticed. I suspect it was made last century. The filigree gives it away completely."

"So there never was a Harmsworth Jewel?"

"Perhaps once." She searched his face. This had to be a blow, no matter how well he appeared to take the news. "I'm sorry, Richard."

He shrugged and his smile held no shadow. "I sought a jewel in Little Derrick. I found one. I've been amply rewarded."

After an hour, their candle burned low and they were no closer to escape.

Breathless, Richard gave up shoving at the altar and stepped back, wiping his hand over his sweaty face. Discouragement weighted his sigh. Before sealing them in, Fairbrother had destroyed the mechanism for moving the stone. The broken stonework was new.

"Richard, you won't shift it," Genevieve said from the step below. With her knife, she'd been checking for chinks in the walls. But down here, safe from weathering, the masonry aligned as perfectly as it had five hundred years ago. "That altar must weigh tons. I doubt a team of oxen could budge it. If you're not careful, you'll reopen your wound."

Leaning against the wall, she brushed back the hair that escaped its string tie. Another item from her seemingly bottomless pockets.

"I don't suppose you packed lunch in your pinafore?" he asked hopefully, trying to lift the despondent atmosphere.

She laughed wryly. She must be as aware as he that every second, their situation worsened. "I didn't prepare for incarceration today. Silly me."

"I'd love to revisit our Oxford picnic."

"Don't torture me." Her smile was reminiscent.

An hour ago, when he'd held her, gasping her release, he'd believed that he couldn't love her more. Now her stalwart spirit made him light-headed with adoration. "That roast chicken was delicious."

"Not to mention the champagne."

"Looking at you makes me feel like I'm drinking champagne."

Her cheeks flushed with the shyness that always clutched at his heart. "I'd swap a dozen bottles of champagne for a tumbler of cold water."

She was right. The greatest danger was thirst. Foreboding oozed through his veins like glacial ice. He wouldn't let Genevieve die. He couldn't bear to lose her. Not now he'd found her. Not now she'd told him she loved him. Every time she spoke those simple words, she filled a river in his soul that had been dry since boyhood.

"There may be another way out," he said without conviction. "Any ideas?"

"I've lost confidence in my ideas since Lord Neville discovered this crypt. I should have guessed a building of this era had an underground chamber."

"Don't be too hard on yourself. The Harmsworth Jewel occupied your attention."

"And the scoundrel who plotted to steal it." She lifted the candle and descended to sit on a tomb. "At least we know the jewel's a modern copy."

"If we don't get out, nobody else will know." Richard clenched his fist against the base of the altar, wishing he could punch it out of the way.

"We'll get out." Her statement rang with faith in him. By God, he'd make sure he justified her trust. She watched as he prowled down the steps.

"How appropriate that a fraud of a baronet should pursue a fraud of a treasure." He sat and slung his arm around her shoulders, leaning his chin on her head. She was warm and soft and rested against him as if he provided inviolable sanctuary. Hope surged. He refused to countenance a universe that permitted this brave girl's destruction.

"You went to enormous lengths to lay your hands on it."

He struggled to recall his reasons for actions that in hindsight seemed lunatic. "Must we talk about this?"

She stroked his cheek. The brush of her fingertips shivered through him. "I love you, but I don't know you."

"You know me better than anyone else." Even Cam, a realization that jolted him.

"I know Christopher Evans."

His arm tightened. "Christopher Evans is more real than Richard Harmsworth ever was."

His cryptic response didn't placate her. She'd honed native curiosity into a weapon. She shifted to study him and her vulnerability scored his heart. "You're always saying things like that. Things I don't understand. I *want* to understand."

A lifetime of pretending that he didn't care about his birth warned him to stay silent, but he owed Genevieve honesty. Not because he'd lied. But because he loved her.

Still he hesitated. The hellish truth was that he suspected that his real self wasn't worth knowing. Certainly not worth loving. He'd long ago recognized that much of his anger at the world's derision stemmed from a deep-seated belief that the world might just be right.

With one finger, she traced a line up his temple where the pulse pounded with fear. "Trust me, Richard."

She made it sound easy, yet telling her what it meant to grow up in scandal's shadow was the most difficult thing he'd ever done. It sliced too close to the man he'd hidden from even his closest friends.

All his life, a sardonic air and an immaculately presented façade had deflected contempt. He couldn't bear to reveal his soul to Genevieve, only to confirm that his pretense at being a shallow popinjay was no pretense at all.

She was right. If he loved her, he had to trust her. Damn it. He stole a jagged breath, gave the terror torturing his gut the cut direct, and flung himself into the void.

Chapter Thirty-Four

"I t sounds insane to admit that this quest started because I lost my temper." Reluctant to reveal his flimsy motives, Richard shifted uncomfortably on the stone tomb. "At a raw moment, some puling cub sneered at my bastardy and I swore I'd show them all. The Harmsworth Jewel confirms the Harmsworth heir. So I'd find the gewgaw and brandish it under every disapproving nose in society. Childish, really."

"I remember those stories in the papers." Genevieve's expression was troubled. "Don't be too hard on yourself. A lifetime of prurient speculation would sting anybody's pride."

"I learned young that a bastard can't afford the luxury of pride." He laughed without amusement. "It's a lesson that needs repeating."

She looked puzzled. "Why is your illegitimacy such widespread knowledge? After all, you inherited the baronetcy."

"Every dunderhead can count. Sir Lester was in St. Petersburg for sixteen months before his wife delivered a healthy boy. Odds were that another man had shared Lady Harmsworth's bed." His gut knotted. He loathed admitting that the world's spite was justified. "Great Aunt Amelia was perfectly right to deny me the jewel."

"What does your mother say?" Genevieve sounded so calm, whereas he was barely capable of reason on this subject. Talking of his bastardy turned him into a mass of howling pain, like a wounded animal.

Richard shrugged as if all this didn't matter, although the devil of it was that it had always mattered too much. "Nothing significant."

"Mrs. Meacham said nobody knows who your real father is."

"My mother has remained remarkably close-lipped." Rancor tinged his answer. "I assume the answer is as appalling as everyone suspects—she swived some groom or traveling gypsy."

To his surprise, Genevieve struggled out of his embrace to regard him accusingly. "You sound like you hate your mother."

Without Genevieve, his arms felt empty. "I do."

"Really?" She sounded skeptical. Wise Genevieve. She knew him too well.

He sighed. "If she'd been a faithful wife, my life would have been easier."

"Perhaps she loved your father." Genevieve was angry, although he couldn't think why. So far in this tale, he'd played innocent bystander.

"I doubt it."

"You're very judgmental."

"You don't know my mother."

"No. But if she has a son as wonderful as you, she can't be all bad."

If he hadn't been so tangled up in misery, her praise might mollify him. "The world calls my mother a whore."

"The world can be wrong," Genevieve said coldly. Although only inches away, she folded into her body, closing off the warm, loving openness.

Old insecurities stabbed. Was he wrong about Genevieve? Of all people, she struck him as someone who might be capable of looking beyond illegitimacy and scandal. Not for the first time, he wished he was Christopher Evans, with Christopher Evans's clean name. He'd long ago discovered the futility of wishing. Alone in his bed at Eton and at last able to stop pretending that the endless abuse didn't distress him, he'd prayed night after night for some twist of heredity to prove him Sir Lester's son.

"Genevieve, does it matter to you that I'm baseborn?" His voice shook, damn it.

She looked appalled. "Surely you know me better than that."

Even as he wanted to believe her, years of insult whispered doubt in his ear. "It's mattered to everyone I've ever known."

Rage flashed in her eyes. "Sedgemoor and the Hillbrooks don't treat you with the contempt you appear to consider your lot."

"They're my friends." And Jonas, Sidonie and Cam were no strangers to scandal.

"So what am I?"

"The woman I love."

His declaration didn't thaw her anger. "Yet you think I'll blame you for something that's not your fault and that has no bearing on the man you are."

He spoke the bitter truth. "I'm the man I am because I'm a bastard."

"Then heaven send us more bastards." Her lips tightened with impatience. "You need to show some forgiveness. Both to yourself and your mother. You talk as though she never said a kind word."

Richard dearly wanted to claim that was the case. But while he'd been vaguely aware of whispers, on the whole, his early years had been a haven of affection and luxury. Then at eight, he went to school and discovered how the wider world despised the offspring of illicit affairs. Especially offspring with the temerity to claim equality with their legitimate schoolfellows. Thank God Richard had found Cam and Jonas, although their friendship, as much mutual protection as meeting of minds, had earned the cruel label "bunch of bastards."

"At Eton, my inferiority became blatantly clear."

He'd suffered his share of beatings, until learning that sharp-tongued indifference discouraged violence. If bullying provoked no visible effect, his peers transferred their attentions to more responsive prey. Richard Harmsworth, arbiter of style, was born from blood and pain and mockery. But he never forgot that his elegance shielded a man inadequate to the role he was born to.

Genevieve's eyes softened with compassion, although her tone remained implacable. "You're no longer that schoolboy. Do you see your mother?"

This inquisition was beyond enough. He slid off the tomb and strode into the darkness. He wanted Genevieve to understand his resentment of his mother, but he had a nasty feeling that explanations would make him sound like that sulky schoolboy she decried. "Not if I can help it."

She rushed after him and caught his arm. "I'm sorry."

However he tried, he couldn't keep Genevieve at a distance. He slumped where he stood, his weariness stemming from childhood. "I'd do something about my bastardy if I could. But it's a wound that never heals."

She stiffened, although he couldn't see her expression. "I don't care about your birth."

"Really?" Sarcasm drenched the word. "Then why are you angry?"

He found himself cradled in warm, soft Genevieve. Her arms curled around his back, her face lay against his bare throat. "I can't stand that the world doesn't recognize how remarkable you are. I can't stand that you're estranged from those closest to you."

Groaning, he pulled her into him. To his astonishment, the wound that never healed didn't feel nearly so agonizing with Genevieve in his arms. "I'm a damned self-pitying fool. I never wanted for anything."

"You never wanted for anything but kindness and love. I had no right to criticize. But I can't imagine your mother doesn't love you."

"That's because you're a paragon and an angel."

Her laugh was choked and he felt hot moisture against his skin. He'd made her cry. He really was a bastard in all senses of the word.

She drew away. In the darkness, he saw only the glint of her eyes and the pale oval of her face. "I love you. Whoever you are. Whatever you call yourself. Whoever your father was." She sounded as decisive as she had when she'd reproached him for misjudging his mother. "You're a wonderful man, Richard. Kind. Perceptive. Clever. Resourceful. Brave. Handsome enough to turn any girl's head. That's what matters. Not what your parents did."

With an unsteady hand, he brushed the tears from her cheeks. A lifetime of self-doubt melted under the blaze of Genevieve's love. With a few words, she'd made him anew.

He tried to sound insouciant, but his voice cracked. "If the paragon and angel Genevieve Barrett rates me so highly, how can I argue?"

Her smile was shaky. "Now come back into the light."

He wanted to tell her that she'd already drawn him from stygian darkness into light. Instead, he kissed her as he'd never kissed her before. She was the most precious thing in the world. He cherished her. He honored her. He loved her more than he ever thought he'd love anyone in his heedless, selfish life. Passion burned. He couldn't touch her without passion. But deeper than passion at this moment ran tenderness, care, his delight in her existence.

They returned to the stone tomb and the guttering candle. Genevieve fumbled in her pocket for the second candle, lighting it from the dying flame.

She smiled at Richard as if she believed he was a hero. Silently he promised her that he'd never let her down. "I now understand why you love Sirius so much."

Confused, he stared at her. "He's a fine dog."

"He's a fine dog of unspecified breeding with a stalwart heart. You're kindred spirits."

"My darling, that's hardly flattering to my noble hound," he said thickly, then frowned and glanced around. "Speaking of Sirius, where is he?"

Concern replaced her smile. "He's been away a long time."

The thought of Sirius coming to grief in this labyrinth was unendurable. Raising the candle, Richard set out ahead of Genevieve into the looming darkness.

Richard's calls summoned only echoes, no bark of recognition. The crypt was huge, a vaulted maze of pillars and tombs and gargoyles fit to give the most prosaic man nightmares.

At last they reached the chamber's end. Genevieve turned to him in frustration. "He can't disappear into thin air. If he hears you calling, he'll come."

That was true. Sirius's manners belied his humble background. "Let's follow this wall and see what we find."

The wall proved impossibly long. Richard began to loathe the industrious monks. With every step, he called to Sirius. Genevieve progressed more slowly behind him, her hand running along the bricks. He bowed to her knowledge of medieval architecture, but a secret passage seemed too much to hope for.

Although she'd just said that she loved him. Miracles could be the order of the day.

"Sirius!" Where the devil was the mutt?

The wall took an illogical turn. Or perhaps Richard's senses failed after all this meandering. When he raised the candle, another line of stone columns extended ahead. "Sirius!"

Silence. Richard started down the hall. A hundred yards down, he heard something in the distance. Could that be a bark? He called again. In this restricted space, sound reverberated, distorting response.

Genevieve joined him. "Is that Sirius?"

"I don't know." He called as loudly as he could. Echoes made it impossible to tell if Sirius answered. Richard stepped forward, then halted. The scrabble of paws was unmistakable. "Listen."

"Is it him?"

"Either it's Sirius or the rats are big enough to eat us." He lifted her hand and kissed it, then passed her the candle. "Sirius!"

Sirius leaped from several feet away, crashing Richard onto the terracotta tiles.

"You're a deuced troublesome fellow, you hairy rogue." Richard laughed under the uproarious welcome, although his arm protested the boisterous greeting. Then abruptly all desire to laugh fled. "Good God."

"What is it, Richard?" The candle lit Genevieve's face from below, lending her a haunted look.

He sat up with new energy. "Sirius's coat. It's wet."

Richard's joyful reunion with Sirius melted Genevieve's heart. No wonder she loved this man. She bent to pat Sirius's shaggy head. The stink of wet dog overpowered the pervasive dust. "Found a puddle, have you?"

Richard's eyes held a strange light. "Darling, you're not thinking this through. If he's wet, he's found water."

Interesting but hardly cause for celebration. "I doubt it's drinkable."

Richard sprang to his feet and caught her hand. His smile was brilliant as he leaned forward to kiss her. "Perhaps not, but it must have fallen since the sixteenth century."

The kiss, however brief, distracted her. His kisses always did. As her head cleared, realization struck and with it, a flare of hope. Could Sirius have saved them? Then grim reality tempered excitement. "It's probably underground seepage. This doesn't mean there's a way out."

"It doesn't mean there isn't. Haven't you noticed how fresh the air is? This part of the crypt isn't nearly as musty. There must be an opening."

"We have to find out where he's been." She tugged the string from her unruly hair and passed it to Richard.

"If you lead us out, Sirius, you'll dine on *foie gras* and pheasant for the rest of your life." Richard tied the makeshift leash to Sirius's collar. His tone became a command. "Home, Sirius. Take us home."

The dog hesitated and Genevieve wondered whether they asked too much. Then with a yip, Sirius trotted down the corridor.

Richard wasn't generally a praying man. His prayers at Eton had gone unanswered too often for him to retain much faith in the Almighty's benevolence. But in Sirius's wake, his head filled with half-coherent pleas for Genevieve's safety.

The dog followed one long corridor, then another, then another. Richard soon lost track. They could travel in a circle. Who knew? At his side Genevieve remained quiet, the candle unwavering in her hand.

After what felt like forever, Genevieve tugged his arm. "Look at the candle, Richard."

Peering ahead, working out the dog's direction, he hadn't noticed the light. The flame flickered wildly. To confirm what he saw, a breeze teased his bare chest. "Go on, Sirius."

The dog broke into a lope, Richard chasing. Genevieve jogged after them. Soon dank and decay tainted the air. Even this bolstered optimism. If the crypt was sealed, nothing should grow.

His heart pounding, Richard extinguished the candle and realized that Genevieve stood in green-tinged shadow. Sirius barked and jerked the leash free. The dog bounded into a low tunnel and disappeared.

Shock held Richard motionless. The lure of escape was so sweet he hardly dared test it and prove himself mistaken.

"Richard—"

He gestured her to silence, superstitiously afraid of voicing his hopes. "Wait here."

He dropped to his knees and crawled into the tiny space, more dog- than man-sized. The ground was sludgy with rotted vegetation. Gradually the tunnel narrowed, the walls cold and wet like clammy flesh. Fear constricting his gut, he closed his eyes and told himself he wasn't trapped.

The tunnel compressed almost to impassibility. Damn it. Had he come so far only to fail? He faltered, panting. This was impossible.

Then the dread of Genevieve's death overcame his instinctive aversion to such restricted space. Drawing a breath fetid with dead plants, he dug his hands deep into the mud. Ignoring his wound, he hauled himself forward in awkward lurches, forcing his way through the crumbling soil.

More prayers. That the tunnel didn't collapse and smother him. That freedom waited at the end. Sirius barked ahead and the sound goaded him on, despite the slicing pain in his arm and the crushing pressure around him.

"Are you all right?" Genevieve called from the crypt, her voice echoing strangely.

"Nearly there," he grunted. He hissed a curse as his hip slammed into a rock.

Dizzying relief flooded him when the tunnel started to widen. He took his first full breath in what felt like hours, although logic insisted it must only be minutes.

A thick wall of vegetation blocked his way. Roughly he shoved it aside, breaking and wrenching with shaking, filthy hands. Then without warning, the sinking sun blinded him.

He slumped over the lip of the tunnel, gasping with exhaustion. "I'm out."

"Thank God," she said from far away. "Shall I follow?"

He lay in a dip of land. All he could see was the blue bowl of sky, framed by greenery.

"Wait, I'll come back. It's a tight fit." An understatement as his bruises, grazes and throbbing arm affirmed. Every cell revolted at returning, but he couldn't let Genevieve struggle alone through that hellish passage.

He snatched one last look at the outside world. Then he gritted his teeth against the pain and crawled into the dark.

After his moments outside, the tunnel seemed grimmer than ever. He heaved himself through the mud for what felt like an eon until he saw Genevieve ahead as a dark shadow. "I'll pull you."

When she gripped his hand with immediate trust, his heart leaped. She was such a gallant woman. He barely credited that she loved him.

They squeezed along the tunnel. This third time, the way seemed even longer. Perhaps because he went backward. At least his prior journeys had smoothed the passage a little.

As they approached the mouth, muted light revealed Genevieve. Dirt matted her hair. A bleeding scratch and the older bruise on her cheek made Richard want to shred Fairbrother's liver.

Only now did he accept that they'd make it. For hours, dread had thrummed a bass note in his soul. Finally he admitted his terror at rotting in that forgotten catacomb. And his greater terror when he contemplated Genevieve suffering the same fate.

He tightened his grip and with her scrambling help, dragged her through the vines. Blessing the sky overhead, he collapsed onto the rough grass.

Eventually Richard turned his head toward Genevieve, sprawled beside him. By Jove, he was in a bad way. The stickler who had scorned a hundred diamonds of the first water was head over heels with a woman who looked like she'd wrestled a mule through a landslide.

Closing his eyes, he let the late sun melt the crypt's chill from his skin. His arm hurt like the very devil, but even that seemed a minor consideration now that he was above ground. A few feet away, he heard Sirius nosing at some leaves as if he hadn't just saved their lives.

Dear God, that had been a close-run thing. Richard basked in the warmth, relishing the birds chirping from the bushes, the rustling leaves, the gentle lap of water.

The gentle lap of water?

Summoning his last strength, he staggered upright to see beyond the sheltered hollow. He started to laugh, descending to the ground and leaning his head on one filthy knee. "Do you know where we are?"

Genevieve didn't shift. "Heaven?"

"I have no doubt that's your destination, my love. I'm not sure it's mine."

She closed her eyes. "If you're not going there, neither am I."

Yet again you rip the ground from beneath my feet with mere words.

Caught on the raw, he bent and kissed her, cradling her dirty face in one hand. She was more fragile than Dresden china, more precious than any jewel, ancient or new. She smelled of rotting vegetation, mud, and sweat. And flowers and female musk. The mixture was astonishingly alluring.

Once she'd struggled to her feet, she released a broken laugh. "Everything comes back to Sedgemoor's pond."

"It does indeed." They were just behind the bank where they'd first kissed. Across the water, trees hid the summer-house. "I wonder if Cam would sell me this corner of the estate."

"I'd like that." Her smile indicated that she too remembered.

"I'll only pay top price if the naked nymph comes with the deal."

"I'm not sure naked nymphs are the duke's to supply," she said drily. She brushed her skirts in a futile attempt to dislodge the caked muck. "I hate to be prosaic, but I'm starving and I'd love a bath."

He rose groaning—that tunnel was a deuced torture chamber; he felt like he'd gone ten rounds with Tom Cribb. "We could swim here."

Her gaze sharpened. "I'd rather plot Lord Neville's downfall."

"A warrior queen to the end." His voice hardened. "Let's head for Cam's and decide how to bring down a lord."

Chapter Thirty-Five

An expressionless footman showed Genevieve to Leighton Court's splendid library, where the Duke of Sedgemoor and Richard waited. Lady Hillbrook had helped her dress, but neither she nor her husband were present now. Which was a pity. She felt comfortable with Lady Hillbrook, whereas His Grace overawed her. He wasn't exactly supercilious, but she felt like a complete peasant compared to his aristocratic perfection.

Night had fallen and the room glowed with candlelight. Upon her entrance, Sirius raised his head from the hearth rug before resuming his snooze.

"Darling, how are you feeling?" Richard strode forward to take her hand. As always, his touch restored failing courage.

He looked much better, and not just because he'd washed and changed. After they'd run across Sedgemoor looking for them in the woods, the duke had brought them here and summoned a doctor. Following the examination, Richard sent a footman upstairs to the bedroom with a note informing her that the bullet had done no lasting damage. Thank heaven.

The endearment made her glance nervously toward where Sedgemoor stood beside the carved marble mantelpiece. She mustered a smile. "Better, thank you."

Richard was dressed for society. The only sign of their travails was the sling supporting his arm. "My valet would despair. Cam's clothes are too big." He addressed the duke. "Lay off the puddings, old man, or you'll soon be as fat as His Majesty."

Sedgemoor raised his claret in an ironic toast to Richard. "I can't help being a fine figure of a fellow, instead of skinny as a blade of grass."

"Well, at least you've been kind enough to feed a starving man." Richard drew Genevieve toward a chair. "Can I fetch you something?"

Chafing dishes crowded one of the library tables. "Yes, please."

She settled upon a brocade chair, the rich silk gown flowing around her like crimson water. She'd never worn such a garment. The bodice was tight. Lydia, the duke's sister, was built on less Amazonian lines.

She turned toward Sedgemoor. "Your Grace, I appreciate your kindness."

"You're most welcome, Miss Barrett." He waved a nonchalant hand. "I'm sorry that our acquaintance begins under adverse circumstances."

Richard passed Genevieve a plate and a glass of wine before returning to select his meal. With difficulty, she stopped herself falling on the food like Sirius on his bowl. She hadn't eaten since breakfast.

"Fairbrother can't get away with this," Richard said to the duke. She'd already sensed that her arrival interrupted an intense discussion.

Sedgemoor frowned. "Mr. Evans—"

Richard looked up sharply. "She knows my real name."

Sedgemoor's lips twitched. "Glad to hear it, if you've progressed to calling Miss Barrett 'darling.'" He must see that she blushed like a tomato. "Miss Barrett, please accept my apologies for abetting this tomfoolery."

"Genevieve knows I'm to blame." Richard dropped to the carpet before Genevieve's chair and leaned against her knees. She stifled the urge to run her fingers through his thick hair. After the day's intimacies, it felt artificial not to touch him.

"Richard had good reasons for what he did," Genevieve said softly.

He straightened with astonishment and turned to stare at her. "I did?"

She wanted to kiss him and tell him that once he'd described his childhood—and the things she'd surmised from what he left unsaid—she'd forgiven his scheming. The duke's presence forestalled such openness.

Her heart ached for the proud, lonely boy. She kicked herself, she who took such unjustified pride in her understanding, that she'd once believed Richard impervious to the doubts and insecurities that afflicted lesser men. His courage in facing down a world that had never welcomed him left her wanting to stand up and cheer. Viewed from that perspective, his pursuit of the Harmsworth Jewel became almost valiant.

Again, the duke's presence made her self-conscious about declarations. "I should have told you the jewel is a copy."

Sedgemoor assumed his full impressive height and regarded her down his long nose. "It is?"

"Didn't you tell him?" Genevieve asked.

Richard shrugged. "We haven't had a chance to share ancillary details."

"That's hardly ancillary." Sedgemoor stepped forward,

his face alight with a mixture of humor and irritation. "This entire idiotic masquerade has been a wild goose chase?"

Richard's laugh was a grunt. "Fate has a sense of humor, don't you agree?"

Genevieve could no longer contain her curiosity. "Have you reported Lord Neville to the law?"

With suspicious concentration, Richard scooped some fricassee onto his fork. He managed his food surprisingly well, given one arm was out of commission. "We can't."

Shock made her catch her breath. "Why on earth not? Lord Neville's dangerous. Someone must stop him."

Richard stood and placed his still full plate on the table before facing her. No trace now of the charming Lothario. "I intend to."

"So report him to a magistrate."

She read regret and determination in Richard's features. "If he's arrested, he'll tar the reputation of anyone ranged against him."

She immediately understood the austere expression. Her appetite evaporating, she too set aside her plate. "You're trying to protect me."

"If Lord Neville slanders your good name, life will become impossible. Not only that, it will hurt your family."

And her hopes for a career. It was difficult for a woman to be taken seriously in an all-male preserve like medieval scholarship. With unsullied virtue, she had a slim chance, especially if producing original and expert work. Should the world doubt her chastity, salacious laughter would howl down everything she did. Bitter disappointment clogged her throat. She could never regret giving herself to Richard, but the price of recklessness was abandoning the future she'd planned.

"I'm sorry, Genevieve," Richard said quietly.

The aching sadness in his voice provided no consolation. Blinking back tears, she stared blindly into the distance. "So we do nothing?"

"Of course not." Richard stood beside the duke. The two men made quite a contrast, one so dark and one so fair, even with dyed hair. "I'll challenge him."

Dear God . . .

She should have expected this. Furiously she surged upright, hardly noticing that she spilled wine on the beautiful gown. Her chagrin about lost dreams crumbled to ash compared to Richard risking his life. "Don't be absurd. Forget my reputation and let the law take its course."

"He won't talk if I kill him first." Richard sounded older than his years.

She'd never loved him more and she'd never felt a stronger urge to hit him with something large and hard. She advanced, itching to shake sense into him. "He might kill you."

Richard shrugged and rescued her listing glass from her clenched fist. "Have some faith, darling. I'm a damned good shot."

"And he's a cheating swine."

"A duel means scandal." Sedgemoor's coolness deflated her anger like a pin to a balloon. "He's Leath's uncle. If you kill him, you'll have to flee the country."

Richard placed her glass safely on a table. "Unless we present our information to the law afterward."

Sedgemoor ran a weary hand through his hair. "How convincing will that look when he's unable to defend himself?"

"So I flee," Richard said with forced casualness. Once his indolent air might have convinced her. No longer. "Fairbrother is a blight upon the landscape. Expunging him is a public service."

Ignoring the duke, she grabbed Richard's good arm with frantic fingers. "Not at the cost of your life or freedom."

"I can't allow him to threaten you."

Her grip tightened. "You needn't act the knight in shining armor, Richard."

Wryness tinged his smile. "When it comes to you, I can't help it. Apparently I've discovered my backbone."

"Don't be an idiot," the duke snapped, setting his glass on the mantel with a click. "You've always been a better man than you pretended. Nobody with any gumption believes your ineffectual fribble act. If I was in trouble, you're the first person I'd turn to."

Amazement flooded Richard's face. He stared at his friend as if awaiting some quip to undercut the tribute. "I—"

Sedgemoor put him out of his misery. "Don't bother answering. You'll laugh it off anyway. I know how you react to anything that smacks of genuine feeling. But given you're determined to fling yourself before Fairbrother's pistol, you should know how highly I value you."

As so often, Richard surprised and impressed her. He crossed the room to clap the duke on the shoulder. He made no attempt to hide how the avowal moved him. "Thank you, Cam. When a man like you says such things—however unjustified—a fellow would be a cur to quibble." He paused. "In case Fairbrother's bullet finds its target, I couldn't ask for a better friend either."

The cold wind of their dilemma tempered the warmth in her heart. "This sounds unpleasantly like a farewell."

The duke faced her. "Richard's right. With Fairbrother at large, you're not safe."

"I can hide." The threat of losing Richard to a bullet constricted her belly with anguished denial.

"What about your career?" Richard asked.

Her smile was shaky. Astounding how profoundly she'd changed since falling in love with him. Her ambitions meant nothing compared to this man's well-being. "My work isn't worth your life."

"Let's not quarrel."

"No, by all means, let's not quarrel," she responded sarcastically. "Far better you get your brains blown out."

He stepped near enough to catch her face between his palms. The heat of his touch warred with the icy fear lancing her heart. "I have no intention of dying. I've got too much to live for."

"We're not alone," she stammered, trying to withdraw.

"Cam's a grown-up. He'll cope." His hold, while gentle, was adamant and his kiss, however brief, tasted like he promised her forever. She stared at him, distraught and dazzled in equal measure. By the time anger revived, he'd turned to his friend. "Will you act as my second?"

"Of course."

"Thank you."

"I'd like to challenge Fairbrother on your behalf."

Richard frowned. "That's not done, is it?"

"It's for the best. You'll murder the blackguard the moment you see him, devil take the rules of honor."

"Richard, don't do this." Genevieve caught his arm, prepared to restrain him physically if she must. "We'll go to the magistrate. Lord Neville will hang and never trouble us again. Surely that's what matters."

The tender sorrow in his smile made her want to cry. "Genevieve, I won't let anything hurt you."

Stupid, stupid man. Rage got the better of discretion. "Losing you will hurt me."

He covered the hand curled around his arm. "You won't lose me."

"I must go tonight," the duke said before she could refute Richard's fatuous statement.

"He's probably run." She clutched at straws, but she'd seize any chance, even the frailest, to save Richard. "After last night, he must know that the duke's awake to his games."

Richard shook his head. "He wants to spread news of our supposed elopement." His grip firmed in reassurance, whereas nothing except his withdrawal from this ludicrous duel could appease her.

The duke spoke to Genevieve who turned to face him. "Miss Barrett, will you stay? Sidonie's here to preserve the proprieties. Or would you prefer to return to the vicarage?"

"She's not leaving my side," Richard said quickly.

She summoned an unsteady smile. "I'd like to stay. May I write my aunt a note telling her where I am?"

"Of course."

"Godspeed, my friend," Richard said softly.

With a brief bow, Sedgemoor left the room.

Chapter Thirty-Six

Cam strode up to Neville Fairbrother's exquisite house, making no attempt to disguise his arrival, and banged the knocker hard. The house was quiet, but every instinct insisted that Fairbrother was in residence.

He slammed the knocker again and this time a footman opened the door. "I am Sedgemoor," he said coldly. "Pray arrange for someone to hold my horse. Inform Lord Neville that I wish to see him."

The ducal manner had its usual effect. Within minutes, he stood in the library. The room was more vitrine for *objets d'art* than refuge for reading. Glass cases crammed with gold, silver, and glittering gems surrounded Cam. One quick glance confirmed that Fairbrother's collection included everything from tiny, exquisite statues of Egyptian pharaohs through heavily embossed platters in Roman silver to intricate medieval ivories and enamels.

Fairbrother rose at Cam's appearance and it was clear that he didn't welcome the interruption. It was also clear that beneath his arrogance, he was wary.

So he damned well should be.

"Lord Neville."

"Your Grace, this call is unexpected." Fairbrother's bluster sat oddly with the scratches on his face.

Without invitation, Cam took one of the leather chairs facing the gilded baroque table where Fairbrother pored over his latest acquisition. The Harmsworth Jewel. Cam had never seen the troublesome artifact, but Richard had shown him drawings. "My lord, you and I are due a serious talk."

Fairbrother's swine-like eyes darted apprehensively around the room. "Indeed?"

"Indeed." Cam leaned his elbows on the arms of his chair and steepled his fingers. Outrage at the thought of Richard and Genevieve suffering a slow death tightened Cam's gut, but his façade remained as calm as if he discussed a tenant with his steward.

"We have no mutual interests."

Cam's lips curved. Fairbrother's unhealthy pallor indicated that the smile's implicit threat hadn't escaped him. "You don't consider attempted murder a matter for concern?"

"Attempted murder?"

"Of course," Cam said almost gently. "When you confine someone as expert in all things medieval as Genevieve Barrett in a crypt, it's prudent to shoot her first."

"I have no idea what you mean." Fairbrother faltered back a step and cast a panicked glance at the closed French doors. Then he retreated with more purpose toward the desk against the wall where he almost certainly kept a gun. "If you truly believe I've tried to kill someone, you'd have the law here."

Cam's eyes sharpened. "You don't want to menace me with a pistol. I am Sedgemoor. I have influence you can't even imagine."

"You're the bastard by-blow of a whore mother."

Cam's smile remained. Fairbrother would inevitably use the scandal to jockey for advantage. At least the man had stopped edging toward the desk. "Ah, the old gossip. So old it hardly matters. Whereas if you're hauled before the courts, the scandal will be fresh. Leath won't relish seeing his uncle tried as a common criminal. And a hanging will quite blot the family escutcheon."

"I won't hang."

"Burglary. Conspiracy. Assault. Attempted rape. Attempted murder. I'm sure those aren't the only charges. Although they're sufficient to dangle you from a rope."

Fairbrother watched him like a rabbit watched a fox. "So why not have me arrested?"

"A lady's reputation is involved."

Fairbrother sneered as he came around the table to stand in front of Cam. "No lady worthy of the name."

Cam's voice remained calm. "Careful. I won't sit quiet while you insult Miss Barrett."

Fairbrother showed no compunction. "We're at *point non plus*, then. If you can't inform the law without soiling Miss Barrett's name, it's best to overlook this entire matter."

"I imagine you think so." Cam paused for effect. "But gentlemen whose honor is impugned have other remedies."

Fairbrother laughed contemptuously. "You can't intend to challenge me, Your Grace. I've done you no wrong, and a man of your status doesn't risk his life over minor peccadillos."

By God, the man must be half lunatic. He'd filled a catalogue of villainies to shame the Devil. "Believe me, if not preempted, I'd happily face you over the barrel of a gun, but someone with more rights has priority. Sir Richard Harmsworth issued the challenge."

Bewilderment replaced Fairbrother's self-satisfaction. "Harmsworth? You jest, sir. I've never met the fellow."

"Indeed you have," Cam said softly. "He's familiar to you as Christopher Evans."

"This is bloody nonsense." Fairbrother finally abandoned all pretense of civility.

Cam's tone cooled. "Miss Barrett asked for Sir Richard's help to protect the jewel." It wasn't the truth but it would suffice.

Fairbrother snickered. "He helped, all right."

"I've warned you."

"There will be a scandal if I accept this gimcrack challenge," he said defiantly, leaning back against the table and folding his massive arms across his chest. Behind him, the jewel glinted malevolently.

"I agree."

Tension seeped from the hulking shoulders. "Then you're hoping to resolve this matter without bloodshed."

"Perhaps." The answer allowed Cam to introduce his scheme for untangling this deuced mess. Richard and Genevieve had better name him godfather to their first baby or he'd have something to say.

"If I keep my mouth shut about what that bastard Evans— no, pardon, Sir Richard—got up to with fair Genevieve, we'll call it quits, shall we?"

"Oh, no, my lord. Nowhere near compensation for the trouble you've caused. I demand the Harmsworth Jewel's return."

"And that's the end of it?"

"It's a start."

"If you're too lily-livered to bring the courts down upon my head and you dislike the alternative of a duel, there's nothing to negotiate." The man's confidence swelled every minute.

"I asked my friend Viscount Hillbrook to look into your activities. Jonas Merrick has resources mere mortals like you and I only dream about. Although I gather unearthing your unsavory dealings required little specialist knowledge."

Fairbrother went as pale as a fish's belly and he sagged against the table. "You're bluffing."

"Jonas came up with quite a list, even in the short time he devoted to the issue. Items stolen from museums joining your collection. Bribery and coercion in pursuit of your mania to possess. An inherited fortune squandered so that you now operate brothels and opium dens to fund your purchases. Violence. Murder. Theft. Fraud. I could continue."

"You can't prove any of this," the man said, but he already looked diminished, as though someone had sucked the air from him.

"Right now, it's merely reports on Hillbrook's desk. But he esteems Sir Richard and he's ready to investigate every last rumor."

"You're blackmailing me to be silent."

"Quite so."

Sweat sheened Fairbrother's jowls. "So let's be clear—if I remain discreet about Miss Barrett, you won't pursue these inquiries."

Cam shook his head with false regret. "Again, far too easy. After all, you tried to kill my friends. Not to mention my friend's dog."

"That mongrel?"

"He didn't deserve the treatment you handed him. But we digress."

"What do you want?"

Cam straightened. This was the important part. This was why he'd come alone. "You will sign your collection over to Miss Barrett. Lord Hillbrook and I will reinstate all stolen items to their rightful owners. Anything you purchased legitimately forms Miss Barrett's dowry."

"Nobody will marry that slut."

Cam leaped to his feet. His fist slammed into the man's gut, smashing him into the gilt and marble table, sliding the massive piece backward. Fairbrother slumped and would have fallen if he hadn't caught the gold chased edge.

"Your decision?" Cam asked pleasantly, opening and closing his bruised hand against his side.

Fairbrother scowled with undisguised hatred. "If I say no?"

"Then you meet Sir Richard at dawn." He paused. "My friend is a crack shot. That's not the alternative I'd choose. Particularly as unless you agree to my terms, I intend your ruin. If I were you, I'd surrender the collection, then make for the Continent."

"You're a cold bugger, Sedgemoor." Fairbrother's gaze swung around the glass cases as if he counted each item.

Cam shrugged. "What's it to be?"

The man seemed smaller, less formidable than he had ten minutes ago. "I'll send the relevant documents tomorrow."

Cam shook his head. "This ends tonight. You'll sign an undertaking to relinquish your collection to Miss Barrett. If you steal even one pawn from a chess set, Hillbrook and I will hunt you down like the feral cur you are."

"Then what?" His hands clutched at the table, the big ugly knuckles shining white.

"You go to France or Italy or hell for all I care. But remember, if I hear one whisper about Genevieve Barrett or any resident of Little Derrick, if I discover you're back to your bad old tricks, if I learn you've set foot on English soil, I will present the evidence I've amassed to the Crown."

"How will I live?"

"That's up to you." Cam ostentatiously checked his gold pocket watch. "My time runs short. Will you sign the paper and go, or would you rather face Sir Richard on the field of honor? Believe me, he's itching to place a bullet in your lardy carcass."

Without a word, Fairbrother trudged across to the desk and opened the top drawer. Cam maintained his relaxed posture, but suspense spurred his pulse. Would the fellow produce a gun? Fairbrother must know that all his schemes came to dust and killing the Duke of Sedgemoor ended any hope of escaping legal consequences. Still, he was a desperate, angry, vengeful man. A cornered rat.

When Fairbrother withdrew a thick sheet of cream paper, Cam silently released his breath. He hadn't been sure his gamble would succeed.

The over-ornate room was silent as Fairbrother scrawled on the paper. Flames crackled in the hearth and candlelight gleamed on the treasure lining the walls. Cam wasn't nearly the connoisseur Genevieve was, but he knew enough to recognize that Fairbrother's collection put his family heirlooms in the shade. Beautiful, costly items surrounded him. Beautiful, costly items that had earned their ransom in blood and misery.

Eventually Fairbrother straightened and shoved the paper toward Cam with a contemptuous gesture. "Here."

"Good." Cam read the document, expecting some trick. But the will, which to all intents it was, appeared straightforward. He glanced up. "And I'll take this." He closed his hand over the Harmsworth Jewel and slipped it into his pocket.

"You're a bastard, Sedgemoor," Fairbrother said in a low, shaking voice.

"So they say." Cam's smile was icy. "Now ring for the footman."

Fairbrother frowned. "Why the devil do you want a footman?"

"Humor me."

Fairbrother shrugged with ill grace and wrenched the bell pull near the desk. The footman who had greeted Cam appeared.

"See His Grace out." Fairbrother stumbled over the title. His outrage boiled closer to the surface. Cam had a feeling that if he asked for that signed paper now, Fairbrother would consign him to hell, whatever the consequences.

"Good evening, my lord." Cam rose with a nonchalance designed to irk.

At the door, he turned back. Only to catch an expression of such despair and fury on Fairbrother's face that briefly he almost pitied the fellow. Fairbrother stared at his priceless objects with such naked pain, it was like he surrendered his children. Then Cam recalled this man's sins, and compassion dissolved into loathing.

Cam strode across the marble hall with its porphyry columns and coffered ceiling. In the huge space, his footsteps echoed eerily. This gaudy house seemed more mausoleum than home. He shook off the breath of evil and ran down the stairs. He tipped the groom holding his horse and mounted.

Instead of galloping off, he ambled along the lime tree avenue. Once away from the house, he circled off the drive toward the back. From here, he could see the gorgeous and oppressive room where he'd confronted Fairbrother.

He reined Gaspard in and bent to pat his glossy black neck, soothing the horse into stillness. The footman drew the curtains, the footman who would swear that when Sedgemoor left, Neville Fairbrother had been in perfect health, if a little bruised around the midriff and bearing abrasions from the previous night.

Darkness cloaked Cam. A faint rustle from the trees. The scent of clean air, purer and fresher than anything he'd breathed in Youngton Hall. A bird fluttered overhead, making him jump. Dear God, his nerves were more on edge than he'd realized.

Ten minutes passed. Half an hour. Still he sat.

Finally he straightened from his slouch and firmed his grip on the reins. It was time to go, to assure Richard and Genevieve that their future was secure from Lord Neville's poison.

It was only then that he heard what he'd waited for.

A single shot rang out from the house, shattering the peaceful night.

Chapter Thirty-Seven

Lord Neville was dead.

Exhausted, dazed, overwhelmed, still aching from her recent trials, Genevieve lay in her luxurious bedroom at Leighton Court and struggled to accept that Lord Neville's evil influence had ended. Even more important, Richard wouldn't perish on the field of honor. Thanks to Sedgemoor, she and the man she loved were safe at last. The duke still made her shy, but she'd never forget what she owed him.

After a couple of hours, Sedgemoor had returned to Leighton Court. But they'd only received confirmation of Lord Neville's death when the local magistrate sent the duke a note as a courtesy to the premier nobleman in the area. Until that moment, Genevieve couldn't trust that the nightmare was over.

The clock struck three with Genevieve staring wide-eyed into the darkness. Sighing, she shifted on the crisp white sheets. She was so weary she felt close to tears, yet still she couldn't sleep. If only Richard was here to hold her against the clamor in her head. In the last two days, she'd lived through so much. Abduction. Losing her virginity. The revelation of Richard's identity. Her father's betrayal. Those blissful stolen moments in the barn. Captivity. Declarations of love. The escape. Lord Neville's final defeat.

She'd never again complain about a dull life.

If she must be restless, why couldn't she bask in the joy of love returned? Instead a quieter moment played ccaselessly in her mind. The doubt and self-hatred in Richard's voice when he spoke of his bastardy.

She'd learned enough about him to realize that for every slight he described, he'd endured a thousand more that he'd never reveal. His long-concealed anguish made her stomach cramp with pity—and anger at those who disparaged him.

She'd once thought him a man who had enjoyed an unfairly easy ride through life, thanks to looks, wealth, and breeding. How appallingly wrong she'd been. How self-satisfied. How self-righteous.

Yet the miracle was that still he said he loved her. And she loved him. More than she loved anything else in the world. She wished she lay waking because she gloried in his love. But a sadder, more onerous truth pounded in her mind as she counted each slow minute toward dawn.

If she loved Richard, she couldn't contribute to his misery.

When Richard entered the library, the sun just peeked above the horizon. Immediately, his attention leveled on Genevieve. She curled up in the bay window, staring pensively out at the dew-laden garden.

"Can't you sleep?" He closed the door behind him. The servants were about, but he assumed that Sedgemoor and his guests were still asleep upstairs. Although he'd heard Consuela crying during the night, so that assumption might be a little optimistic for Jonas and Sidonie.

Genevieve turned toward him, the glow in her eyes setting his heart aflame. "No."

Desire slammed through him. Unfortunately, he couldn't do a damned thing about it.

He'd dressed before coming downstairs, but she looked as though she'd just risen from her bed. Her beautiful hair lay loose and she wore an extravagant green silk dressing gown. He loved to see her lush beauty arrayed in rich fabrics and colors like this or like last night's gown. She'd always been a jewel. She'd only lacked the right setting to do her justice.

"Me either." His step light—he was in love, his darling loved him back, and the sinister forces that had threatened their lives and happiness had receded, he hoped forever—he crossed to her side.

She raised her arms. "Kiss me, Richard."

"With pleasure."

Heat. Passion. *Love.* Eventually he raised his head and cradled her against him. He must look insufferably smug, but he couldn't help it. To think that this magnificent woman loved him.

"We can't make love," she said breathlessly. "Anyone could come in."

He pretended shock. "Why, Miss Barrett, the thought never crossed my mind."

With a low laugh, she pressed closer. "I'm sure."

"I can't tell you how often I watched you stitching away on your window seat and wanted to have my way with you."

"You're a wicked man," she said in a tone that told him she loved him.

He caught the hand fisted against his shoulder. "What have you got there?"

Her fingers unfolded to reveal the Harmsworth Jewel. Cam had passed it to her last night. Once it had offered

Richard a preternatural connection to a heritage that he now accepted wasn't his by blood. And never would be. The realization was remarkably liberating.

He stared at the gold and enamel artifact. "How powerful our imaginations are. When I thought the jewel was real, it was magical. Now however beautiful it is, it's just an object."

"I'm giving it to you."

His head jerked up. "It doesn't prove anything about my birth."

To his regret, she pulled away. His knowledge of her love was so new that any distance felt like a danger to his happiness. Then he caught her grave expression and knew that the chill trickling down his backbone didn't entirely result from clinging insecurities. "Genevieve, what is it?"

She stood. The light strengthened, revealing that the silver had left her eyes. Instead they were a flat gray, like the sea on a rainy day. "Only you and I know that the jewel is a copy."

He frowned, not sure where she was going. "Cam does."

"You could swear him to silence."

Deeply perturbed now, he too rose. "Why on earth would I do that? Once your article is published, the secret will be out."

Her stare was unwavering. "I'm withdrawing my article."

Shocked, he stepped back, bumping his legs against the edge of the seat. "What the hell is this?"

Her shoulders were as straight as a ruler. She looked like she faced a firing squad. "My article will harm you. I'm not going to publish it."

Genevieve saw that Richard didn't understand. Which was odd. Usually he was, if anything, too quick to pick up on things.

"Harm me?" He reached out to touch her before, thank goodness, hesitating. Despite knowing that this was her only course of action, she wasn't sure she was strong enough to persevere. If Richard cajoled her with tenderness or passion, she'd weaken.

She couldn't weaken.

During last night's long, dark watch, she'd realized that if she loved Richard Harmsworth, she couldn't expose the truth about the Harmsworth Jewel. His words in the crypt, about a fraud of a baronet pursuing a fraud of a treasure, had haunted her. She couldn't invite the world's spite to his door.

"Richard, all your life you've suffered because of your birth. Turning the Harmsworth Jewel into a *cause célèbre* will only reopen old wounds."

His lips twisted. "The gossip never goes away, my love. Your article won't change that."

She shook her head. "It gives the world another stick for beating you."

He frowned. "What about your career?"

She twined her arms around herself. It was warm for October, but she was as cold as if she stood in a freezing north wind. After struggling to reach this decision, she thought she'd come to terms with her choice. Here, surrendering her dreams, she felt slowly and painfully crushed in a giant fist. "I won't use my work to your detriment."

"People will always snicker about my birth. You deserve your moment in the sun." His tone developed an edge. "You've already sacrificed yourself for your father. You won't sacrifice yourself for me."

She fought tears. No joy could compare to her love for Richard. But she'd so looked forward to claiming a place in the wider world. Why was it that the two things she wanted,

Richard's happiness and her personal fulfillment, had to clash? It seemed bitterly unfair.

The complaint of a spoilt child. *Time to grow up, Genevieve.*

Shame steadied her voice. "That's not your decision to make. When I go home, I'll write to Dr. Partridge and tell him that I was mistaken about the jewel being a forgery."

"You're not mistaken," Richard said harshly.

No, she wasn't. But the image of the tormented boy building such powerful defenses against a malicious world broke her heart. She couldn't love Richard and expose him to public ridicule, whatever it cost her.

"You should be pleased." She knew by his unimpressed expression that her attempt at a smile was a rank failure. "You've succeeded in what you came to Little Derrick to do. You can now wave the jewel under the nose of anyone who dares to deride you and nobody will guess it's not the real thing."

If anything, he looked angrier. "It will be a lie."

Her own temper stirred. "That should be no impediment. It's not as though lying isn't second nature to you."

He whitened and retreated another step. "I suppose I deserve that."

Eaten by guilt, she wanted to snatch the words back. But it was too late. She stared at him helplessly, wondering why the space between them suddenly felt like a thousand miles instead of a few feet. "This is what you wanted."

"I was a damned fool," he said bitterly. "How the devil did you expect me to react to this ludicrous offer?"

"I thought you'd be grateful," she muttered.

His expression darkened. "Did you really? Apparently your opinion of me hasn't changed since our first meeting."

She flinched. "When you've had time to think—"

"I still won't accept this unnecessary act of self-flagellation."

She turned away, unable to bear the wretchedness and frustrated anger in his face. Right now, he thought of her welfare, not his own. She loved him for that, but it reinforced her decision. "I might come across something else that will make a splash in scholarly circles."

"Nothing to compare with exposing the legendary Harmsworth Jewel as a fraud."

No, nothing like that. Such discoveries were unique. But how could she regret saving Richard from hurt? Her hand shaking, she placed the jewel on one of the heavy mahogany tables that filed down the center of the long room. "Take it. Do what you originally intended. Use it to compel the world's respect."

"A jewel can't earn me respect. Since I've come to Little Derrick, I've learned the world's opinion doesn't matter to me. Only yours does."

She turned back, blinking away tears. "You have my respect. You know that."

In his pale face, his mouth was stern. "I can't let you do this, Genevieve."

"You have no right to *let* me do anything," she snapped. Antagonism was easier to handle than devastation. Right now, perhaps it was true that all he cared about was her love. But that wouldn't last. Not when he returned to his glittering ballrooms and society friends. Then he'd hate that she'd exposed him to fresh mockery.

Perhaps, God forbid, he'd even come to hate her. She couldn't endure that.

His eyes narrowed. "Do you want to fight about this?"

"There's nothing to fight about." She glared at him and raised her chin defiantly. "My mind's made up."

She waited for more arguments, but he stared at her as if she was a stranger. His closed expression cut sharper than a knife.

"Well, that's it, then," he said in a clipped tone. "Of course, your decision is the only one that counts. Yet again, the independent, self-sufficient Miss Barrett goes her own way."

She recoiled at the bite in his tone, but couldn't back down. "I'm a woman alone. I have to make my own decisions."

How in heaven's name had everything come to this? Only a few moments ago, he'd held her in his arms.

"If you're alone, it's because you want it that way." The muscle flickered in his cheek, always sign of strong emotion, and she realized that in trying to save him from hurt, she'd hurt him.

She stood silent, unable to summon words insisting that she didn't want to be alone, she wanted to be with him. Yesterday Richard had told her that he loved her and she thought she'd never feel lonely again. Today she stared at him across an impassable gulf and felt lonelier than she ever had in her life.

"I have to go to London with Cam." He stalked toward the table. His voice was unemotional, as if he'd never called her his darling. The knife stabbed deeper. "He's in this mess because of my dashed stupidity. There will be questions about Fairbrother, legal issues."

He paused and she wondered if he meant to make some conciliatory gesture. Her hands curled at her sides as she fought the urge to reach after him and tell him she'd do whatever he asked. In this case, what he asked would injure him. She couldn't countenance that.

Genevieve turned away and stared out the window at Leighton Court's elaborate gardens. Although tears prevented her from seeing them. Was this how everything ended? A few sharp words and Richard retreating to London, and with that, the joy was done?

He continued, still in that same neutral tone. "Promise that you won't do anything until you hear from me."

"I can't wait. Dr. Partridge is preparing to publish." She struggled to match Richard's uninvolved manner, but her voice emerged raw with misery. "I won't change my mind. As I said, this is purely up to me."

After a weighty pause, he answered. This time even his well-practiced nonchalance couldn't hide the anger vibrating under his words. "As you wish."

Dear Lord, it wasn't as she wished. She turned to ask Richard to wait, to beg him to let her explain, although surely he must know the reasons for what she did.

He was gone. Her gaze fell upon the library table. He'd taken the Harmsworth Jewel.

Richard was halfway to London before his temper eased enough for his mind to make sense of this morning's disaster. He didn't see Genevieve before leaving. He'd dashed off a note to Cam saying he'd be in London, then he'd returned to the vicarage for his carriage and a change of clothes. The phaeton now hurtled east at a pace that sent the mud flying.

How dare Genevieve sacrifice her dreams for him? He wanted to give her a good shake and tell her to wake up to herself. He wanted to kiss her into a stupor until questions of right and wrong no longer mattered.

But after several hours of furious driving, he began to see that she'd made the offer out of love, foolish girl. It was an act of such wholehearted generosity, he could hardly comprehend it.

Gratitude made him no more likely to accept her

self-denial. Genevieve underestimated how she'd changed him. His old misguided self had crouched behind an imperturbable façade. Now that Genevieve loved him for the man he was, the world's derision had lost its sting.

He'd damn well show her that in loving Richard Harmsworth, she gave up nothing. One hand slid into his pocket to touch the Harmsworth Jewel. He no longer needed it to shore up his pride, but the trinket would yet prove its value.

Chapter Thirty-Eight

First Genevieve noticed the dog.

From the parlor window, she saw Sirius trot past in the late afternoon light. Nerves set her pulse racing. If Sirius appeared, Richard couldn't be far behind.

She'd picked up her embroidery, but the sight of her elephant peony made her want to cry, so instead she stared moodily outside. Hecuba curled beside her, as out of sorts as her mistress. Autumn drew to a close. Since her last meeting with Richard, Genevieve had felt cold to the bone. Although that wasn't altogether the season's fault.

As if summoned by her thoughts, the stylish phaeton turned into the back lane. When she saw Richard, bundled into a caped coat, his hat at a jaunty angle, her heart hiccupped. As he passed, she caught a flash of his face. His features were set and determined. He looked more like the man who had rescued her from Lord Neville than the man who had mocked her inept stitchery.

"Who is that, dear?" her aunt asked from her chair near the fire.

"Sir Richard," she said without turning. The carriage disappeared in a cloud of dust.

"That's nice."

Curious, Genevieve glanced at Aunt Lucy. She sounded remarkably calm about the famous beau's visit. A distinct contrast to her excitement when Genevieve had told her that Christopher Evans was really the fabulously wealthy baronet Richard Harmsworth. Genevieve had taken her cue from Sedgemoor and repeated the story about Richard guarding the Harmsworth Jewel from Lord Neville. Lord Neville who had killed himself a fortnight ago to escape prosecution for theft.

"You don't seem surprised," she said flatly.

Her aunt laid aside her knitting and shot her a withering look. "Of course he's come back, Genevieve. Don't be a henwit."

Well, that put her in her place, she thought, flopping back against the window embrasure. She hadn't been nearly so certain she'd see him again. After all, she hadn't heard from Richard since their quarrel.

Unexpectedly it was Sedgemoor who had sent her a couple of notes informing her of developments. The inquest into Lord Neville's death had brought in a verdict of suicide. No alternate theories had arisen. Greengrass, named as a person of interest, had vanished without trace.

Thanks to Lord Hillbrook, the world now knew the scope of Lord Neville's criminal activities. No wonder the man had lived in the country where he could display his ill-gotten gains without questions. No suspicion in Lord Neville's suicide had fallen on either Richard Harmsworth or Camden Rothermere. As far as Genevieve knew, her name was never mentioned.

She'd pored over the London papers, seeking details of

the brouhaha that engulfed the Fairbrothers, reaching as high as Lord Neville's top-lofty nephew, the Marquess of Leath. Actually if truth were told, she'd searched like a love-struck adolescent for the merest mention of Richard Harmsworth. Every time she saw his name, in connection with the Fairbrother scandal or detailing his appearance at some glamorous event, their hours together receded further into the realm of fantasy.

She couldn't imagine a man who hobnobbed with the king telling her that he loved her. She couldn't imagine such a man returning to wrench her from the melancholy limbo that had gripped her since his departure.

If she'd ever felt herself above the common run of her sex, she felt that no longer. She was as capable of making a fool of herself over a man as any naïve dairymaid or giggly miss at Almack's. She couldn't even find comfort anymore in her dreams of scholarly acclaim.

Richard had made no promises, no plans for the future. She couldn't accuse him of raising false hopes. But she loved him. Hope, false or real, had become the breath of life. With every day of her lover's absence, that breath became fainter. Until she'd convinced herself that everything was over between them. Even worse, they'd parted in rancor.

Yet here he was, rolling along in his carriage as though he hadn't left her to lonely torment for fourteen whole days. Was he here to convince her to publish her article? Or out of politeness? After all, he'd deceived everyone in Little Derrick. His scruples must insist upon apologizing to the Barretts for his falsehoods.

If he apologized to her, she honestly thought she'd brain him with her sewing box.

Dorcas appeared. She looked like someone had struck her with a cricket bat. "Sir Richard Harmsworth, missus."

"Please send him in," Aunt Lucy said before Genevieve could respond.

Dorcas performed a shaky curtsy and held the door open. Richard strolled into the tiny parlor and Genevieve understood why Dorcas acted like she'd witnessed a heavenly apparition. For all her turmoil, Genevieve felt rather that way herself.

"Mrs. Warren, your servant." He swept off his hat and bowed to Aunt Lucy with an elegance that contrasted sharply with this rundown room. He turned to Genevieve. "Miss Barrett, a pleasure to meet you again."

"Yes," she said faintly, standing and feeling completely inadequate to handling this resplendent creature.

He wore a royal blue coat, and a gray-and-white-striped waistcoat that fitted him within an inch. His faun breeches displayed not a wrinkle and his boots were so shiny that she'd see her face more clearly in their black leather than in her mirror upstairs. A gold fob glinted in his pocket and a sapphire pin the color of his eyes adorned his impossibly complex neck cloth.

If this was what he usually looked like, she could understand his shock when she'd accused him of overdressing as Christopher Evans. The man who stared at her with a quizzical light in his beautiful eyes belonged in a painting by Raeburn or Lawrence. Hecuba sprang down with more spirit than she'd displayed in a fortnight and twined around his long legs.

"Sir Richard, how good of you to call." Her aunt rose to lift the purring cat and shot Genevieve an annoyed glance, wordlessly insisting that she gather herself. "Would you like tea?"

"How kind," he responded smoothly.

Genevieve supposed he'd always possessed this effortless

assurance. When he'd first arrived at the vicarage, she remembered wanting to puncture his conceit. Today he looked as out of place in their untidy parlor as she would dancing onstage at the Theatre Royal.

A silence descended and he sent Genevieve a questioning look. Her aunt struggled to restrain a wriggling Hecuba.

"I'll see about a fresh pot. Genevieve, will you entertain our guest?" Aunt Lucy's voice developed an edge. "Perhaps he'd like to sit down after his journey from London."

Genevieve continued to gape at Richard like a rag-mannered hoyden. Or even more mortifying, like a starving urchin outside a pie stall. This gorgeous man couldn't have told her he loved her or kissed her or dragged her to safety through stinking mud. Somewhere there must be another Richard Harmsworth. The man she knew well enough to tease and scold and love.

"I can't claim to have come so far, Mrs. Warren. I'm at Leighton Court for the next few nights."

"Is His Grace in residence? I hadn't heard."

"No. But he's given me the run of the place."

"Please sit down," her aunt said. "I won't be long and you and Genevieve know each other so well."

As she retreated to her window seat, heat tinged Genevieve's cheeks at her aunt's unintentional double entendre. She and Richard did indeed know each other, in ways a vicar's daughter should never know a man to whom she wasn't married.

Genevieve stared into her lap, feeling awkward. She'd never been tongue-tied with Richard, even when she believed he was a lying thief. Especially not then. But this man was a stranger.

She heard the parlor door close.

"Alone at last."

She jerked her head up. He'd chosen a chair to her right. His eyes brimmed with laughter and she didn't trust that note of fond exasperation, just because she so desperately wanted to hear it. "Don't mock me."

"Why not? You're acting like a ninnyhammer."

"Charming," she snapped. "You're blond again."

The change in his hair was part of what left her so unsettled. The gleaming gold suited him much better than muddy brown. But she couldn't relate to this shining Apollo, even as her heart clenched with hopeless love. She wanted Christopher Evans back. She could imagine Christopher Evans needing Genevieve Barrett in his life. She couldn't picture this epitome of fashion sparing a glance for her rumpled person.

Self-consciously he touched his hair without ruffling its perfection. It was like he was made of marble and paint and enamel, not flesh at all. She struggled to recall the hot press of their bodies. The memory was hazy.

"I can't say I miss that damned sticky paste." When she didn't reply, he sighed. "I'm sorry I took so long to return. It's been a devil of a few weeks, dealing with Fairbrother's death and ensuring the scandal never touched you."

"Thank you," she said ungraciously.

She hated that he saw her so clearly. What she really wanted was for him to sweep her into his arms and kiss her and tell her that he loved her and that he forgave her for being a witch last time they were together. How she wished she wore her gold silk instead of this faded blue muslin. Except her good dress was seasons out of date and couldn't compete with his splendor.

He leaned forward and for one breathless moment, she wondered if he'd take her hand. "Where's your father?"

Her breath escaped in an exhalation of bewilderment. "He's been in Oxford since Lord Neville's death."

His patron's suicide had devastated Ezekiel Barrett. He'd categorically refused to believe the reports of illegal activities, not to mention the attempt on Genevieve's life.

"Genevieve—"

She stood on shaky legs. "I suppose you've left Sirius at the stable. I'll go and see him."

"Genevieve, I'm sorry I didn't adequately appreciate what you offered to do for me."

It seemed he did mean to apologize. Was that indeed why he was here? "It's of no importance."

Annoyance darkened his features and fleetingly he looked like her Richard. "Damn it, yes, it is important. I've got something to tell you."

Oh, no. That sentence never boded well. She braced for bad news, even as frogs the size of ponies jumped about in her stomach. "What?"

He slid a hand into his coat and produced a letter. "Read this."

Not sure of his purpose, she accepted the sealed paper with a shaking hand. Did he say farewell in writing? "Is it from you?"

He scowled. "Why the devil should I write to you? I'm right here."

For how long? He'd stayed away two weeks without a word. And she remembered Mrs. Meacham's magazines saying that he sought a high-born wife.

A faint smile warmed his expression. "I promise it won't bite."

Reluctantly she opened the letter, then gasped in surprise when she saw the heading. She sank back onto the window seat. "It's from the British Museum."

His smile intensified. "Yes, it is."

Curiosity forced its way through the fog of misery that

had enveloped her since he'd marched away in a temper. "It invites me to lecture next month." She raised her head and stared at him in confusion. "I don't understand."

He stood. "I showed them the jewel and told them what a genius you are. Dr. Partridge had given me a copy of the article so I had more than my limited eloquence to bolster my claims. The trustees were slavering to have you address them before I'd finished."

"But—"

He swept over her quibbling. "You won't surrender your dreams because of me, Genevieve."

"I wrote to Dr. Partridge withdrawing the article."

"He's merely delayed publication while you reconsidered. I told him you had some final threads to tie up."

"You visited him?"

"He's not the world's most scintillating company."

No, he wasn't. She blinked at Richard in speechless admiration.

He stepped toward her. "Don't be angry. You'll have everything you ever wanted."

Except you.

The thought went unvoiced. He still hadn't mentioned love.

He eyed her with uncharacteristic diffidence. "Are you angry?"

"I feel like I've been carried away in a whirlwind." She glanced down at the letter on her lap. "The British Museum?"

His smile conveyed satisfaction. "You can't say no. If you do, I'll look like a deuced fool."

"It feels unreal."

"You'll be famous."

Famous and alone. Right now, that seemed a punishment

rather than a reward. "But it will bring the Harmsworth name into disrepute."

He shrugged. "We Harmsworths are used to that." He paused. "Don't deny me the pleasure of seeing you take your rightful place in the world, Genevieve. Between lawyers and magistrates, I've spent the last two weeks chasing dry-as-dust scholars. If you cheat me of my triumph, I'll sulk until Christmas."

So like him to trivialize his massive efforts on her behalf. She'd be churlish to refuse something that he'd taken so much trouble over. She didn't underestimate the obstacles to gaining her a public hearing at such a prestigious institution.

She'd once called him St. George—now he'd set himself to slay all the dragons standing in the way of her success. Her objections to exposing the jewel's origins persisted, but his gargantuan efforts proved that he could live with any consequences.

His advocacy left her winded, astonished, moved. After a lifetime of dealing with the closed minds of male academics, she could imagine the battle he'd fought even to get the authorities at the museum to listen, let alone accept her as a fellow expert.

She should be grateful. She was. But he didn't act the lover and he'd had a fortnight back in his real world. Was this extravagant gesture meant to celebrate his love or mark his departure? The most likely answer was that he'd decided his idyll in Little Derrick was over. Not that it had been much of an idyll, with homicidal noblemen, voluble vicars, and prickly bluestockings wherever he looked.

"Thank you." She struggled to sound pleased. "It was kind of you to do this. And to come all this way to tell me in person."

His mouth flattened. "I'm not bloody kind."

He caught her hand in an uncompromising grip. His level regard indicated that he meant business. No trace of teasing now. His shoulders straightened, then to her amazement, he dropped to one knee, still clutching her hand.

"What on earth are you doing?" she asked breathlessly, sliding back against the windowsill. His touch still set her pulses leaping. More powerfully after days without him.

"Be quiet, Genevieve. For two weeks, I've shored up my courage. Your caprices won't divert me."

"Caprices?" she repeated on a rising note, then fell silent when she met his gaze. He stared at her as if he'd never seen a woman before. Nervously she raised her free hand to her cheek. "Have I got something on my face?"

The intensity drained from his expression. "No. You're beautiful. You're always beautiful."

Her heart crashed against her ribs so hard that it must surely shatter. "Stop these mad antics."

His hand tightened to the verge of pain. "Mad or not, I love you and I can't live without you. Will you do me the incomparable honor of becoming my wife?"

The breath jammed in her throat and she ripped her hand free. In forbidden dreams, she'd imagined this moment. Now it arrived, she found herself completely flummoxed. All her old fears about dwindling into a wife rose like a wave to swamp her hopes for a future with Richard. She could perhaps conquer those doubts—after all, hadn't he just demonstrated his wholehearted support for her ambitions? But the prospect of marrying this dazzling creature who watched her so unwaveringly terrified her.

"You never mentioned marriage," she choked out, her hands fluttering like some nitwit heroine's in a play. Dear God, every moment proved she lacked the sophistication to become Lady Harmsworth.

"Of course I intend marriage." He frowned faintly. "When we were in the crypt, I distinctly remember saying that I wanted to marry you."

"You were joking," she said miserably. "You're always joking."

"Not always. I wasn't joking when I said that I love you."

"Two weeks ago."

His laugh was a dismissive snort. "I know you think me a shallow sod, but I doubt a fortnight would make even the shallowest sod forget the woman he wants to spend his life with." All amusement evaporated. "Or have you changed? Have you decided you don't love me?"

She didn't answer. Admitting her feelings left her too vulnerable when she remained torn and unsure. She recalled the bride of impeccable pedigree. "You have to marry to restore the Harmsworth prestige."

"I have to marry where I love."

It was a good answer, but still she wasn't convinced. "I won't fit into your world."

He rose, towering over her, his expression severe. "How do you know?"

"Look at you." Her quivering anguish was audible. She stood too. She felt too much at a disadvantage sitting. "You're dressed for a ball at St. James and I'm a bookish frump."

"I wouldn't be allowed into a ball wearing breeches. Not done, don't you know?"

His humor cut her on the raw. She swung away and stared blindly out the window. "Don't laugh at me."

She heard him shift closer. Her skin tightened with longing for his touch, even as she braced against slumping into his arms and telling him that she'd take him under any circumstances, as long as he never left. Truly pathetic.

"I'm sorry," he said quietly. "I probably should have

toned down the clothes, but devil take it, I'm proposing. A man ought to look his best when he asks a woman to marry him. I can't believe that you're refusing me because of what I'm wearing."

Put like that, her objections sounded insane. But she understood her qualms, and she had an inkling he did too. "I haven't refused you," she muttered. "Yet."

She started when his hand slid around her waist, although he made no attempt to coax her closer. "Does that mean there's hope?"

She sniffed. Curse him, she was crying. "That means I know it's a mistake to marry you." She blinked away stinging tears and turned without breaking his hold. "Richard, I know I'm making a muddle of this and that you must think I'm off my head, but I come from humble circumstances and you move in the highest circles. I'm direct and difficult and odd. I'm not the wife Sir Richard Harmsworth deserves."

To her astonishment, anger turned his blue eyes black. "You're the only wife I want. You put every other woman into the shade. You'll have London at your feet within a week. After you've given your lecture and your article is published, everyone will wonder what you see in a dunderhead like me." His expression darkened. "Or have you decided that you can't bear to marry a bastard?"

She stared at him, too astonished even to cry. "Of course not. I love you. I don't care who your parents are."

"And don't you think I love you, whether you come to me in a pinafore with a hundred pockets, or a silk gown, or a damned hessian sack?" His expression became breathtakingly grave. "Genevieve, you're the only woman I've ever loved. If I must dress like a farmhand the rest of my days, I'll do it as long as you become my bride."

A choked laugh escaped. "Now I know you must love me."

He drew her inexorably nearer. "Of course I love you. The question is—do you love me?"

"I told you I did, didn't I?" she said gruffly, placing her hands on the lapels of his spectacular coat. She still thought she ought to wash before she touched him, but she had an idea that the suggestion might annoy him. Right now, she didn't want him annoyed. Not when the glint in his eyes said that he was about to kiss her. At last.

"In between a lot of other twaddle." He paused. "Do I need to go on my knees again?"

She shook her head. "No."

"Does that mean you'll marry me? Because you know I don't have a hope of happiness away from you, don't you?"

Her heart slowed to a steady rhythm. She'd been nervous and afraid and unsure and, yes, piqued that he'd stayed away for two weeks when she'd been so lonely. The unimportant clamor receded. This was the man she wanted. This was the man she would have.

"For God's sake, sweetheart, stop torturing me and say yes."

He looked desperate and unsure. Which she rather liked. It reminded her that he was as vulnerable to her as she was to him. Hard to believe when he looked like he did. Then she recalled that he'd spent a lifetime cultivating this elegance as a defense. His handsome exterior—much as she appreciated it—wasn't the real Richard. The real Richard was brave and good and had a loyal and loving heart. Which it seemed he placed at her feet. Lucky her.

"Will you kiss me?" she asked huskily.

"Now?"

She nodded, her lips curving. She didn't feel inadequate anymore. She felt beautiful and adored and capable of holding onto this fascinating, wonderful man. "Now."

"Your aunt could come in," he drawled without shifting.

"Let her." Although her aunt's absence proved suspiciously lengthy. Aunt Lucy must be waiting until things were settled before she reappeared to offer congratulations. She'd long ago guessed that her niece was head over heels in love with their former lodger.

"Will you say yes if I kiss you?"

"I certainly won't if you don't kiss me."

He sighed. "You're impossible."

With his free hand, he tipped her chin up. He leaned down and pressed his lips to hers. Immediate heat bloomed and she melted against him, kissing him back with all the love in her heart. By the time he paused for breath, she felt off-kilter and misty-eyed and ready to waltz around the room singing.

Slowly she opened her eyes and stared up at Richard. He looked as if that kiss had flung him into infinity too. Good.

Another smile curled her lips and she stroked his cheek. "Richard, I love you with all my heart. Of course I'll marry you."

Epilogue

London, April 1828

I shouldn't be here."

Genevieve stopped studying the magnificent Turner over the alabaster mantelpiece and eyed her husband with loving impatience. "Of course you should."

Richard swung into another turn, pacing toward the end of the gracious drawing room decorated in the modish rococo revival style. It said something for the changes Genevieve had undergone since becoming Lady Harmsworth six months ago that she knew what was fashionable and what wasn't. One result of marrying an arbiter of elegance.

"This can serve no purpose."

"Then we'll pay our respects and leave," she said calmly.

He usually wasn't skittish, but she'd long ago realized that belying his casual manner, when he cared, he cared to the depths of his being. He cared about his friends. He cared about his wife, thank goodness. And much as he loathed admitting it, he cared about his mother.

The woman who had invited them to her Mayfair house this afternoon.

Genevieve had been surprised when Richard wrote to Augusta, the Dowager Lady Harmsworth, to inform her of his marriage. A week after he'd proposed, she and Richard had wed at Little Derrick by special license. Dr. Barrett had returned from Oxford to perform the ceremony.

The church had been packed with well-wishers. Sedgemoor and his sister Lydia with her husband. The Hillbrooks. The villagers, including George. Her aunt, who told everyone that she'd promoted the match from the first. Aunt Lucy now lived at Polliton Place in Norfolk, Richard's family seat, where she flirted like a giddy girl with a handsome local squire.

That morning in Little Derrick had been Genevieve's last cordial encounter with her father. Once her article appeared and she'd given the first of several well-received lectures, his pique had been boundless. He'd never forgive her for breaking away, even as he basked in his new status as a baronet's father-in-law. Since the wedding, her father had renounced parish duties to accept a place at his old college.

Genevieve's article had created a flurry in academic circles and had led to numerous invitations to investigate heirlooms of doubtful provenance. She'd been right to fear some backlash as the Harmsworth name again stirred talk. But she'd soon realized that Richard hadn't exaggerated when he claimed he didn't care a fig for society's approval. The malice had quickly faded when it became clear to the world that the bastard baronet and his eccentric wife were beyond the old scandal's reach.

Genevieve and Richard had spent their first six months of marriage traveling. A honeymoon in Italy became a tour of medieval sites in Spain and France. So magical to see places she'd read about all her life. Even more magical to see them in the company of the man she loved.

She'd wondered whether her husband's lukewarm interest in the Middle Ages would survive imprisonment in the crypt. But he'd escorted her with good grace. When she'd quizzed him on his tolerance, he'd swept her into bed, then pointed out that when she was happy, she was amenable to making him happy. Scholarship hadn't fully occupied their time, she smiled to recall.

"You're laughing at me."

Heat tinged her cheeks. "I was thinking about that inn above Roncesvalles."

He ceased pacing and regarded her with sudden interest. "Were you indeed, you saucy wench?"

"The painting reminds me of the landscape." Which was a complete lie, although now she checked the canvas, the rugged scenery conveyed a hint of the Pyrenees.

"I'm sure." He prowled toward her, his expression intent.

Dear Lord. "Richard, you can't tumble me here. Your mother may come in any moment."

"To Hades with my mother." He slid his arms around her waist. "I want to kiss my wife."

"A laudable ambition, my son."

Genevieve gasped with embarrassment and struggled to pull free. Richard tensed, but didn't release her. Instead he turned slightly, like a step in a waltz, and stared over Genevieve's head at the woman in the doorway. "I'm glad you think so, Mother."

He sounded like the supercilious rake who had provoked Genevieve's dislike at the vicarage. But the Dowager Lady Harmsworth couldn't see how his hands tightened to bruising around Genevieve's hips or hear the hitch in his breath.

"Richard, let me go," Genevieve whispered urgently, pushing at his shoulders. Her face was on fire. This wasn't how she wanted to meet her mother-in-law. She'd told Richard he should see his mother alone, the first time he called on her in sixteen years. But he'd insisted upon Genevieve's presence and she, recognizing vulnerability beneath his stubbornness, had agreed.

Now she wasn't certain she'd made the right decision.

To her relief, Richard's grip eased and she extricated herself, smoothing the skirt on her dashing teal dress. She retreated a few steps, then faced the woman whose actions had exerted such baleful influence over her husband's life.

She wasn't sure what she'd expected. Beauty certainly, and beauty there was. Augusta Harmsworth must be in her fifties, but her bone structure and slender figure made her a striking woman. What surprised Genevieve was that she didn't look like her son. Where Richard was all golden fairness, Augusta was dark. Raven hair, arching black brows, eyes that seemed at this distance as dark as night.

Genevieve knew better than to expect maternal warmth. After all, Augusta had avoided her son as far as possible since he'd started university. But there was a wariness about this woman that made Genevieve hesitate before speaking. She glanced at Richard standing motionless beside her. While he didn't share his mother's features, something in his set expression echoed Augusta's.

Augusta swept in with a commanding manner that reminded Genevieve how this woman had dazzled countless foreign courts. In louche Continental circles, the Harmsworth scandal had added piquancy to her presence. She wore an azure silk gown that must have come from Paris. Richard had inherited his instinct for style from his mother.

"Pray, don't let my arrival forestall your plans," Augusta said coolly.

Richard took Genevieve's gloved hand and led her to the sofa. "My wife is still a little shy, madam."

Genevieve stifled the urge to kick him. When she'd agreed to this, it hadn't occurred to her that she might become a bone for the two formidable Harmsworths to quarrel over.

Lady Augusta approached and sank into the chair opposite the sofa with a grace that made Genevieve green with envy. Since marrying Richard, she'd learned a lot. These days, she made a fair show of navigating society. But never would she manage such poise. Particularly in a meeting that must be difficult for anyone with liquid thicker than iced water in her veins. For all Augusta's unruffled façade, something about the line of her shoulders indicated turbulent emotion constrained by an iron will.

"Thank you for telling me about your wedding," Augusta said.

Richard leaned against the mantelpiece with a nonchalance that didn't convince Genevieve. "It seemed appropriate."

Augusta arched her eyebrows but didn't respond. Instead she turned to Genevieve. "My son has forgotten that it's appropriate to make introductions. I, my dear, am your notorious mother-in-law. And you are my son's distinguished wife. I hear you're the toast of academia. I attended your lecture at the Royal Society. Very impressive."

Genevieve saw Richard start with surprise. She was surprised herself. And too concerned about her husband's reactions to this meeting to feel particularly flattered.

"I didn't see you," he said.

A faint smile curved Augusta's lips. "I made sure that you didn't." She turned back to Genevieve. "Good for you, showing the men up at their own game. And soon you'll be consulting at the British Museum."

Richard stared at his mother as though she'd sprouted a tail and wings. Augusta must have lofty connections. The British Museum offer had only come yesterday.

"We're in early stages of negotiations, my lady," Genevieve said calmly, although her hand closed nervously around the Harmsworth Jewel which hung around her neck.

Richard had set the relic into a pendant and presented it to her as a wedding gift. She always wore it as a badge of his love and all they'd endured to achieve happiness. To her amazement, a craze for jewelry in the medieval style had arisen as a result. Who would have thought a bookish country mouse like her could set a fashion?

"I believe they will have a happy outcome." Lady Augusta's smile remained. Cool, contained, but not, thank goodness, hostile. She surveyed Richard. "I congratulate you on choosing such a clever wife. I must admit it was unexpected—I imagined you'd marry some brainless chit who would bore you silly within a week."

Richard looked astonished, as well he might. It became clear that while the Dowager Lady Harmsworth hadn't maintained communication with her son, she'd kept a close eye on his activities. He shifted to stand behind Genevieve and placed one hand on her shoulder, curling his fingers over the skin between her neck and gown. Silently she willed her strength into him. "Once I met Genevieve, I couldn't marry anyone else."

He made no attempt to mask his sincerity. For a long moment, his mother studied him. Her smile became more natural. "I'm glad you found each other. There's nothing more fatal than an unhappy marriage."

Before Richard could respond to that provocative statement, the door behind Augusta opened and a team of footmen set out tea. Genevieve's hand crept up to hold Richard's. Once she'd have taken his self-assurance at face value, but not now. Beneath his serene exterior, this meeting stirred emotions that had tormented him since childhood. Behind her, he vibrated with tension.

Once they were alone, Augusta didn't pour the tea. The delicate sandwiches and cakes remained untouched.

Augusta's finely carved jaw set into a determined line that reminded Genevieve of her husband. The woman glared at Richard in exasperation. "Why don't you ask me? You know that's why you're here."

Richard's hand tightened around Genevieve's, but his voice remained steady. "You've never answered before."

Through a bristling pause, Augusta studied her son as if she saw past the gorgeous shell to the unhappiness within. Genevieve knew that the joy he'd found in marriage had healed many of his wounds, but while his father's identity remained a mystery, one last wound remained.

"You weren't ready to hear before." Another pause. "Now when I see you with a woman you love, I wonder if you've changed."

"The fact that I'm here indicates that I've changed," he bit out.

"Richard, ask me." It sounded like a plea, if such an imperious creature could lower herself to begging.

Genevieve gripped his hand. Without looking at him, she sensed his turmoil. He inhaled unsteadily before he spoke. "Very well. Will you tell me about my father?"

For a moment, Genevieve wondered whether Augusta meant to refuse. She had a horrible premonition that this was a spiteful game. Then Augusta lifted a golden locket over her head and extended the necklace toward her son. "This man is your father, Richard."

Genevieve squeezed Richard's hand in reassurance, then released him so that he could move around the sofa toward his mother. "What is his name?"

"Major Thomas Fraser."

Richard's mother no longer looked quite so composed. Her lips were compressed and lines that Genevieve hadn't noticed before appeared around her eyes. Her barely concealed agitation made Genevieve warm toward her. She wasn't quite the chill, distant harpy Richard had painted.

Richard accepted the locket and spent a few moments opening it, his hands shook so badly. Genevieve bit back the urge to go to him. This wasn't about her, much as she loved him. This was something he needed to resolve with his mother. Although, by heaven, if Augusta hurt him, Genevieve would stab her with a cake fork.

When he finally looked at the locket, Richard went as pale as paper. The dread that this encounter would result in damage rather than renewal jammed in Genevieve's throat.

Augusta watched him steadily. Genevieve glanced away from the naked regret and anguish in the woman's eyes. She suddenly understood that whatever had driven a wedge between Richard and his mother, it wasn't lack of love.

"Thomas Fraser." Richard's voice held no trace of its usual lightness. To Genevieve, it seemed that he struggled to look away from the picture inside. "Tell me about him."

"He was a brave man."

The muscle in Richard's cheek twitched erratically. "Was? He's dead, then?"

Augusta sat upright, as though facing an inquisition. Genevieve supposed that she did. "He died on a mission to France in 1794."

Richard grew even paler. Worried, Genevieve rose and shifted to his side. Blindly he reached for her hand, but his attention remained on his mother. "That was the year I was born."

"Yes."

"Tell me."

Genevieve sensed his roiling reactions. Pain, certainly. Anger. Curiosity avid as a fever.

Augusta's lip quivered. It was the first weakness she'd displayed and Genevieve realized that she suffered too. "Please sit down. This isn't easy. Especially with you looming over me like an ax about to fall."

Genevieve waited for Richard to say that it wasn't easy for him either. He remained silent. When he and Genevieve sat on the sofa, she drew his hand across her lap, holding hard to bolster his courage.

Augusta's eyes faltered from her son's face and she spoke in a low voice. Richard leaned forward as if striving to catch and keep every word. The need in his expression sliced at Genevieve's heart.

"My parents were ambitious. They arranged my marriage to Lester Harmsworth when I was only seventeen." Augusta paused. "I was already in love with a young lieutenant from a good family, but sadly, he wasn't rich. We planned to run away together, but he was posted to India and my maid confessed our plans. In the end, I buckled to pressure and wed where I was bid."

She stopped and glanced quickly at her son, as if expecting criticism. After a crackling silence, Augusta continued, her voice even lower. "I didn't see my young lieutenant for five years. When we finally met again, he was a major with a fortune in prize money. He came to London while Sir Lester was in St. Petersburg."

"So you broke your marriage vows," Richard said softly, but with such bitterness that Genevieve flinched.

Augusta was as ashen as her son. "I was a wife in name only."

"Because you didn't love your husband?"

She shook her head. "No. Because Sir Lester was incapable of the marital act. In any true sense, Thomas Fraser was my husband."

"Good God!" Richard's hand clenched over Genevieve's.

"Lady Harmsworth—" Genevieve protested, speaking for the first time in what felt like hours.

Augusta raised a trembling hand. "Please. I've waited almost thirty-four years to say this. I can't stop now." Her hand returned to fist in her lap until her knuckles gleamed white. "You know what love is like."

It was an appeal for understanding. Genevieve wondered whether Richard could rise above his history to respond. However touching the circumstances leading to his birth, for years he'd paid for what this woman had done with a man to whom she wasn't married.

"Yes, I do." It was tacit acknowledgement that he couldn't despise his mother for her sins. Genevieve loved him then more than she ever had. She blinked away tears.

His mother must have recognized his words as a concession too, because her anxiety faded, replaced by a grief that was no kinder for being over thirty years old. "We couldn't stay away from each other. We had plans to elope to America and make a life together. He'd sell his commission, although a brilliant career beckoned."

"Presumably he thought you were worth it," Richard said with no hint of a sneer.

Augusta's faint smile made her look very young and Genevieve had a glimpse of the girl Thomas Fraser had loved so desperately. "He said he did." She stopped and visibly fought for control. "But he was committed to one more mission.

France was in chaos. Thousands murdered. Robespierre mad with blood. They sent Thomas there in secret, but he was betrayed. I've never discovered the full truth. After all, I had no official standing in his life. I was merely his mistress."

A tear trickled down her cheek. "His pregnant mistress. Just after Thomas left for France, I discovered that I carried his child." She brushed the tear away. "You, my son."

Augusta visibly gathered herself to finish the tragic tale. "Sir Lester returned from St. Petersburg to a fine baby boy. He had no hope of a child of his loins, so he accepted you as his heir. He loved you. I hope you remember that."

Richard stared across the room, but Genevieve knew he sifted memories. "Yes, he was kind to me. I grieved when he died."

Augusta's mouth contracted. "I couldn't save you from scandal. After all, everyone can count and no child grows in its mother's womb for sixteen months. I can't even blame you for hating me. After all, my sin fell on your innocent head. But when I heard that you were madly in love with your wife, I had to tell you and... and beg forgiveness."

It was the first truly humble thing she'd said.

Another silence fell. One heavy with years of resentment and regret. Richard had much to blame his mother for and only an afternoon's confession to place on the other side of the balance. Genevieve longed to hold him close, to tell him that none of this mattered compared to the wonderful man he was, to insist that whatever decision he made, she was on his side. But under Augusta's tormented dark gaze, she stayed silent.

Richard kissed the hand he held. Then he released Genevieve and rose.

Genevieve's muscles tightened until she trembled on the edge of the sofa. Dear heaven, did he mean to storm out?

Augusta had cost him so much happiness, and he'd nurtured a lifetime of rancor.

He passed Genevieve the locket. She glanced at the tiny, exquisite painting and bit back a shocked gasp. If one disregarded the old-fashioned powdered wig, the man staring from the miniature was Richard. No wonder he'd been so moved to see it.

The tension between mother and son drew her gaze from Thomas Fraser's handsome face. Augusta's eyes were lowered as if she awaited condemnation. Richard still hadn't moved. The disregarded tea table stretched between them like a thorny barrier.

Genevieve's heart melted with compassion for Augusta. How could it not? But her main concern in this encounter remained Richard. How must he feel after today's revelations?

When he stepped across to his mother, it was as if the earth quaked beneath Genevieve's feet. Her hands fisted at her sides as she told herself not to go after him, not to beg him to be kind to this woman who had endured so much. She had to trust Richard to choose his next move.

Let him choose wisely, she prayed silently. Let him chose the action that rids his heart of poison.

Unblinking she watched him approach his mother. Augusta slowly raised her eyes. Genevieve read in her face that she awaited castigation. After all, how could a belated confession compensate for such pain?

With his characteristic grace, Richard dropped to his knees by his mother's chair. "I'm sorry for your heartbreak, Mother. I'm sorry that I was such a blind, self-righteous, contemptible ass all these years. I'm sorry it's taken me until now to ask your forgiveness."

Augusta straightened in astonishment. "Richard?"

"I sincerely beg your pardon." He embraced his mother with a naturalness that scoured Genevieve's heart.

"My son—" Augusta choked. She buried her face in Richard's broad, capable shoulder. The proud, beautiful woman who had offered such a frosty welcome began to cry, sobs muffled against her son's coat.

Torn between joy and sorrow, Genevieve watched mother and son. They had so much time to make up. Their reconciliation wouldn't change the world's view of the old scandal. Nonetheless, something inside her flowered into gratitude. Richard and Augusta had found their path. They would survive. Better. They would triumph. Genevieve felt privileged to witness this raw, true occasion when her husband conquered his demons.

Eyes dark with emotion, Richard glanced up at Genevieve. His smile was distinctly shaky, but it conveyed his depth of emotion. Genevieve released a choked laugh and lifted her hand to dash moisture from her cheeks.

"I love you," she mouthed silently.

"And I love you," he said softly, firming his grip around his mother's shoulders.

He extended his hand toward Genevieve, an invitation to share this extraordinary moment. On shaky legs, she rose and stumbled across to enfold Richard and his mother in her arms. The man she loved had made peace with his past. Now a shining future beckoned.

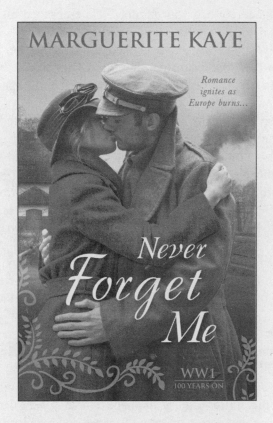

Aa a war blazes across Europe, three couples find a love
that is powerful enough to overcome all the odds.
Travel with the characters on their journey of
passion and drama during World War I.

**Three wonderful books in one from top
historical author Marguerite Kaye.**

**Get your copy today at:
www.millsandboon.co.uk**

0714/MB486

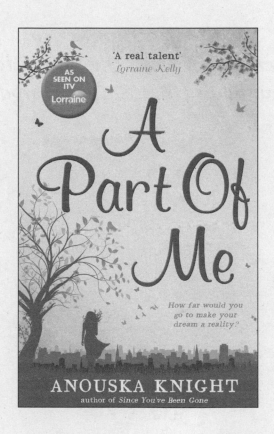

Anouska Knight's first book, *Since You've Been Gone*,
was a smash hit and crowned the winner of Lorraine's
Racy Reads. Anouska returns with *A Part of Me*,
which is one not to be missed!

Get your copy today at:
www.millsandboon.co.uk

Make it a summer to remember with the fantastic new book from Sarah Morgan

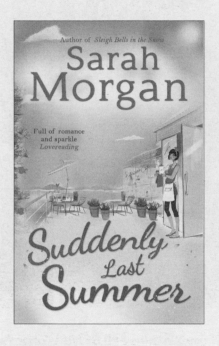

Fiery French chef Elise Philippe has just heard that the delectable Sean O'Neil is back in town. After their electrifying night together last summer, can she stick to her one-night rule?

Coming soon at millsandboon.co.uk

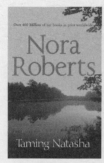
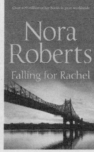
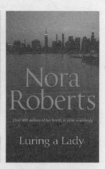
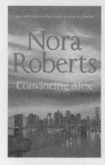
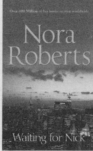
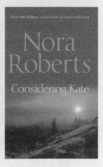

Get ready to meet the MacKade family...

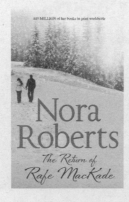

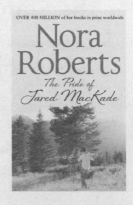

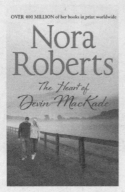

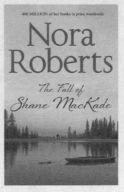

'The most successful
author on planet Earth'
—*Washington Post*

www.millsandboon.co.uk

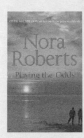
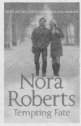
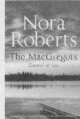
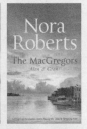

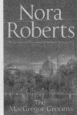
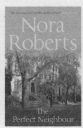
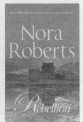

Discover more romance at

www.millsandboon.co.uk

- ❤ WIN great prizes in our exclusive competitions
- ❤ BUY new titles before they hit the shops
- ❤ BROWSE new books and REVIEW your favourites
- ❤ SAVE on new books with the Mills & Boon® Bookclub™
- ❤ DISCOVER new authors

PLUS, to chat about your favourite reads, get the latest news and find special offers:

- Find us on facebook.com/millsandboon
- Follow us on twitter.com/millsandboonuk
- ❤ Sign up to our newsletter at millsandboon.co.uk